praise for elizabeth ellen

"Ellen walks on at least five different tightropes, handling the difficult themes of teenage angst, family conflicts, and trauma with deft skill. Brilliant."

— *Booklist*

"Gossip, delusion, sapphic mania, Britney Spears—*American Thighs* has everything I want from a novel in Elizabeth Ellen's inimitable style. It's fearless, it's propulsive, it's wildly entertaining. I devoured this novel."

— Anna Dorn, author of *Perfume & Pain*

"Furious, hilarious, frantic, messy, *American Thighs* is the *Moby-Dick* for our present crazed moment, questing after everything precious and innocent we've destroyed. Open it up and get out of its way."

— Daniel Handler (AKA Lemony Snicket), author of *A Series of Unfortunate Events*

"Elizabeth Ellen's *American Thighs* is an elegy for American girlhood, for the way in which we are squeezed in the vise of pop culture and the male gaze, and for the way we increasingly have little choice but to wild the fuck OUT. Elizabeth Ellen is one of the most fearless, gripping writers out there, writing the way Bret Easton Ellis would if he had actual balls. I started panting on page 1 of this book, and I still haven't caught my breath."

— Lindsay Hunter, author of *Hot Springs Drive*

american thighs

American Thighs
Copyright © 2025 by Elizabeth Ellen
Cover by Matthew Revert
ISBN 9781960988355 (paperback)

CLASH Books
Troy, NY
clashbooks.com
Distributed by Consortium
All rights reserved.

First Edition: 2025
Printed in the United States of America

for Miley
And Brandy
And Lindsay
And Amanda

and, most especially…
for Brad Renfro and River Phoenix
(R.I.P.)

"I was so celebrated for being a child. I think I held on to that immaturity for a very long time. It was the thing that made me special."

— Christina Ricci

"I do want to go to the prom. Or several proms, hopefully. That's my goal. I've been to the Emmy's, but prom—that's where it's at. [Laughs]"

— Kiernan Shipka, child actress, *Mad Men*

"I had my first drink at age nine, began smoking marijuana at ten, and at twelve took up cocaine."

— Drew Barrymore, *Little Girl Lost*

"I feel like most kids like me end up going down a spiral of depression, and the world is sitting there looking at them through their phones laughing and making jokes and making memes…"

— Willow Smith

"I would cut and burn myself… yes, I tried to kill myself many times."

— Paris Jackson

"I was playing with Barbies at 13 and at 14, I'm in Japan, emancipated."

— Gisele Bündchen

Q: audience member:
"What is the biggest sacrifice you've had to make?"

A: MACI:
"Mine would be just your youth. You go from being, like, sixteen to thirty, within nine months."

— *Teen Mom*, Season One, Finale Special with Dr. Drew

"I was very privileged in my own life to be able to go to New York, make mistakes, and have scary situations happen to me—make wrong decisions, choose wrong people to do things with… without the whole world putting a magnifying glass on [me]. And she's never had that opportunity.

What happens is, you make a mistake and the whole world is watching you; they beat up on you. Or, they're not even mistakes, sometimes. It's just called growing up."

— Madonna speaking about Britney Spears on
Britney: for the record, 2008

"I also had to accept a certain amount of responsibility. I'd been egging him on for years about the girls at Winwood, asking if he'd seen this one in her tight little skirt or that one in her black velvet top. Tracy had been a staple of our gossip for well over a year at that point. It was easier than you might imagine to forget she was fifteen. Spend enough time in a high school, and you forget what fifteen *means*."

— Tom Perrotta, *Election*

american thighs

elizabeth ellen

CLASH
FICTION

waste of space

. . .

kappa18

101 Fans

Impersonating your daughter and pretending to be a high school student when you're 31 years old is pathetic

11 JAN 2016 9:02 AM

·FAVE

·SHARE

·MORE

RowRowRowYourBoat

650 Fans·...last one out, turn off the lights.

...if she's so bored can't she just have an affair?

s

Evolution is going to take a drastic turn for the worse from here on out.........how anyone could bring life in to this world is just beyond my comprehension. Get some cats.

16 JAN 2016 2:38 PM

· FAVE

· SHARE

Rixie Jones 2 months ago
> wow there are some messed up ppl out there arent there?
> Upvote

Confusion 2 months ago
> I'm glad her daughter isn't being raised by her.
> Upvote

First let me just say... What the F***? She couldn't be *responsible* for her own daughter, who is in the grandmother's custody, but she will steal her identity. Waste of space.

By the way, if you need to "relive your childhood" because you think it was "denied you", MAYBE you should have thought of that before you became pregnant at age 16-17.

On what planet would this woman pass for 15????

We need a new law: You must have an IQ above a certain level before you can have unprotected sex.

Her defense will be she has some psychological syndrome or is a victim of something that causes her to commit fraud. Gotta feel bad for the daughter who has a her as a mom.
> 11 JAN 2016 6:28 AM
> · FAVE
> ·SHARE

ANISSA GRANT

It was even easier than I thought.

I remember reading this quote from this semi-famous director in *The New York Times*. Or maybe it was in *Elle* magazine. I don't remember. And who cares anyway? He was a douche, the director, I mean. You definitely *heard things…* about him, I mean. But the quote was good, the quote was something about how people *want* to be hustled, how they *want* to suspend their disbelief.

Which makes it easy. Which accounts, I think, for most of what happened that fall and early winter at Dobson High in Elkheart, Indiana, population, I don't know: twelve?

MRS. STONE

I don't know. I didn't notice anything out of the ordinary. It's so hard to tell with teenagers; some come in here looking like babies, looking prepubescent, and others look twenty-six. Look like they're in college already. Grad school. Look like my husband the day I married him. Are we supposed to question each one of them? Assume they're lying about the information they've provided the school? Do background checks? Visit their homes?

She was very sweet, soft-spoken. That's what I remember about Tatum. I had no reason to assume she was lying. Why would I think she was lying?

ANISSA GRANT

I stood there in the office a second longer, hoping Mrs. Stone would look up. I'd rehearsed this whole back story, practiced my lines over and over, prepared more for this day than any audition I'd ever been on, like, *Hi, my name's Tatum, my mom and I just moved here from California so she can take care of her great aunt Cecil who's dying of cancer because she doesn't have any other living relatives because she never married or had children even though everyone tried to warn her about never marrying or having children because who would take care of her in her old age and now look, it's my mom,* and it was all going to waste. All I got out was the Hi, my name's Tatum part out before Mrs. Stone started nodding and signing my papers.

I couldn't believe it. I'd spent three weeks going to tanning salons and the gym and getting my hair highlighted with the perfect "California" sun streaks. I'd watched popular YouTube videos of teenagers putting on makeup and gone to the drugstore and Sephora and stocked up on every brand they liked, all the Kylie lip kit shit knockoffs, practiced putting it on in my bathroom mirror, took selfies and videos of myself to see how I looked, to notice what I was doing wrong, what didn't look right, to change it and make it better. I never really got into makeup. Maybe because most of my youth was spent in a makeup chair, bored out of my mind, reading a book while some makeup artist with a cigarette in her mouth cemented my face with layers of foundation until I could barely move it or recognize myself.

Mrs. Stone signed my papers and told me to go down to the gym and get my picture taken for my School ID.

I was almost disappointed.

I was twirling my hair like I'd seen teenagers on TV do. Like I'd watched Tate do a million times. Like I remembered doing years and years and years ago.

But Mrs. Stone didn't seem to notice and there was another girl waiting behind me, so I grabbed my papers and walked out of the office and down the hall, slump-shouldered, uneasy, like a sixteen-year-old, like a high school sophomore, like *the new girl, the new bitch: Tatum.*

I passed a teacher. A couple students.

More audience members. More auditions.

More hair twirling.

A slow down-the-hall slink emoting boredom. Emulating over-it-ness.

Improvisation.

I really wanted a cigarette, but I was improvising calmness, or meekness, or *somethingness*. sixteen-year-old-girlness.

PRINCIPAL PITT

I had a lot more on my plate, on my mind, then. The students at a neighboring school district were starting to kill themselves: to jump from the tops of buildings, to walk in front of trains. You knew it was only a matter of time… But, still, you tried to get out in front of it, to ward it off, to keep your kids safe. It was all on account of YouTube. As a principal, as a father myself, I hated YouTube. It didn't seem anything good ever came of it. Justin Bieber? Are you kidding? Is this a joke? That's what I asked myself the first time my daughter emailed me a link to him, to one of his songs. I'm not gonna lie: I thought *he* was a *she*. Then there were all the conspiracy theories: 9/11 being an "inside job"; the Earth being flat; the Beatles' imposters. Then, even worse, these idiotic teen challenges. There was the Cinnamon Challenge and the Pass-Out Challenge and the most ludicrous of all: the Tide-pod Challenge—some teens actually fried the things first, in frickin' skillets on their stovetops, if you can believe that. Of course, that didn't make them anymore palatable, any more *edible*. Or I'm assuming it didn't. It's not like I've actually *tried* them or anything. They just looked like idiots, biting into them, the blue running down their chins. Like, Jesus, couldn't they just smoke some pot and drink some of their parents' liquor and play with each other's privates after school like we did when we were teenagers in the 80s? But we had ridden all that out. We, the administration, the teachers, Mrs. Stone, Leslie, and I. We had watched the videos of our kids ingesting teaspoons of cinnamon sans beverages when we weren't home, when we were working to make money to buy their name-brand canisters of cinnamon. Sure, some had ended up at the E.R. Or at least that was what the internet said. Cinnamon in their lungs, I think? Who the hell knows. There were always so many things to worry about, to think about, I never had the time to delve very deeply into any of them. I just prayed nothing really bad would happen to any of the kids at Dobson. And now this ludicrous Russian Blue Whale shit. The goddamn Blue Whale Challenge. Now the fun and games were over. Now teens were actually *dying*. Killing themselves. Cuz some stupid internet game told them to. Cuz their lives were so devoid of meaning. Cuz they were so bored and mistook boredom and maybe loneliness—the loneliness of self-alienation, of not leaving one's bedroom but preferring to sit on one's bed, thumbing one's phone rather than getting drunk, rather than getting laid—for depression, for losing the will to live. So they took the Blue Whale Challenge because no one else—certainly not their parents—were offering them any rules or guidance or boundaries—only these peer-created challenges offered anything like that. ("Wake up in the middle of the night." "Watch a scary movie." "Carve a whale into your arm." "Kill yourself.") Peers who were strangers—peers who might live in other countries, speak another language, but peers, nonetheless.

So, yeah, I wasn't really paying that close of attention to the new girl at school that September. I was watching our students' arms for the outlines of whales. I was more intent on keeping our students from acting as mindless lemmings, apocalyptic zombies, following in the footsteps of their peers down the road, at that backwoods, hick school, Clearfork. Not that we aren't hicks. I get it. Especially now, now that the whole world is looking at our little town, our tiny school district. We're the most infamous hicks now, I guess. Right up there with Cousin Eddie from the *Vacation* movies. Emptying our shitter right into your middle class yuppie sewer. Stinking up your carefully-cultivated pristine world with our waste.

TATE GRANT

While Anissa was, I guess, starting school in some Midwest podunk town in some Midwest podunk state we didn't know the eff where, I was having my first real life high school experience at the same high school Paris Jackson went to in Sherman Oaks. You know she was a cheerleader and everything, too, right? Paris Jackson, I mean. Paris Jackson was, *is*: THE. SHIT. I've always admired Paris Jackson. To go through everything she's gone through... So publicly, everyone around the world fucking staring at her at her father's funeral and everything... And to come out the other side, okay... to come out as fucking beautiful and cool and shit as her... it gives me goals. Paris gives me hope. And now I was at her fucking high school, walking down the same fucking halls she walked down just a couple years before. It was like fucking magic or some shit. It was like fucking fire.

COACH W

I saw her walking down the hall a week or so before school started: School ID photo day. There's only about a hundred and eighty students per grade here at Dobson High so it's hard to miss the new ones. They sort of stand out like a red thumb.

She looked like any other of our pretty sophomores, just a little more golden, a bit more California. Or maybe I'm falsely remembering the Californianess, given what I know now. She was pretty but not gorgeous. Pretty in a plain way, if that makes sense. Sweet-looking, but not the center of attention or anything. Not like Taylor Ragner. Taylor was always center of attention at Dobson, even though she was only a sophomore. She'd been the center of attention since day one of her freshman year. Even us teachers talked about her. You'd be surprised, probably, if you knew how much teachers talk about students. A lot less now, due to all of the PC stuff, but it used to be all the time, a regular thing. Who was boning who and all that and the other. I swear the high school students were having way more sex than we were, every goddamn year, but that's another story. I digress.

I don't know *why* Taylor was so special, it's hard to put into words, to explain to someone who hasn't met her.

She just had that certain special oof quality. Like Marilyn Monroe or, in more recent terms: JLO.

Sorry, I'm the acting teacher, also. My references are a little old school. Selena Gomez? Is she still current? Is she still relevant? Like her, I guess, then. Taylor Ragner was like the Selena Gomez of Dobson High. She even looked a little like her, too, now that I think about it. Or maybe it's Ariana Grande I'm thinking of. Demi Lovato?

She had that, pardon my French, Latina ass. You know her mom was from… fuck, where is her mom from? Columbia? Venezuela? Puerto Rico? I really can't remember. You got me drinkin here and fuck if I can remember shit. She had that ass, too, though, Anabel, Taylor's mom, did.

Anyway, Anissa, or, *Tatum*, as we knew her, as she *presented* herself then, was just another attractive new student that day. We had no way of knowing how much or how quickly she would impact most, if not *all*, of our lives. My life, for fuck's sake. My fuckin' life, man. Fuck.

ANISSA GRANT

Maybe I was crazy. Like they say. Maybe I'm *nuts*. I can't explain to you what I was doing there. It was a compulsion. That's the only word I can think of. It was a compulsion, born of all those *other years*, my unnatural, Hollywood childhood and teen years and everything after that: Quinn, my mother, Tate, *all of it*.

Anyway, I was compulsed. Compelled. Whatever.

ROBIN GRANT

I know I'm portrayed as the MOMMIE DEAREST in the media now, the cliché stage mom, the cold bitch, the nag, the alcoholic mother being "raised by her daughter." Brooke Shields' mother. Maybe Natalie Woods' mama, too? Why is it only the mothers of actresses are portrayed this way? You never hear about Justin Timberlake's mom. Or Ryan Gosling's. or Leonardo's? I think it's something to do with inherent misogyny. Not only in the portrayal of the stage *mom*, but specifically in the stage mom of the female child, of the young adult actress. I don't know, maybe sons don't talk, maybe they don't complain so much, either. I don't know, I've never had a son. Or maybe society doesn't feel a need to protect boys, young men, to keep them innocent. Maybe boys, young men, are lib-er-ate-ed, by their young maleness.

Females are so much more delicate, you see, prone to being controlled and overrun, ma-nip-u-lated. That's what that stereotype is telling us. Male actors, even young ones, adolescents, aren't portrayed that way in the media, because even as adolescents, males are thought of as strong-willed, incapable of manipulation.

Well, Anissa may have been introverted, but she wasn't weak-willed. She told me no many times. *Many* times. And I listened to her. I did.

She didn't need to do what she did.

Or maybe her doing it is another example of her strong will. Her independent spirit.

I couldn't have controlled her if I'd wanted to.

You can't control a storm cloud. You can only get out of its way.

COACH HARDEN

Yes, we were all aware of Coach Wellsley's, of Colton's... leeringness, shall we say?

You'd catch him looking a little too intently at a girl in the hall, at Taylor, usually, to be honest. But I guess I thought he was harmless. You know, we just sort of accepted things back then. Back in 2015... and one of the things we accepted was men leer at women, and at teen girls. And to be honest, pretty much everyone leered at Taylor.

And I'd always say to the girls, to the girls on my cheer team, of which Taylor was one, "You know, you can tell me *anything*, if anyone ever bothers you or makes you feel uncomfortable, in school or at home, another student or a teacher or a family member... *anyone*. Please, come to me. I promise we'll keep it confidential."

No one ever did.

I'm not sure what I would have done if they had... I guess I would have had to figure that out.

But no one ever did. So it was a non-issue. Or, maybe I should have made it an issue anyway, asked Coach Wellsley what was up, if he was okay, if he needed help...

But that's a hard thing to do. A very hard thing to do. Especially in 2015. Especially in every year before then, before now.

ANISSA GRANT

I got to the gym and got in line. I was behind a girl with long brown hair, the kind of thick, wavy brunette hair you want to run your fingers through. The kind of hair you see in shampoo commercials. The kind you want to lean forward to smell. Which I did. Lean forward to smell. Which was what I was doing when she suddenly whirled around. I jumped back. I don't know if she noticed or not. I knew who she was, of course.

I tried to act casual. Twirled my hair.

TAYLOR RAGNER

I met Tatum on picture ID day. That's like a week or so before school starts. It's like the most boring day of the year. I turned around to say something to whoever was in line behind me. It didn't matter who it was. I was just so fucking bored. I would have talked to anyone at that point. Well, anyone but Todd Rucker, who was in front of me and giving off the worst fucking shitsmells as usual.

So in part I turned around to avoid smelling him.

That's when I realized the girl behind me was new. I'd never seen her before. I knew everyone in the school, even the invisibles, that most people don't notice. The Victoria Bakers and Shelby Andersons and Nova Parkers, etc. I'm very observant, even though people want to think I'm too self-involved to notice anyone but myself. They want me to be a cliché. The fucking Latina cheerleader. Half fucking Latina. My dad, SCOTT, is as white as they come. El-oh-el. They want me to be all kinds of fucking things I'm not, that I never was. I wish that song "Even the Homecoming Queen Cries" or whatever it's called had been around then, maybe for two seconds someone would have listened…*Whatever*.

Tatum was pretty. But not like threateningly pretty or anything. Not that I'd be threatened. I welcomed a new pretty face. I was bored of all the old ones. I was effing *bored* of my friends and boyfriend and the teachers and my parents.

Tatum arriving at Dobson was like the best gift I could be given right then.

I was soooooo effing happy to see her in that moment.

Even if she *was* wearing some weird Aeropostale shit and twirling her hair like a goddamn freshman.

ANISSA GRANT

When Taylor whirled around it was like how in *The Godfather* they say Michael was hit by the thunderbolt in Sicily. When he meets that other woman, not Kay. Not the boring WASP back home in America waiting patiently like a fool for years for his return. The sexy, young Sicilian woman. The one he falls madly, instantly, in love with; marries. Apollonia, I think her name was… like Prince's former lover.

Anyway. It was like that. Like my internal organs were punctured with a huge knitting needle and joined to hers.

It's only happened to me once before. The thunderbolt. Years ago. With Quinn.

I didn't think it was possible to be hit twice in one lifetime.

COACH W

The internet and social media had a *Rear Window* feel to it. Everyone in town and at school seemed to know shit about each other they probably shouldn't have known. And we teachers probably knew shit we shouldn't have known. What the inside of students' bedrooms looked like, what they wore to bed, what time they went to bed, what they listened to while falling asleep, what they wore to work out in, what their faces looked like while working out, what podcasts they listened to, what Netflix shows they watched, who they planned to vote for, what they ate for dinner, what drugs they took, what flavor vape they smoked, who was getting a BJ—pardon my French—and from whom.

I, as a teacher, of course, tried to keep all my personal shit to myself. I didn't post anything that wasn't related to my job as teacher or coach. I was Jimmy Stewart, holed up in a wheelchair staring out at them. I stared through the window of my computer screen at all of them while making sure no one could see in my window/screen at me. I kept my personal shit on lock as long as I could.

Anyway, it'd been a pretty long while since anyone had thought to give me a BJ! I can tell you that. [laughs]

ANISSA GRANT

I wasn't expecting it, is what I mean. Or maybe I was. maybe that's a lie. Maybe I was *hoping*, but not counting on it… maybe the thought had crossed my mind… all those recent nights, online…

Of course I already knew her name (Taylor Ragner), her age (fifteen), her boyfriend's name (Cam Spencer), her boyfriend's age (eighteen—as of last

Thursday), that she cheered, that he played football, that she was gorgeous, that he was a dick, that she was popular, that he thought he ruled this school and Taylor too, that she was perfect…

I'd been following her social medias, watching her YouTube videos for a month at this point. There were a shitton of them with titles like "How to make the cheer team" and "How to Apply Makeup for Homecoming" and "How to Be 'That Bitch' at Your High School."

I'd done my homework.

And now here she was. Face to face, finally. In person. Even more fucking gorgeous than I ever could have imagined watching her from afar, studying her online. Talking to me. It took me a second to hear what she was saying. I had to first process her face, her dark hair, her green eyes. She looked a little like she could be an offspring or descendent of Elvis. She had that drawl of Elvis's too. Like she was southern, though I didn't think Indiana counted as the south. Even southern Indiana. which was so close to the Kentucky border.

When I came back into focus she was still talking. She was complaining about one of the photographers. There were three separate lines, three different people taking the pictures.

"I hope I don't get that bitch again this year," she said, nodding toward a middle aged woman with glasses and a fine line grimace. "Last year she tried to sabotage my school pic. She pushed my hair behind my ears at the last second and took the picture when I wasn't even ready. It was hideous. I demanded she take it again, of course, and she gave me that stink face she has on now. But I didn't care. I'm not going to go around with a hideous School ID for nine months, you know?"

TAYLOR RAGNER

She said her name was Tatum and that she was from California. I said why the eff would anyone move from L.A. to this shithole town in Indiana. I told her my goal was to move anywhere after high school, to get the fuck out of this town. And she shrugged and said she and her mom were on the run from her dad who was abusive and alcoholic and also she had a great aunt or something who was sick and her mom was a nurse and going to take care of her or something. I don't know. I wasn't listening to that whole story that closely. I was mildly interested but I was more interested in taking a good photograph for my School ID.

I didn't want that bitch fucking it up again. So when the bitch barked, "Next!" I nudged Tatum. I said, "You go ahead," and sort of gave her a push.

Then I waited for the nice dopey guy on the right. I knew I could make sure he took the picture I wanted. I knew he wouldn't put up a fight. I knew he'd do whatever *I* said.

COACH W

Of course, I already knew what Taylor's bedroom looked like. I expect most of us at Elkheart—teachers and students alike—did. She filmed most of her YouTube tutorials in it: "My Cheerleading Makeup Routine," "What's In My Cheerleading Bag," "How to Make the Cheerleading Team," shit like that. She got a lot of views, probably from all over, not just us at Elkheart, were watching her put on lipgloss, two coats of mascara, doing deep stretches on her front lawn, the splits in her childhood bedroom, on her cute, little, fuzzy purple bedroom rug that matched the purple bow in her bouncy hair. Pervs all over the country, most likely. And a few young women interested in cheerleading, too, I guess.

The video with the most views, oddly, was one she'd titled, "Getting Ready for School." I don't know why it was so popular or viewed. Maybe because it showed her straight out of bed, in her Victoria's Secret sweats and tank top, hair messy, eyes sleepy, looking how she'd look, you imagined, if you woke up next to her, after a night sleeping beside her, after a night... by the end of the video, of course, she looked just how she looked when I passed her in the halls at school: perfectly made up, hair in a ponytail or down in curls. But it was the way she looked at the beginning of the video that I suspect was the reason it had so many views. I know, if I'm being honest, and why shouldn't I be at this point, it was the reason I'd watched it so many times. I rarely made it past the blow drying part of the video, if you know what I mean. That was two and a half minutes in and by then we'd seen her get out of bed, brush her hair, and get in the shower. You didn't see her get in the shower, of course, but she said she was going to and then next thing you saw was her in a bathrobe with her hair all long and wet, holding all those beads of water, some of which ran down her face into her robe. Her lips looked wet too, whether or not they were. By the time she plugged in her hairdryer I was already *there*, if you know what I mean. It was all just too much: the dripping, heavy hair, the wet morning lips, natural, without any shit on them yet, the light pink terrycloth robe that always promised to fall open, even if it never did, or only did in your imagination, her perfect, youthful breasts—sized D, at least, I'm guessing—exposed, her hands busy, too busy to catch her robe, blow-drying her hair.

It was like an old outtake from *Family Ties*. What we all wanted desperately to see, then, but never got to: Mallory Keaton alone in her bedroom, getting ready for school.

TATE GRANT

The first thing I did after Anissa left was change my name. And the second thing I did was get my mom, or, I guess, grandma—*fuck*, I still shit that up—Robin, I call her Robin now, it's just easier—I got Robin to get me an audition for this new teen TV show. My whole life I've wanted to be an actress and for my whole life my mom and sister—shit!—my *grandma* and *mom*—have been against me acting. Or, I guess, I know now it was mainly just Anissa who was against it. Because *Robin* is all gung ho, 100%.

ROBIN GRANT

Anissa likes to blame me. For everything that happened. For the fight and everything after. But it wasn't like I said it on purpose. I hadn't premeditated telling Tate, is what I mean. Though, Lord knows, she was getting old enough to start figuring some things out for herself. I was really surprised she hadn't asked more questions by then, anyway. It was like walking on eggshells all the time, truthfully. I was always waiting for her to figure us out. So in a way, it's been a kind of relief. A huge relief, really. not to have to keep up this lie another fifteen years.

One slip of the tongue and everything was finally out on the table.

So while I regret *how* it happened—the nastiness of the fight with Anissa —I don't regret *that* it happened. If that makes sense.

CAM SPENCER

I hated Taylor's videos, hated that she made them and that anyone— any lowlife—could watch them, could watch *my girlfriend* in her short shorts, down on the ground, doing the splits and all that cheer and gymnastics shit. I told her all the time how many creeps there were out there, how many pervs and pedophiles and sickos there were online but she just shrugged it off. She was getting so many *views*, she said.

"This is what I've been building toward for three years, Cam," she said.

"An audience. People not just here in Elkheart, but around the country, watch. You're just being a jealous boyfriend. You're just being a frickin' asshole."

I wasn't, though. I was honestly worried about all the men watching. I don't think she thought about them. I think she thought it was all innocent teen girls like her interested in cheer who were watching. Not that Tay was innocent. But... well, you know what I mean.

ANISSA GRANT

I wasn't sure if I should wait for Taylor or not, after my picture was taken. It wasn't great, but whatever: it was a high school ID which sort of thrilled me, which was the reason I was here. I wanted to keep talking to her but I didn't want to seem desperate. So I sort of hesitated, looked around, and then started walking real slow, giving her time to catch up. Which was when I ran into Cam and Chase, who were standing right outside the gymnasium in the hall. I was walking slow, with my head sort of down, twirling my hair. I didn't make eye contact, but they called to me, anyway.

CAM SPENCER

I met Tatum on picture day. She was walking out of the gymnasium alone. She wasn't the hottest chick I'd ever seen—that was Taylor, hands down, no competition—but she was cute, and more importantly, she was *new*. New pussy. *Strange*... I was chilling in the hall with Chase waiting on Coach Wellsley to start football practice, waiting on Taylor. She'd texted me she was in line to get her picture taken. I figured I'd surprise her when she came out.

Chase and I looked at each other when Tatum walked out, though. We didn't have to use words to communicate. I knew what he was thinking and I knew he knew what I was thinking. We'd been best friends for ten years, since third grade, which was when I was held back a year, put in Chase's class.

Chase called her over. Since he was single. He'd broken up with whatsher-bitch over the summer, like I'd advised him to.

ANISSA GRANT

I think it was Chase who waved me over. Who said, "hey," or something else clever like that. They were both tall and built, Chase and Cam, and I knew they were both seniors and football players, something Taylor confirmed for me—me nodding, pretending to learn this information for the first time—a few minutes later in the parking lot.

I wasn't used to interacting with people my age. Or, with people who weren't my mother's age, I guess, is what I mean.

I wasn't used to talking to boys or men, either. It'd been so long since I'd talked to Quinn. I hadn't really had an interest. Since then, I guess.

But Chase seemed friendly. Friendlier than Cam, anyway. And he was cute. Like the sweet guy on a teen TV show. Like the one guy who's somehow cute *and nice*.

CHASE WHITING

Cam nudged me so I called her over. The new girl. Tatum. I wasn't looking for a girlfriend. I'd only been single a month. I wanted to ride out senior year unattached. But Tatum was pretty—blonde and tan and she didn't seem too affected, she was pretty chill and cool. Unlike my last girlfriend. Unlike most of the girls at Dobson.

She said she was from L.A. and living here temporarily and she didn't have any friends yet, she'd just been hanging out in the apartment alone while her mom was taking care of an aunt or something.

She had a nice smile.

TAYLOR RAGNER

I walked out of the gymnasium and saw the new girl talking to Cam and Chase. I'd already forgotten her name. It was something weird I'd never heard before.

I wasn't worried about Cam liking her. It would have almost been a gift if he had. Over the summer I'd gone away to cheerleading camp with Makayla and the other girls and I'd been so worried I was going to miss him so much and then I barely missed him at all. It was actually such a relief not to have to touch base with him constantly since phones weren't allowed at camp. I could breathe for goddamn once. I don't think I realized how much Cam was suffocating me until I wasn't with him 24/7.

I walked up to where the three of them were standing and grabbed the new girl by the arm and said, "She's mine, hands off," and walked her out of the school to the parking lot.

Cam yelled, "Hey!"

And I yelled back, "I'll see you after football practice, Cam!"

And kept walking.

ANISSA GRANT

I was surprised when Taylor came out and grabbed my arm. I wasn't used to being touched. Her hands were small and soft and well-manicured. Her nails were painted a pastel pink. Later, she would complain it was hard to find any polish that matched the school colors, which were purple and white, other than purple and white. "Which is so fucking boring," she'd say. "How many years of my life must I be expected to wear the same two colors? It's obnoxious. It's deadening. I feel dead inside half the time."

I let her lead me out into the parking lot and to a curb where we sat and she lit a cigarette. "Don't tell Cam," she said and rolled her eyes.

She asked me if I cheered and I said no, but that I'd taken dance and gymnastics since I was little and she said, "Great, try outs are Friday and you should come."

Of course, I already knew when tryouts were, where and what time. I'd already been practicing my cheers for two weeks. I knew who all the cheerleaders were, the main football players, some of the teachers, the coaches, the principal… I'd been looking at Facebook and Instagram and Snapchat since I got to Elkheart. Social media made it so easy to learn who everyone in town was before you met anyone in town. Like a TV show about teens. One you watched every night.

I hadn't made a profile for myself yet.

I figured I'd do that tonight, after I got home and looked to see what Tate was up to.

I don't know how to explain to you the dichotomy going on inside of me. It's been this way my whole life, pretty much, though. So I was used to it. I always felt both super old and super young at the same time. A child actor has to mature really quickly. From the time you're like five or even younger you have to be mature and understand things about how the adult world works and interact with a lot of adults and act adult-like in a way normal children don't. You have to have things like self-discipline and a work ethic.

When you're *five*. You might be the main breadwinner in your family. The person with the biggest, or only, paycheck. But then when you go through puberty, when you come out on the other side, sometimes something happens, you can regress. Suddenly, you're fifteen but people treat you like you're thirty and so by the time you're actually an adult, eighteen and twenty and twenty-five, you're like, *hey, what happened? Did we just skip over my whole adolescence?* And then you get pregnant as a teenager and that adds another whole dynamic. Because then you truly are like a thirty-year-old, taking care of a baby 24/7, even though you're sixteen.

I don't know. It's hard to explain if you haven't lived it. Maybe it's not even about growing up a child actor, either, because I read this quote from Kanye in *Harper's Bazaar* where he says kind of the same thing. He says something like, "I'm a mix of a fourteen-year-old high schooler and a 60-year-old guy. It can never fall into the thirties or the forties. It has to be 100 % sixty or 100% fourteen, no in between."

Yeah, it's kind of like that. And earlier in my life it'd been the former—me being sixteen and feeling thirty. And now it was the latter. So fucking sue me—for feeling fifteen, or sixteen, or whatever. Or, someone already has. The government, I guess, it is. The state of Indiana. So fuck me. Fuck.

TAYLOR RAGNER

I looked over at Tatum. She looked so sweet and innocent, just standing there quietly, head down, swirling on her Dr. Pepper lip gloss like she didn't have a fucking clue what was going on. She seemed like the type who'd never popped a Xanax or molly or had an abortion. You have to drive an hour to get one if you have the misfortune of growing up in Elkheart, but that doesn't stop anyone. It's common knowledge Keisha Finefrock has had two already. If she keeps it up they might as well give her a punch card. Buy nine abortions and your tenth is free. Not that I care. I don't give two ships or a truck how many abortions Keisha has, I just can't figure out why she can't seem to get her hands on a morning-after pill. Like, Keisha, it's *not that hard*. I offered to help Tatum practice for tryouts. I wondered if she was still a virgin. She had that look, like she'd never had a dick in her mouth. I used to look like that too, a long time ago. Before Cam came around and stuck his in mine. He made me watch porn with him so I'd know what he liked. All that choking and gagging shit. I pretended to like it too but what asshole *likes it* when her eyes are watering cuz her boyfriend's dick is halfway down her throat and her main thought is *don't puke, don't puke, please don't puke.* Tatum just seemed different. I wanted her on the team so I'd have someone new to talk to. I was so fucking bored all the time. I'd been surrounded by the same people since grade school. it was getting so old. Same girls on the team since junior high. Same basic cheers. But what else was there to do around here? other than sucking your boyfriend's dick in the front seat of his dad's F-150 trying to gag sexily—strings of saliva and all that shit—but not puke. You had to have some way of filling your time so you didn't end up slitting your wrists like the kids at Munson High down the road were starting to do. Two suicides since school let out in June.

It was all anybody *didn't* talk about.

That and the fact the boys barely went down on us. Cam went down on me twice. I remember exactly where we were, the specific days, my surroundings, because it was so rare, because eating pussy, I guess, isn't a top search on Pornhub. Go figure.

Do you know how many dick-sucking videos my friends and I watched at sleepovers, trying to perfect our techniques in middle school? A fuckload. How many pussy-eating videos do you think Cam and the other members of the football team watched to prep for going down on us? Zero? Or if they watched any, it was probably on accident. Like somehow one sneaked in on Pornhub.

I had to fake coming both times. It was just too pathetic. His weak-ass cunnilingus techniques. At some point you just have to let both yourselves off the hook and fake it so it can end, so you can both be done with it.

"That was so good, baby," I told him both times after, patting his head, which was still between my legs.

He didn't have a fucking clue I'd faked. He smiled real wide like he knew he was the pussy-eating king of Elkheart. The Dobson High king of cunnilingus. I just smiled back. It wasn't like some of it hadn't felt kinda good. It was like a bad massage. It still feels better than no massage at all, right? That's how Cam's cunnilingus felt. Like, this is okay. This is alright. I'm not gonna fucking come but this is aight.

Then he kissed me, of course. Something else he'd learned in porn. Stuck his tongue with my juices covering it in my mouth. It didn't taste bad. Actually, I tasted pretty good. Even without the pineapple juice cleanse Makayla had told me she was on at the time. Ninth grade and our primary goals were how our pussy tasted for our boyfriends and how well we could fake an orgasm so they'd believe they had skillz they didn't have. Jesus.

TATE GRANT

Since Anissa had left things had really started happening for me. It'd only been three months and already I'd gotten three commercials and an audition for a show based on a Stephen King novel. It was a remake. I think Drew Barrymore was in the original.

I was trying not to think about Anissa, to be honest.

I just wanted to concentrate on acting, on my career, which I was finally allowed to have now that Anissa was gone. She'd always been staunchly against me acting. She was always all big sis protector of me and, for some reason I never understood, Mom always listened to her. I always chalked it up to Anissa having been the sole moneymaker in the family for so long. Like whoever is bringing home the money makes the rules, even if that person is ten and Macaulay Culkin. That was what I *thought*, anyway.

I thought it was selfish of Anissa to leave without telling us where she was going. I refused to waste time worrying about her; *where* she was, *how* she was, all of that. I was trying not to care. I was trying to focus on *me*, for once. I figured eventually she'd come back or call or something.

JAIME KING (model/actress)

I'd always wondered what happened to Rachel. Sorry, another name. I know. She's had so many over the years. At least I've just had Jamie and Jaime. But when I knew Tatum/Anissa she was Rachel Grant. A young—*very young*—actress and sometime model. She was, like, fourteen, when I was nineteen. I'd started modeling when I was fourteen, too, so I knew how it could be, what it was like… shit was fucked up. Adults offering you cocaine, heroin… sex. All of it. The fashion world doesn't care if you're a minor, a child: thirteen, fourteen, fifteen. Hollywood doesn't give *a fuck*. If you're old enough to make money, if you're old enough for them to sell you somehow, you're old enough for everything else, I guess, is what they figure, and what fourteen-year-old doesn't want to make money and make her own decisions and "do" *everything else*?

So we hung out a couple times. After shoots. She had this real iconicness but also an overlookedness. Sort of like Chloe Sevigny. Who also did a shoot with us once back then. Like either one of them could blend into a crowd of teens behind a rural 7-Eleven but could also look like the coolest chick ever, the coolest girl in the world, in the right photograph, with the right photographer or director, you know?

I heard some rumors about her and Quinn James around then, right after the times we were hanging out, and then after that I didn't hear anything for so long, I sort of forgot about her, we all did, I think, we all sort of forgot about her—"Rachel Grant"—until now. Until fucking now. Wow. What the fuck. *What*. The. *Fuck*. Rachel.

KATE MOSS (supermodel)

I didn't meet Johnny for a couple years after I met Rachel. She was still Rachel then. Just another young, teen model like me. Like all of us. You know, Johnny was in his early thirties when he and I started screwing around or dating or wanking or whatever. I think Quinn was only, like, twenty-one, or something, when Rachel and he did that movie together. She was still a teenager, but whatever. That's Hollywood. You *are* the age you're playing on screen and Quinn was playing seventeen. They were teenagers in love and on the run in the Old West in that film, I think. Quinn was so bloody gorgeous, goddamn beautiful. I would have given anything to shag Quinn James. He was definitely as beautiful as Johnny. Maybe more so. I think he was more beautiful, actually, now that I think about it. More beautiful, more vulnerable, more troubled, more in trouble...

Fuck's sake. Quinn James was so bloody beautiful. I still get sad just thinking about it, thinking about him. Wank off.

TAYLOR RAGNER

I smoked a cigarette and Tatum hit it a puff or two. I had a Diet Coke I'd bought from the vending machine in the gym and I opened that and we shared that, too.

Makayla walked by with Matt and waved and then did a double take to see who I was talking to. I knew she'd be jealous but so what. I wasn't her property any more than Cam's. I was tired of feeling like I belonged to these people just because we were all stuck in the same school system together for thirteen years.

ANISSA GRANT

I drove back to my apartment thinking how well everything had gone at the school. How easy. Piece of cake. My first interaction at the school and I'd already met Taylor Ragner and Cam Spencer and Chase Whiting. I parked my car—a ten-year-old used Taurus I'd bought off a guy on Craigslist in Iowa—in the lot in the back of the complex and walked without touching my hair into my apartment.

I'd moved in a few weeks earlier. There were only two apartment complexes in Elkheart so it was pretty easy to choose. I picked the apartments that weren't right next to the bowling alley and Al's Pizza, the only bar in town. I figured that was where the majority of the wife-beaters lived. I was looking for something quieter. I didn't deal well with conflict.

The apartment wasn't bad. It was tan carpet and white walls and two bedrooms and one bath. There was a sliding door in the living room area that led to a tiny patio and I planned on buying a plant to stick out there. One of the bedrooms was considerably larger than the other and I made that bedroom "Mother's room." and fixed up the smaller one the way I liked it with a mattress on the floor and a lamp and a small bureau/desk thing, all of which I'd also gotten off Craigslist.

I hadn't had a room to myself since Tate was born.

I'd gone to the mall and bought some posters of Miley and Beyonce and Drake and that one guy from One Direction to hang on my bedroom walls.

I'd bought a larger bed for Mother's room. A cheap grey couch and black glass coffee table for the living room.

I got a Diet Coke from the fridge and a bag of pretzels and sat on the mattress and opened my laptop. I went first to Tate's social media accounts. She had five of them but I could only see three because two were set to private. Since I'd last looked the night before she'd uploaded two new photographs of herself—one on the set of a movie and one hanging out with girlfriends in her bedroom, which used to be *our bedroom*. I could tell she'd changed it around a lot, taken down pictures I'd hung up, gotten new duvet covers. I wasn't completely sure but I thought it looked like she'd even painted the walls. They looked lighter. Purpler, somehow. She looked like she was dressing more confidently, showing off her curves more. She was self-conscious of her chest. She used to always wear loose t-shirts and high necked blouses to hide it. She thought her boobs were too big, sloppy. Not *classy*. Now it seemed like she was wearing tank tops and lower cut tops like a normal teenager.

That's all I'd ever wanted her to be: a *normal teenager*.

TATE GRANT

I'd gotten cast on this new sick teen show *Freaky Friday*. It was based on the same basic premise as the old school Lindsay Lohan movie, which was, I guess? based on a book from like the 80s or 60s or something? Anyway, the showrunner was the guy who'd directed *Spring Breakers* with Selena Gomez and Vanessa Hudgens and everyone wanted to be in it because it was going to be so much darker and effed up than the Lindsay Lohan Disney version. The tagline was, "Putting the *freaky* back in Fridays," and in it the teen daughter in the mom's body goes out and does crack and meth and shit and the mom in the teen daughter's body fucks some high school boys—a black football player and a wannabe white gangsta, etc.—shit was gonna be so sick and messed up and somehow I'd gotten the lead. Somehow I'd gotten cast in Lindsay's role. Rumor was Justin Bieber was going to have a cameo in it at some point, too. it was the best thing that had ever happened to me! I didn't have time to be a cheerleader now but I was over that anyway. Acting was so much more exciting. Acting was everything. Everything was falling into fucking place finally. Now that Anissa was gone. Now that I was fucking free to make my own decisions. Now that I was fucking free.

I wasn't yet legally emancipated but I was thinking about it. I was considering my options. One thing at a time, though, right? One day at a motherfucking time, bitches. [holds up the peace sign to indicate 'peacing out']

ANISSA GRANT

The first thing I'd done when I'd gotten to Elkheart in July before school started, was to find the cemetery where Quinn was buried. It'd been fifteen years since he'd died, since I'd seen him, and I hadn't been with anyone else or loved anyone else or dated anyone else. I was still fucking pissed at him for abandoning me; for leaving me with my alcoholic mother, our infant daughter... I stopped wanting to act after that. I stopped wanting to leave the house, or to get dressed, or to do anything, really, except watch old movies and take care of our daughter and think about Quinn.

I took a pack of cigarettes and a bottle of Jamison to his grave and lay down on top of it, sort of how Madonna lays down over her mother's grave in *Truth or Dare*, if you've seen that. I smoked two of the cigarettes and drank a couple long swigs of the whiskey and left the rest for Quinn. There was graffiti and trash all over his grave, which seemed fitting; which seemed like he wouldn't have minded, would have liked, even. I kissed his grandmother's headstone next to his. I'd never met her but he'd talked about her every time he got drunk or high and we were alone. His mother had abandoned him when he was three months old and his grandma had raised him. His father split, too. He was practically an orphan. It was hard to stay mad at him, because he was so childlike, so vulnerable and lonely and innocent, under the semi-tough exterior: the teen boy angst shit, the self-destructive delinquent act. You just couldn't help loving him. Also, he was real in a land of phonies. Like Kevin Federline probably seemed to Britney at the time they met. Or maybe *I* was the Kevin Federline in Quinn's world. I don't know. We were both fucked up and had trust issues, we'd both been shitted on by multiple people all our lives. Part of me wanted to die when he died. Part of me did.

ROBIN GRANT

Since my daughter had left I'd finally gotten Tate some auditions. Anissa, or, *Tatum* as you know her, was always staunchly against her being in the business, on account of what happened to Tate's father, I guess. It just never made sense to me, to be honest. Tate was a beautiful, mature, natural actress. I knew she'd do well right away. I knew she'd be successful. Maybe that's what Anissa was afraid of.

Anissa could have been successful.

Anissa was always her own worst enemy, as they say.

She'd tell you it was me, that I was her worst enemy, but you wouldn't know that looking at photographs of the two of us the first ten years of her life.

We were inseparable.

Best buddies.

She was perfect back then; she'd been perfect since birth, which was why I'd gotten her into commercials right away. The baby food commercial and then her face on a box. And then everyone wanted her to play their child on TV and in the movies. She was just so easy to work with, so malleable, so unafraid. I got flack for letting her take roles some people considered too "sexual" at a young age. But it was always because she begged me to let her take them.

Anissa was my perfect little angel baby. We didn't have any other family. Her father and my parents weren't in our life. It was just us. Just she and I against the world, like that old Helen Reddy song. We even shared a bedroom the first few years of her life, until she started booking bigger roles, movies. She hated sleeping alone. She slept with me and then for a brief time she slept with Quinn and then she slept with Tate.

WINONA RYDER (actress)

I only met Rachel Grant once. This was a long, long time ago. Late 90s? She was trying out for a role in *Girl, Interrupted*. The chicken-eating girl. It was this character, this teen girl with an eating disorder, who ate nothing but whole chickens. Roasted. Anyway, I think she got it. I think she actually got the part but then at the same time she found out she'd been cast in that movie with Quinn, Quinn's last movie, turns out... she would have been great in *Girl* but I'm sure she's glad she made the movie with Quinn instead. I mean... I don't know...

It's just so tragic. Like if Johnny had died while we were dating...

Ugh, I don't even want to think about it.

I don't know how you go on after something like that.

It makes total sense she left Hollywood. Or stopped acting, at least.

I don't think I could have gone on acting if Johnny had died back then.

Anyway, the part went to Brittany Murphy—RIP, Brittany; RIP, Quinn; fuck, we lost so many great actors, actresses...—and I never ran into Rachel again. But I remember her being very young and very sweet; very quiet. Sort of how I'd been ten years earlier.

We're ten years apart. Maybe a couple more. Something like that.

Anyway, thank god Johnny didn't die.

He just dated Kate Moss. Tore up some hotel rooms. He was passionate. Johnny was always very passionate. I always heard the same of Quinn James. He and Johnny were friends, actually. But I never met him. But I heard he was a lot like Johnny. Very into music and his work and women and... *passionate*. I guess that sort of thing can go one way or the other... Thank god for Johnny it didn't go Quinn's way. At least, *not all the way* Quinn's way...

Though no one will ever forget Quinn James now.

Not that anyone will ever forget Johnny, either.

ANISSA GRANT

It was scary alone in that apartment at night, sleeping alone for the first time in my life. Thankfully, I had Quinn's gun. We'd been taught how to shoot for his last movie, which was a western. We'd been taught to shoot and to ride horses. I kept the gun behind the mattress where I could reach it if I needed it. I'd left just enough space between the wall and mattress. I'd put a throw pillow down on the floor in case anyone noticed. Not that anyone was ever going to be allowed in my bedroom, allowed in this apartment. Just in case, I don't know, some drunk wandered in the sliding glass door some night. Just in case I needed to shoot somebody. I didn't even know what kind it was; I could never remember. But I had it. Just in case.

JULIET TAYLOR (casting director)

I remember Rachel Grant, sure. She was supposed to be the next Winona Ryder. The next Gwyneth Paltrow. That's how they were trying to sell her (to me). I remember I was casting some movie… god, I can't remember which one now, this was so long ago, the 90s for christ's sake. Maybe a Woody Allen? I don't know. Anyway, I remember her mother bringing her in. Her mother was her manager, her agent, everything. All of it. They were inseparable. Super codependent. I think I remember hearing they even slept in the same bed, that they had since Rachel was a baby. Who knows if that's true. I've heard crazier shit though, in Hollywood. That's for sure.

And, no. I never heard about Rachel and Quinn James. I don't think most people knew about that. Certainly not about a baby! Who knew Quinn James had a kid? Did Quinn even know? Wouldn't he have died before she was born? I'm just trying to do the math…

MAKAYLA RICHEY

I'd seen Taylor talking to the new girl after school. I figured out right away what was going on, what was happening. Taylor and I had been best friends for forever but ever since Chase and I broke up, things had felt different. She didn't like Matt. Or Cam didn't like Matt. Or Chase didn't like me. Or Cam hated my guts.

I knew right then and there I was being replaced. I told Matt, "Look at that bitch." And he said, "Which one?" and I said, "Exactly. Fuck them. Come on." And we kept walking. We walked right on by. But I knew what was up. That was the day I decided… I knew.

ANISSA GRANT

After I looked through all of Tate's social media accounts I could access, I started looking at the accounts of people from Dobson High. I'd bookmarked a few already: Taylor's and Chase's and Cam's and some other girls from the cheerleading team: Keisha and Sam and Whitney and Brooke.

Now I looked for that Makayla girl Taylor had talked to in the parking lot. Another cheerleader. I didn't know how I'd missed her in all my research. She was cute, petite, maybe 5' 2" with a short blonde bob. I found her Instagram and her Twitter. It looked like she had some YouTube videos too. She wanted to be a singer. Most of her videos only had fifty or a hundred views. A couple had less. They were all covers of popular songs on the radio at the time: Kesha and Miley Cyrus and Adele. The Adele ones were the hardest to watch. Someone should have told her you need formal training to attempt an Adele song, much less three Adele songs. Taylor had made a comment under the Kesha video. "Killin' it as usual, Kayla!" she'd written and put a bunch of exclamation points and little black hearts.

I'd sung once in a movie but the songs were low key, were more almost quiet humming than an actual song. There were lyrics but the director had told me to for the most part ignore them. that's what my character would do anyway, he said. I was supposed to be strumming a guitar also but I didn't know guitar. They had some guy show me and I did my best and later they dubbed in someone else playing.

I started looking backwards at Taylor's Instagram photos. It was getting dark out and I went and got a beer, took my clothes off, got comfortable. You weren't supposed to smoke in apartments anymore but I opened the window and did anyway. I remembered reading a quote from either Sean Penn or Johnny Depp somewhere how they wished they had more holes in their bodies to smoke from. I thought that was pretty funny and pretty accurate. Of course I hadn't smoked in years, either. Not since the last time I'd been with Quinn. The second I'd found out I was pregnant (with Tate) I'd quit everything: smoking, drinking, even coffee and sugar.

I kept scrolling farther back waiting for a time period before Cam but I guess there wasn't one. Instagram hadn't been around that long or not as long as Cam at least.

I made an account for myself. Uploaded a photo I'd recently taken of myself at the apartment complex pool that was in the middle of the parking lot. There were a bunch of cars in the background. In the photo I'm wearing an American flag bikini I bought at a Walmart in Iowa. Same town where I got my car.

I didn't have any other photos I wanted to use. I figured I'd take some with Taylor soon and after that everyone at school would add me.

I captioned my pool selfie "new girl" and followed Taylor. A few seconds later she followed me back. I lit another cigarette, smiling.

So far I'd only played a high school student in the movies.

Turns out it wasn't that different irl.

TAYLOR RAGNER

Having a new girl at school was the best thing to happen to me all summer. You hardly ever get new students in a small town like Elkheart. It's the same two hundred kids from kindergarten to high school graduation, everyone in their safe respective cliché, unless one of the fat girls like Bethany Baker suddenly loses a bunch of weight over a summer and moves up a group because suddenly all the guys want to fuck her and all the guys wanting to fuck her makes all the girls want to hang around her. hat happened last year.

Losing enough weight can make you excitingly like a new girl.

I couldn't wait for school to start to show off my new BFF Tatum.

She was new and shiny and mysterious. I looked at her social media account but it seemed like she'd just made it, like she hadn't had it before moving to Elkheart. Like she was a totally brand new human being with no past.

Which was exciting because I could make her into whoever I wanted her to be.

And I had plans for who I wanted her to be.

Or maybe I had plans for who I'd always wanted to be but never thought I could be until Tatum moved to town.

Plus, she looked real hot in her American flag bikini. Like a girl in a Kid Rock video when I was little, before Kid Rock was a racist or an asshole or a republican or old or all of the above. Cam still listened to him. He said his music was good for working out to. Eye roll. OH-kay, Cam. Whatever.

ANISSA GRANT

I was obsessed with this kinda old song—old meaning it'd come out three years earlier or something, I think. Tove Lo's "Habits" (Stay High). I'd somehow stumbled upon the video one night a couple weeks earlier and it really spoke to me. I watched it over and over, studying Tove Lo's face as she becomes more and more intoxicated, sadder and sadder, until finally she's alone, drunk off her ass, crying in a bathroom stall. That's kinda how I felt inside. I was beginning to realize I'd never really mourned Quinn's death, I'd never really been allowed to, because no one was supposed to know about us, because I had this little baby to raise, Quinn's baby, but I couldn't tell anyone she was Quinn's baby, or I felt I shouldn't...

Now I just related so hard to that song. I listened to it constantly and thought of Quinn. I started drinking while listening to the song and thinking of Quinn. Pretty much the first two weeks I was in town, after I made it to Elkheart, I was drunk all the time, singing that song, drunk, alone, crying in my new shitty-ass apartment, instead of a bathroom stall. My favorite line was the one about throwing up in the bathtub. I may have, in fact, thrown up in a bathtub. I hadn't been alone since Quinn died. I was still processing his death. I'd put mourning him on hold to raise this little baby he left me with. Once I started mourning, though, finally, I couldn't stop. I saw his face everywhere now, again. I kept driving by the cemetery, sometimes I stopped, sometimes I just kept driving.

"I gotta stay high, all the time, to keep you off my mind."

"Spend my days locked in a haze tryin to forget you, babe, I fall back down."

"Gotta stay high, all my life, to forget I'm missing you."

Yeah... Ummm... I don't think there's any other song that speaks to me more than that one. In some ways, the person you love most in the world dying, or, leaving you, is all the permission you need to completely fuck up your life, to do whatever you want or to *not do* anything. you know?

I was finally giving myself permission—fifteen years later.

CAM SPENCER

It was the Friday before school started and I was at Kmart with my brother Gage. He was buying beer for us, for a cookout we were having later with Chase and guys from the team. First Gage said he needed socks so I was wandering, bored, around, waiting, when I saw the new girl, Tatum, walking around by herself. She was wearing cutoffs and a tank top and you could see way more of her body than you could the first time I saw her on School ID day when she'd been wearing a skirt and some sort of blousey top thing. There wasn't much there, in the tit department. I mean, Taylor was practically a double D. Taylor had the most perfect tits you've ever seen in your goddamn life. Taylor had the most perfect everything. But like Chris Rock says, even if you have the hottest woman in the world, the top supermodel, after a while, it gets old, you crave something new. Like, even Jay Z gets bored of fucking Beyonce, right? I wasn't exactly craving but, you know… And Tatum had killer legs, like really toned and shit. And a nice ass. Especially in those cut offs. What did I care if she didn't have any tits?

It was one in the afternoon and the cookout wasn't until six. I walked over to her and said hey and asked her what she was doing and she said nothing. Her car keys were hanging out of her pocket and I said, you drive? And she said, yeah, she had recently turned sixteen, got her license soon as she and her mom moved to Indiana, and I don't know why, maybe because Taylor and I had had another fight that morning, maybe because it was really hot, like the hottest day that summer, and the heat always makes me extra horny, but I asked her if she wanted me to show her the reservoir, the lake all the kids went to to hang out. I told her we could take some of the beer Gage was buying. A six-pack or whatever.

It wasn't planned at all. It was just a chance occurrence. Happenstance or whatever it is Coach Wellsley is always talking about. Her ass looked real good in those cutoffs. Even if they were from Aeropostale, which is, like, really lame.

ANISSA GRANT

I don't know why I said yes to Cam. Does there have to be a reason? I wasn't expecting to see him, I guess. I was at Kmart buying a plant for my patio and another box of Twinkies. He caught me off guard. I knew he was Taylor's boyfriend. And I wanted to be Taylor's friend. But I'd only met her that once and she hadn't seemed that into him anyway and anyway we were just going to go see the lake, hang out, drink a couple beers. It was like I was inside that Tove Lo video now.

This was why I'd moved to Indiana. For these types of *experiences*. Shit you could write about in your *journal*, if you were that kind of person (I'm not). Ways of forgetting Quinn, of forgetting who I was, of forgetting the history of Hollywood, of L.A., forgetting.

Cam was acting a lot sweeter toward me when we ran into each other in Kmart than he had at the school with Chase.

Maybe when he was with Chase he let Chase be the nice guy.

Anyway, he was kinda hot in a frat boy/douchebag way and I didn't have anything else to do, other than eat Twinkies and throw up in my bathtub.

"Okay," I said, shrugging my shoulders, feeling very Tove Lo about the whole thing, about Cam, and Cam said, "one second," and got the beer from his brother and got in the passenger seat of my car, my new houseplant on the floor between his feet, Twinkies in a plastic bag on the back seat, and told me where to drive.

Is this where I mention I'd only ever fucked one guy?

ANONYMOUS DIRECTOR

I think for the most part, people had forgotten about "Rachel Grant," or, you know, Tatum, Anissa. (Rachel Grant was who she was billed as so that's still how I tend to remember her). I mean, it'd been... what... twelve years? oh, longer? fifteen? longer? since her last film, the one she made with Quinn... Hollywood isn't exactly known for its long-term memory. Most people— actors and so forth—get six months. Six months to stay relevant. Unless you're goddamn Tom Cruise or Angelina Jolie or something. And Rachel Grant was never Tom Cruise. Quinn James could have been Tom Cruise, if he'd wanted to be. But Rachel, Rachel, I don't think ever had that full star quality. That charisma. She was a great actress. She could fully and convincingly envelop any character. But most people didn't even know her name. They confused her with other actresses of similar name and with a similar lack of defining persona or brand, shall we say, at the time. There were three of them then that all sort of ran together in your mind: Rachel Grant, Raquel Janson, and Jasmine Granderson. All quality actresses. All boring public personalities.

I mean, off-screen, Rachel could be really awkward and almost off-putting. Like, you might hire her for a film—I didn't, but you might— because she was a hard worker and a good actress who wouldn't give you shit, who wouldn't become a major pain in your ass like most big name actresses could be and were—but you might not because of her total lack of recognition as a personality, as anyone you wanted to read about in *People* or *US Weekly* or, later, follow on Twitter or Instagram, as someone who could sell a film. Did you ever see that clip of her on Letterman back in the 90s? Oh, man. She was just so stiff and dull. And this was in an era when you had Drew fucking Barrymore climbing up on Letterman's desk and lifting her shirt. She fucking flashed Dave her tits—Drew did. And then you have Rachel just sitting there, hands in lap, wanting to talk about her *craft*. Dave couldn't get anything out of her. It wasn't even funny in an awkward way. It just wasn't funny. She just wasn't made for the PR side of the business. The persona side. She was devoid of persona. Everything she had went into the characters she played. Otherwise she was an empty shell. Or so it seemed from her appearances on Letterman and *The Today Show* and some parties we both attended back in the day. I don't think she even did coke. When *everyone* was doing coke. Maybe if she'd done some coke she would have developed a person-*ality*. But, so, yeah. Rachel Grant wasn't really on anyone's radar anymore. The only reason you really even thought about her was if you were thinking about what actresses Quinn had fucked and most people weren't even aware he and Rachel had been a thing, ever, so, most people just didn't think of her anymore. Ever. At all. Until now. Of course.

CAM SPENCER

She was acting cool that day, not how she'd act later: like a *bitch*.

I'd never done anything like this, never even kissed anyone but Taylor in the three years we'd been going out. I wouldn't have had the chance, Taylor knew everyone and everyone knew Taylor and I were going out.

And girls were afraid of Taylor.

And to be honest, I'd never been tempted. Not *really*. Not more than jerking off to the fantasy of being with someone else knowing you would never actually do it. I loved Taylor. But we'd had that fight, and she could be such an annoying bitch sometimes, too.

And Tatum being new, something felt different. I mean, if we hadn't run into each other that day at Kmart, I don't think anything would have ever happened.

But it was August and hot as fuck and we sat in the grass by the lake, drinking the beers, and I got a little drunk and I think Tatum was a little drunk. You know girls: lightweights.

I said, "Have you ever been skinny dipping?" and she shook her head, no, and I said, "Come on then, let's do it!"

And we started taking off our clothes and running toward the water, which was something Taylor would never do *then*. Taylor would be too afraid someone would see us, that she'd ruin her perfect reputation. I guess Tatum didn't have a reputation yet… that's sort of ironic, I guess, to think about now, her *reputation*… haha… given everything that's happened, but anyway, she was fast. I was behind her, running, checking out her bod, which was tight, which was tan and tight, and her little titties, they weren't bad either… Only weird thing was she had a bush, a big fucking afro bush. Maybe that was cool out in California, but no one in Indiana I knew of had pubes. Taylor had been waxed even as a virgin. Hell, she'd probably been waxed since she sprouted her first pube. Even all us guys shaved, balls too. Pubic hair was just so… I don't know, I just never thought about it because you never saw it.

Then again, she had those little titties with the dark nipples and I couldn't wait to get my mouth on them. I started sprinting to catch up. I'd had a couple beers. I was kinda drunk. Hella hard.

ANISSA GRANT

I hadn't been naked with another person in a long time. The first time Quinn and I got together I got drunk and ended up telling him he was the hottest guy I'd ever met. Which was *true* (and saying a lot in *Hollywood*), but *still*. He sort of smirked and said, "Thanks—you're special, too." I was fifteen and he was twenty-one. He said, "I get that a lot." But he wasn't all conceited about it. It was just a fact. Like the fact he loved heroin. Like the fact everyone in Hollywood including me knew he would die soon. Maybe that made him even hotter.

I was drunk enough to look down at Cam's dick. It was bouncing.

It was like a scene I'd freeze-framed from *Porky's*, a movie my mother'd made me watch years ago when I was auditioning for the role of a high school popular girl. I didn't get it.

Staring at Cam—at another man's body—just made me miss Quinn even more. Quinn had the delicate body of a druggie; a "coke body," he called it. He rarely ate. He smoked at least three packs of cigarettes a day, on top of whatever drugs he was doing. Coke. Amphetamines. Whatever. He barely weighed more than me and I had an eating disorder. Also, I missed his beautiful cock. Even his cock was somehow angelic.

Cam wasn't the hottest guy I'd ever met, not even close. Cam was a frat boy, in comparison. Dull, thick, muscular in a way that wasn't *that* interesting.

His dick was fine.

"Suck it," he said, moving his hips, sort of thrusting them forward. Quinn had never told me expressly to suck his dick. He'd never had to—I was nothing if not eager, but I don't think he would have anyway. He was a gentleman, like that. But I got down on my knees in the sand. I was playing a role. I was saying yes to life. Whatever. But I wasn't going to swallow. I planned to pull my mouth away just in time for Cam to come on my face, but then some got in my mouth, anyway. He started coming when I wasn't ready, out of nowhere, and I swallowed some without realizing what was happening, my brain was slow to catch up, and then I pulled away and some got in my eye. I was sure this was something Cam had watched a thousand times in porn, something he thought was really cool, super *hot*. Coming in a chick's eye.

"Sorry," he sort of laughed. I wiped at my eye with the back of my hand, swallowed. My mouth tasted salty, chlorine'y. Like I'd just been in a pool.

"Whatever," I said, rolling my eyes, the eye that was still wet with his come. Then, almost immediately, after he'd taken a few more swigs of a warm beer, handing the backwash to me, he turned me around so that my back was to him, and shoved his dick up in me, doggy-style, there on the waterfront. How romantic, I thought, eyes rolling, again, in my head. I came, anyway, with my eyes already rolled backward. I figured one stereotype was true, at least: teen boys can fuck and fuck.

Immediately, I felt sorry for Taylor. What if she thought this was what sex was supposed to be like? Cam coming on her face, in her eye. What if she married Cam and this was what she had to deal with the rest of her life? Frat bro sex. Married to a fucking douchebag who wore knock off Brooks Brothers shirts and Polo cologne for fifty years before dying, bloated, balding, of a heart attack, while fucking someone else on some fucking cheap drug he saw advertised on TV to make his dick harder. I couldn't stomach this fate for my beautiful perfect Taylor Ragner. I couldn't fucking stand to think of her marrying Cam. It made me physically ill. I vomited into the bushes. I vomited Cam's come into the grass on all fours like an actual dog.

"Sorry," I sort of laughed. "Must have been the warm beer."

CAM SPENCER

She fucking puked right after we finished. I didn't take it personally. Girls can't handle their alcohol, I figured. Taylor was always puking, too. And just that one thought—of Taylor puking—made me miss her so much.

And I knew that this had been a one-time thing, that it would never happen again; *could* never happen again. I don't know what I'd been thinking. All of a sudden this new girl didn't look so good to me. All of a sudden she looked like a basic bitch and in my head Taylor was an angel and I was the stupidest moron on the planet. Maybe it was the 'roids my brother had given me, that made me act so stupid sometimes, like that day, like thinking it was a good idea to fuck the new girl at the lake. Man, was that fucking stupid. Chase would definitely have bitched me out if he could see me. Chase was always coming at me with morals and shit like that, like he was a fucking altar boy or some shit. He wasn't even Catholic but he could guilt you real good like he was. He shoulda been a priest, that's what I always thought, what I always told him, too. "You should be a goddamn priest, with your morals and your guilt and your goodness." He'd just smile and shake his head. "No way, man," he'd say. "I'm not good. You don't know. I'm not good at all."

ANISSA GRANT

After I finished vomiting I laid down next to Cam on my stomach. It felt good to be in the grass, in the sun. I was still a little drunk. I'd rinsed my mouth with a fresh beer.

I said, "Don't you date Taylor Ragner?"

High school and Hollywood have that in common: you always refer to people by both their first and last names.

"Yeah," Cam said. "I do. So, like, we can *never tell anyone about this*. This *never* happened."

"Of course," I said.

He didn't hate me yet, in that moment by the lake. That would come later, once school started and Taylor and I became best friends.

"Our little secret," I said. I'd turned over onto my back and he bent down and kissed me, closed mouth, no tongue. He was probably still thinking of the puke. It was the last time I kissed him. His lips were dry, chapped. My mouth still tasted like his come and my vomit, warm beer.

I wanted the next person I kissed to be his girlfriend, Taylor. But it wouldn't exactly work out that way. Life doesn't always go as planned.

TAYLOR RAGNER

I invited Tatum over the Saturday before school started to go over some cheers with her. I wanted to get to know her better, also. I wanted to make sure she felt some loyalty to me before school started and all the other girls tried to claim her for themselves.

At first my mom really liked her. She asked her a ton of questions about California and L.A. and her mom and all that. Tatum answered politely but vaguely. Something about moving to California with her mom when she was little to escape an alcoholic, older father. Something about having done a couple commercials when she was little. Something about being home-schooled. Something about being an only child. Being lonely. Not knowing how to interact with her peers.

After she left my mom said Tatum seemed smart and interesting. She said she was polite and mature for her age.

I didn't give a shit about polite or mature or what my mom thought about anything.

I dragged Tatum into my room and locked the door so we could have some privacy. My mom was the type to eavesdrop and be all up in your business. It's because my father was always away on business trips. They didn't sleep in the same room anymore. And my older brother was away at college, dealing drugs and running poker games to pay for his own addiction to amphetamines, which I think my mother knew but pretended not to. Which left all her focus on me.

The year before I'd slit my wrists and taken twenty Motrin because I couldn't handle being under her constant watch. I'd been in the hospital a few days and gone to counseling but it was over the summer so not that many people knew, surprisingly. My mother had promised to give me some room, some breathing space, but like I said, that was a year ago and she was starting to close in on me again, up my ass about Cam and me and Makayla and me and making sure I was preparing for college aps by doing extracurriculars and taking the right classes and volunteering somewhere I could brag about in a college entry essay.

The thing was, I didn't even know if I wanted to go to college. At least not right away. But I couldn't tell her that.

I couldn't tell her anything, which is why she resorted to eavesdropping and trying to control me and micromanage my life as much as possible.

I prayed every night she'd meet a man (*or woman*) and have an affair.

I thought maybe I could convince Coach Wellsley, who was a loser and divorced or a loser who never married—no one really knew, once school started. He was a loser but some girls at school thought he was cute in a total loser way. Our options for teacher fantasies were extremely limited.

It felt like my only hope. *He* felt like my only hope.

Get. Mom. Laid.

Get. Mom. Off. My. Ass.

I'd seen Coach Wellsley looking at it—my ass, I figured he'd like my mom's too. In her knock off Lululemon yoga pants she was always wearing. God knows my fucking dad never looked anymore. Who knows whose ass he looked at, but it wasn't my mom's.

ANISSA GRANT

Taylor's house was in the subdivision with the town's community pool. I didn't imagine it was open too many days a year but it was open that first day I drove to Taylor's to practice cheers. It wasn't much bigger than the pool at my apartment complex and it sat on top of this small hill surrounded by allotment houses. I could see a lifeguard chair and a bunch of sideways bicycles and chubby kids and scrawny kids running around on the cement as I drove by. It looked like about two hundred kids in a pool built for twenty. It looked like an outtake from *Gummo* where all the huffers take a break from huffing to go swimming.

In L.A. everyone has a pool so there are rarely more than four people in one at any given time. I couldn't imagine the amount of urine in a pool with that many people, the amount of chlorine it must take to kill all the bacteria and sickness and baby shit.

Taylor's house was a ranch like all the other houses in the subdivision but a little bit bigger, a little bit nicer. She told me later that once her dad started making more money, started traveling a lot, they'd added on to the house instead of moving into a bigger one because her mom didn't want to move away from their neighbors: a whole new wing in the back, finished the basement with carpeting and paneling, put in a master bedroom bathroom so they no longer all had to share.

It was a Midwest teen dream. A Katy Perry video set.

Taylor's mom was in the kitchen making sun tea when I got there so I had to hang out and do the parent thing for a few minutes before Taylor and I could go to her room. Taylor's mom looked like an *SNL* actress doing a sketch of a suburban housewife making sun tea while secretly wishing she was still sixteen and getting laid on a regular basis. Like the mom in *Mean Girls*. Like she probably had extensions in her hair and injections in her lips. She probably owned Christie Brinkley's book on looking like an 80s swimsuit model well into your sixties. Like that was her Bible. That and every Kardashian's Instagram page. I wondered if she'd thought about getting cheek injections, butt implants. So many women in L.A. had them. All of it: butt implants, cheek injections, lip injections, breast implants, Botox, lasering, labia sculpting, asshole bleaching... you can't imagine the procedures available an aging woman in California with a bit of disposable income.

And by aging I mean twenty-two. Twenty-three.

Taylor's mom's face looked a little Botox'y when you got up close. A little frozen. She smiled and half her mouth went up and one eyebrow. I figured the "doctors" in the Midwest didn't quite have it all figured out yet, how to inject a woman's face without completely immobilizing it, without making her look like a Real Housewife of Elkheart, Indiana cast member.

"Who's your new friend, Tay-Tay," her mom said, staring at me. I was staring at the wooden cross on the kitchen wall behind her.

"Jesus, I asked you not to call me that, Mom. It's bad enough when Cam does."

"I'm sorry, baby," her mom said, in a voice you use to talk to a toddler. Or a man who's paying to have sex with you.

"Mom! *God*!" Taylor said. She made some other noises and rolled her eyes and grabbed my arm, grabbed my wrist. I smiled back at her mom as she drug me down the hall.

TAYLOR RAGNER

God, my mom was so embarrassing. I'd told her over and over not to get any work done. Even her hair was ridiculous. Like, nothing says I'm desperate to look younger than curled hair extensions that reach your ass. I wanted to rip them out whenever I saw her, burn them in our new fireplace, but it was fake too. Everything in this house was fake as fuck. My mom and her stupid baby voice most of all. I couldn't take it anymore. I grabbed Tatum and led her down the hall to my room.

"Don't bother us!" I yelled at my mom. "We're practicing."

"Sorry about that," I told Tatum. "My mom's a little psycho."

"No worries," Tatum said. "My mom is a little psycho too. You'll see if she's ever around."

"You're lucky," I said. "That she's not. I wish my mom had a sick aunt."

Then I realized that probably sounded shitty.

"I mean, to keep her busy and not up my ass all the time."

"I know what you meant. No worries. Moms are assholes."

"Yeah."

TATE GRANT

I was still a virgin when Anissa left. How could I have been anything else? Anissa and Robin never let me out of the house alone.

I never even knew what was up with Anissa—I remember thinking, like, is *she* a virgin too? El-oh-el. I had no clue. No one in our house talked about sex. There were three of us females living there together and sex was like this thing that didn't exist. I didn't know how Anissa or I even got born! I think for a long time I believed, like, that stork shit. Like in *Dumbo*—a movie, coincidentally or not, they made me watch *a lot*. Or, like, artificial insemination. Not, like, the Virgin Mary. Not, like, God artificially inseminated my mo… Robin. But, like, maybe she'd gone to a sperm bank. Fifteen, sixteen years apart gone and got artificially knocked up?

How the fuck was I supposed to know?

I just knew something wasn't right.

Shit was weird.

Where were the dads?

Shit was fucked up.

And I was a fifteen-year-old virgin. Which felt *really old* in Hollywood.

ANISSA GRANT

Taylor's room was just the same as it was in all her videos.

I already knew she had a bird because you could always hear it chirping somewhere just off screen while she was talking to the camera in her YouTube videos, but now I could see it: he was one of those little green canaries. At least I think he was a canary. Something like that. I didn't ask.

Anyway, I knew her rug was purple. Her bed cover purple. Her bed canopy purple. But I pretended to look around. To take it all in.

"I like your rug," I told her, which was maybe the dumbest thing I could have said.

"Thanks," she said. "I hate purple but it's the school color and my mom is, like, *obsessed* with me showing school spirit. I think she was a cheerleader or something in Puerto Rico before my grandparents moved her here and she never got over it."

I kept looking around the room at all the parts that had been off camera in the videos. Her name was spelled out in big, purple, bubble letters on the wall next to photographs of her and her brothers and parents and another one of her and Cam and another of her and the Dobson High cheerleading squad and a bunch of ribbons for gymnastics and cheerleading competitions.

"Oh, *god*," she said, rolling her eyes. "How embarrassing my life is; sorry."

I didn't know what she was talking about. She had the perfect suburban life, as far as I was concerned. She had the life I'd only ever fantasized about, tried to mimic on film. I mean, aside from her boyfriend, Cam, who'd been inside me less than twenty-four hours ago and who I could kind of still taste in my mouth.

I didn't notice the scars until later: they were on her arms and inner thighs.

"I'm just not a happy person," she told me that first day alone in her room but immediately after making that admission she'd shrugged her shoulders and smiled and said, "What the fuck am I talking about? I'm a spoiled fucking half-Latina Disney princess. I have everything I want!"

I didn't know what to say to either declaration so I just shrugged back. "I wouldn't know about either," I said. "I've lived a very isolated life so far."

She was sitting on the bed biting at her hangnails.

"You seem cool to me," I added. I was standing looking at the photograph of her with her family. They were all wearing white like they were expecting an angel to ascend them to heaven immediately following the family photo shoot. Or like they were in Scientology.

Anyway, in the living room was a picture of Jesus with some sort of palm frond stuck behind it, which I guess meant they were Catholic.

I hadn't thought of my own mother in a few hours, which, honestly, was a relief.

There were photographs of the two of us smiling on sets when I was younger. The one that stuck out in my head was the one of us on the movie where I played a child prostitute. I was eleven and even more flat-chested. It was like 1995 or something but the movie was set in the '30s, during the Great Depression. Kurt Cobain had been dead a few months. I had Nirvana posters all over my room. I sang "Rape Me" while crying alone in the shower. I was a very angsty eleven-year-old. But maybe it turns out, all eleven-year-olds are angsty. Or think they are. Drew Barrymore was already practically a drunk at eleven *and smoking weed*. Anthony Kiedis wrote his dad a note asking if he could have sex with his *dad's girlfriend* when he was eleven. The girlfriend was like nineteen and his dad said yes. Anthony smoked weed at age eleven, too. I know. I read his book. Twice. Also, maybe he was at a club with me and Quinn once or twice. It's hard to remember. After a while all the scrawny druggie boys from L.A. sort of run together.

"I'm not cool," Taylor said. She was wearing plaid cotton shorts and her thighs were spread out on the bed in a way I found excruciating.

I sort of wanted to kneel down between them.

I could see some faint stretch marks. Some less faint marks where she'd carved out her pain.

I imagined running my tongue over them. I had a thing for any sort of imperfection on a beautiful girl: cellulite, little tiny pimples, a birthmark, razor wounds.

But I remained standing and she said, "So you want to see some fucking cheers?" and she got out her laptop to show me some videos. I sat down beside her on the bed and she smelled like a Victoria's Secret Pink store. Like cotton candy and bubble gum.

It made me want a cigarette so bad.

Instead, I pinched the sides of my legs as hard as I could.

TAYLOR RAGNER

We were out in my backyard practicing cheers when my little brother Jimmy came out to watch us. Jimmy was six, about to start first grade. His whole life he'd been like my shadow, following me around the house, into my room, wanting me to put makeup on him, to paint his nails. He said he wanted to be a cheerleader like me when he grew up.

Mom would always just laugh it off but Dad would get annoyed and leave the room or make some sort of disparaging comment about encouraging him and normalizing "it." Like he thought if we didn't indulge Jimmy's wants, like me painting his fingernails or letting him dress up in my old cheer uniform, he'd stop wanting to do these things. He'd suddenly become super hyper-masculine and athletic like my dad and older brother.

It made me so mad that Dad couldn't just accept Jimmy the way he was, instead of fearing him or fearing how he was different from other little boys or different even from him.

Tatum was so good with Jimmy. She showed him how to do some gymnastics, a backbend and side splits. He tried to mimic all our cheers, too. He got so sad when it was time for Tatum to leave. He kept saying, "Where's

Tay?" after she left, which was also what he called me so it was confusing but really sweet, too.

He liked Cam but not like that. Cam always tried to play ball with him or watch some boy cartoon like Sponge Bob and Jimmy just wanted to watch girls' stuff. Jimmy really just wanted to be a girl.

ANABEL RAGNER

I met Tatum the weekend before school started. Taylor had her over to help her with some cheers. She seemed normal enough. More mature, maybe, than some of the other girls. But also, in a way, less so.

Taylor seemed excited about her. That's mostly what I noticed. Taylor couldn't stop talking about her after that.

I thought maybe it would be good for her.

She'd been depressed the last year or so.

There was the incident you've read about, I'm sure. I don't want to go into that right now. But we'd had some hard times with Taylor.

I watched them doing cheers in our backyard that afternoon as I sipped my sun tea.

Jimmy was out there with them, of course. He always followed Big Sis around and tried to do whatever she did. He seemed to like Tatum, too. He couldn't stop talking about her either, to be honest.

I was just happy for a break from both of them.

I was reading a book I'd gotten at the library about preparing your high school student for college applications. It went year by year, Freshman, Sophomore, etc., and listed what you should be doing each of those years. If you want to get into a good school. If you don't want to end up at a community college or whatever. Not that there's anything wrong with community colleges. That's where Taylor's father and I met. But I always pictured Taylor going somewhere more… academic. like Duke or Northwestern or Harvard. But mostly Duke. For some reason Duke had been a fantasy of mine. Duke seemed even more regal than the northeastern schools to me.

I looked through the Freshman year chapters. We were already so far behind. There was already so much to catch up on.

ANISSA GRANT

On the way home from Taylor's house I stopped at the mall. It was much smaller than the malls I was used to going to in California. For one, there was no food court, just a Starbucks and a Mrs. Fields cookies stuck in the middle, and some weird regional Greek restaurant chain next to the Macy's.

I went to American Eagle and Victoria's Secret and Forever 21 and bought a couple more tank tops and button-up plaid shirts and lip glosses and cologne sprays in pink bottles.

I went to Hollister which was a store made to look like a California surf shop. You entered one side if you were a boy and the other if you were a girl and both sides had loud music and smelled like coconut suntan lotion. I thought I saw the Makayla girl Taylor had talked to outside the school on photo day working behind the counter but I wasn't sure. I picked out a handful of denim skirts and jeans and went into the dressing room area to try them on. That guy Chase, Cam's friend, was working the dressing rooms. I wasn't sure if he remembered me. He was tall, taller than Cam, and leaner than Cam, with light brown hair and green eyes. He smiled and asked me how many items and I made a fast count and said six. He was wearing a tight-fitted v-neck t-shirt and I could tell his nipples were hard from the A/C.

When I came back out of the dressing room he asked me how they'd worked out, meaning the clothes I'd tried on, and I said fine and handed him the ones I didn't want. I said thanks and he said no problem and we stood there smiling at each other dumbly for a few seconds and when I turned around, that Makayla chick was standing there, observing the whole interaction. I didn't see why she cared, though, because I thought Taylor said she was with that guy Matt we'd seen her walking into the school with.

CHASE WHITING

When I saw Tatum at the mall that day before school, I thought she was prettier than I'd remembered. But maybe I hadn't remembered much from the first time I saw her because she was with Taylor and I was with Cam and Taylor and Cam had a way of outshining everyone else around them. She had a nice smile. And she looked Californian. And she pissed off Makayla who for some reason acted territorial about me even though we were broken up and I was pretty sure she was screwing Matt Reynolds now.

I liked her the most for pissing off Makayla.

No matter what Cam said I didn't want a girlfriend, but I thought Tatum could be interesting to hang with. I sort of looked forward to seeing her at school all weekend after that.

ANISSA GRANT

Anyway, after Hollister I went to Sephora and stole a blue mascara and a purple lipstick so I would have school pride and so I could feel like a real teenager. I'd never stolen anything before. Not even a set prop or anything; I always asked or they just gave me stuff after a film wrapped. I was sure walking out someone was going to come running after me. Call out "Miss" or tap me on the shoulder or something like I'd seen in movies. 95% of what I know about life I've watched in movies or on TV, or in preparing for roles I'd auditioned for and sometimes gotten for TV shows and movies. I'd never played the sort of teen girl who steals shit from malls, though, so I hadn't method acted being the sort of teen girl who steals shit from malls.

I went back to the apartment and shut the blinds and got in my bed with my laptop and two Diet Cokes and my cigarettes. I got online and Googled "cheerleading tryouts" and "cheerleading competitions" and looked for the most popular videos. I wanted to take my cheerleading opportunity seriously. It was half the reason I'd moved from California.

I stumbled onto this one site that claimed to be *what every young woman should know about high school cheerleading* and said shit like, "High school cheerleading is where the fun begins!" (right, that's why I'm here) and "High school cheerleading tryouts can be one of the most exciting times in a girl's life." (we'll see) and "Being a cheerleader in high school can be one of the most 'looked-up-to' activities a person can be involved in, but it can be hard work too. You will find that there's much more to being a cheerleader than just being 'cute' and 'popular.'" (not so sure) And lastly, "You will more than likely be given a list of rules that you must abide by throughout the year to remain on the cheerleading squad." (mmmm)

Then I got on YouTube. The first video I watched was called "high school cheer tryout video" (not even a capitalization) and had 137,000 views. But it was mostly a lot of "competitive cheering"—multiple backflipping, something called "flying partnerstunts," and something else called "stunting basing." This was probably the sort of "cheering" you did in at a larger high school, in a major city or something. Or at least in a town with a population higher than five thousand, which was a high estimate for Elkheart, Indiana.

Luckily, the stage mom that she was, my mother enrolled me in dance, gymnastics, and whatever other classes she could sign me up for from age two onward. I knew most of the basic moves and what I didn't know or had forgotten, I retaught myself via the YouTube videos. I'd played a teenage runaway stripper in one of the last movies I'd made, ten years ago. I was fairly confident going into tryouts. I just had to remember to at least *act* confident 24/7. Anyway, Taylor had been a cheerleader all through middle school and freshman year and she said I would make it in easy, no problem.

"Besides," she said. "Wait til you see all the lameos and butterfaces who try out. It's fucking pathetic. I don't know what they're thinking. Like, they're going to represent our school? I don't think so."

COACH W

I'd been teaching and coaching at Dobson High about ten years. I taught English *and* History and every now and then they let me teach acting too. Every once in a while they let me put on a school play. Neither was in our permanent budget. Our permanent budget was shit. It allowed for football and basketball and that was about it, as far as "the arts" goes. A long, long time ago I fancied myself an actor. I thought I would make it out of Elkheart, find my way to Hollywood, sign into the movies like signing in at the DMV. Believe it or not, I'd been semi-good looking once. Before all the alcohol and cigarettes. The years of living alone and drinking myself into oblivion because Hollywood, it turns out, didn't want me. It took about two weeks to find this out and years to recover from the realization, all the I wasn'ts. I wasn't good looking enough. I wasn't talented enough. I wasn't charismatic enough. I wasn't driven *enough*. The best and worst part was, my best friend who went out there with me was all of those things. Of course, that didn't stop his self-destructiveness, it just fed it. Now he had the money to feed his self-annihilating heart all the meth and heroin and coke it wanted, demanded. It was painful to watch—both his success and his deterioration—from back here in Elkheart. That was where football came in handy. I'd watch the boys I was coaching pummeling the shit out of each other and remember his and my better years. The summers we spent drinking beers and smoking cigarettes out on the football field in the middle of the night. The autumn nights we pummeled boys like us from neighboring shithole towns. Luke Perry was from one of them. Luke Perry was from the tiniest little shithole town, that was how we'd gotten the idea to go to Hollywood, following Luke Perry.

Goddamn, motherfucking Luke Perry, may he—and my friend—rest in peace.

ANISSA GRANT

The first day of school I just kept thinking about what Taylor had said in her video about smiling. Taylor had the best smile.

That morning before school I stood in the apartment bathroom practicing my smile for two full minutes.

I wanted to make a good first impression on my new classmates, on the faculty and administration.

I wanted to come across as a peppy and energetic person like Taylor.

I tried to do the exercises some actors like to do on sets. I asked myself, *what's my motivation?*

That was easy. Live the life I was never allowed to live the first time around.

Make the cheer team, go to prom.

Have a popular best friend like Taylor Ragner.

Make a nice, sweet, good-looking football player like Chase Whiting fall in love with me.

It was the American dream.

That's what I wanted.

I wanted my slice of teen-aged American pie. I wanted what Michael Jackson never got. What Drew Barrymore missed out on.

Michael made sure his daughter Paris went to high school, was a cheerleader, at least.

COACH W

I think one of the reasons Taylor was so popular was because she was one of those early bloomers, shall we say, who basically looked like a grown woman in eighth grade. Which isn't exactly a good thing. I think it can kind of be a curse. People assume things about you when you're fifteen and look like Taylor Ragner.

It was similar with the new girl, Tatum Grant. She wasn't built like Taylor but she had a maturity to her, poise, the way she carried herself.

To be honest, if I saw the two of them at a gas station—Taylor and Tatum—I would think Taylor was about twenty-six and Tatum was maybe twenty.

The world works on what it assumes about a person based on her looks. For a long time my grandma believed Mariah Carey was white. I remember the day I walked into her house and she said, "Mariah Carey is marrying a black man."

She was lying on the couch in her quilted housecoat and she pointed a finger at the TV.

I looked at the TV and looked at my Nana and I said, "Nana, Mariah Carey is black."

You should have seen my Nana's face.

That's the face a lot of teachers and students had later, myself included, when the news started reporting about Tatum.

ANISSA GRANT

I'd watched and studied all of Taylor's YouTube videos. I watched them and then watched them again, taking notes, preparing, as I used to, for a film, for a movie role.

I practiced all her cheers and stretches and makeup applications and hair tutorials. But also I practiced *smiling*. In some ways this was much harder than the stretches and cheerleading moves. Remembering to smile is *really hard*, especially when you've been a recluse like me for fifteen years.

It honestly felt good to have a role to play again, someone else to be besides boring me.

Most of the roles I'd taken in the first sixteen years of my life had been girls and young women not too unlike me: serious, introverted females. Awkward and shy girls. Loners. Losers. The ones others pick on. Smiling wasn't required much for most of my roles.

Even in my last film, *The Westerners*, the one with Quinn, we were playing teen runaways during the Old West time period. We were serious as a heart attack. Young lovers surviving together in no man's land, fighting off rogue cowboys and Indians and wolves and so forth, together. How many times do you see Juliet smile or laugh? In Romeo & Juliet, I mean. I mean, does she *ever*? I don't remember if she does. I don't remember Claire Danes smiling all that much. Or whoever that actress was in the 60s version, either.

So, anyway, smiling was something I had to practice. As much or more than I practiced cheers. As much or more than I practiced applying makeup, doing my hair.

I was used to being very serious like Juliet.

My young Romeo had died, like he was supposed to, and somehow I'd survived, when I shouldn't have.

It was hard to smile knowing you shouldn't have survived, that you shouldn't be here, that you should be dead and buried in a grave next to your Romeo.

I'd heard how actresses who had once been pageant girls put Vaseline on their teeth for auditions, to make smiling easier.

I bought a jar of Vaseline at Walgreens, applied a line of it across my top front teeth.

Then I hit "play" one last time on Taylor's face. It was at the end of her "How to Make Cheer Team" video. It had a lot of views. Like twenty-thousand or something, I forget, and it's way more by now, of course, since everything that's happened. I clicked on her perfect peppy face:

"DO SMILE A WHOLE LOT. Make sure you're never NOT SMILING, Show you're a peppy energetic person, be very happy, introduce yourself, show you're confident 24/7! WHAT CAN YOU BRING TO THE SQUAD? Volunteer to help the coach at all times. Project your voice. DON'T COMPLAIN don't talk back. Don't be gossipy. don't be late."

I stared at Taylor, then, I stared into the mirror. Taylor was smiling and I wasn't. I looked at Taylor again, then back in the mirror: tried to will my mouth into the same sort of effortless grin as hers, but mine was full of effort. Stiff. Unnatural.

I practiced this multiple times a day. I filmed myself talking, "DO SMILE A WHOLE LOT." pretending to be Taylor. I filmed myself smiling. "SHOW YOU'RE CONFIDENT 24/7!"

I smiled.

"BE VERY HAPPY!"

I smiled into the mirror, tried to project happiness, even if I didn't know what it was.

I didn't yet know how unhappy Taylor was.

I didn't know yet she was just faking, too.

MRS. STONE

That first day of school I remember I had to sit Tatum down, go over the school dress code with her. She showed up to school in a thin-strapped tank top and a very short mini skirt that left little to the imagination, if you know what I mean.

Mr. Pitt, the principal, asked me to speak with her.

He had a hard time talking to the girls.

They sort of didn't listen to him too well.

He sort of let them walk all over him. The pretty ones, I mean. The ones who challenged the dress code on a regular basis.

I took her behind the counter and I said, "Honey, there's a two finger rule on the straps and a fingertip length rule on skirts and shorts." I demonstrated by letting my arms hang at my sides, showing how far down my fingertips reached on my thighs.

"But I have really long arms," she said, demonstrating. I think she was purposefully lengthening her arms, like hunching over a bit.

"And anyway, I bet the boys don't have this sort of scrutiny over what they wear. They can probably wear whatever they want because *no one cares*," she said. "Nobody's up their asses about how far above their knees their shorts hit or how you can see the outline of their... *you know*... through their athletic pants and shorts and whatever."

It was true. There wasn't much in the way of rules for how the boys dressed. No profanity. No perverse or drug-related images. That was about it.

Chase and Cam pretty much wore whatever they wanted. Basketball shorts in winter...

"We don't want you girls to be a distraction for the boys in class," I said, something Mr. Pitt had said to me repeatedly. "The girls are a distraction, Mrs. Stone."

I thought I heard Tatum mutter something like, "That's bullshit," under her breath but when I turned to look straight ahead at her she was just smiling that big cat-eating grin smile of hers.

ANISSA GRANT

Of course, I knew my skirt was too short, the tank top straps too thin. I figured day one was the day to push all the boundaries, all the school's rules. Or at least the ones regarding what a *girl* can and can't wear.

As I was walking out of the office, Taylor was walking in. Same deal. Same short skirt, same tank top situation. Same male distraction, temptation, Eve and the apple, all that Biblical female as temptress, female as class distraction for boys bullshit.

Taylor and I rolled our eyes at each other. Fucking sexist school bullshit, Day One.

CHASE WHITING

I saw Tatum in the halls between classes the first day of school. Makayla was trying to talk to me and I sort of lifted a hand to wave and smiled and Tatum lifted a hand and smiled back.

"How annoying," Makayla said, rolling her eyes. "I'm just praying new bitch doesn't try and go out for cheer."

I ignored Makayla as usual.

She always still had a hand placed somewhere on me. Cam said I should fuck her again—"just to fuck with her, bro; to fuck with Matt, brah"—but I didn't have an interest. Cam was always telling me who to have sex with, living vicariously through me.

The strange thing was he never told me to try and hook up with Tatum. He didn't seem to like Tatum very much. He'd already texted me what a bitch she was. I guess he'd run into her or something. Maybe he didn't like that she and Taylor were already close. Maybe he was threatened by their friendship.

Cam was always feeling threatened by someone with regard to his girlfriend.

One time I gave Taylor a ride home from school when Cam was at a dentist appointment and Cam found out about it and flipped his shit. Calling me up yelling and accusing me of trying to fuck his girlfriend behind his back.

It was actually kind of a sickness with him.

He was otherwise a nice guy. Well, nice guy might be stretching it. But when it came to Taylor, he could definitely get a little crazy.

ANISSA GRANT

Taylor and I had two classes together, Geometry before lunch and Acting after. Geometry was my second hour and we sat in side-by-side desks and passed notes the whole time.

Taylor was friends with everyone or everyone thought they were friends with Taylor, including the teachers and Principal Pitt.

I sort of got introduced to a lot of people that day on account of Taylor walking me around. My face hurt from the smile I'd plastered on it. I think I smiled more that first day of school than all the days of my life before that day combined.

I was glad Cam was a senior so I wouldn't have any classes with him. I'd already run into him twice in the halls and both times I'd tried to smile and wave but he'd pretty much ignored me, gave me a half smirk the first time and immediately started talking to the person standing next to him the second. He was treating me like an ex even though we hadn't dated.

I was hoping he'd play it a little cooler when Taylor was around. I mean, it sort of screamed "we fucked" the way he was treating me.

Chase, on the other hand, was a total sweetheart. But it was going to be hard to be friends with Chase now that Cam seemed to hate my guts.

CAM SPENCER

I didn't like that Taylor was going out of her way to be best friends with Tatum. It'd been a huge mistake to fuck that girl, *obviously*. I didn't trust her at all. She kept trying to smile and wave at me and I kept ignoring her. I didn't know what she wanted. What shit she might try and pull. Why she was even here. What was going on in that little female brain of hers.

I didn't want anyone jeopardizing what I had with Taylor.

I'd wanted to marry Taylor Ragner since the first day I laid eyes on her in ninth grade and I wasn't going to let some out-of-state, fake basic bitch get in the way of our dreams.

It bothered me that Chase seemed to like her but on the other hand, maybe he could preoccupy her. Keep her a little distanced from Taylor. I didn't want them lezzing out together, scissoring and fingering behind my back.

TAYLOR RAGNER

To be honest, I think Cam was jealous of Tatum from day one. I was just trying to be a good friend. She was the new girl. I was showing her around, introducing her to everyone. I remember at lunch he sort of pouted. Sat at our table but ate his protein silently, not even talking to Chase. He was giving me the cold shoulder. He was being a fucking baby as usual. Any time I didn't give him one hundred percent of my attentions, he pouted. It was getting really boring. I was over catering to his insecurities. I acted like I didn't notice his pouting. I took Tatum by the hand around the cafeteria, introducing her to more people. I introduced her to the other girls on the cheer team. I introduced her to the football guys. I introduced her to the student council kids. The band geeks. The goth nerds. Pretty much everyone.

It was a big deal, having a new student at our school. Especially one as pretty and cool as Tatum. Especially someone from CALIFORNIA. We never had anyone move in from out of state.

So yeah, by the end of lunch that first day Cam was pretty pissed. I kept asking him what the fuck was wrong and he kept muttering nothing but he would barely look at me; he was being such a tool. I was just so bored of it. He was being so boring. He definitely pushed me to wanting to hang out with Tatum more.

I mean, who would you rather hang out with after school? Your moping, treating you like you'd done something wrong when you hadn't boyfriend or the cool new girl everyone wants to talk to and be friends with?

Yeah, it was a no-brainer.

COACH W

I had both Tatum and Taylor in my afternoon Acting class. Right from day one they were super flirtatious with each other. Holding hands and sitting close to one another, whispering and laughing, sharing jokes, like girls in high school will do, playing with same-sex flirtations, bisexual impulses. I hadn't seen Taylor that happy in a while. Everyone sort of knew she'd gone through a rough patch the year before, been hospitalized and stuff over the summer. We pretended we didn't know, but we all knew.

No one blamed Cam, of course. I sort of felt sorry for him, actually. He was the guy who supposedly had it all but I'd known other guys in high school like that, guys other guys are jealous of, and they're often miserable. Because once you "have it all," you don't have much reason to justify feeling sad or depressed. So when you do, you have a tendency to beat yourself up for it.

Kurt Cobain style.

I was worried Cam was one of the guys who peaked in high school: football quarterback, good-looking jock, not much going for him.

If he wasn't careful he could end up selling cars like his dad the rest of his life. You know that old Kid Rock lyric, "Never wanted to sell cars cuz my dad was a dick."

Anyway, Tatum was an interesting young woman. Different somehow than my other students. Even while she was holding hands and laughing with Taylor, I could see a seriousness underneath that smiling exterior. She looked familiar in a way I couldn't explain. I felt drawn to her in a way that scared me.

Of course, I'd witnessed my share of teacher/student affairs over the years. That sort of thing used to go on a lot ten years ago, you know. Back before it was all over the news. Back before you got labeled a sex offender if you got caught. Like pissing outside behind a tree or a truck. It was a different world then. Or it's a different world now, however you want to look at it. I knew some guys back in the day that divorced their wives to marry their students. And they're still married today! Crazy shit that doesn't fly anymore. Tell it to their kids. Mary Kay Letourneau style. Haha. That's obviously an extreme case. The dude was, what? Eleven? Twelve? Can you imagine? I mean, most men *can* imagine… that's the thing. You flip the gender and what do you get? Van Halen's "Hot for Teacher," that's what!

TAYLOR RAGNER

Coach W was harmless. Just another horny adult male. We were surrounded by horny adult males in Elkheart. You saw them in the stands every Friday night, every football game. Some were hornier than others. Some watched you the whole game when they should have been watching the football players. Some tried to make eye contact with you. Others seemed not to even realize how fucking pervy they were being, staring the shit out of you the entire game. People's dads. People's grandpas. Fucking perverts. Fucking men who'd been fucking the same woman for twenty, thirty, fifty years. Men who wanted some tight, teen pussy.

Sometimes I got off on that. Stuck my chest out, arched my back further.

Sometimes it disgusted me.

Most of the time I tried not to think about it.

I waved back at Coach W in the halls, flirted back with him in class, after class, whatever. Part of me felt sorry for him. I knew he'd gone to Hollywood. Obviously that hadn't worked out cuz he was back here living in this shit town with the rest of us. And he wasn't married. And who knew the last time he'd gotten laid. He was a sad, broken man. I felt sorry for him, so I flirted a little. It wasn't like he thought I was going to fuck him. No way he could have possibly thought that. For one thing, he knew Cam. He knew Cam would murder him if he ever tried to *actually* fuck me. MURDER. Everyone at Dobson knew Cam would murder anyone who tried to fuck me.

Well, everyone but the new girl. Haha. Everyone but Tatum.

ANISSA GRANT

After school Taylor took me to meet Ms. Harden, the cheerleading coach. She was a petite woman, maybe 5' 3", with a short mousy bob and she was *built*. Like, built built. Like she had more muscles and harder muscles than Cam or Chase or even Coach W. I guess she'd been in the Army or Navy or something.

"Yeah," Taylor said later, after we left her office. "She's gotta be a dyke, right?"

"We all flirt with her because, like, why not?"

"Anyway, she seemed to like you."

Taylor winked at me and stuck her tongue out between her two fingers, middle and fore.

She said tryouts were this Friday. She said we should probably do more practices. She said we should go to my apartment this time, so her mom wouldn't be on our dicks.

TAYLOR RAGNER

I wanted to see where Tatum lived, what her mom was like, so we went over to her place after school. it was that new apartment complex on the other side of town. I knew a couple people who lived there; people who sold drugs, mostly. Guys who had been friends of my brother, before he went off to "college."

It was your typical two bedroom. Her mom wasn't home. Tatum said she was hardly ever home; that she often stayed over at her great aunt's house because her great aunt was dying of cancer. I was like, "Lucky bitch. My mom is like always home."

Which was true. My mom didn't have anything else going on in her life. I would have been so grateful for a sick aunt, a dying relative. I couldn't bite a hangnail without my mother commenting on it, riding my ass about it.

Tatum said it used to be that way for her, too, before her aunt got sick and they moved to Indiana. She said her mom had been up her ass in California but so far here she hardly ever saw her.

I looked around the apartment. There was a photograph of Tatum with a beautiful girl, maybe our age, maybe a bit younger. In the photograph they were sitting on someone's bed together and Tatum's arm was around the girl and they looked pretty intimate. I don't know why my instinct was to feel jealous. Jealous and curious. A little possessive. I guess I felt how Cam always feels. Like a dick. I didn't have any right. Yet. To feel that way. I didn't say anything. But I didn't like looking at that picture.

ANISSA GRANT

It already felt funny lying to Taylor. Wrong. Like lying to myself. Kind of. She saw a photograph of Tate and me and asked who it was and I said it was my best friend in California, Daria. I don't know why I said Daria. Taylor seemed appropriately jealous of Tate, which was a plus, but I still felt kind of shitty about lying to her.

That's how I felt about everything: kind of.

It was hard for me to have a definitive feeling.

Since Quinn died, anyway.

We were sitting on the carpet in front of the screen door, smoking butts and drinking Diet Cokes after practice, and Taylor was talking about Cam, what a shithead he was.

"But Chase is so sweet and I think he likes you," she said.

I tried not to agree too fervently with the Cam part and sort of blushed appropriately with the Chase part.

"I'm going to text him right now," she said, meaning Chase. "We should double date this weekend."

I sort of nodded and flicked my ash.

One of the druggies walked by on the path to the pool outside.

He was good-looking, in a druggie way. Not exactly like Quinn. Quinn was a beautiful druggie; an angel.

I didn't really care one way or the other about Chase but if spending time with him meant spending more time with Taylor, I was in.

She had a mole on the inside of her right thigh, which was bent to push her foot up under her. She was sitting on it, which raised her ass a little off the ground. She was arranging her hair all to one side with her left hand as she scrolled her phone with her right.

She was a perfect teen-aged goddess.

TATE GRANT

We hadn't heard anything from Anissa since the night of the fight.

I tried to push it all out of my mind as much as possible.

Everything else was going so well for me.

I didn't want to get caught up in any negativity when my life was filling up with so much positiveness since Anissa had left.

It was like her presence had been a bad luck charm my whole life. And now that she was gone, the bad luck was gone with her.

I know that sounds mean to say but sometimes the truth is mean.

To be honest, I kinda didn't want her to come back. At least not until I got my career going far enough that she couldn't do anything to stop it. Or jinx it. Or, you know. Whatever.

I was binge-watching and reading all the various versions of *Freaky Friday* in preparation for my role. I was studying *Spring Breakers* too.

I stood in front of the mirror for hours in various bathing suits, staring, wondering if I was going to be as good as Lindsay, as iconic as Selena. Selena had more Instagram followers than anyone in the world. I wondered what that must feel like, having that much power, even if she looked pretty powerless sometimes because of the on/off thing with Bieber.

I barely had any followers yet. Mostly because when Anissa was here, I wasn't allowed to be on any social media platforms or even have an iPhone. Honestly, it was like living in pilgrim times. Or like those women they find living in basements of serial killers. Or in a hole in the ground in the backyard.

It was all pretty fine until I started going through puberty. That's when Anissa started getting overly protective, not wanting me to go outside, not wanting me to do anything but sit with her and watch old movies from like the 90s, listen to old music. Nirvana and Fiona Apple and shit.

ROBIN GRANT

I'll admit, it was a bad fight.

The worst we'd ever had.

I regret losing my temper, losing control.

But looking back, even from this short of distance, I can already see how necessary it was.

Anissa blames me for everything between her and Tate.

I mean, I know it was wrong of me to blurt it out, the truth about Anissa and Tate and Quinn and all of that, but at the same time, what's resulted since Tate heard the truth has been nothing but positive.

Aside from Anissa leaving, obviously.

But… I mean… I hate to say this of my own daughter, but, I think Anissa's leaving has been the best thing for Tate, right now, anyway.

Tate has blossomed in a way I never thought possible. She's just so confident and outgoing and social in a way Anissa never was. Anissa was always withdrawn and shy off-set. I could barely ever get her out of her bedroom, she barely ever wanted to talk to me unless I was driving her to a studio or helping her with her lines.

Tate, on the other hand, is chatty with everyone. And everyone loves Tate because of it.

When Anissa lived here, I think Tate felt like she had to be loyal to her, which in her mind meant being withdrawn like her. I don't think Tate ever wanted to be, I don't think it was her personality to be, but she was so loyal to Anissa… for years, of course, they'd been inseparable. Best friends. "Sisters."

ANISSA GRANT

After Taylor left I got online to look at Tate's social media accounts as usual.

I looked at them at least twice a day. First thing in the morning when I woke up—since the time difference meant missing Tate's end of the night posts—and again in the evening.

There were always at least two new photos, usually more.

I didn't recognize any of the girls in the photographs with her since she was going to a new school.

She didn't have any photographs with me either.

And it looked like she had a whole new wardrobe. Mother must have taken her shopping. And she was wearing makeup. And curling her hair. blowing it dry.

There was a picture of her wearing a Hole shirt and I was sure it was mine. I'd left it in the closet. I wondered if it smelled like me. if she noticed.

She was making the "metal" sign with her hand, middle two fingers down, outside fingers up.

The day before she'd been in a Marilyn Manson shirt I didn't recognize. I didn't remember buying. I wondered if it was Quinn's. If somehow Mother had found it and given it to Tate. He would have been about the same size. He was so thin. He barely weighed more than me. He had Tate's blue eyes. Mine are a dull hazel/green.

COACH W

The first suicide happened day one. Or, night one, rather. Out on the railroad tracks. Chen Lee. I think her family was Chinese. Or maybe they were Korean. Or Thai? I know that's bad, that I'm not sure. To be fair, I'd never had her as a student.

Over the summer there had been a couple teen deaths they attributed to suicide at a neighboring school district. Falls from parking structures that could have been accidental or on purpose. Alcohol had been involved in at least one of the cases. So it was hard to say.

Chen left a note for her family with a bag of gifts by the railroad track.

The teachers found out about it the next day. Day two of the school year.

Principal Pitt called us into his office. He didn't want the students finding out. He was worried about copycatters. But it was impossible they wouldn't find out on their own, anyway, someone pointed out, so we decided it was better to tell them ourselves, to spin it as positive as possible.

Only, how the hell do you spin a suicide positively?

Yeah, I didn't know either.

And Principal Pitt left it up to each of us in Period One to tell the students.

CAM SPENCER

Everyone in first hour was pretending to be sad about Chin Lee. Or whatever her name was but no one really was. I don't think she had a single friend. I'd never talked to her. And to be honest, I didn't really care that she'd jumped in front of a train. I had a couple other things on my mind: like Taylor and Tatum. They were already inseparable. As I'd predicted they would be. There was a part of me that worried about Taylor's... *sexual orientation*, I guess. She used to be really into Makayla but I didn't think Makayla was into her the way she wanted. Like, Makayla totally worshipped her. She would have done anything for her. For Taylor to like her. But she wasn't going for the fish sticks. Makayla was probably too afraid to look at her own vagina, let alone Taylor's.

Taylor told me on the way to school she wanted to go on some double date Saturday night with Chase and Tatum.

I knew Chase would be psyched. I was pretty sure he liked Tatum. For whatever reason. But I wasn't looking forward to spending any more time with her. I didn't like watching her with my girlfriend. It was bad enough at school. Walking through the halls like a pair of dykes with their hands all over each other.

It was only going to get worse if Tatum made cheer.

Then I'd have to watch them together at every game, too.

I just wanted the year to be over already, to be graduated. I wanted Taylor to be a senior too so we could graduate together, start our life together. Away from all these kids. Be our own little family.

TAYLOR RAGNER

I felt so bad for Chen. She'd been in some of my classes in middle school. She was always so quiet and sweet, diligent, a good student.

I didn't know why she'd do it.

Rumors were already circulating that she was trans or a lesbian.

Even in 2015 it wasn't easy being gay in a small town in Indiana.

We didn't have an LGBTQ group at our school or anything.

Guys still got called fags all the time. Cam was constantly joking that I was a dyke. I'd sort of started to worry I might be asexual. I secretly dreaded having sex with Cam. I guess he could kind of tell even though I tried to fake it as good as possible.

I don't know why I couldn't just break up with him. It's so hard in a small town when you're fifteen and have been dating the school quarterback for two and a half years. Breaking up with him would have been some major school drama. Not to mention home life drama.

Cam was graduating this year. I figured I'd wait it out. Break up with him after this year, if I couldn't get him to break up with me before then.

ANISSA GRANT

I didn't know why Taylor and Cam were even a couple.

It seemed like she never wanted to spend any time with him.

I felt kind of bad for him, actually, because she kept dragging me around with her everywhere and ignoring him.

At lunch the second day he kept trying to talk to her, and she kept rebuffing him, telling him she'd talk to him after school.

But then after school she said we had to practice more cheers.

She said she wouldn't live if I didn't make the team.

That she'd quit if I didn't make it.

Because, she said, she was so bored of all the other girls.

She was so bored, so bored, so bored.

I nodded my head. I understood boredom. Boredom was why I was here.

I fingered myself to Taylor's boredom later that day, alone after school. Taylor's bored face was the sexiest. I tasted my fingers after. Imagining they'd been inside her.

CAM SPENCER

At lunch Taylor was super clingy with Tatum in a way she hadn't been with me in a long time, constantly holding her hand, super affectionate, practically sitting on her lap.

It didn't seem appropriate, given that we were all supposed to be mourning Chin Lee's loss or whatever.

She'd barely even kiss me anymore. We hadn't fucked since way before school started. It was gross to think about, but I thought the last time I'd had sex had been with Tatum at the lake. It'd only been ten days but it felt like a scene out of a movie—a horror movie—I'd watched, not something that had happened to me.

I wasn't too worried about Tatum telling Taylor though because that would make Taylor hate Tatum as much as me. Maybe more.

Tatum wouldn't risk that.

I could already tell.

We were locked inside this secret together.

It was okay for me to hate her.

She wasn't going to say shit.

ANISSA GRANT

That night Chase called me. He must have gotten my number from Taylor. We talked on the phone for two hours. He was so sweet, just like Taylor had said. I wondered why she hadn't gone out with him instead of Cam. Maybe she wasn't Chase's type. Maybe she was one of those people who says they want a normal, sweet person but then go for the asshole narcissist instead.

Chase spent a lot of time talking about Chen Lee. He said he couldn't stop thinking about her, that she'd been in his classes, they'd been lab partners in Chemistry II the year before. She'd always smelled clean, good, like Tide or Downy, he said. Like his Grandma's house. I thought that a strange remark to make. That a teen boy should be attracted to or remember a girl smelling like laundry detergent. The cleanliness. The purity.

I texted Taylor about Chase talking a lot about Chen Lee's death and she told me Chase's mom had died suddenly, in her sleep, a couple years before. An undetected bleeding ulcer or something.

She'd been one of those super outgoing, energetic types, Taylor said, which made it even more unexpected.

Death must have been something Chase thought a lot about.

We had that in common, at least.

After Chase and I hung up I put in a movie I'd been in a long time ago. I played a high school cheerleader in it. They'd brought a former NFL cheer coach to the set. She'd taught us five or six simple cheers. Nothing fancy. Nothing acrobatic. I wasn't the main cheerleader or anything. Just one of the backgrounds. I could still remember the cheers, though. I got up out of bed and stood and did the motions along with myself in the movie. I was smoking a cigarette and drinking a beer. I drove a town over to purchase alcohol. I didn't want anyone in Elkheart to think I was using a fake ID.

I made a mental note to buy some Downy next time I went to the grocery store.

Something within me felt maternal toward Chase Whiting after that. I just wanted him to rest his head in my lap. I just wanted to smooth the hair from his eyes. I just wanted to smell like Downy fabric softener while doing the above mentioned activities.

TAYLOR RAGNER

Cam wouldn't leave me alone that week. The more I wanted my space the more he hounded me, tried to kiss me at school, called me, texted me. I couldn't breathe. He was driving me crazy. He tried to finger me in the car after school on Thursday. I told him I had my period even though I didn't. I just didn't want him touching me for some reason.

Friday he picked me up for school and on the way there he straight up asked me, "So are you a dyke now or what?"

I just laughed. Obviously if I was a dyke I'd always been a dyke. Cam could be so dumb sometimes.

But the truth was I didn't know what I was. I was still trying to figure that out. Part of me wanted another girl to hit on Cam so I could decide if I was jealous or not. If I still cared.

There was a time I would have gone redneck crazy on anyone's ass who dared to fuck with him.

But now I just found myself looking forward to Friday night, Tatum sleeping over after tryouts.

I just hoped she made the team. She *had* to make the team. I was prepared to threaten to quit if she didn't.

ANISSA GRANT

Naturally I woke up with my period the morning of tryouts. The night before I'd found a single white hair in my pubic region, pulled it out with a pair of tweezers. It hurt like a bitch but whatever. Beauty is pain, as my mother always said while ripping a brush through my constant nest of tangles. I didn't have any white or grey hairs on my head yet, thank god. I looked and looked, in my big magnifying mirror, every night for like fifteen minutes, parting my hair like a chimp. Only I wasn't looking for bugs to eat. But something worse. Something that would betray my true age.

I worried every time Taylor was up close in good lighting.

I searched out bad lighting, stayed in shadows, shade.

Like the older woman in the Tennessee Williams play.

Like Johnny Depp in *21 Jump Street*.

My only consolation was the fact people constantly believed I was approximately ten years younger than I was.

The last time I'd gone to Vegas with Mom, I'd been carded at Blackjack tables twice. "Sorry," the one dealer smiled. "I thought you were fifteen."

Okay, so, fourteen years younger.

I was wearing two super plus tampons and a maxi pad, all at the same time, all day long. My periods were beyond heavy. I was the only person I'd ever known, aside from my mother, who had to shove two super-sized tampons in at once to control her flow.

I wondered if Tate was the same way.

She'd only had her period a year. She'd been a late bloomer in that regard. I'd still been eleven, almost twelve, when I got mine.

Tate looked exactly her age. That morning when I'd checked her social media there was a photo of her on a set with other actors who were obviously supposed to be teenagers but only Tate looked like an actual teen. I could spot the adult actors a mile away. When I made the high school cheer movie everyone on set was in their mid-twenties. One dude was thirty-two.

You see what you want to see, nine times out of ten.

Thank god.

I hoped Ms. Harden wanted to see a sixteen-year-old cheerleader when she saw me.

COACH W

I had all three of them: Tatum, Taylor and Chase in my fifth hour after lunch. I was concerned about Chase. He was the sweetest kid, but I'd seen the light go out in him after his mother passed. I mentioned my concerns to other teachers but they didn't see it. They thought he was fine, same old friendly, outgoing, caring Chase.

I was rooting for Chase and Tatum to become a couple. It seemed the natural outcome, given their levels of beauty and popularity and that they were both currently single.

But Tatum seemed more into Taylor. Or Taylor seemed to be distracting Tatum. I couldn't tell which.

Chase was a third wheel to all their conversations and flirtations. That much was obvious.

COACH HARDEN

Taylor had introduced me to the new girl, Tatum, earlier in the week. She was fine, friendly enough. Smiled a lot. A LOT. I don't think I ever saw her not smiling. And her teeth glistened, like she had shit on them. Slime.

I knew the girls all thought I was a lesbian, a big bull dyke. Which of course I was. I *am*. But they acted silly about it, like I thought I was fooling them. Flirted shamelessly with me. Thought I wanted to see their teenage asses all the time. Flipped their skirts at me. It was funny. I didn't mind. I laughed. But I wasn't into teen girls. That was Coach W's scene, I'm guessing. The male teacher thing.

ANISSA GRANT

Friday after school I went with Taylor to the bathroom to get ready for tryouts. I'd been practicing all week with Taylor and alone in my apartment. I had a good gymnastic background to 'fall back on.' I had played a cheerleader in a movie, but I couldn't tell Coach Harden that. I changed my plugs and changed my panty liners and got ready. I was shaking like a leaf. I hadn't been this nervous in years, since my last movie audition. A long time ago.

This was what I'd been waiting for. Why I'd moved across the country. Why I was here. That American Country Love Song shit. "Cheerleaders and quarterbacks." Taylor and Cam.

I felt like I was going to throw up.

And then I did.

TAYLOR RAGNER

Tatum was really nervous. Super nervous. She threw up in the bathroom right before tryouts. It was kind of gross because I was standing right there with her when she started to hurl but she made it into a stall, thank god. But then at tryouts she did great. She did awesome and amazing!

I could tell Ms. Harden and the other girls were impressed.

There was no way she wasn't making the team!

MAKAYLA RICHEY

I didn't think Tatum was anything special. I didn't see what Taylor saw in her, other than that she was new. Fresh blood.

Taylor and I'd been friends since first grade. We grew up in the same neighborhood. Went to all the same schools, had the same teachers. Slept at each other's houses. Cheered together. Dated best friends. Were inseparable.

We'd had our first falling out the summer before Tatum arrived.

Taylor thought I'd been flirting with Cam, was into Cam, which wasn't true at all... I was still totally into Chase and she knew it. But Cam was nice to me, and Chase wasn't, so I sometimes talked to Cam to try to get to Chase.

But I was sure we'd get over it, be best friends again, once school started.

But then Tatum came and instead of making up with me, Taylor glommed on to the new girl.

Now Taylor and Tatum were the new school BFFs.

And I was stuck with Brooke and Whitney. Queens of the preps. *I* was the fucking third wheel to a pair of stuck-up do-nothings. What the fuck.

ANISSA GRANT

I got the feeling Makayla didn't like me. All the other girls at tryouts were so cool and chill—Keisha, Whitney, Mallory, Brooke... but Makayla definitely didn't like me. I guess because she and Taylor used to be best friends. Taylor told me not to worry about it, but how could I not worry about it? Makayla was team captain. She was Ms. Harden's right-hand girl. Taylor joked she was the one who had to masturbate Ms. Harden every week after the game.

TAYLOR RAGNER

I could tell Makayla was jealous but so what. That was her problem. Things hadn't been good with us long before Tatum moved to town. She'd been a little too comfortable with my boyfriend a few too many times. She was supposed to be my friend and every time I turned around, at a party or whatever, she was practically in Cam's lap. Over summer I'd gotten sick of it. The final straw was a pool party at Chase's house. I'd come out of the bathroom to find Makayla pushing her tits up in Cam's face. She was drunk, of course. But so what. I never pushed my tongue in Matt's mouth when I was fucked up. I had respect.

That's the thing, Makayla didn't have any respect, for herself or for other people.

I was tired of dealing with her.

She'd been a mess ever since she started taking Xanax every day to 'cope' with school and Matt and shit.

I guess I should have been more empathetic but she'd tested me too many times. I just didn't care anymore.

I was so happy Tatum was going to be on the team.

COACH HARDEN

There was something about the new girl, Tatum, now that I really looked at her...

Her audition was flawless. It was a no-brainer she'd make the team.

There was a familiarity to her, though, I couldn't place.

And she seemed more mature than the other girls.

In a way I couldn't articulate.

Later, when I caught her and Coach W in a compromising position, I wasn't shocked. It didn't seem like a student/teacher thing. Because something about Tatum didn't seem like a student.

But you get girls like that every few years... young women, sixteen, seventeen, who seem like twenty-five-year-olds. Who are very mature, physically and mentally. Who don't seem to belong in high school with the rest of the kids.

There are boys like that, too.

You recheck their IDs, pause to study their faces.

You'd swear they were twenty-six. Twenty-seven.

But their birth certificates say otherwise.

Their paperwork says they're sixteen.

[shrugs]

MAKAYLA RICHEY

As usual, Coach Harden had a pool party at her house for all the cheerleaders.

The only other girl I actually liked, besides Taylor, was Mallory Swindell.

She was a senior, had cheered all four years and middle school too.

I hung with her and Coach Harden, mostly that day.

I was already sick of watching Taylor fawn over Tatum. I think we all were, honestly.

I didn't have anything against girls being with girls *like that* but I felt like they were just doing it for *the show*, you know what I mean? The spectacle. For something for people to talk about. To piss off Cam.

They were in Coach Harden's bathroom for a long time together. Half the party. None of us knew what they were doing in there. I, for one, didn't feel like giving them the attention they obviously wanted by going in there to check.

I sat eating Doritos and drinking Diet Mountain Dew with Ms. Harden and Mallory on the side of the pool, talked about upcoming cheer competitions, camp next summer.

That was another thing, I didn't think Taylor was serious about cheer anymore. It seemed like she was just doing it to show off her bisexual friendship with Tatum in front of the whole school. The whole next week they walked through the school together arm in arm or hand in hand. They hugged and kissed on the mouth whenever they saw each other. Made a big display of their affections.

It was like that quote from Shakespeare or whoever my dad always quoted: me thinks thou doest protest too much. Or whatever.

TAYLOR RAGNER

Everyone at the cheer pool party was acting so lame. Maybe they always had and I just hadn't noticed. Being around Tatum made me notice everything in a way I hadn't before she moved here, like I saw our school and the people in it and myself through her eyes and we were all so lame!

It was a real eye-opener. I suddenly saw how boring and repressed and *basic* we all were.

I couldn't wait to get out of this town, to move west, to California where Tatum had come from.

I wanted to be more like her. Even though she was modest and shy. She was also mature and worldly and just seemed so much cooler than anyone else I'd ever known, even though I couldn't put my finger on exactly why.

At the pool party I pulled her into Coach Harden's bathroom and pulled a flask of whiskey I'd stole out of my brother's room out of my purse and we sat on the floor, our backs against the tub, taking sips from the flask.

Our legs were leaning against one another and the whiskey was making my cheeks burn.

I said, "Ohmygod, I'm so hot, are you hot?"

And Tatum said yes.

"Come on," I said, and pulled her up by the hand and led her back outside to the pool.

"Take off your clothes and let's get in the hot tub," I said.

I could feel everyone else's eyes on us.

On our bodies. The pervs.

That's the thing I've noticed about repression, it makes perverts out of everyone.

ANISSA GRANT

At Coach Harden's pool party for the cheerleaders, Taylor took me into the bathroom and locked the door. I didn't know what she was going to do next. I just stood there, nervous, waiting to see. My nipples were hard from the chills I always got when I was nervous and I could feel the lining of my bathing suit dampening, which sometimes happens too.

There was definitely some sort of tension between us I'd never felt before or I'd felt something similar before with Quinn, I thought, but I wasn't sure, because that was so long ago.

I felt like I was being woken to some sort of other world, some sort of feelings I'd never experienced before.

But then Taylor sat down in front of Coach Harden's shower and pulled me down beside her and we just sat there drinking from a flask and staring at Coach Harden's toiletries. There weren't many, as you can imagine. Secret deodorant. A man's razor. A bottle of Scope. Some shaving cream foam in a can.

Taylor was sort of giggling and not making sense and I giggled too because I could tell something was funny even though I wasn't exactly in on the joke.

It felt good to be alone in the bathroom with Taylor. To be chosen out of all those girls.

And then Taylor wanted to get in the hot tub and I followed her out to the patio, took off my t-shirt and shorts and tried not to stare when Taylor took off hers.

Her breasts were larger than you thought they'd be, way larger than mine. Heavy.

Her hips also.

I had a flash of our chests naked pressed together in the water, bobbing.

But then Coach Harden yelled out, "Be careful! You're not supposed to mix alcohol and heat!"

And Taylor said, "Ha Ha, Coach Harden. You know we're not drinking."

And I remembered where we were, I remembered all the other girls watching.

And that Taylor was fifteen. Even though she seemed a lot older. Or I seemed a lot younger. I couldn't decide which. It didn't matter.

And then Taylor swam over and sat on my lap.

I was grateful to be in the water.

Like a boy with an erection.

Like a girl with a sticky white substance in her bathing suit.

COACH HARDEN

When I was growing up you couldn't even think about liking a girl or being affectionate with a girl.

I was that weird third grader who wore shorts under my dresses and who looked like a boy in drag in them anyway.

One time I had this girl Kim over after school. No one else was home and we put in the *Grease* soundtrack and danced all over my bedroom, singing the songs together, duetting... and then there was this moment... I don't know how it happened, who initiated it, but we kissed... like Sandy and Danny in the movie. And there was tongue and everything. Just like I'd always imagined. This was in sixth grade. Maybe seventh.

But the next day at school Kim pretended like it hadn't happened and it never happened again. I didn't kiss another female for ten years after that, until grad school in Milwaukee. Most of my life I felt like a perv because what I fantasized about was considered weird, unnatural, not 'normal.'

Girls have it so much easier now. Even though I realize it's still not "normal" or it wouldn't be a topic of conversation. I wouldn't have mothers suggesting to me it's "merely experimentation." Their faces wouldn't get that weird look when I suggest to them their daughters might benefit from an LGBTQ meeting. That they might also.

They fight it. Which lends a sense of shame still to the girls. To us.

I didn't know what was happening between Tatum and Taylor—if it was just a close, affectionate friendship or more than that. It wasn't my business. Unless one of the girls came to me, made it my business.

I tried to give them what I would have wanted: privacy.

MALLORY SWINDELL

Makayla kept trying to convince me that Taylor and Tatum were hooking up but I thought she was just jealous that Taylor was best friends with someone else now and not her. That's what happens when you break up in a small town. Doesn't matter if it's with a boyfriend or one of your girl friends. It's a big frickin' deal. And everyone knows about it and everyone has an opinion. Except me. I didn't really care. But I pretended to for Makayla's sake. So she'd shut up about it. Or that was the hope. She never really did shut up about it, though. In some ways, looking back, she was as obsessive as Cam was about it, about Taylor.

I guess Taylor brought out that quality in people. Male and female.

She brought it out in Tatum, that's for sure.

And Coach W.

And a whole list of other people at our school and in our community.

I was just a quiet observer, a silent bystander.

TAYLOR RAGNER

Tatum was driving me home from Coach Harden's but it wasn't that late and I didn't want to go home yet. I didn't want to be bored in my bedroom, alone, again.

"Let's do something crazy!" I said.

"Like what?"

"I don't know... like, drive by Coach W's house? That old perv. See what the hell he does alone in his house at night."

"Ewwww."

"I know. But it'll be fun. Please? Just turn right here, at the light. Pleeeeeease?"

Tatum turned right, and I smiled my wickedest, shit-eating smile.

ANISSA GRANT

We were still in our wet suits. Taylor's was clinging to her. She'd thrown on some denim shorts, overtop her bottoms, but no shirt, just her bikini top, and her hair was sort of half-dried, half-wet, crunchy from the chlorine. She was so beautiful. It was a chore not to stare openly at her. I had to be aware of myself at all times whenever I was around her. I couldn't let my guard down.

I was wearing my American flag bikini.

Taylor was wearing a white bikini top that let her nipples shine through.

She wanted to drive by Coach W's house.

I wanted to do whatever Taylor wanted to do.

So we drove by Coach W's.

"Park here," Taylor said. Which turned out to be a few houses from his.

We got out of the car in our bare feet. My flip flops were on the backseat. Taylor lit a cigarette, took a drag and handed it to me.

"Okay, so here's the plan," she said.

The plan was to sneak around to the back of his house and peer in the windows. It sounded like a terrible plan but I wasn't going to tell Taylor that. I was going to shut up and do whatever Taylor wanted to do.

"Okay," I said, taking another drag off Taylor's Marlboro Light.

And the next thing I knew we were crouched down beside one another in Coach W's bushes and Taylor's hand was on my knee, steadying herself, and her breath was still hot from the whiskey. I could feel it on my cheek as she whispered to me.

"*Ohmygod*," she said. "There he is."

Ninety-nine point four degrees. I didn't mind.

There he was: a thirtysomething, out-of-shape teacher in his semi-finished basement, semi-working out, I think to Tool. Or Pavement. Or Rage. I always got those three bands mixed up. He had a beer gut, of course. And he was wearing a muscle shirt, *of course*. Men don't make any sense half the time.

"*Ohmygod*, what if he'd been jerking off?!" Taylor whispered. More hot whiskey breath. Ninety-nine point two. Her hand was still on my leg but now a little further up my thigh.

"What if," I said. "I'm sure if we stick around long enough that's up next."

"Ewwwwwww."

"You're the one who brought us here," I said.

"Come on," she said. "Let's go to the graveyard." She was already pulling me up, pulling my hand, pulling me toward the car.

Which is how we ended up at the cemetery together, staring down at Quinn's headstone, Taylor's arm locked through mine.

It's strange how life goes sometimes.

Smoking Marlboro Lights with your new teenaged best friend at the grave sight of your former teenaged soul mate, your first crush, your BD, your Romeo.

"I guess he was super hot," Taylor said.

"I guess."

"Such a shame."

"Yeah."

TAYLOR RAGNER

I don't know what I would have done if Coach W had been jacking it the night Tatum and I drove to his house. I'd seen Cam jack off, *of course*, on Facetime, plenty of times. But seeing your teacher? Ugh. Gross. I don't know why I wanted to go there. There wasn't much else to do. Spy on teachers and other students. Park at the reservoir. Drink at the graveyard.

There was this stupid old legend. Mary Jane. Everyone talked about. Mary Jane's grave. She was supposed to have been this witch, burned at the stake, a hundred years ago, or something. I can't remember why. Just that she was young and pissed off. So you were supposed to go to her grave and say her name three times and wait for her to grab you or something. Obviously, it was just a bunch of bullshit guys told girls when they brought them here to get them all scared and clinging to their dicks but whatever.

That's what I told Tatum.

After we looked at Quinn James's grave. The other local legend. He wasn't literally burned at the stake but pretty much. I wondered if anyone got out of Elkheart alive. If I would. If I could.

ANISSA GRANT

Taylor kept taking my hand, pulling me places. She pulled me to and from Coach W's house and then she pulled me around the graveyard. I kept waiting for cops to show up, ask for my ID. I had the fake one and the real one and I knew if they ever figured out the fake one was fake I was in serious trouble. The gig would be up. No more Elkheart high school. No more cheer team. No more Taylor Ragner. I couldn't let that happen. I had to keep my shit together. Not fuck up.

I let Taylor pull me across the grass—we were still barefoot—to this cleared area with an old broken headstone you couldn't read anymore.

"This is it," Taylor said. "Mary Jane's grave. Are you scared?"

I wasn't scared, not of Mary Jane, anyway, but I pretended to be, for Taylor's sake.

"Yeah," I said. "Look, I have goose pimples."

Which was true. I did have goose pimples. All up and down both arms. On my legs. But not from Mary Jane's grave. Or the cool autumn air. I had goose pimples from standing so close to Taylor, from Taylor holding my hand.

"Oh shit, yeah," Taylor said, her green eyes blazing like a Coldplay song. No one can ever figure out what color my eyes are: Blue. Grey. Green. They seem to change all the fucking time like a mood ring. I'm fucking moody. Sue me. Haha. Inside joke.

"Come on," she said, taking my hand again. She had a newly lit cigarette in her mouth. She was every country love song ever written. I didn't know what she saw in me.

TAYLOR RAGNER

My mom was blowing up my phone by the time we got back to Tatum's car. There wasn't any service in the graveyard, but I couldn't tell my mom that.

"Okay, Mom, Jesus Christ, I'll be home in a minute," I said. I had my mom on speaker, so Tatum could hear what a total psycho spaz she was.

"Sorry about that," I told Tatum after she hung up.

"Don't worry about it," she said. She was driving and maybe she winked at me. I wasn't sure if it was a deliberate wink or if she was just blinking hard because she had shit in her eye. Anyway, she pulled up along the sidewalk in front of my house and I didn't want to get out of the car but I had to. I had to go inside and face my psycho mom.

"See you tomorrow," Tatum said, smiling. She had a nice smile.

"Yeah," I said. "See ya!"

I don't know what made me grab her tit. I just sort of grabbed it and squeezed and laughed and got out of the car.

Maybe I'm the one who's psycho.

I don't know.

Tatum didn't seem to mind too much, though.

She just sort of sat there, grinning. In her American flag bikini top. Like it was the fourth of July or some shit.

"Bye!" she yelled at me and I turned around one last time before I made it up the steps to my front door.

"Bye!" I yelled.

I don't know why but for a second it felt like I was getting dropped off after a date, like I didn't want to say goodbye, like I didn't want the night to end.

Maybe that made me a lesbo. Like Cam said. Maybe it just made me like Tatum. I didn't know. It was so hard to tell anything anymore, living in a diorama in Elkheart. Living in a fucking snowglobe for everyone to watch and observe and jerk it to.

ANISSA GRANT

I was never going to let anything happen between Taylor and me.

I'd decided that Day One.

That hadn't been part of the deal I made with myself when I left L.A. The deal was cheerleading, friendship, Prom, drama club. That sort of thing. The promise was life in a small town. Middle class. Middle America. Apple pie and bonfires and football players and dances. Being sixteen again. A second chance at a first kiss. Innocent flirtations. Light inebriations. Nothing too crazy. Nothing criminal.

Like that guy who wrote *Fast Times at Ridgemont High*. That director. He's pretty famous. *Almost Famous*. Haha. LOL. A lot of people don't know this—that there was even a book or anything—but he went "undercover" in a high school... I had the book, or, my mom had it. On the back jacket of the book it said he "lightly dated" or something like that. Which I took to mean he made out with high school chicks but didn't have sex with them. Maybe he just fingered them. Ate them out. No penetration. I think he was twenty-two. Twenty-three. At the time. Something like that.

That night after I dropped Taylor off I came home and tried on my cheerleading uniform first thing. I danced around in it in the mirror, took photographs of myself in it, made a video of the cheer I'd done for tryouts.

I couldn't wait to wear it to school on Friday. Game days cheerleaders wore their uniforms all day. Then there was a pep rally last period, to get the whole school hype for the big game that night.

I fell asleep in my uniform. My hair smelled like chlorine.

After we'd crawled out of the hot tub, Taylor had pushed me into the pool, then jumped in after me. Everything was so carefree and frivolous. She'd wrapped her arms around my neck, then pushed me under like a boy does his little sister, laughing the whole time. I could hear her even underwater. Laughing while I couldn't breathe.

I couldn't be angry with her.

I didn't understand how I would ever be angry with her.

I dreamed about Taylor in a bathtub filled with rose petals like the father in *American Beauty*.

Except the bathtub wasn't filled with rose petals.

And I wasn't a forty-five-year-old man.

In my dream *I* was the one in the bathtub and Taylor was the one who climbed in *with me*.

My mouth was the one red with petals. And Taylor's hair was short like a boy's and her mouth was filled with snails.

COACH HARDEN

The strange thing about teaching Sex Ed in schools is how many parents worry about their sons being *gay* but don't seem to worry about their sons being rapists or sexual assaulters or abusers. I thought we should talk about all that, have discussions with both the girls and boys about physical and emotional and sexual abuse. But no one wanted me to go *there*, to talk about that.

"Just stick to Sex Ed, Coach Harden," that's what Principal Pitt said. "Rape is sort of a taboo subject. It's a little too uncomfortable for parents to hear about, like we're saying their son could be a rapist, you know? No one wants to think about that, to hear us talk about that."

Exactly, I thought. Which is exactly why we *should*?

TAYLOR RAGNER

My mom was on my ass the second I walked through the door. I just wanted to go to my room, finish the whiskey in Tyler's flask. I knew my makeup was running from swimming in the pool with Tatum. I knew she'd ask me about it, try and smell my breath.

"Weren't you going to see Cam tonight?" she said. She had me cornered in the kitchen, which was between where you entered the house from the garage and my bedroom.

"I don't know," I said. I didn't know why I said that. "No," I said. "Who cares anyway. If you want to see Cam so bad, if you're so worried about it, you go on a date with him."

I swear to god, sometimes I could swear she was in love with my boyfriend. He totally fucked with it, too; was extra nice to her, always took her side, always called her by her first name, always acted like I was rushing him out the door. It was just one more annoying thing about Cam. And one more annoying thing about my mother. The two of them combined could be *really fucking annoying*.

"Well I was just wondering if everything was okay between you two, it seems like you've hardly seen him the last couple weeks is all."

"And that's my business, Mom, not yours. How often I see my boyfriend, *if* I see my boyfriend, if I even *have* a boyfriend."

God, she was fucking annoying. I grabbed a Diet Coke out of the fridge and went to my bedroom and closed the door.

It wasn't my problem she was home alone again on a Friday night. That my dad was out of town "on a business trip" again as usual.

I hated my dad for leaving my mom alone. For making me deal with her. For making me the one to feel sorry for, to feel guilty for going out and having a life. For having a boyfriend. For having sex and a good time.

The men in this house solved problems by leaving. My brother too. I loved Tyler but he left for college and never looked back. Like never ever. He didn't come home for weekends or for holidays. He stayed at his university or went home with his college girlfriend every break. I couldn't say I blamed him, really. But I hated him for it anyway.

For leaving me alone with *her*.

MAKAYLA RICHEY

I don't know who started calling them "T&T." If they started it or someone else.

That would be so lame, if they somehow started it.

All I know is, people starting referring to them like that.

As this one thing: T&T.

I know it pissed Cam off.

Then again, everything seemed to piss off Cam.

It was probably the steroids.

ANISSA GRANT

Taylor texted me that night. "Fucking hate my home life. My mom is fucking psycho."

I didn't see it until the next morning. I'd fallen asleep with the light on again.

In the morning I texted back, "All moms are psycho. And every teen hates her home life or she'd never want to leave."

"I can't wait to fucking leave," Taylor replied. "SMW," Taylor texted.

SMW was a joke between us. *Slit my wrists.*

"Don't SYW," I said. "You'll need them for cheering Friday. You can't let the school or football team down. LOL."

"Right. God. I'm so selfish. What was I thinking."

Which was when I got a text from Chase.

"So I hear we're going on a double date with Cam and Tay Saturday night?"

I texted Taylor, "Double date Sat? Chase texting me…"

"Oh yeah," Taylor said. "Forgot to tell you. ;)"

"Sounds good," I replied to Chase. I added a heart emoji.

He replied with a thumbs up emoji.

I guess that meant we were going on a date.

My calendar was filling up the way I'd always dreamed it would: first football game of the season Friday night, double date with football players Saturday night. Hanging with Taylor every day after school for cheer practice.

I'd have to deal with Cam's death stare all night but whatever. He's the one who asked me to go to the lake. He was the one who decided he wanted to fuck me. I just went along for the ride. Figuratively and literally.

CHASE WHITING

I spent Sunday with Cam at his house, working out in his basement and eating dinner with his family. His mom liked to fawn over me. I knew she felt sorry for me, since my mom had died. She was always baking extra brownies and cookies and sending them home with me for my brothers and dad and me. She and my mom used to be room mothers together when we were little, back when we were in elementary school, before Cam's mom got her law degree, got real serious about the law.

Cam was going off about Taylor again as usual. Things weren't good between them again I guess. He was blaming Tatum of course. Saying if she'd never moved to town everything would be fine between him and Tay. I nodded and tried to be supportive even though I knew things hadn't been fine between them for a while. I liked them both independent of the other but as a couple they could both be insane and annoying.

We talked about going on a double date with Tay and Tatum the next weekend. Taylor had set it all up. I was fine with it. Tatum was attractive and seemed nice enough. Cam of course thought otherwise.

"Maybe if you guys start dating she'll leave Taylor alone for once," Cam said.

"Maybe," I said. I didn't like the pressure he was trying to put on me to distract his girlfriend by dating someone I wasn't sure I wanted to date.

"I mean, Tatum might be a bitch but she's alright looking. Fuckable or whatever," Cam said. He was standing there holding weights and his arms were bulging and his eyes were wide and I wondered if he was using his older brother's Adderall again. Or his steroids. Gage had a whole pharmacy of pills at all times.

"I'm not trying to fuck her," I said.

"Why not?" Cam said. "*You faggot.*"

"I just don't know her like that yet," I said.

I hated when Cam called me a fag. I hated that word. He was always accusing everyone of being gay. Taylor. Me. His brother.

I didn't know what I was. I was still trying to figure that out.

"Well, whatever, man," Cam said. "You can't hold onto your V-card forever."

Cam was twelve when he lost his virginity to a babysitter.

He'd told me this a million times. She was eighteen. A senior at Dobson. A cheerleader. Of course. She was there to watch his baby brother who was two and asleep in his room. I guess they didn't trust Cam to watch his own brother.

Cam said they did it doggy style in the basement.

Cam said they did it a couple times after that also and then she went away to college and he never saw her again.

He'd already had sex with a couple other girls when he met Taylor. Taylor was thirteen. Cam was sixteen. I didn't know if that was legal or not. It's hard to keep up with the specificities of the laws.

Here I was seventeen, a football player, and I still hadn't had sex.

I guess that's weird, right?

I don't know. It'd just never felt right.

I didn't want to just have sex to have it.

I wanted to like the person I was with. Call me crazy. Or a fag. Or whatever.

CAM SPENCER

I didn't understand why Chase was being such a pussy as usual. Why he was dragging his heels about Tatum. Dragging his dick. Why he was always such a prude.

I couldn't stop looking at old photos on social media of Tay and me and thinking about how great things used to be.

I just wanted things to be great between us again.

I wanted it to just be her and me forever without these other people causing problems in our relationship.

I was glad I had Taylor's mom on my side, at least.

Sometimes my own mom would make jokes to Taylor like, "When are you going to break up with my son? We all agree you're out of his league." Haha. So fucking hilarious. I wanted to kill her when she said shit like that. I wanted to murder everyone in my family who laughed, which was all of them.

I knew everyone including Taylor thought she was smarter and more ambitious than me. I got it. They didn't have to hit me over the head with it.

I was the dumb jock and she was the beautiful, smart, Harvard bound, Honor Roll student who would drop me the second she left Elkheart.

Taylor used to tell me that wasn't true, that she loved me and believed in me and that together we would stay or leave this town.

I used to believe her.

I think she used to believe herself.

I think she really did believe in me, in us, once.

Now I couldn't ever tell what she was thinking, what she believed.

I could only feel her distancing herself from me.

Or trying to.

I needed Chase to do me this one solid. To help a homie out.

I just wanted this double date to go well Saturday.

It felt like so much was riding on it.

For them and for us.

I would even be nice to Tatum. I was going to be extra nice to that bitch.

TAYLOR RAGNER

Cam called me up crying Sunday night. He was starting to have a lot of emotions.

For once I felt sorry for him. I knew I'd been being a bitch, distant. Cold.

I let him pick me up and take me to dinner.

He was being so sweet, like he was when we first started dating.

He took me to Millington, which was a bigger town ten miles up the road, to Outback for steaks. Except I got chicken. Cam got a filet, though.

I just couldn't eat that much red meat. But it was nice of him to take me there.

He said he'd written me a poem, too.

I was shocked. I'd never known Cam to read a book or to write anything. I usually had to write his papers for him for school.

The poem was all about young love and puppies and me.

Like it literally metaphorized puppies.

Cam seemed so vulnerable when he read it to me. I felt my heart opening to him again.

After we went to the Motel Six and Cam got us a room since he was eighteen. We hadn't been alone together in a while. My mom kept texting me to ask when I'd be home. I was supposed to be home by ten on a school night but she made exceptions for Cam. Especially now that she was worried we'd break up.

Cam paid for a porn on the TV in the room and I felt my heart closing up again and then my vagina. He always picked porns where girls choked on guys' dicks. It made me feel sick. I just wanted to get out of there so I acted like I was into it and Cam didn't seem to notice. It'd been forever since I came with Cam. I masturbated a lot instead.

I texted Tatum on the way home.

"Who are you texting?" Cam said.

"My mom," I said. It wasn't a lie because I did text her too.

"Cam is being insane again," I texted Tatum. *on top of everything else.*

This was another inside joke between us, like SMW. OTOEE.

Which was when I realized I didn't have any inside jokes with Cam anymore.

Which made me sad.

Being around Cam was making me sad almost every time now.

It sucked. I didn't want to break his heart.

I kept thinking maybe it would pass.

That I was going through a weird stage.

If I wasn't asexual.

I was going to be sixteen soon.

Maybe things would become clearer then.

ANISSA GRANT

Sunday night I scrolled through Tate's social media accounts. I had started looking at the social media accounts of her friends also. It seemed like they were always partying, at a club or a friend's house or a fancy restaurant in West Hollywood. I wondered if my mom had any limits for her, if she was making it to school every day on time, if she was drinking and doing drugs.

Well, it was clear from the photographs she was drinking.

I was desperate for any info I could find. It was getting harder, being out of contact with Tate.

Things had gotten so bad between us after she turned 14.

It'd felt like we were best friends until then and then overnight it felt like she never wanted to be around me anymore, never wanted to tell me what was happening in her life.

And then after the big blow up fight with Mom last year, it seemed like Tate hated me. And why wouldn't she?

I could have killed Mom for telling Tate everything without clearing it with me first. After she'd been the one to insist we keep the secret from Tate all those years.

I'd never wanted to lie to Tate once. Not once in her life.

But Mom had convinced me it was the right thing to do.
And now it'd backfired. Now I'd lost Tate and she still had her.
Like she'd fucking planned it out that way all along from day one.

In one of the most recent photos of Tate she is, I swear to god, sitting by the pool at the Chateau Marmont with a group of people who all look like fashion models or Macaulay Culkin. I recognize the pool from when Quinn took me there. Sometimes I think Tate looks like Quinn. Like the way she holds a cigarette now. Quinn smoked menthols and they almost killed me first thing in the morning. Quinn had the most beautiful hands. Like Tate's.

Sometimes I reach a point where I can't look at photographs of Tate anymore because I start to feel like crying and I don't want to cry anymore. I told myself I wouldn't cry in the Midwest. Compartmentalizing.

Maybe it's fucked up, focusing on, obsessing over Taylor because I can't think of Tate. Playing this new role, Tatum, sixteen-year-old sophomore at Dobson High. Method acting in Elkheart, Indiana.

I guess I'm just like fucking Sheryl Crowe now. I can't cry anymore.

CAM SPENCER

Just when I thought things finally might be getting a little better, just when Taylor finally gave me a glimpse of fucking hope, Sunday night, deep inside her again, inside her sweet warm pussy, my face buried in her hair, smelling her shampoo, she shut me out cold again Monday morning. And Tuesday. And Wednesday.

Every day after school it was "I can't. I have cheer practice and then I'm hanging out with Tatum." I didn't get it. I had football practice too but I still had time for Tay. I would always make time for her. Now I had to watch my girlfriend pass me in the halls with Tatum, wave her hand at me like I was just some other asshole she didn't give a fuck about. I was trying to be patient, trying not to push her farther away, but it was getting harder every day. I was jacking off twice a day, every day, working out all night in the basement.

Everything I had was riding on Chase.

He had to hook up with Tatum so the two of them would start dating so I could have my fucking girlfriend back.

It was driving me crazy. Thinking of everything depending on Chase. On his heterosexuality, which was always in question.

I needed to have another talk with him.

So he'd finally get how fucking important this was.

TAYLOR RAGNER

As if it wasn't bad enough with Cam on my dick, now I was having to fend off Coach W too. Any time he could catch me alone, which, was hardly ever but somehow he managed, he was flirting with me, touching my arm, touching my leg…

I'd heard rumors about him, how he had a thing for freshmen. Which was even more disturbing than a teacher having a thing for a senior. Who might at least be legal.

Looking back, I guess he had been sort of insistent the year before I try out for the school musical. But Cam and I were inseparable then, I guess. Now that I was trying to get some space, it left room for Coach W to try and weasel himself in too. Fuck. I had two fuckboys on my ass. Hounding me.

Thursday after school I told Tatum about it. About how Coach W kept cornering me.

Normally, I would have told Cam but I didn't need Cam all up in my face blaming me about it, telling me I'd welcomed the flirting and aggression by being too nice or too outgoing or by acting like a slut or a whore. Rich words considering I'd never slept with anyone but him and he'd slept with half a dozen girls before me, and those were just the ones I knew about.

Tatum was so much cooler, anyway.

Tatum told me not to worry about it, that she'd distract Coach W.

"What do you mean by that?" I'd said.

We were smoking cigs in my car by the lake. Cam used to take me there after school. We were listening to Rihanna. We'd just smoked a blunt I'd gotten from Chase.

I wished Cam would smoke weed and relax but he never would.

He said he didn't like "that stuff," that it made him paranoid. As if he needed help in that area. Sometimes he was like a fucking young republican. So uptight and angry.

"I don't know," Tatum said. She was leaned back in the passenger seat. Like, she had the seat rolled all the way back. And her eyes were slits and she was grinning.

"Just don't fucking worry about it," she said. "I got you."

"Oh, you do, do you?" I said. I was sitting sideways in my seat with my legs across hers and my feet sticking out her window.

"Yeah," she said. Her eyes were closed. She was dancing to Rihanna with her eyes closed and her seat reclined all the way back. Meaning, she was doing something with her arms and hands out in front of her but the rest of her was perfectly chill.

"I'm going to cut all my fucking hair off," I said.

"Yeah," she said.

"Maybe Cam and Coach W will leave me alone then."

"Doubt it," she said.

"But maybe," she said.

"Maybe they're into that," she said.

"Into what?" I said.

"The Britney crazy girl look," she said.

"A lot of guys are into crazy," she said.

"Some girls also," she said.

I didn't know what the fuck she was talking about. If she was flirting with me or if I was just high or what.

"Like, shave it?" I said.

"Yeah," she said. "You could look hot with a shaved head."

"LOL, right," I said. "They'd kick me off the cheer team."

"I'd shave mine too, like in solidarity."

"Like a friend of a cancer patient?"

"Yeah, fuck 'em."

"Fuck 'em."

We sat there a good while like that listening to Rihanna, totally faded.

ANISSA GRANT

I remember back when Quinn and I first met, on the set of *The Westerners*... I remember still thinking acting would save me. I still believed in it then. This was before I saw what it was doing to Quinn. Had done to Quinn.

Maybe that's too easy. Maybe he would have self-destructed with or without Hollywood. He told me his parents had both been in and out of prison his whole life. Most likely he would have been in and out of prison, too, if he hadn't accidentally become an actor, if he hadn't been sort of plucked off the street by a casting agent walking through his town when he was ten or eleven, the beautiful preteen boy with the beautiful preteen angelical face that was also just a little dirty. Just a tiny bit hoodlum. But mostly angelic. 99% innocence. 1% delinquent.

And yet here I am, acting my ass off in Elkheart, Indiana. Playing a role, because being myself is too fucking uncomfortable. *Who the fuck am I, anyway?* I asked myself that question for fifteen years. I never got an answer. When you act, you have all the answers. You have a character mapped out for you on the page, in your head, all her characteristics, her ticks, her motivations. You come up with all of them, write them down in a notebook, you come up with her favorite songs, her favorite color, her favorite fucking party dip. "It's all in the details that don't show up on film," an acting coach told me once.

I looked at Tate's Instagram now and wondered how this would all turn out for her. I prayed it would turn out better than it had for her mother and father. I prayed she would never end up like her dad, like Quinn. I had promised him I wouldn't let our baby get eaten by Hollywood. He'd made me promise. He'd held my face in his hands and said, "Say it, baby. Say you'll never let our child be an actor. You'll never let them sell their body like us, like we do." I knew by body he meant soul. I knew he wasn't much longer for this world. I grabbed hold of his hands, which were still on either side of my face, plastered to my cheeks. I grabbed hold of him and said, "I promise."

Now here I was breaking that promise. (I'm sorry, Quinn.)

But what could I do?

What can I do, Quinn? Your daughter, our daughter, she has her own mind. She wants what we wanted. What we thought would save us. There's nothing I can do or say to stop her. If you were alive I think you'd get this, Quinn. If you were fucking alive.

Don't lay down and die. Hey, hey. I know what to do. Oh, baby, fly away, to Malibu.

I always thought of that song by Hole now when I thought of Quinn.

Quinn had been obsessed with Kurt Cobain. He had the date of Kurt's death tatted on his side, under his arm. Kurt was some kind of god to Quinn. And now Quinn was some kind of god to other young men, teen boys… it was so weird. Sometimes I'd see Quinn's face staring back at me on some nineteen-year-old's bicep while standing in line at Starbucks. Before I left L.A., I mean. All these young actor wannabes. Quinn James wannabes. He was the James Dean of our generation. He was a tattoo artist's rendering now. I wondered if anyone had the date of Quinn's death tatted on him—or her—now. It made me a little sick to think about. I hoped no one did. I hoped if they did it was hidden under their arm where I wouldn't have to look at it.

I knew what it was like now to be Kurt Cobain's mom, sister, Courtney. Always chasing a ghost. Always being reminded of an angel you can't ever touch again.

It was the same for Sean Lennon.

It was a different way to live: in a relationship with the dead.

Maybe that's another reason I had to get out of L.A. Get out of myself. Become someone else. Full time. 24/7. Or at least, 12/7. Actually, it was just easier to try and method act 24/7. Whenever I wasn't method acting I was thinking about Tate, looking at her social medias, missing her… that was hard as shit. Obsessing over someone online that you can't talk to irl. Like an ex or a celebrity. So mostly I didn't. Mostly I stayed in my role as sixteen-year-old Tatum Grant. Things were just so much easier for me that way. And the longer I was her, the more hours a day I allowed myself to be her, the harder it was to switch back.

I almost never wanted to switch back.

Just every once in a while to make sure Tate was still okay.

But less and less.

I'll admit: switching back to my real self was becoming less and less attractive, more and more a problem. That's how people go crazy, isn't it? Leading a double life. It was becoming harder and harder. I looked at Tate's social medias less and less. Updating mine here in Elkheart more and more. Selfies of me. Photos of me and Taylor. Me as Tatum. T&T. The halls of Dobson High.

TATE GRANT

I didn't know how Anissa and Mom lived with themselves for fifteen years like that, keeping such a huge secret from me, such crucial information *about me* like that. I mean, how did it not just slip out? How did they sleep at night knowing we were all three living such a huge lie?

I was still trying to process it all...

It was taking a long time to even make the flip in my head, from thinking of my grandma as my mom and my mom as my sister. Jack Nicholson shit. But he was in his 30s when he found out. Not a vulnerable teenaged boy.

Who knows when they were planning on telling me, when I might have found out. If they hadn't had that big blow up fight six months ago.

If Mom, or 'Grandma', hadn't gotten so pissed at Anissa, at my *mother*, that she totally forgot I was there or just didn't care anymore, for once, and just started going on and on about how she'd had to raise me as her own because Anissa had gotten knocked up as a teenager, as a fifteen-year-old, by an older, drug-addicted actor who died, who od'd, two months before I was even born.

"Good choices, Anissa!" Mom had said. Mom. Grandma. I still couldn't make the transition in my head, really. I still called her "Mom," still thought of Anissa as Anissa, as my sister...

The only good thing to come of all that was I now had a dad. Even if he was dead. I had a name and a face. Before that they would never tell me anything about my father. Anissa didn't have one, why did I need one? The implication was that Mom just somehow kept being immaculately impregnated. Or getting pregnant from one night stands with men she didn't even bother getting the names of. It was ridiculous. It was so much better knowing Quinn James was my father. Even if it was weird as fuck that Anissa was my mother. I didn't know if I'd ever get used to that.

But I started reading about my father, started watching all his movies... except the one with my mom in it, his last one. I wasn't ready for that. I didn't know if I'd ever be ready. If I'd ever watch that film.

ROBIN GRANT

Of course we'd gotten the idea from Jack Nicholson's story, about how he hadn't known until he was in his late thirties or maybe even into his forties that the person he believed to be his mother was actually his grandmother and the person he thought was his sister was, in fact, his mother.

And he found out after they both died. (His actual mother must have died young.) I'd read an article in which Jack was quoted as saying he was happy they'd kept that secret from him and that he admired their strength to do so for all those years.

It didn't seem like Tate was going to be expressing admiration for Anissa or myself anytime soon.

Of course, maybe it was on account we didn't have the strength to keep the secret to our own deaths. In a weakened state—angry with Anissa—I broke the secret. Maybe that was more damaging than holding it in, at that point. Maybe Tate wasn't actually mad we'd kept the secret so long but that we'd revealed it so soon.

ANISSA GRANT

I remembered back in 2007 or so when Britney 'went crazy,' shaved her head, took to a car with an umbrella. I'd felt like that most of my life. Like I'd wanted to act out like that, to rebel, from being the perfect daughter, the perfect child actor, never a complaint, always go to dance lessons, always go to voice lessons… just this whole Groundhog's Day existence.

The closest I came to rebelling was that year with Quinn. Not even a full year.

And I paid for that. After that my life got even more controlled, even more claustrophobic. My mom was more up my ass than ever. Because now I had a child. Now I was someone's mother, even though I wasn't allowed, really, to be her mother. I still had to behave as though I were. To live my life in this very controlled manner.

But I kept dreaming of a way out.

I always knew I had to get out or I'd die.

In *Britney: for the record*, toward the end of the documentary, Britney's friends come up with a surprise for her. And she doesn't know what it is and you the viewer don't know what it is. She's driven in a van out to the middle of nowhere. Out where there's some cows and some barren land and not much else. They tell her they're going for a hike. For a picnic. To look at cows.

The film cuts to an interviewer asking her when the last time she felt free was and Britney pauses, looks out the window, and says, "when I got to drive my car."

And then the film cuts back to the van in the middle of nowhere and Britney saying, "Is that my car? Is that my car?" And then you see her driving her convertible, solo, out on the open road, around these sharp curves, in the California or Nevada sun. Two hours from Vegas. Middle of nowhere.

And Britney is ostensibly smiling. We don't know. We don't get a close-up.

And Britney is ostensibly free. For an hour or two or however long they let her drive her car before she has to get back in the van and the car has to be driven back by someone else, someone not Britney Spears.

I felt like *that Britney*, the one driving her convertible, the hours I was driving through the Midwest, driving to Elkheart, Indiana.

I felt free in a way I'd never felt in my life before. I want Tate to feel that. Someday. One day.

TATE GRANT

I'd changed my name almost as soon as I found out. I still had the same legal name but my stage name now was Kaylin Jennings-James. I don't know where I got Kaylin. Maybe I made it up. It sounds similar to other names I've heard before but I don't know that I've heard that exact name or seen it spelled that exact way.

Jennings was my mom's, or, my grandma's maiden name.

And of course James was my father's name. It was actually his middle name. His real last name which I read on Wikipedia was Henderson. But Quinn James sounded better, I guess. More outlawish. More badass and masculine.

I loved being Kaylin Jennings-James.

Renaming myself felt like the beginning of taking back control, of taking hold of my own destiny. It was right after I changed my name I started getting parts, got the commercials and the first small role in a film and now the TV series.

I don't think any of this would be happening if Anissa and Mom hadn't gotten in that fight, if Anissa hadn't left town.

She was always against me acting, anyway. She was always so negative about Hollywood and the film industry and I get it now, I get that my dad died in it. But I honestly feel like he probably would have died being a truck driver. Or a garbage man. I think his childhood had fucked him up so bad, his mom and dad, it didn't matter where he lived or what he did for a living. He was an addict. He was probably bipolar.

But he was so fucking cool.

And maybe acting, being in films, helped save him, kept him alive longer than he would have been had he stayed in Indiana.

Who fucking knows? You can't know what might have happened if.

But I was glad Anissa was gone if she was just going to be a nag and a Debbie Downer about me acting because I loved acting. I loved it more than I'd ever loved anything in my life. I loved everything about it. Sitting in makeup, waiting in my trailer, talking to other actors and other people on set, the grips and the camera guys, the makeup artists and hair people. I loved the fans and going out at night, going to places like the Chateau Marmont. Getting to wear designer's clothes to parties and premiers.

I didn't ever want to stop acting.

I wanted my dad to be proud of me. I know that sounds silly or fucked up to say. But it's the truth. I felt like he was watching over me now, hanging around sets making sure I was okay. Making sure I got good lighting and good lines. I felt like he'd be happy I was an actress. That I was carrying on the family tradition.

People liked knowing I was Quinn James' daughter.

No one had known he had a baby.

I felt the love when they found out I was his.

They'd had all this love for him all these years since he died and now they could finally express it. I dug being the recipient of that love.

I think it would have freaked Anissa out.

Which is why she never made it public knowledge I existed.

Barely anyone had known she existed, in Quinn's life, I mean.

She was a very secretive private person. I'm the exact opposite. I want to share my father with the world through my acting, keep him alive to an extent, as much as I can, through me.

TATUM GRANT

I hadn't smoked pot in a long time. "Since Quinn," right, go figure. My life had been on fucking hold and I hadn't even realized it. Or I'd realized it but I hadn't cared. Depression. What a racket.

Taylor and I got pretty stoned. Like, I can't feel my face stoned. I had her drop me back off at school. I wanted to confront Coach W when no one else was around, after school hours. I knew he stayed late, getting the set and wardrobe and script ready for the fall play and shit.

I got in the school by the side door, which was always unlocked until like nine or ten at night.

I walked down to the theater high as fuck. I forgot I wasn't sixteen. It's so easy to regress back into high school adolescence, especially when you're constantly *in a high school,* surrounded by adolescents. I was always forgetting I wasn't sixteen now.

I didn't have a plan other than distracting Coach W from Taylor.

I was ready to sacrifice myself if necessary.

Any means necessary, bitches.

Taylor had enough shit to deal with just dealing with Cam Spencer.

She didn't need this shit, too.

I was much better prepared to deal with "this shit," as I came to think of Coach W.

COACH W

Sometimes I think people are looking for inappropriate behavior from a teacher. They read into too much. I liked Taylor. You couldn't help recognizing she was beautiful and smart and charismatic. But that's it. I wasn't a moron. I wasn't trying to jeopardize my career at Dobson High. Or my life in Elkheart. You couldn't take a shit in the men's room as a teacher in this town without everyone in town knowing.

When I was a kid going to Elkheart Junior High we had this teacher Mr. A. I don't know what it is about male teachers that no one can pronounce their last names. I never had a female teacher go by the first initial of her last name. But I digress. Mr. A. was our most popular teacher. Taught World History to seventh and eighth graders. Also coached boys' track and field. He was a bachelor. Middle-aged. Maybe forty. Maybe forty-five. I don't know. It was all the same to me as a thirteen-year-old. I ran track. Most of us ran track just so we could hang out with Mr. A, to be honest. He was super charismatic and talked to you like you were an adult, treated you like a peer. Maybe that's a mistake. I guess now that's frowned upon. But it made us feel special and mature and like we were being taken seriously.

There was some slightly weird stuff too. He made you undress for weigh ins. Completely nude. And then turn around so he could get a look at you. He said it was for…

He never touched me or any of my friends, that I know of.

Later, after he killed himself, rumor was a boy or a boy's mom had complained to the school. About inappropriate touching. Light petting, I think they called it in the papers.

He hung himself before it could go any farther.

The case, I mean.

I guess we'll never know, if he actually molested anyone or not.

And you can draw your own conclusions on the nude weigh ins.

Personally, I didn't think it was that big of a deal.

Weighing how nice he was and how important he made you feel.

For once in your stupid adolescent life.

I loved Mr. A but I didn't want my life to end like that. Alone in a rented house. The beginnings of a small town's hysteria circling me.

Me the center of allegations and…

So, yeah, I was well aware of my relationship to students at Dobson High. Of the line I had to walk. Every day I walked it. Any high school teacher who tells you he or she has never been sexually attracted to a student is either lying to you or lying to her or himself. Or is seriously repressed or asexual.

But then Tatum came to school. Tatum was unlike the other high school girls. Tatum was aggressive.

It was like this other buddy friend of mine who'd been adopted as a baby. People would always ask him, his whole life, if he ever wanted to look for his birth parents and he always, without hesitating, said no. He had wonderful adoptive parents. He couldn't do better. What would be the point. Then when he was about thirty-five, his bio family started looking for him. He'd never even considered that as a possibility. He'd always felt confident in his decision not to look for them. But they kept trying. One year. The next. And it started wearing on him. He wasn't so sure anymore that he didn't want to know.

I'd never factored in the possibility a high school girl would pursue *me*.

Sometimes if you're not prepared for shit in life, you respond differently than you might if you'd anticipated, if you'd planned ahead.

Shit comes out of left field. And what the fuck.

Tatum came out of left field. And, seriously, what the fuck.

Suddenly, I wasn't so confident I'd "never fuck a high school student," if I'm being honest. And I guess I am.

ANISSA GRANT

I wasn't going to let Coach W fuck with Taylor. And I figured I had nothing to lose. Coach W thought I was a sixteen-year-old girl and obviously believed fifteen and sixteen-year-old girls were easily seduced and even easier controlled.

Taylor had told me he kept cornering her when no one else was around, talking about her role in the upcoming musical; how he wanted to give her the lead, how perfect she'd be for it, if only...

He can tell you now he never had any intention of blah blah blah.

But clichés and stereotypes are typically based on *something*.

I didn't want Taylor to be that something. A cliché.

I figured I'd see for myself what Coach W was capable of, what lines he would or wouldn't cross.

I also am aware what he says now.

How he claims he always knew I wasn't sixteen.

Bullshit he knew.

You think he would have gotten it up that fast, his dick would have gotten that hard, if he didn't believe I was jailbait, underage, not barely legal but 100% illegal?

I don't either.

I was still high AF when I waltzed into the theater at six pm on a Thursday.

I was wearing my athletic shorts and tank top from cheer practice. My hair was in a fucking ponytail, how much more cliché could I have gotten, how much more could I have played the part.

It was like a goddamn audition in there.

For a high school acting teacher, he didn't know shit about acting or actresses.

He couldn't read when he was being played.

I sidled up to him. "Hey, Coach W," I said in a southern accent I didn't have. (You can pick one up in a small Midwestern town; particularly if you frequent gas stations late at night for cigarettes and boxed wine.)

We shot the shit for a few minutes, me pretending to be interested in upcoming tryouts. I wanted to make sure no one was hiding in a utility closet or up in the lighting/audio booth. No other ingénues, on deck for that evening.

When it was clear we were alone, I pulled a note from the Juliette Lewis school of high school student acting and took hold of Coach W's forefinger, slid it into my mouth, directing it toward the back of my throat.

Maybe I actually was interested in trying out for the fall play.

I was pretty sure I could get a lead role.

Maybe I had the subconscious teacher/student fantasy just like I had the conscious cheerleader/football player fantasy. Just like I had the Homecoming and prom fantasies.

Coach W practically shot in his pants. Which made me reconsider how many times this had happened for him. Meaning, maybe it hadn't.

He wasn't a bad looking man.

He looked a little like Rob Lowe if Rob Lowe couldn't afford a personal trainer and a personal chef and a personal makeup artist.

I was kind of surprised when I realized my underwear was getting wet. Maybe I actually wanted to fuck Coach W. Compared to Cam, he had a sense of humor, at least.

He said, "Yeah, I saw the *Cape Fear* remake, too, Tatum."

I laughed with his fucking finger still in my mouth. It was a good thing it wasn't his dick because I'm pretty sure I bit down on it when I guffawed.

I was checking off boxes left and right: make friends with the popular kids, make cheerleading team, bang a football player, bang your drama coach.

And it was only week two of school.

COACH W

I wish I could tell you I felt good about fucking Tatum. The truth is the second she left the shame set in, grabbed me by the nuts, and didn't let go.

I went to Target, bought a fifth of whiskey. Went to the gas station, bought a pack of cigarettes. Even though I was supposed to be sober, supposed to have given up smoking. I smoked four on the drive home, listening to Rage, fucking thrashing.

The dirty little secret no one wants to tell you, no teacher, anyway, is how these "kids"—*kids* who can procreate, by the way; kids who fuck *each other* like rabbits, let's not forget—can become your friends. In some cases, your closest friends, maybe your only friends, for four years.

Taylor, Cam, Chase, Tatum, Matt, Makayla… they were all the people I talked to the most that year. The people I spent the most time with. Around. Of course you develop feelings. You'd have to be a sociopath *not* to.

The next year or two or four, another group of high schoolers are my friends. And the cycle repeats. Maybe that sounds fucked up to you. I don't know what else to tell you. Just the truth.

ANISSA GRANT

I'd driven home from school thinking how I couldn't wait to text Taylor, tell her everything that had happened. But once I got there, lit a cigarette, thought about it a little longer, I wasn't so sure I *should* tell her.

I didn't want Coach W to get in trouble but also I wasn't sure Taylor would think it was a cool move, fucking the drama coach.

What if she thought it was disgusting? That *I* was disgusting. Or what if she told Cam and Cam got Coach W in trouble. I mean, his fucking aunt worked at the school and knew everything about everyone.

Also, to be honest, I wasn't sure I never wanted to fuck Coach W again.

He was only the second man I'd ever had sex with (not counting Cam).

There was something about the way he'd held my hair, wrapped it around my neck, that I liked. I kept touching it, my neck, now, wondering what Coach W was doing, what he thought of what had happened, if he was punishing himself. He seemed like the sort to punish himself.

I got a can of frosting from the pantry and a box of graham crackers and made "sandwiches" out of them the way my mom had done when I was little. I ate one while smoking a Marlboro Light and stuck the rest in the fridge for later. They were better chilled. Like white wine. Ha ha.

You're starting to think I'm crazy but everyone's crazy when you get to know them, right? Like how every family's weird.

I took what was left of the frosting tub into the bedroom and got out my laptop and got online to look at Taylor's social medias and Cam's and Chase's and mine.

I took a selfie in bed with the can of frosting, uploaded it. Wrote a caption: *Sweet as shit.*

Cam was the first person to like it, which I figured was a "fuck you" like.

He had posted a photo of himself "pumping iron" with Chase and I "fuck you back" liked it.

I'd recently read an article quoting a young Arnold Schwarzenegger saying that pumping iron felt like coming.

An hour later Taylor changed her profile pic from one of her and Cam to one of she and I we'd taken in the car earlier, her feet over my lap.

I waited for Cam to lose his mind.

Of course he "liked" it.

Which meant he was probably plotting my murder as I sat eating my vanilla frosting in my bed with an enormous spoon meant for... I don't know what that spoon was meant for, actually.

COACH W

I stopped at Subway, got two footlongs. I was ravenous. I was terrified I was going to lose my job.

Believe it or not, I'd never fucked a student before. Never even really come close.

I had this long-term off and on girlfriend, Macy, but we'd been dating so long we barely ever had sex anymore. Mostly, now, we were off.

More than losing my job, I was terrified I was going to lose my entire life.

Nothing had been right since Quinn died. Or really, nothing had been right since Quinn had left town when we were fourteen. Stupid fucking Hollywood talent scout. Took my best friend.

And now here I was blaming me fucking a high school girl on Quinn leaving twenty years earlier.

Pathetic.

I was a fucking loser.

But tell me something I didn't know. You think any divorced, middle-aged, high school teacher with a fifth of whiskey, a pack of cigarettes, and two foot-long meatball sandwiches on the seat beside him thinks he's a winner?

Maybe a part of me wanted to get caught, to get it over with: my total and utter downfall, I mean. My excommunication from the community. So the fear would end.

Quinn came back to visit his grandma one summer, four summers after he left. We were fifteen. He'd already been in four or five movies at this point and was getting ready to film another. He had all this money. Like, literal bills falling out of his pockets. He kept shoving them on me. Hundred dollar bills. What he really wanted was to feel like a small town thug again, the way we'd been headed when he left. We rode bikes out to the reservoir. He was on my brother's. He kept almost falling off lighting cigarettes, lighting a joint. I kept trying not to stare at him. I never had any close friends after he left. I mean, I had *friends*... I was on the football team and the basketball team... but it wasn't the same. I'd known Quinn since before kindergarten. We'd grown up on the same street. We'd constantly slept over at each other's houses. His grandma was like my second mom, or second grandma. He and his grandma loved each other so much it was insane. His actual parents were so fucked up on drugs, in and out of jail, he hardly ever saw them and when he did it wasn't good. They'd try to bum money off him and tell him he wasn't the big hotshot he thought he was, that he was just a piece of shit like them, how the apple doesn't fall far from the tree, that sort of fucked up shit. I was around for some of it. It was real bad. But as long as they weren't around, things were fine. His grandma made us cookies and shepherd's pie and anything Quinn wanted.

Anyway, that day, we rode bikes out to the reservoir, getting high as fuck on the way there. And then once we were there we were like, okay, so now what? Which was when Quinn decided we should borrow this houseboat. Not steal it, mind you, just borrow it a while. Take her out on the water. Free her, so to speak. I was too high to object. Not that I would have objected to Quinn anyway. I always went along with whatever he suggested. It was hard to say no to Quinn. Mostly cuz you never wanted to. Of course we got caught, busted. Someone called the cops. It was in the papers. Like, national papers. On account of Quinn being in movies, that one movie, especially, the one he'd left town to make when he was eleven. I still have some of the newspapers somewhere in a bin under my bed.

That wasn't the last time I saw him, of course. Once I turned eighteen I drove out to Hollywood, tried to make it like he did; failed real quick. But it was the last time we hung out like kids in our hometown. The last time we really felt like brothers.

Quinn's life was dark. You could see the inevitable outcome barreling at him like the train in *Stand by Me*.

But he didn't have the agility to dodge it like the boys on the tracks.

Or maybe he just didn't want to.

He was just gonna stand there while the train came faster and faster.

He was a speed freak.

An adrenaline junkie.

A cowboy junkie.

A drugstore cowboy.

Your basic addict.

BAM!

Maybe this was what was happening to me now. Maybe I was dark, too, darker than I'd ever cared to admit. Or maybe the darkness calls each of us at different times in our lives.

This was what I was thinking when suddenly my phone rang.

It wasn't darkness calling. It was just Macy.

I let it go to voicemail.

TAYLOR RAGNER

I knew as soon as I changed my profile pic, Cam would have something to say about it. That's how petty he could be. That's how petty he *was*.

The closer I got to Tatum the more he tried to control me the more he pushed me away the closer I got to Tatum.

It was a nasty little circle.

I scrolled through Tatum's online photos, her social media history. It only went back a few weeks. Til she moved here.

Where was her life before Elkheart?

Her friends and family?

While I was looking at her social media account, she changed her profile pic to be the one of us together also. The same photo I'd used for my profile pic.

I smiled knowing how mad it would make Cam but also because I realized looking at the photo how happy I looked, how happy I was for once. I don't think I'd been really happy for a while. A few months. Over a year.

Honestly, I wasn't sure I'd ever been that happy.

Maybe once, a long time ago, when my brother and I were little, our parents still acting *like parents*.

Sometimes they let me sleep in my brother's room with him. I remember feeling so safe and warm in his bed.

I hated sleeping alone.

I hated *being alone*, period.

I was going to ask Tatum to spend the night Friday, game night. I didn't want to spend another night alone in the house with my mom. I could hear her crying all night long some nights. It was fucking disgusting. I didn't understand why she didn't just leave my father. Get a job. Get a life. Get the fuck out of this house. I couldn't wait to get the fuck out of that house.

I stuck cotton balls in my ears. I needed new headphones. The kind that canceled out your mom sobbing. The kind that let you forget you're still only fifteen and not in control of your own life.

Juliet was thirteen, "almost fourteen."

That's what Coach W said.

If that puts things in perspective.

Maybe that's why so many teens kill themselves. Or develop eating disorders. Because you can't legalize suicide or anorexia. Sometimes suicide or starving yourself are your only options for autonomy.

Listen to me, I sound like I'm writing a goddamn speech for Government.

I sound like a fucking teen movie heroine.

"AND THAT'S WHEN I SHOWED THE POPULAR KIDS HOW DUMB THEY ARE. AND THAT'S WHEN THE HOT GUY LIKED ME."

[eye roll]

Gag.

Anyway, I was the popular kid. And the hot guy already liked me.

That was the problem.

Fuck my life.

I'm an asshole.

Friday was our first game of the season. It was the first day we got to wear our cheer uniforms to school. Taylor stopped by to help me with my face stencil—a mustang, to give me a bow for my hair in school colors—purple and white.

I closed the master bedroom door.

"Shhh," I said when I answered Taylor's knock, holding my purple manicured nail to my lip. "We have to be quiet, my mom's sleeping."

I pulled her into my bedroom and closed the door, went into the bathroom.

Taylor smelled good, like Jennifer Aniston's cologne they sold at Target.

Her hair was curled and pulled into a ponytail and her uniform swished when she walked and I wanted to reach my hand up under it and grab what was under there but of course I couldn't. I didn't put my mouth on hers either, though I thought about that too.

In the bright bathroom lighting I could see the tiny pimples she complained about under her foundation. I found something about them so sexy.

I found Taylor's imperfections attractive.

The small cellulite on the backs of her thighs.

The tiny pimples you could only see if you were super close to Taylor.

Maybe it was the intimacy with which you needed to observe these imperfections.

I understood how hard it must have been for Coach W (or any other living male) to be in close proximity to Taylor.

Your natural instinct was to try and possess her.

"Lift your chin," she said, taking my face in her hands. "Turn your cheek," she said, turning my jaw in her palm.

I wanted her to guide me this way, always. To move and rearrange my bones at her will.

When she was finished I had a cartoon horse on one side of my face and a purple cheer thingy on my other.

Just like Taylor.

Then she pulled my hair into a limper version of a ponytail—I hadn't gotten up early enough to curl it—and wrapped it in the purple and white ribbons. Got her makeup out of her purse and applied purple shadow to my lids, a purplish tint to my lips.

"Here," she said, handing me a Kleenex. "Blot."

I slid the tissue between my lips while making eye contact with Taylor.

"Perfect," she said, taking a step back to admire her handy work.

"If things don't work out, you could get a job as a makeup artist," I said.

Not knowing what *things* were. What *working out* meant.

"Right," she said. "Instead of Harvard," she said. She laughed. I laughed too even though I wasn't sure which part was the joke.

"Come on," she said, pulling me by the hand. "Let's go or we won't have time to smoke before school."

By the time we pulled into the Dobson High parking lot we were both high as fuck.

It was beginning to be a pattern.

I felt Taylor pulling me down the hallway, toward our lockers, past Coach W and Cam and Chase and Makayla and everyone who hated me for coming between them and Taylor.

It felt like I was grinning. Everyone else felt comparatively somber. Monotone. Static. It felt like only Taylor and I were moving.

"OH my god," Taylor said. "Don't let Cam see me, we can't let Cam talk to us, he can't know we're high or he'll totally freak out about it, he'll totally call my mom or pull some narc shit. He's so fucking stupid sometimes, such a cop."

I couldn't stop grinning. We ran into the restroom. I splashed water on my face.

We took deep breaths in front of the mirror.

"Pull it together, Taylor Ragner," Taylor told herself.

I couldn't see her tiny pimples in this lighting and I missed them. I couldn't see her cellulite either. I wouldn't get another glimpse until later that evening, alone in Taylor's bedroom after the game. That was a lot of hours, between then and now.

But I was a cheerleader, goddamn it. And that's why I was here.

Swish swish,

I walked down the hall and into my first class, my head held high.

Every female secretly wants to be what I was. It was like being Miss America or a Victoria's Secret model. It was like being Kendall Jenner. Or Kylie, at least.

CAM SPENCER

I kept texting Taylor and she kept not responding or responding "k" or with just a smiley face emoji or a heart, but no words.

It was driving me crazy but Chase said not to think about Taylor right now because we had our first game that night and then after the game I could see Taylor, talk to her face to face. We always went to a party after the game and tonight Chase was having one in his barn because his dad had to go out of town on business. The whole school was going. Well, the whole school minus the losers who didn't ever go to parties.

We were playing Clearfork, a team we were sure to beat.

I just wanted the game to be over so it'd be time to talk to Taylor. I was hoping we'd both be in a good mood, get a little drunk and chillax, find a room at Chase's to be alone in. Reconnect. Fall back in love. Or at least take our clothes off. At least fuck.

TAYLOR RAGNER

I texted Tatum from first hour to see if she wanted to sleepover at my house after the game and party that night. Cam was blowing up my phone as usual. Trying to make plans with me for after the game.

I wanted to go to Chase's party but I planned on going with Tatum. I planned on socializing and talking to *everyone*, not just Cam. He could be so goddamn needy, so isolating. I didn't know what his problem was lately. He used to be fun and social, too. That's why I'd been so into him. He was so popular, the life of every party. Now he just wanted to sulk and try to get me alone so we could talk all night. I was so sick of talking about our future and our relationship and blah blah blah.

I was a fucking sophomore in high school. Maybe he was ready to leave, maybe he was a senior, a super senior, already eighteen, but that wasn't my problem. I wasn't the one who'd sought out a freshman when I was a junior. A *second year* junior.

I just wanted to cheer and party and drink some beers with my friends.

I didn't need my boyfriend acting like he owned me, acting like my dad, wherever the fuck my dad was. I didn't need either one of them, to be honest. Maybe I was better off without both, was what I was starting to think.

ANISSA GRANT

I got a text from Taylor in first hour asking me to sleepover.

I smiled and put my phone away so Ms. Corwin wouldn't take it.

I sat in my seat staring at the board thinking of how much closer Taylor and I would be after tonight.

I'd never spent the night at friend's house. I'd never even had a friend sleep over.

I wasn't allowed. Mother didn't trust other people, anyone outside the family.

I was glad she was different with Tate, had different rules, or less of them. Or Tate ignored them.

I'd seen a new pic of Tate that morning before Taylor came over. Tate at the Santa Monica pier with a guy who looked a little like Quinn. Like, when I first clicked on the photo I inhaled sharply, because he so closely resembled Quinn. For a brief second I forgot Quinn was dead. I forgot Tate wasn't me.

They weren't holding hands or anything so I didn't know if this guy was just a friend or another actor or what.

I couldn't tell from the photo if he was an adult or a teen.

Tate hadn't tagged him or named him.

Tate was wearing a Lana Del Rey cropped tee and the guy had a tattoo of a spider on his hand, which Quinn never would have had. Quinn was terrified of spiders. Once he ran out of a hotel room we were staying in because he saw one in the bathroom. I had to go in and capture it in a plastic cup and carry it outside. It probably didn't help that he was on something at the time. I don't even know what. Prescription pills. Acid. You never knew with Quinn. You just buckled up. Crossed your fingers. Hoped for the best.

It all happened so fast. He was here and we were here and he was gone.

I didn't have time to digest or analyze until later.

Now when I look back I see it all in his eyes, in the photographs of us together. I can see he is about to leave. That he's barely there as it is. He's already almost gone.

COACH W

It was our first home game, Friday, and the cheerleaders were all in uniform all day for the pep rally in the afternoon.

I watched Tatum swish by me in the hall several times before I had her and Taylor for acting class in fifth hour. Swish, swish.

I'd had the whole night to think about what had happened but then Friday morning they'd called a staff meeting to tell us another student had committed suicide the night before. Lance Hershner had gone out to the same train tracks at the same time as Chen Lee, jumped in front of the same train. Principal Pitt wasn't sure how or when to tell the students. We were all worried even more now about copycatters. Suicides amongst teens could run in clusters like any other fad. Which seems stupid to say aloud but it was true. We'd all read about other towns, one in California, for instance, where students kept jumping off the top of this one parking structure until they finally had to tear it down. And the suicides stopped. Amazingly. But five kids died before they made that decision, to destroy a perfectly good parking structure.

Anyway, Lance Hershner's killing himself kept me from thinking about my own problems for a day. Distracted me from wondering what was going to happen or not happen between me and Tatum now that what had happened the night before had happened.

I postponed thinking about it till the end of the weekend.

That's about how long the effects of someone else's suicide last, to be honest.

Two and a half days. Tops.

Unless you're another suicidal teenager, which was why Principal Pitt had called the meeting. We couldn't destroy the train tracks. So we were trying to come up with other options.

For now we were supposed to talk to students. As a whole and individually.

Watch for anyone we thought might be vulnerable.

Anyone showing signs of identifying with Lance Hershner or Chen Lee.

But then Taylor and Tatum came into my fifth hour holding hands as usual, and like the disgusting male human I am, I found myself fantasizing about having sex with the two of them. Or about watching the two of them having sex.

I couldn't even focus on the two student suicides long enough to stop being a perv for five minutes.

Thanks testosterone!

It was the goddamn cheer uniforms. I couldn't understand why they kept making Catholic school uniforms and cheer uniforms to play into male fantasies of what teen girls should look like. Why they hadn't reconfigured them, redesigned them, to be less... sexy.

It was like dangling a large steak in front of a lion and shaming him for wanting to eat it, telling him he had to be vegan or he was immoral.

I wanted to scream at someone at the school, whoever was in charge of the cheerleaders' uniforms, stop dangling the fucking meat!

Or stop expecting me to be vegan!

Anyway, the meat had already been half eaten by high school male students; Cam and Matt and the others.

So it was okay for them to eat the meat but not me.

This is turning into a horrible analogy, fuck.

Equating teen girls with steaks. And teen boys with lions.

Forget all that.

Forget I said anything.

ANISSA GRANT

I'd been too busy to think about Coach W until I was actually in his class. Which I know sounds impossible.

The school was somber even though it was a game day on account of Lance Hershner. They announced it at lunch, his death. We cheerleaders stayed in our uniforms but it felt morbid. Like a horror movie set.

Like our uniforms were drenched in dried blood like in an alternate version of *Carrie*.

Or like we were cheerleaders in a Nirvana video. All Goth'd out and unsmiling and shit.

It never occurred to me Quinn was on heroin even though he had a Kurt Cobain tattoo on his arm.

What a dope I was.

How fucking ignorant.

Coach W kept spacing out and staring at Taylor and me like *he* was on heroin.

We were supposed to be doing trust exercises in class.

You know, take turns falling into each other's arms.

Of course Taylor and I were partners.

Of course Coach W used Taylor to demonstrate the exercise to the class.

She fell backward into his arms and for a second he looked like he was going to cream his pants. He looked how he'd looked with his dick in my mouth the night before which now felt a million light years away.

I probably looked similarly when Taylor fell into my arms, though, so I shouldn't be so judgmental.

It was a slow-motion movie scene with her skirt floating up and her ponytail hanging in the air defying gravity and me catching her before she hit the ground, me rescuing her, being the hero for three seconds.

Then I had to fall into Taylor's arms and I was hesitant. It wasn't that I didn't trust her, that I thought she wouldn't catch me, I just... I don't know. I panicked at the last second and caught myself, stood back up.

"What the hell, Tatum?" Taylor said. "You don't trust me?"

I mean, did she really expect me to? We hadn't even spent the night at each other's houses yet.

I was still the new girl at school.

I think the thing was more that I didn't trust myself.

Or I was still unsure what I was doing here, what my long-term goal was, what I was allowing to happen…

Maybe to be perfectly sentimental about it and overly metaphorical, I was afraid of being too vulnerable around Taylor, of literally falling for her…

God, when did I become a contestant on *The Bachelor* speaking to the camera?

Taylor wasn't happy until every single person in the school made themselves vulnerable to her so she could stomp on their hearts.

Haha. What a cynical thought to have.

I turned around to look at Taylor. She was still looking at me like, WTF?

She was standing with her feet hips distance apart, solidly, like she was grounding herself to catch a large load. My fat ass.

I smiled sheepishly, gave her a half-hearted thumbs up, turned back around and readied myself to *let go* as much as you can ready yourself for total submission and possible emotional annihilation.

I felt myself falling in slow motion the way I had felt myself catching Taylor.

One second I was falling, falling, falling, in a dream state, as in a literal dream, and then the next I was hitting the ground, my ass pummeled by the cold linoleum or ceramic or whatever-that-substance-was tile of Coach W's classroom.

After I landed, sort of caught myself with my hands which felt smacked with blood, enlivened with contact, with catching me, I looked back and up at Taylor, like WTF?

She was standing nonchalantly, biting a hangnail.

"Next time, trust me," she said.

Like, wtf? What did that mean?

"What? What are you talking about?"

"I let you fall because I could see you didn't trust me to catch you," she said. As though that was the most logical explanation for what had happened, as though I was a moron not to see that.

What a strange way to make a lesson. I worried for her future offspring. For her fucked up sadistic parenting.

I glanced up at Coach W and he also had the wtf look on his face.

And then the bell rang and everyone started running to their next class.

So I got up off of the floor, followed Taylor down the hall. Watched her swish off to her next hour. After that was the pep assembly.

My ass hurt as I walked down the hall.

My first public cheer and I'd be wincing in pain all because I hadn't made myself 100 % vulnerable to the great Taylor Ragner.

Fuck me.

TAYLOR RAGNER

The pep assembly was the last hour of the day. All the students piled into the gym and Principal Pitt said some words and Chase and Cam and the other football players all got up and talked about taking down Clearfork and how the Mustangs would dominate them and everything else. I felt Cam staring at me. Trying to catch my eye, to get my attention. Which made me not want to look at him for some reason.

Instead I winked at Tatum. I could tell she was really nervous, being that it was her first time actually cheering and all.

But she did great. All we had to were some of our most basic cheers anyway. Nothing fancy or gymnastic. No one cared that much.

We could have stood still for all they cared. Well, except for Coach W. He seemed extra into it. He was smiling this dopey smile, tapping his foot. He was such a nerd. Such a loser. It almost made you want to give him a blowjob or something. Except then he'd become instantly obsessed with you because his life was probably pathetic and lonely and all about television and internet porn and Doritos.

COACH HARDEN

Of course, we all saw Coach Wellsley practically foaming at the mouth at the pep rally. He and the other male teachers at Dobson were constantly foaming at the mouth. Wiping their mouths on the backs of their sleeves. Acting like idiots, like dogs in heat.

I could only imagine how it'd been twenty years earlier.

When *gay people* were thought of as moral degenerates.

Not that plenty of people didn't *still* think of us that way.

[eye roll]

But now people like Coach Wellsley might be looked at that way, too.

ANISSA GRANT

I'd been so nervous all day, I couldn't eat lunch or anything even, and then it was over in like five seconds. And Chase came over to tell me how great I was and gave me a hug and he smelled so nice, like aftershave or the beach, Hollister or whatever. And Cam continued to scowl at me as usual. So I scowled back at him. It was so hard to believe we'd had sex, that he had ever been inside me.

It felt like we'd always been enemies. And not the kind of enemies who fuck every now and then when the tension gets real bad.

After, Taylor and the other cheerleaders and Coach Harden and I went to Big Boy for the salad and soup bar before the game. And then we had a few minutes to run home and freshen up.

Taylor and I split up for the first time since that morning. She'd told me to pack an overnight bag and bring it with me when she picked me up in an hour.

I got online quick enough to see a new pic of Tate standing in front of the church of Scientology. So she was playing a young woman in a cult now? Or had she become an actual Scientologist in my absence. Who knew what crazy shit went down after I left.

My mom was not a normal human by any stretch of the imagination.

I'm surprised we weren't in a cult already.

Maybe we were but a cult of three. Mom being the leader.

My childhood—though so much of it took place on sets—was so isolated.

I don't think I ever had a real friend other than my mother.

And isn't that the point of having a cult or a cult leader?

That they become your only need for socializing?

I wondered how long it would take for Tate to realize my mother was playing at letting her be independent. I didn't think there was any way my mom would allow actual autonomy. There had to be a limit to her newfound generosity with rules and curfews and such.

There was bound to be a supreme blow up between Mom and Tate at some point.

Tate was too stubborn and strong willed.

I'd been a mouse, limp, meek.

The sort of person who will one day inherit the earth but until that day will suffer silently in her own invisibility.

It was pathetic.

But that was then and this is now, as Judy Blume once famously said. Or was that S. E. Hinton.

ROBIN GRANT

It'd been a few months since Anissa left and Tate and I were getting along great. Better than ever. Like the old days with Anissa.

Tate was filming a new TV show and still doing commercials and at her new school and happy as a clam.

She kept asking me about Quinn, though… I wasn't sure what or how much to tell her. I told her not to believe what she read on the internet. I knew she was reading everything she could find. She wanted me to take her to the cemetery where Quinn was buried with his grandma, but I wasn't sure that was such a good idea. Anissa was already mad enough at me. I thought she'd probably want to be the one to take her. If and when she ever returned from wherever it was she was. I'd sort of stopped waiting for her to contact us. Stopped checking my phone every five minutes. Stopped looking for her handwriting in the mailbox.

I don't know if Tate stopped waiting. Tate was the sort of young woman who didn't necessarily let you know all her feelings. She liked projecting an image of perfectionism. Like she had it all together, all the time. Sort of like me.

Anissa was never interested in projecting anything. A particular image or persona. She sort of went out of her way to not have one. To be as vanilla as possible. While still getting second billing in a film with Quinn James.

You'd be hard-pressed to find any other actress who costarred with Quinn in his last five years who can still walk down Hollywood Boulevard unnoticed or unknown or undetected.

Anissa just has that sort of personality, that look: she could be your neighbor or the girl at school you barely noticed existing.

She doesn't stand out in any particular way.

Unlike Tate. Tate, like Quinn, is incapable of blending in.

That was the source of much of Quinn's problems. He was the opposite of Anissa. He couldn't walk out of a hotel room without six people in the hallway noticing and probably offering him drugs. He couldn't fill his car with gas without being asked to sign a dozen autographs. And this was before the internet and social media and everything.

Can you imagine Quinn James' life today?

He couldn't handle the attention and fame then.

It's a hard life. It takes a special kind of person.

I don't know if Tate's that kind of person. It remains to be seen.

But it wasn't for Anissa. Or Anissa wasn't for it.

And maybe I did push her, in retrospect.

It's hard to know when your child's been in the business since she was a baby.

When they're doing it because they want to and when they're doing it because you want them to.

Ask Jade Barrymore and Terri Shields about it. We've all gotten shit.

TATE GRANT

Every once in a while something would remind me of Anissa but mostly I didn't have time to think about her. I didn't really have a scenario for where she went, what she was doing, you know? It's not like Mom and I... Grandma... Robin and I thought something bad had happened to her. We knew she'd left because of the fight, so we figured she'd gone off somewhere to find herself or to cool off or to just get some space and when she'd done that, she'd be back.

For the first time in my life I was *in love* so that was where my head was at. My boyfriend, Josh. I was *obsessed*. He was one of the writers on the show. He was only 23 when we started dating. Or... being friends. Or whatever. I mean, he wanted everyone to think we were just friends. It was easier that way, he said. Since I was still legally underage. Even if it was Hollywood and so normal rules don't really apply. I mean, you never went to a Hollywood bar or party and saw young actors or actresses—people you knew were under twenty-one—getting carded.

Mostly, we made out in his car on breaks because he had tinted windows or my trailer or he'd sneak me up to his condo on weekends or late at night if I snuck out which I did more and more.

Sometimes it freaked him out I was only fifteen, if he thought about it, but I told him I felt like an eighty-year-old man inside so it wasn't that big a deal.

Anyway, it wasn't like he was that mature or something. He'd worked mainly for Judd Apatow before this. So. You know. What-*the-fuck*-ever, dude. Twenty-three going on fifteen.

TAYLOR RAGNER

By the time Tatum and I got to Chase's party it was already lit. We'd gone to the reservoir and smoked together first and next thing you knew, two hours had gone by.

As soon as we walked into the barn Cam was on me. "Where have you been? It's already eleven o'clock. I've been here since ten waiting for you!" Like he's my fucking mom or something instead of my boyfriend which was fucking annoying because I already was fucking annoyed at my mom for acting like that.

"I was with Tatum at the reservoir," I said. "So what?"

He sort of got a weird look on his face then. I don't know what that was about. Tatum was over at the fire talking to Chase. And Makayla was hanging on Chase as usual even though her boyfriend Matt was also at the party, across the room. This school, this town, was so incestuous. I had to get out.

Cam begged me to go to the house, into the kitchen with him, to get more beer and to talk to him.

I went, reluctantly. I thought maybe I would just break up with him. Get it over with. But then I remembered Homecoming was coming up and it felt like I should wait. As much not to hurt Cam as anything else. I mean, I could have gone with Tatum, if that's all it was about. But a part of me *did* feel bad for Cam. For pulling away. For wanting distance. Of course I felt guilty about that. Cam was my first boyfriend. My first kiss. My first fuck. He was always going to mean *something* to me.

"Come here," he said. We were standing in the entranceway to Chase's house. It was weird because there was a family portrait and it was weird seeing Chase's mom in it now that she was dead. It made me want to cry or be sick, looking at it.

Maybe that's why I was feeling so vulnerable. I let Cam pull me upstairs to Chase's room. We'd done it in there before, at other barn parties. Cam said Chase didn't mind. He claimed Chase told him to go ahead and use it. We hadn't been up there since the funeral and the first thing I noticed was a photograph of Chase with his mom that I swore hadn't been there before. It made me sad again. I felt like crying all of a sudden.

"What's the matter?" Cam said.

"I just feel bad for Chase," I said, nodding at the photograph on the dresser.

"Yeah," Cam said. "It's been a rough year."

"And now the suicides," I said.

I hadn't really dealt with them yet either. All of a sudden everything was hitting me. The heaviness of all the deaths in our small town in recent months.

"I know," Cam said. "That's why we need each other even more now. I need you, Taylor."

He was on his knees and I was sitting on Chase's bed. It was made meticulously of course. Cam's was never made. Neither was mine, to be honest.

I was a little bit terrified he was going to ask me to marry him right then for a second. But I'd told him over and over not to even think of proposing till we were graduated from college.

I leaned forward to meet his lips. I was still pretty high but I hadn't had anything to drink. Cam was a little drunk. I could always tell because his face was pinker, a little blotchy, and he was talking sentimentally, needily.

His mouth still tasted good. Cold, like the beer. Foamy.

We kissed again, longer this time, and Cam laid down on top of me on Chase's bed. I could feel him, pressing into me. I didn't have to fake it this time. He didn't need porn either.

But pretty soon after, almost the second we finished, I was annoyed by it again. His possessiveness. His treating me like property. His rules and demands.

He got dressed in Chase's bedroom and I told him I needed a minute. I told him I'd be down soon and I went into the bathroom just to sit on the edge of the bathtub a second. Just to catch my breath.

ANISSA GRANT

I didn't know where Taylor went but I noticed Cam wasn't anywhere to be seen either so I assumed they'd gone somewhere together.

I stood around the fire talking to Chase and listening to Halsey.

We both liked her. We both followed her on Instagram and Snapchat and Twitter.

Chase was a little drunk. I could tell by how much he was talking and by how sleepy his eyes were. They were sort of cute all half-shut like that. You couldn't help falling a little in love with him in the same way you can't help falling in love with a puppy dog or a kitten or any baby animal.

He said he was going to wait until the next night, when we were on our double date with Cam and Taylor to ask me, but did I want to go with him to Homecoming.

I think Makayla heard because she sort of gave me the stink eye. I pretended she wasn't there. It was becoming a habit.

Inside, I was fucking melting. Just like I always knew I would. Like I was Molly Ringwald or something. But better. Cuz this wasn't happening on a film set. This was fucking happening for real. *For real* for real. No simulation. No fed lines.

"Of course I'll go to Homecoming with you, Chase," I said, grinning up at him like I'd practiced a thousand times in my bathroom mirror. "It'd be my honor."

Maybe I was overdoing it a bit but what the fuck. I was high. And this was what I'd driven all the way to bumfuck Indiana for, left my family, gave up my identity and risked imprisonment for. To go to fucking Homecoming. With a fucking football player. And now it was actually happening. I wasn't sixteen and pregnant anymore. I wasn't missing out on life anymore.

And I was so happy.

Like John Hughes 80s happy.

Like Molly Ringwald at the end of *Pretty in Pink* happy.
Like *what the fuck am I going to wear to Homecoming* happy.

TATE GRANT

Maybe it was on account of dating an older boy, man, whatever. Maybe it was a sadistic way of getting back at Anissa for leaving. Maybe I was just sick of everyone on social media. I was already getting why my dad did what he did, why he couldn't handle Hollywood or stardom or what-the-fuck-ever.

I don't know. I just stopped updating my Instagram and Facebook and whatever else. I just let it all go…

TAYLOR RAGNER

I found Tatum all cuddled up with Chase by the fire and for a second I felt some emotion I hadn't felt in a very long time, since Cam and I started dating. It surprised me. That I was sort of… jealous… of Chase or Tatum or both of them. I wasn't sure which. I couldn't put my finger on why I was feeling what I was feeling I just knew that I was.

It kind of excited me, if I'm being totally honest. To have a feeling, I mean.

I went over and cut in between them.

"What's going on here," I said, sitting down on Tatum's lap.

"Chase just asked me to Homecoming," Tatum said, beaming.

I had to turn around to face her and our faces were so close we could have kissed if one of us had been drunker.

"Oh, good," I said. "Now we can all go to dinner together beforehand and get a limo together and everything."

I kind of felt like the only reason I was even into going to Homecoming anymore was on account of Tatum. If she hadn't moved to town I don't know what I would have done, if I'd have even gone or gone with someone other than Cam or what.

Maybe I would have gone with Chase, who knows.

Chase and I had made out once at a party in middle school when I was in sixth grade. I'd always had a tiny crush on him even if part of me thought he might be gay or at least bisexual.

Chase got us each a beer and we were having such a good time, just chilling by the fire, and then Cam walked in. [eye roll]

CAM SPENCER

When I walked back into the barn my girlfriend was sitting on Tatum's lap and my best friend had just asked Tatum to Homecoming. If I'd known that week before school started how in my shit that girl would be, I never would have taken her to the lake, that's for sure. It sure wasn't worth this. The sex we had, the bad head she gave me.

Now I had to stand there and pretend to like this cunt and make conversation like we were friends. I could tell she didn't like me either. I just couldn't tell if Taylor could tell. I think Chase knew but I didn't care if he did.

I just didn't want to ruin things with Taylor any more than they already were, especially not because of anything to do with Tatum.

I didn't want Tatum coming between us but that's exactly what she was doing.

I'd stopped in the kitchen on the way back down to the barn and done a couple shots with Matt who was fighting as usual with Makayla so I was sort of fired up.

I said, "Hey, how about giving me back my girlfriend," to Tatum and reached for Taylor's wrist. I didn't mean to pull her that hard or anything. *Obviously*. I just meant to joke around, to playfully win her back over to my side. She used to like it when I was "the alpha male" as she called it. She used to like my aggressive, masculine side. But this time she yelled "let go of me" or "get off of me" and dramatically pulled her arm away, holding it as if in a sling with her other arm, and both Chase and Tatum right away acted sorry for her, like *I* was the bad guy, and tried to pull her back.

"Honestly, Cam," Taylor said then. "I'm barely your girlfriend right now so you better watch how you're treating me. You're acting like a teen dad on *16 & Pregnant*. You're being a total shit."

"Jesus, Taylor, I'm sorry," I said. For fuck's sake, the girl still had my cum inside her. You'd think that might make her feel some type of way about me but noooooo. It just made her even pissier, even more stuck up, an even bigger cunt.

I'd about had it, with her and with all of them. I started walking toward my car which was when Chase ran up to stop me.

"You can't drive right now, Cam," he said and tried to get the keys from me.

"Damn it, Chase, let me alone," I said.

I was about ready to punch him but I knew that would just give Taylor the ultimate reason to break up with me. And, yeah, I wasn't an idiot, I knew she was looking for any reason to break up with me. It was pretty fucking obvious.

"I'm fine," I said. "Really, I'm not even drunk."

But I could see Taylor and Tatum walking past us across the lawn to Taylor's car.

I could see they were leaving so I decided "fuck it" I'd stay.

"Alright, man," I said and turned back around toward the barn.

"Cool, come on, man, don't worry about it, don't worry about her," Chase said, which was when I really started worrying. Hearing someone else acknowledge things weren't right between us out loud. Outside of my own head.

"What do you mean?" I said. "Worry about what?"

"Nothing, man," Chase said. "Nothing, Cam, come on, let's just go back to the party and have another drink and chill out."

I stood there a second thinking about it, considering my options.

Makayla was standing there giving me the "I'll fuck you look" which was the same look she gave Chase and pretty much every guy who wasn't Matt. Every football player at least.

"Let's get that bottle of Jack down here," I said to Chase, but looking at Makayla.

I was feeling sort of neglected and unappreciated. I was feeling like I needed a drink. It was our senior year, for fuck's sake. I wasn't going to let some female ruin it. Like Jay Z says: I got 99 problems but the bitch ain't gonna be one.

Even though she kind of already was.

TAYLOR RAGNER

After that I didn't feel like being at the party anymore so I grabbed Tatum by the hand and we left. I didn't want to go home yet either though so I took her to the Denny's on the other side of town by the mall where Cam and I used to go when I didn't want to go home yet. We ordered coffee and cheese sticks and fries.

I sat in a booth across from Tatum for two hours, drinking coffee and asking her questions about her childhood.

She was so mysterious. It was like aliens just dropped her in Elkheart one night over the summer. Or like she was born a fifteen-year-old in Elkheart.

Except I knew she came from California. Or, I guess I didn't *know*, as Cam liked to point out. "That's what she *says*, Tay. But who knows, she could be making it all up," he had told me a few nights before during one of his paranoid rants. "She could be from anywhere. Be anybody. How would we know?"

I'd told him he was crazy, rolled my eyes and laughed it off, but he had a point.

What *was* she doing here? She said her mom worked long hours for her great aunt but wouldn't she be home sometimes? And where was her dad?

There were so many questions and not that many answers.

ANISSA GRANT

I had decided at some point shortly after meeting Taylor that I would never lie to her. So even though I wasn't looking to reveal much about my life before Elkheart to anyone, including her, when she started asking me direct questions that night at Denny's, I couldn't lie to her.

I told her about my mom and me moving to California when I was a baby and how I'd never known my dad—how my mom had gotten me into commercials as a baby, for baby food and how that had led to small roles in movies and TV shows when I was a child.

She asked me if I'd liked acting, if I missed it, and I said I thought I had once but it was hard to remember.

I didn't tell her exactly how long it'd been. That it'd been almost fifteen years.

I waited nervously for her to ask if I'd had a different name as an actress or if she might have seen anything I was in but she didn't ask either of those questions.

Maybe she felt like she'd asked enough questions for one night.

I asked her what she wanted to do after high school and she sort of looked off out the window of Denny's into the parking lot and her face was so soft and so determined, like an actress in an old black and white movie with a soft lens, and I could have sat, just staring at her, all night, waiting for her to answer.

TAYLOR RAGNER

I couldn't bring myself (yet) to tell Tatum the truth because I don't think I was ready to say it out loud myself.

It's scary when you realize you don't belong in the town you're born into. When you don't belong in your family or with your friends. Or with your boyfriend.

I didn't know how I was going to get from A to B or from A to Z, I just knew I had to.

I knew I didn't want to be part of this town much longer.

Maybe that was how Tatum had felt back in L.A.

Maybe that was part of what she couldn't or wasn't telling me.

I stared across the table at her.

I'd never met anyone like her.

She was so weird, and her weirdness was what I liked most about her.

It already felt like I would know her a long time, maybe forever.

She was eating a cheese stick dipped in ranch and I smiled at her and her whole face lit up even though she couldn't say anything because her mouth was stuffed with cheese.

ANISSA GRANT

On the drive home I was acutely aware—as I always was—of Taylor's thighs spread out on the imitation leather seat beneath her. Just as I was aware of my desire to spread myself out between them.

We went back to her house and Taylor put a finger to her lips and we snuck in like we were going to be in trouble. It wasn't that late. Midnight, maybe.

Later, sitting in the middle of her bed in her room, her thighs once again a thrilling distraction for me, she told me it wasn't that she'd be in trouble. She just didn't want to have a conversation with her mother right then. She was just happier to avoid her altogether.

I sat down on the bed beside her. We were both wearing V.S. Pink boxer shorts and tank tops. We'd picked them out together during one of our joint after school ventures to the mall.

Taylor said she was super tired and turned out the light. Taylor said good night and turned on her side behind me, facing my back. I could feel her breath on my shoulder. Hot and heavy. I closed my eyes and thought of leaning back into her but restrained myself, made myself "light as a feather, stiff as a board," like the slumber party game. I'd never been to a slumber party but once in a teen horror movie we'd played that game.

This was my first time sleeping with a girl who wasn't Tate.

For a second I worried what would happen if in my sleep, unconscious, I turned to face Taylor, draped an arm over her, pushed my face too close.

But then I must have fallen asleep.

When I woke, Taylor was turned on her other side, away from me, and I felt lonely, but I didn't want to creep her out so I stayed facing the opposite side and tried to will myself back to sleep, tried to will myself not to miss Taylor. Even though she was right behind me.

ANABEL RAGNER

Saturday morning Tatum Grant was in my kitchen. I didn't know what to think. Obviously, she'd slept over, without Taylor asking me.

Taylor and I had texted at 11 or 11:30 and she'd told me she was at Denny's with Tatum and would be home soon. She hadn't mentioned anything about Tatum coming home with her.

It shouldn't have been a big deal. Taylor used to have Makayla and other girls on the squad spend the night a lot, before the whole… before she was hospitalized.

But she hadn't had anyone spend the night in six months. Since.

And even though Tatum was a nice girl, I felt like there was something weird about her.

Maybe it was just that I didn't know her parents.

I knew everyone's parents. For better or worse, we all knew each other and knew each other's business.

Tatum was the unknown.

And she was real quiet around me. She didn't say much directly to me.

She sat next to Taylor or she sat next to Jolie and played with her.

I have to admit, Jolie loved her. Tatum was very maternal toward Jolie, brushing her hair and playing with her with her Barbies on the floor and talking to her, asking her questions like a teacher.

Whenever I tried to catch her eye, though, she quickly looked away.

And whenever I asked her questions—about her family and her dreams and goals—she dodged them.

It was weird. Something wasn't right. I was onto her.

ANISSA GRANT

Taylor had told me about the name change a week or so earlier: Jimmy to Jolie. And the pronoun change too: he to she, his to hers.

I wasn't sure if this was something they'd changed at the beginning of the school year or after but it didn't matter to me either way.

In some ways, Jolie reminded me of Tate at that age.

And I was used to playing the role of big sister.

It just came naturally to me now.

Being a mom was the strange one, because I'd never been "Mom." I'd always just been Anissa. *Mom* had been "Mom." For both of us.

We'd played out our roles so well with Tate for fifteen years, it became so

I almost forgot I was her true biological mother, that I'd been pregnant once, that Quinn and I had conceived her ourselves.

Honestly, it's been strange, making the adjustment now back to thinking of myself as Tate's mom rather than as her sister.

Maybe this is another part of why I fled.

I didn't know how to make that transition, how it would impact Tate and me.

Fear of the unknown is a powerful fear.

Maybe the most powerful one of all.

Speaking of which, Tate hadn't updated any of her social media accounts in three days. Normally, there were updates a couple, three times each day. I didn't know what was going on. I was trying not to panic, trying not to think about it.

TAYLOR RAGNER

I could tell my mom was suspicious of Tatum and maybe it was sort of me being rebellious, having her over. Or it was icing on the cake, pissing off my mom.

I made sure to pull Tatum around the kitchen by the hand, to sit real close to her at the counter so our legs touched.

I knew what my mom was wondering. I liked keeping her guessing. I wanted her to get the message that this was *my life*, that *I* and *it* was some-thing she no longer had control over.

Tatum had told me the night before about actresses she knew who had emancipated themselves from their parents when they were fourteen, fifteen…

She said it was hard if you weren't an actress, though. If you didn't make a million dollars a year, because the whole point was to prove to a judge you could financially take care of yourself. That's why you almost never ran into a legally emancipated fifteen-year-old outside of Hollywood. Here in the Midwest I think they just call them runaways.

Couch surfers.

Sex workers.

ANISSA GRANT

We went back to Taylor's room to get dressed after breakfast. She shut the door and took off her tank top. Then she took off her bra. I didn't make direct eye contact, with her tits, I mean.

"I'm gonna hop in the shower real quick," she said. "Do whatever." She made a motion with her arm, like waved it around the room.

I picked up her bra off the back of her chair, read the label: 32DD. Fuck.

I walked around, picking up the framed photographs of her and Cam at various school functions and family gatherings, wondering what it felt like to be Taylor's boyfriend, to take her virginity, to touch her tits, to be inside of her.

The last thing I did before I heard the water shut off was steal one of Taylor's hair ties. What I really wanted to steal was one of her t-shirts, so I could sleep in it, but I thought she might notice something like a t-shirt if it went missing. But a hair tie, probably not. Girls are always losing hair ties. In their boyfriends' cars, in their cheer bags, in their beds... I took the one she'd used to pull her hair back when we woke up, the one she'd just pulled out of her hair before she walked out of the room, topless, to take her shower. I held it to my nose; it still smelled like Taylor's hair. I wrapped it around my wrist, up under my sweatshirt sleeve, knowing I'd sleep with it on later.

TAYLOR RAGNER

When I came back in my room after my shower Tatum was standing there, awkward as fuck, like I'd caught her going through my stuff even though she was just standing around. Part of me wondered if she *had* been going through my stuff. My underwear and bras and shit. I couldn't tell if I hoped she had or hadn't. I still wasn't completely sure how I felt about Tatum.

I had a towel wrapped around my hips and I took the other towel off my head, bent at the waist, and shook out my hair.

I knew what I was doing, of course.

I'd been doing it to Cam for three years.

Part of me found teasing a person more exciting than actually doing anything with them. I know maybe that sounds bad. A girl always gets shit for being a tease. But I don't mean it like that. I mean it more like... actually, I don't know how I mean it. I just know I liked the way Tatum's face looked when I shook out my hair. Like Cam's did when I sat on his lap in public, at Applebee's or in front of my mom or his dad or whatever. Like a little bit of agony mixed with a little bit of pleasure. Like they couldn't make up their minds which.

ANISSA GRANT

I'd never been with a girl. I'd only ever been with Quinn.

I couldn't tell what Taylor was thinking, if she was aware the effect she was having on me, if that was the point. It seemed like she was but how could I know for sure?

She'd never mentioned being with a girl.

I went back to my apartment and got on my laptop and searched for "girl on girl" porn. There was a video of two girls waking up in bed together after a night of heavy partying. The one girl wanted the other girl to get up and help her clean. She made the girl coffee to nudge her out of bed. They stood on a balcony somewhere sunny like L.A. and drank their coffee out of mugs in their thongs and see-through tank tops. The see-through tank tops reminded me of Taylor's see through bra. It was all real staged bullshit—real fake as fuck—but still I got real good and wet about it anyway.

I was thinking of Taylor's ass, how perfect and pristine and tight it must be.

I was thinking how I wanted to slide a finger inside of it while mouthing other parts of her: her breasts and her mouth and her clit.

I thought she probably had a very fat clitoris because her areolas were so large.

I thought about how inexperienced I was but how with Taylor it didn't seem like it would matter.

I thought about how her face would look from the perspective of being down between her thighs, those great American thighs. I wanted to watch her face as I brought her to climax. I wanted to watch as ecstasy washed over her great American girl-next-door cheeks and lips and chin.

I thought of all this while watching the two women on my laptop and sliding the dildo in and out of me. I hadn't peed when I got home because I'd read once, in some famous romance novel, that not urinating made your orgasm stronger. That was probably some level of bullshit too. But whatever. I came hard.

I lay there a bit wondering if Taylor was making herself come, too, if she had a dildo, if she watched girl on girl porn, if she had pissed first or held it like I did.

ANABEL RAGNER

What no one knew, not my husband, not Taylor, was I'd had this college thing with a girl for a couple months years ago. I know, right? College bisexual, how cliché. It wasn't quite like that back then. Making out with another girl at a bar when super drunk at one in the morning for guys to get hard was kind of okay. But other than that, being bi or lesbian was still taboo. Especially in the Midwest.

But the girl had kinda/sorta broken my heart. We'd met in an English class and gone to a concert together, a country duo who were popular then. The venue was walkable from our apartments on campus so we'd drank a lot of wine coolers, done tequila shots at the concert hall bar.

My apartment was closer so we'd both gone back there to crash. We could barely walk down the sidewalk. We were holding each other up.

By the time we made it to my apartment she had to throw up. I held her hair crouched on my bathroom floor, wiped her mouth, gave her some Scope to gargle with, and put her in bed beside me.

In the morning I woke to her hand between my legs. I turned my head back to face hers and we kissed. I was still drunk from the night before. I was already seeing Taylor's dad but very casually and he was busy with getting his business degree and partying with the bros. We didn't see each other all that much then, couple times a week at most. Red flags.

This girl and I hooked up about four times before she told me she couldn't do it anymore, and after that we stopped hanging out altogether, even as friends. She said she felt guilty, she came from a very religious family, etc.

I said I understood. I came from the same. I had no intention of ever telling anyone about what had happened, of "coming out" or anything like that because I didn't think I was gay or even bi, really. It was just something with this one girl.

But I hadn't wanted it to end so quick. Or I wanted to be the one to say when we were done.

I'd pass her sometimes on campus. We'd wave and say hi but that was it.

I never told Taylor about this. A mom has to have some secrets to herself.

With Jimmy, or *Jolie,* as she now likes to be called, it was different. It wasn't a matter of just sexual orientation. Jolie wasn't gay, she was a girl. I always believed that. Even from the time she was a toddler. I think God just made a mistake the day she was born.

She just wasn't meant to be a boy.

Taylor was very clearly a girl. Taylor was a girl who liked boys. Maybe she wasn't as into Cam anymore. Maybe she just needed to find a different guy. But as I could attest, trying to find love or even lust with another girl never works out. Maybe in Hollywood it can, but not here. Not in God's country.

And anyway, I wanted grandchildren! I wanted a million little grandbabies.

I hated to put so much pressure on Taylor but Taylor had been my traditional baby girl. Taylor's life was all planned out: college, Cam, babies. God's country.

ANISSA GRANT

I wish I could say it was an hour or two later that I went to Tate's Instagram to check on her. I'd gotten up, pulled the dildo out and washed it in the bathroom sink, wrapped it in a towel, went back to the bed and clicked on Tate's name. I had her Instagram bookmarked, of course. But there wasn't anything new. Still, just a photo of her and her high school friends eating lunch at some trendy L.A. outdoor café on their lunch hour. That was from Tuesday and now it was Saturday and where the fuck was she? What the fuck was Tate doing?

How long was I going to have to try not to think about it?

How long was she going to make me pay?

CAM SPENCER

Taylor had set up this double date with Chase and Tatum and the four of us went to the Plymouth Street Fair. I was a little hungover from the night before, from Chase's party, but I got some Gatorade and worked out and rallied.

I'd had another little pep talk, man to man, bro to bro, while working out with Chase.

He claimed to like Tatum, to find her attractive and nice. I don't know why he thought that but I hoped he actually did, that he wasn't just bullshitting me. I really needed Tatum distracted right now.

I really needed time with my girlfriend, *alone*.

I think Chase liked Tatum because she was from California and he'd been talking about moving there for years, since middle school at least. It was his dream to go to UCLA or USC. Working at Hollister in the mall was the closest he got to the beach here in Elkheart.

I think once his mom died he had nothing holding him here anymore.

Every year a portion of the school left for college and never came back. Or they came back on breaks to see family and to brag about their new lives outside of Elkheart.

Everyone in town hated them, though.

I knew we hated them for getting out. That secretly we all probably wanted to leave.

But I loved Elkheart.

I wanted to raise my family right here with Taylor.

I was perfectly happy in the middle of the Midwest, growing old here with my girl and my family and the people I'd known since I hadn't known anything.

On the top of the Ferris wheel I grabbed Taylor's hand and got down on one knee in the middle of the car. It shook and Taylor screamed, "Get up! Cam, what are you doing? Oh my god!"

I kissed her hand and laughed and sat back on the seat beside her. I was just joking then but I was planning on asking Taylor to marry me on her graduation day in two years. I had a ring on layaway at JCPenney. I figured I'd almost have it paid off by then.

Taylor looked so beautiful up at the top of the Ferris wheel with the nighttime lights at dusk. Her long dark hair haloed by the sunset. Her sleepy, heavy-lidded green eyes crinkling at the corners the way I liked when she smiled.

In the photos my mom had taken of me for my senior year, Taylor is in a few of them with me. In one, I'm sitting down in the farm field where we shot the photos and Taylor's crouched down in a dress behind me, her left arm on my left shoulder, her left knee pressed against my hip, the right side of her face pressed against my back. I have that photograph hanging on the wall of my bedroom, over my bed.

The one I keep in my wallet is of me standing in the field, holding Taylor, her legs wrapped around my waist, her cheek pressed to my forehead.

I swear to you she is an angel, when she wants to be, when she stops fighting me, stops fighting life.

And every second of surrender with Taylor is worth all the time spent fighting.

So far, at least.

And I can't imagine it ever wouldn't be.

There's no way I can even begin to think of my life without Taylor as the main star.

TAYLOR RAGNER

Cam was being super sweet at the fair, winning me stuffed animals and going on the Ferris wheel with me and buying me an elephant ear and lemonade. And it was kind of nice, like the old Cam and Taylor. Like back when I was in middle school dating the high school boy, the football player.

We were trying to give Chase and Tatum time to get to know each other better. We peered over our Ferris wheel car and saw them down below us in a lower car and waved.

It didn't seem like Tatum liked Chase as much as she liked me so I wasn't too worried about it.

Also I swore Chase was gay so it didn't seem like it was going to go much farther than friends, anyway.

I was okay with them hanging out and holding hands and kissing...

But I didn't want to imagine anything else happening between Tatum and Chase, which I guess should have told me something. Should have clued me in to what was happening. If I had thought about it longer than a second. But there were always so many things to think about.

And the main one was what to do about Cam.

ANISSA GRANT

Chase was so sweet. He bought me cotton candy and we rode on the bumper cars together and the Gravitron.

I'd never been to a real carnival before, only one on a TV set and as usual, everything was a lot different in reality than it was on a film set. For one, I almost threw up when we walked off the Gravitron. I had to sit down on a bench and Chase rubbed my back and then got me a corn dog to eat.

It's funny how quickly you can become normalized to something, to a new environment or to viewing yourself a new way.

Mom joked when I was younger that she worried she'd have to perform an exorcism at the end of a movie shoot to get her daughter back. When I got older she made me see a psychiatrist. Sometimes I worried I had no soul or personality of my own, that I just took on whatever character I was playing so fully because I had no personality or character myself.

I'd read, doing research for a role, that undercover cops and investigators sometimes fell in love with the people they were following or investigating. It happened enough that they had all these rules in place to try and prevent it happening but it still happened. Cops still got fired and cases were ruined by a police or undercover officer going too far, with a prostitute or with a suspect.

Your emotions are too easy to fuck with. Your heart doesn't understand the difference between acting and real life.

My mom told me when I was three I made this movie where I played this divorced guy's daughter and whenever I had to see him off-set I'd insist on calling him Daddy just like when we were acting. Mom told me, "He'd say very earnestly to you, 'I'm not Daddy, I'm Steve.' And you'd just whine and sort of pretend to cry or maybe you cried. I don't know. It was so hard to tell with you. And you'd say, 'I don't want you to be Steve, I want you to be Daddy' and it kind of broke my heart. Since you didn't have a daddy, you know."

I wondered what would happen if Taylor and I got "off-set," if we ever left Elkheart.

I wondered if I could fall in love with Chase. I didn't think I could but he was so sweet it didn't matter.

CHASE WHITING

I knew it was important to Cam to have some time alone with Taylor even though we were on an official "double date." He'd only impressed that upon me about a dozen times in the past twenty-four hours. The whole morning lifting weights in my basement.

The night before he'd gotten blackout drunk and things had gone a little too far with Makayla, who I thought had passed out on the couch in the living room after Matt and she got in another big fight and Matt left. Cam had passed out in a reclining chair there also and I'd thrown blankets over both of them and gone up to bed.

An hour or so later I woke up so thirsty from all the alcohol I guess I'd also drank and I'd crept down the stairs to get some water and found Makayla giving Cam a blowjob. The thing was, I couldn't tell if Cam was even awake. It appeared, in the dark, that his eyes were closed and he didn't seem to be moving his arms or hands or saying anything or doing any of the things a man might normally do when conscious and the recipient of oral sex.

To be honest, I wasn't sure he remembered that it'd happened in the morning. He didn't mention it and it seems like something he'd be freaking out about if he remembered. It seemed like something he'd be terrified of Taylor finding out.

I was honestly afraid to bring it up. So I didn't. I just kept quiet and waited to see if Makayla was going to tell anyone. Or everyone. If it was going to get back to Taylor. And if she would care or not.

TAYLOR RAGNER

Because the fair was sponsored by the Catholic church, there were Pro-life balloons and stickers and t-shirts everywhere.

Cam and I had had a scare once when a condom broke. We'd had to go and get the Plan B pill. There was no way I was having his baby in high school. I didn't even know if I wanted to have his baby period. At least, lately I'd started to wonder. I used to think I did. I used to say I wanted to have three of them. And Cam would joke, no, four.

After that I got on oral contraceptives. But I hated them. They made me moody and gain weight. Then I started questioning marriage as an institution, and the Pro-life movement as an extension of the pro-marriage movement.

I don't know when I got so cynical. Haha. Maybe when my dad stopped coming home. Or when my mom got so sad. Which I guess was around the same time. which I guess is when I started questioning my relationship with Cam. Which I guess was when I ended up hospitalized. Which was pretty soon before Tatum moved to town.

I guess it's all been a superstorm or whatever that is they call it.

Anyway, I didn't want their fucking balloons.

ANISSA GRANT

I was just happy Taylor and Cam were off doing their own thing for a minute so I didn't have to deal with Cam staring me down whenever Taylor wasn't looking.

I couldn't tell if he was secretly obsessed with me or just plain hated me. But either way, it was disconcerting.

Chase and I did the cake walk three times and won a pink Barbie cake and I asked him if he minded if we gave it to Jolie and he said of course not.

I had the feeling both Chase and I knew we were being set up and that neither one of us was really into the other as more than friends and we were both okay with that or on the same page.

I wasn't sure why or how he was friends with Cam but I guess they'd just been friends so long, since they were in kindergarten, Chase said, so it didn't matter how unalike they were. And they still, for now at least, had football in common.

"I'm ready to be done with football, though," Chase said. We were on the Ferris wheel and Chase had his arm around me but in a brotherly manner, not a romantic one. "It's hard for me to get that aggressive anymore. It's easy for Cam. He doesn't exactly have to work at it."

He laughed but I wondered if by "anymore" he meant since his mom had died or just since he'd grown up somewhat, had outgrown the childish aggressions of his youth.

"What do you want to do after high school?" I asked.

We were almost at the top now. Even Elkheart is beautiful from the top of a Ferris wheel in a Catholic church parking lot.

"I don't know," he said. "Get out of here."

I smiled and said yeah even though I'd just gotten here, even though I'd moved here from a state most people dream of going to. One day.

I don't know why but I took Chase's hand and squeezed it and said, "You will. I know it."

And he smiled and squeezed my hand back.

"Thank you," he said.

"No problem," I said.

And that was our unspoken pact of friendship. That was the moment I knew I could trust Chase. And I think, I hope, he knew he could trust me, too.

MAKAYLA RICHEY

Matt and I saw Cam and Taylor and Chase and Tatum at the fair Friday night. They all looked so pathetically happy. So fucking clueless and dumb, it almost made me want to do this thing right then. Confront Cam right there in the Catholic church parking lot.

Show him the video. See what he had to say about it. See what he told

Taylor, how he defended it… But I knew I had to be patient. Play it out in the right time frame if I wanted the major impact.

I watched Taylor and Tatum join hands walking down the main street, Chase and Cam following behind like their personal assistants, like the Beta males they'd turned into.

I couldn't wait for Taylor to see the video. I wanted to be able to watch her face when she watched it even though that was impossible.

I still remembered all the nights we'd slept over at each other's houses, all the times we'd promised to be "best friends 4-ever!" to go to the same college, be roommates, all of it… what a crock of shit that was.

I grabbed Matt's hand. "Come on," I said. "Let's go win some goldfish."

But that just made me think about the time Taylor and I had won, like, three goldfish each when we were eleven or twelve, the first time our moms let us walk around the fair by ourselves.

"Never mind," I told Matt, as we stood staring at the half-dead fish barely moving in their tiny plastic bowls.

"I changed my mind. Fuck goldfish," I said.

"Whatever, dude," Matt said, shrugging his shoulders at the carnie worker.

Matt was a fucking beta male, too, of course. A football-playing beta male who did whatever I wanted and wore NF and Logic t-shirts. [eye roll]

In some ways I was beginning to see that Taylor Ragner was the biggest alpha male in this school. Cam used to be, but he was slipping. He was falling for Taylor's shit. It was sort of sad when you thought about it. The great Cam Spencer seceding his powers. Letting his insecurities (read: Tatum Grant) get the better of him.

COACH W

I took Macy on what turned out to be our final date to the fair where we promptly ran into Tatum and Chase who seemed also to be on a date.

I said, "Hi" and they said, "Hi," and I introduced Macy and Macy said, "Hi."

Tatum and I were avoiding eye contact but trying to make it seem—I think—as though we weren't. So we sort of dodged our eyes toward and away from one another. I don't think Chase or Macy noticed.

I think Macy sensed I was about to break up with her because she was being overly nice and really affectionate in a way that, honestly, made me uncomfortable. She was making this hard on me on purpose and as the night wore on, that started to piss me off, to backfire on Macy, because as it got later and later, and Macy was more and more physically demonstrative, I got more and more pissed, and it only strengthened my resolve to break up with her.

Like I said, we were barely having sex, anyway. We barely saw each other. What was it to her if we broke up? Why should she care? I didn't get why she cared.

Maybe I resented her caring. Maybe that was it.

I don't know.

Maybe I had a real thing for Tatum.

Maybe that was really what this was about.

As much as I didn't want to admit that.

To myself.

Anyway, I took her home. I dropped her off at her house and told her I didn't think it was a good idea if we saw each other anymore. Of course she cried a little bit. Asked if she'd done anything wrong. I should have felt something. I should have felt bad. But I didn't. I'd already steeled my heart against her, I guess.

Honestly, I really didn't give a fuck. *Literally.*

ANISSA GRANT

Taylor and I texted back and forth every night before bed now. Just like, "heeeeyy I'm falling asleep lol" or "ttyl, bae." Shit like that. High school best friend shit.

But that night after the fair I'd had a little whiskey, a little Jack Daniels I'd picked up on the drive back to the apartment along with some cigarettes, and I texted Taylor, "sweet dreams, don't let the bed bugs bite, xoxo." I was filling her phone with every cliché I could think of. I figured soon enough she'd figure out I was crazy, start backing away. But so far she just seemed to roll with it. I don't know, it was crazy to me—for some reason, she seemed to genuinely like me.

She texted back, "U2 ☺."

Like the band. Even though she probably didn't know who the fuck U2 was or if she did, she probably didn't fuck with any of their songs. She probably didn't know who the fuck Bono was.

"U2 ☺" was the best text I'd ever gotten up until that point. Because I knew it meant, "Sweet dreams" to me, too.

TAYLOR RAGNER

Of course, Cam told me sweet dreams too all the time. Cam told me sweet dreams almost every night. And it meant nothing to me now. Like how when he would call me and he'd literally say, "love you," every five seconds like how some people say um, and expect me to say it back every time, too, like, "love you, too." He said it so much it lost its meaning. It was more like a tic or something. Like he had Tourette's or whatever that one thing is people get who shout out bad words in public.

But when Tatum said it, when Tatum texted me, "sweet dreams xoxo don't let the bed bugs bite," I made a note of it in my head, the date, the time… I wanted always to remember the first time she'd said it.

I was making a note now of all our firsts.

TATE GRANT

I didn't really want to go to Homecoming but my high school friends were insisting. I mean, I obviously couldn't take Josh to a high school dance. Like, here's my twenty-three-year-old boyfriend, come arrest him. LOL.

I guess a part of me kind of did want to go. I just felt bad I couldn't go with my boyfriend.

But after being home-schooled my whole life, for fifteen years, it was sort of exciting to do something normal teens do, even if it was a kind of lame tradition.

Luckily my two best friends—Roman and Gia—didn't have dates either, so we decided to go together. Roman rented a tux and I bought this total fire men's suit from Prada and Gia borrowed—or *stole*—her mom's Halston gown from the 70s. Or maybe it was her grandmother's. Anyway. It was hot.

I was pretty sure Paris had gone to Homecoming and prom both when she was here so wtf. #fire.

ANISSA GRANT

Taylor wanted to go to a mall in South Bend to look for dresses and shoes. She said she wanted to get to the mall when it opened so I picked her up at 9:30 on Saturday. It was another way of not thinking about Tate, another way of not obsessing over her Instagram, either.

"My mom's fucking stuuuu-pid," Taylor was saying. "She doesn't even know I took this."

She held up her mom's Visa. Grinned.

"No wonder my dad has been having affairs since I was ten or like, probably before that even. Who even knows if Jolie is his. Oh wait. That doesn't make sense if he's the one cheating, does it?"

"I don't think so," I said and we both laughed.

We went through the McDonalds' drive-thru before getting on the highway, got McGriddles and hashbrowns, ate them while smoking cigarettes. Old school.

TAYLOR RAGNER

That Saturday before Homecoming we went to Kensington Town Center to try on dresses and get our makeup done.

In the "family lounge" I pulled Tatum inside and locked the door. I had mini bottles of alcohol in my purse I'd taken from my grandma's stash in her basement bar. I handed Tatum a small bottle of Stolichnaya and I drank down a mini bottle of tequila.

"Okay," I said. "Now we're ready!"

"Ready for what?" she said, her cheeks flush with booze.

"To look beautiful, of course, duh!" I said.

"Oh yeah," she said. "Oh, right."

I pulled her in front of the mirror next to me. "Smile," I said. I held my phone at hip level to take the picture. I grabbed a handful of her tit with my other hand. I knew that would make Cam mad. I knew he'd see it on my Instagram and be pissed off.

I took her by the hand and pulled her out into the mall and onto the escalator. I knew what people were thinking.

I leaned over to her on the escalator and kissed her on the mouth.

She almost fell backward.

She tasted like me because she was wearing my Victoria's Secret Pink lip gloss in cherry berry. I figured that was what it was like for Cam to kiss me.

I kissed her again. She tasted good as shit.

ANISSA GRANT

"You know, this makeup was invented for drag queens," Taylor told me as we approached the MAC counter. "And for theater people."

I knew, of course, but I pretended not to; I wanted Taylor to be the one to tell me.

"Yeah," Taylor said. "We're going to be so dragged out. We're going to look so fucking theatrical."

Fifteen minutes later I was wearing toxic green eye shadow and Taylor was wearing neon pink eyeliner and we both looked like Debbie Harry or a Warhol screen queen or an 80s dance icon.

"I love it," Taylor said, admiring her New Wave look in the mirror. "I'm so fucking bored of Elkheart and all the basic bitches. I mean, there's just no way you want *this*," she said, holding her arm out and sweeping it left and right. "There's just no fucking way. I don't believe you."

I smiled and shrugged my shoulders. She couldn't know how much better my life was here, with her in it. There was no way she could know. There was no way I was going to tell her, either.

"Come here," she said, and we stood side by side in the mirror again, tongues stuck out like that guy in KISS, fingers in a V around our tongues, picture taken.

"Bad ass bitches," Taylor said. Which is also how she captioned the photo.

I just want to reiterate, the first fifteen years of my life were lived according to my manager mother's wishes. Out for work, in seclusion (with her) otherwise.

The next fifteen were lived in seclusion/mourning, as Tate's mother/sister, as Quinn's unofficial widow.

I think this explains a lot. My emotional or mental retardation, I mean.

CAM SPENCER

That Saturday I was home working out in the basement my father designed for himself and my brother and me to lift weights. It was a family thing. My father was buffer than any of us, with less body fat. One entire wall of the basement was mirror. My father was a carpenter also. All of us were good with our hands because of him. Could fix things like our cars ourselves; change the oil and all that shit. I thought it was embarrassing when a guy had to hire someone for what could easily be done yourself. Like building a table. We were a family of alpha males. Even my mom, who is kind of a big shot attorney, is an alpha male. You wouldn't want to fuck with her, I mean. Or go up against her in a court of law.

Anyway, I was home working out and checking my phone to see what pics Taylor posted from her little shopping spree with Tatum in the city that day.

I knew she was *trying* to make me jealous by the way she was acting in the pictures she was taking, all super flirtatious and touchy with Tatum. What else was new?

So I didn't say anything.

Sometimes being an alpha male means keeping your fucking mouth shut.

After I got done working out I got online to look at the engagement ring I'd picked out for Taylor again. I'd spent a lot of the money I'd saved working for my dad on that ring. It was fucking gorgeous: 14 k gold w tiny diamond chips all around. I was getting an inscription put on the inside of it where it would meet the flesh of Taylor's finger: *I promise I'm yours.* In little tiny script. In the smallest font you can imagine. I liked imagining the letters pressed into her perfect ivory skin, leaving the words on her finger like a tattoo. Or a branding. Something permanent.

TAYLOR RAGNER

The dresses we ended up picking were so fucking sick. From Sak's. Mine was floor length, ivory, satin, with a plunging neckline, sort of disco'y, classy as fuck.

Tatum's was black, short, strapless, sequined. She was lucky because she was flat chested so everything looked high fashion on her. Nothing ever looked slutty. I was forever getting in trouble at school because of my curves. Everything I wore looked slutty even if I didn't mean it to.

I found her the perfect fishnets with the seam up the back and five inch heels to wear with it. I think I dressed her the way I wanted to dress but I was afraid to because Cam and my mom would bitch too much about it if I looked too punk and not traditional enough.

Tatum didn't have to worry about a mom or boyfriend since she didn't technically have a boyfriend and her mom was 24/7 with her aunt, taking care of her in her dying days or some shit. I don't know if I believed that anymore. Part of me thought Tatum's mom was a serious drug addict but that didn't make sense either. How they lived, how they paid rent, if her mom was on meth or heroin or whatever. So I didn't waste much of my time thinking about it, trying to figure it out. My mom was the one who did that. Since she didn't have a life or a husband, since she had so much fucking time on her hands.

But Tatum and I looked fucking sick standing side by side in the Sak's dressing room mirror.

Something in me imagined myself on the floor on my knees, drunkenly ripping her fishnets.

Maybe it was the heels she was wearing. She was so much taller than me in them. She was a tower. She was intimidating as shit.

ANABEL RAGNER

Taylor came home with a dress that costs three times the price I told her she could spend. It was ridiculous. It was only Homecoming, for chrissake. She was only a *sophomore*. We couldn't dole out this kind of money for three Homecomings and three proms. It was ridiculous.

Of course, had I known she wouldn't make it to Prom that year, or any other year, for that matter, that this would be her only Homecoming, I wouldn't have minded. I would have told her to spend more. I would have encouraged them to rent a limo like she wanted. She hated going in Cam's truck.

ANISSA GRANT

When I finally got back to my apartment that Sunday I got on my laptop right away. I was so worried about Tate. I'd been able to compartmentalize her "disappearance" while I was with Taylor and Jolie at Taylor's house, but the second I was in my car, alone, I was overcome with anxiety, thinking about it. I didn't know what I would do if Tate hadn't posted an update by the time I got online to look. If I would try to get a hold of my mom or what. I prayed really hard the whole way home from Taylor's because I didn't want to have to call my mom but I had to know if Tate was okay.

As everyone knows/has been well documented by now, there is a history of drug abuse and suicide in both Quinn's and my family. Quinn's death had been ruled "an accidental overdose" but I wasn't so sure. I'd never been sure. I think he'd been suicidal since he was at least ten years old. He'd told me a story once about how he'd tried to commit suicide by jumping off a rock into a river when he was ten and his dad went to prison for a second time. His mom had told him it was his fault, if you can believe that. Blamed it on them needing money to raise him. Of course the truth was they needed money for drugs. The way Quinn told it both his mother and his father were hardcore drug addicts and had been since before he was born. I don't know if he was born addicted but if he wasn't he was lucky. That's why his grandma pretty much raised him. Raised him and died ten days after his overdose. I never met her but Quinn showed me pictures and told me stories. I think she was the only person he ever trusted in his whole life including me.

Anyway, I worried constantly that Tate may have inherited suicidal tendencies or an addictive personality or be bipolar.

I was holding my breath when I got online that Sunday morning. I was pulling out strands of my hair to prevent me from clenching my teeth.

CAM SPENCER

Taylor had a fucking hickey on her neck. Of course she fucking lied to me about it, denied it was a hickey, told me she'd burned herself with her curling iron.

Fucking right she did. I knew it was from Tatum. The two of them fooling around in the mall dressing room and who knows where else. Playing this high school lesbo game for everyone to see.

God forbid *I* leave a mark anywhere on Taylor, though, and I'd have hell to pay. I'd never hear the end of it.

But Tatum Grant, Tatum could do no wrong, in Taylor's eyes.

It was fucking retarded. Sorry, I'm not very PC. I truly do not give any fucks right now. You can truly get in line to kiss my ass if you don't like the way I talk right now.

Fuckin' bitches.

TATE GRANT

I figured Anissa was probably watching me, spying on me online. Stalking me or whatever. Wherever she was.

She didn't deserve to know I was safe. I woke up one day last week and realized all this. I woke up one day last week and thought *FUCK. HER.*

I don't know where the fuck she is, what the fuck she's doing, so why the fuck should she know where I am, what I'm doing.

I told my friends not to post any photos of me for a few days because I was up for a big movie role.

For the first time in my life I missed having a dad. It's like, when you don't know who your dad is he doesn't exist. You just don't have a dad. You just appeared one day out of thin air. Now that I knew I did and who he was I couldn't stop thinking about him. And I was mad at Anissa for never having told me. That's a fucked up sentence, but you know what I mean. All those years I didn't know who Quinn James was, let alone he was *my father*. That's seriously fucked up. I didn't understand why Anissa didn't want me to know, why she'd wanted to keep me from my dad.

ROBIN GRANT

I knew what Tate was doing. I, too, saw that she wasn't updating her social media. I knew that was because of Anissa. To pay her back for leaving. I didn't say anything. I didn't blame her. And, besides, Anissa knew our numbers. Anissa could have reached us if she was that worried. If she was *that* concerned. We hadn't gone anywhere, We hadn't changed our numbers. She could call *us* anytime. *Any* time.

She was obsessing over her dad now too, the way her mother had obsessed over him years before.

I have to admit, I never got it. I never got the Quinn James obsession thing.

But I never got James Dean either.

Now, Elvis—Elvis I got.

But Quinn James and James Dean were a little too effeminate for me.

ANISSA GRANT

I got online and there was nothing. Still no update since the week before, five days now. No one had even tagged Tate in any new photos that I could see. I stared at Tate's most recent pictures and updates from the week before, looking for clues. Did she look thinner? Did she have a bruise? Dark circles under her eyes? A hickey? Cuts on her arms? I searched every part of her. Searched the paraphernalia on the tabletops in the photos. Searched the other people visible in the frame. All I could see was a bottle of Xanax, a pack of cigarettes and what looked like maybe a bottle of vodka. Maybe a dusting of cocaine on a glass tabletop. Nothing that out of line for a teenager. Especially for a teenager in Hollywood. For a child actress. I was surprised I didn't see any coke, actually. Didn't see any older men who looked like they could be drug dealers. Or young men who looked like drug dealers. I saw a bunch of young actresses. I guess one of them could have been a drug dealer. Hell, Tate could be a drug dealer. Drug dealers came in all genders, ages and sizes now. You couldn't cast a "type" for that role anymore.

I lit a cigarette and opened a beer and stared out the sliding glass door. A man walked by, someone had told me was on the sex offenders registry. He looked normal enough. I mean, I didn't feel any more or less afraid of him than I did of any other male. He had some tats and smiled a lot. I figured he was probably on the registry for something stupid like having a girlfriend who was under eighteen when he was nineteen or twenty. Or for urinating in public. Or jacking off in a movie theater.

I didn't know what to do about Tate. What to think. I figured if something was *really wrong* I'd know sooner or later because there were no secrets in Hollywood. Even a minor teen actress would suddenly qualify for TMZ if she stopped showing up to work due to drug use or turning runaway teen or something like that.

I googled her name and searched the results and nothing came up, nothing out of the ordinary, just her normal IMDB stuff. Movie and TV announcements and stuff like that.

So I got drunk and looked at Dobson high social medias and passed out early.

Monday started Spirit Week.

I needed to be well-rested.

COACH W

It was Spirit Week at school. The five days leading up to Homecoming. There would be games at lunch, decorative pins to purchase in support of the school, cookies, brownies, cakes, and each day had a different "theme" by which the students could dress up if they so chose. As the acting teacher I often took part in the festivities, dressed accordingly.

This year the student council had decided on the following five themes for the five days: pajama day, hippie day, freaks or geeks day, purple and white (school colors) day and finally: rock or hip hop day.

So Monday morning there I was standing in the hall in my bathrobe and slippers. Of course I was wearing a pair of jeans and a button down underneath. I wasn't a total perv. I wasn't looking to get fired from my job. Yet.

There I was watching a sea of teenagers float by me in flannel pajama bottoms featuring everything from Warner Brothers cartoon characters to the Dobson High Mustang. Some of the guys wore robes, a handful of girls wore boxers and were sent down to the office for measurement by Mrs. Stone to determine if they met the required length above the knee.

I'd admittedly been a wreck since the "incident" with Tatum. I was equally terrified of getting fired and thus avoiding any sort of future interaction with her and terrified of never having another "interaction" with her.

The whole thing had reinforced how pathetic my life was, what a loser I was, still single in my late thirties. Still renting. Normally I kept drinking to the weekends but since the incident I'd been picking up a six-pack every day after work. *Fuck it*, was my general thought process now. Which is maybe a dangerous thought process to indulge when you're a male high school teacher. Unless you literally don't give a fuck. And it was starting to look like I didn't.

So there I was standing in the hall, greeting students, monitoring the Spirit Week day one outfits, when Taylor and Tatum strode by, arm in arm, wearing matching cropped tees with the Dobson Mustang featured across the chest, tight, and thin cotton pajama bottoms that seemed to be a size too small, a second skin to their perfectly rounded backsides. They had put their hair in pigtails. The perfect American male fantasy embodiment walking around freely in the halls.

And strutting through the hall right behind them, the hood of his plush velour Rocky Balboa robe pulled up around his large head, was Cam Spencer, giving wide cheese smiles to his peers who weren't really peers, in his mind, anyway.

All of a sudden I was a man in need of a flask. I'd never drank on the job, of course, but I suddenly felt the need to be that teacher who you think might. About whom you're not sure. Is that alcohol on his breath, you might ask yourself? Or are you crazy, imagining things?

No, I'd say with a smile, you're not imagining anything. I'm that pathetic loser, fucking my student, drinking on the job, jacking off in the faculty lounge.

Welcome to my life, as the pop song goes.

Or, no, wait. That's welcome to my *house*.

Whatever that means.

Yeah, welcome.

CAM SPENCER

There was a lot going on that week. It was school Spirit Week and at the end of it the big Homecoming game and dance. We had extra long practices planned all week. We had school spirit days to dress for.

But I was in a good mood. A better mood than I'd been in since school started, because things were better with me and Taylor. Saturday night after our double date we'd dropped Chase and Tatum off at their houses and gone to the lake, just the two of us, for a couple hours, and Taylor was so sweet, and it reaffirmed for me our love, our future together. Plus, word was I was a shoo-in for Homecoming King. And even though Taylor couldn't be queen, because she wasn't a senior, it would still make Homecoming extra special.

And then Monday right before lunch I got a text from Makayla. And there was an image attached to it. Something told me I didn't want to open it. Something told me to just delete the whole thing, without reading it or looking at it. But of course I had to open it. It was just sitting there on my phone like a bad omen. Like a noose ready for my neck.

TAYLOR RAGNER

Spirit Week was always my favorite week of the school year. I loved dressing up all week in the different themes and I loved Homecoming. And things were good with me and Cam for once and things were perfect with me and Tatum. I had the best of both worlds: a cool boyfriend to go to Homecoming with and a hot best friend to make out with.

Saturday night I'd decided to be nice to Cam, to quit judging him so hard and give him another chance. It was his senior year and it was already going so fast and pretty soon it'd be over and he'd be gone, off to college, hopefully, and we wouldn't see each other that much and then I figured I'd miss him. And even if I didn't, I wouldn't regret the time we dated in high school, going to Homecoming and his senior prom and all of that.

Then I got the text from Makayla. I was walking to meet Tatum in the cafeteria for lunch. I opened it and looked at the pic and threw my phone at the brick wall in the hall. A bunch of kids ducked and stared at me.

"What?!" I said. "Haven't you ever seen a woman pissed off before? Jesus. Don't act so fucking surprised."

I went over and picked up my phone. The screen was shattered. Perfect. Now I wouldn't have to look at my boyfriend's dick in that whore's mouth.

ANISSA GRANT

I found Taylor crying in the bathroom outside the cafeteria. Someone had come and gotten me. I forget who. Just some freshman girl. Taylor had summoned her to go and get me because she'd broken her phone and couldn't text or call me.

I ran into the bathroom worried she was sick or had hurt herself.

She was sitting in a stall on a toilet and her face was in her hands and her pigtails were lopsided and she was shaking her head and saying, "That bitch. That bitch," over and over.

I crouched down next to her and asked her what was wrong. I took her hand in mine and gave it a kiss. Of course I'd never seen Taylor cry before. It'd never even crossed my mind that she could.

"That fucking whore," she said. "That fucking bitch took a pic of Cam's dick in her mouth and sent it to me and Cam."

The funny thing was, that didn't really surprise me. What surprised me was Taylor being this upset about it, crying and everything.

I'd thought from the way she talked she was just biding her time until after Homecoming to break up with Cam anyway.

Which was when Cam came knocking on the door of the girls' bathroom, calling Taylor's name. "Taylor, I know you're in there," he said. "Can I come in? I want to talk to you. Please, let me talk to you."

I looked at Taylor to see what she wanted to do and she looked at me and nodded.

I really hoped I hadn't misjudged this relationship. I hoped this wasn't one of those constant fight and makeup deals where you keep thinking this will be the last time and it never is. I'd met couples like that. They never truly broke up. *Ever.* It was so fucking annoying.

"Okay," I said. "You have two minutes. I'll wait outside."

And I left the bathroom and stood out in the hall, waiting to see what would happen next. Which was when I saw Makayla walk by with Keisha and Whitney, two other girls on the cheer team.

CAM SPENCER

I didn't have any memory of what happened. Nothing. Not one image. Not one word of dialogue. I remembered standing in the barn drinking with Chase and I remember Makayla being there, in the periphery, somewhere near our elbows, she was short, tiny, but I remember Matt, her boyfriend, being there too... I must have been blacked out. I wouldn't have believed it had happened either if Makayla hadn't taken a picture of it. I don't know why she hated Taylor and me so much. I don't know why Chase let me pass out in the same room as that conniving bitch. She'd been obsessed with Taylor for years, which was okay when they were friends. But now that Taylor was closer to Tatum, it seemed to drive Makayla to do insane things. Like framing me for cheating. Like taking a photo of giving me a blowjob I didn't even remember. It's clear in the photo I'm passed out. If our genders were reversed, I think this would very clearly be rape.

But try convincing your girlfriend of that. Especially when you and she had another big blow up fight the night in question and she left the party early and when she left, you and the *person*—and I'm using that term loosely — question were still both very much not passed out.

CHASE WHITING

It must have happened right after I went back up the stairs. Makayla posing Cam to take the picture. I could have punched myself for leaving them alone together. Twice. I don't know what I was thinking. Why I didn't just take Cam up to my room with me, why I didn't insist Matt take Makayla with him when he left that night.

Why I watched from the stairs and didn't do anything. I mean, that I do know. My buddy was getting a blow job. Was I supposed to interrupt the scene, inquire as to his level of intoxication, his ability to consent? An eighteen-year-old football player?

How could I know this was some *Weekend at Bernie's* level blowjob shit?

MAKAYLA RICHEY

I don't know why the fuck Tatum cared, why she came at me in the cafeteria, made a huge public display and shit. It wasn't *her* boyfriend. She'd only known Taylor a couple weeks at this point. What was her fucking problem. Why was she acting like Taylor's guardian angel? I knew something was weird between them then, when Tatum threatened me. When she stuck her disgusting finger in my face and promised to "end" me for what I'd done to Taylor. Typical female shit. Blaming me for Cam's wanting to fuck me. He was all over me that night after they left. They didn't see it. He was all up in my tits and after Matt left, he even kissed me. Sounds like a real true blue boyfriend, huh? Like he wouldn't have fucked me sober? Yeah, right. Cam Spencer was thirsty as fuck because his girlfriend was constantly throwing him shade. That was Taylor's own fault, not mine. If they hadn't been fighting and shit, Cam wouldn't have been at Chase's house without her in the first place. He would have left with Taylor. Instead of Taylor leaving with her new best lesbo buddy. Instead of Taylor and Tatum going off and doing whatever scissorshit they did when they spent the night at each other's houses.

But it was easier to blame me. To call me a slut and a whore. To tell me to stay away from Cam, like I was trying to steal him away.

Please. I wouldn't have wanted Cam even if he was single.

Chase was the one I wanted, but rumor, now, was he was gay.

Which was another problem in and of itself.

If I could have gotten *his dick* in my mouth, don't you think I would have?

COACH W

By the end of Monday, the whole school was talking about the picture on Cam's phone. Including Principal Pitt.

We'd all seen recent news stories of high school kids being charged with child pornography for sending nude or partially nude photos of themselves to other teens in texts. Hell, there was even a case of a student being charged for *receiving* such a photo even though the teen in question didn't ask for the photo or even want it.

What we did *not* know yet, but what we would learn in about an hour, was that not only had Makayla taken the photograph, she'd taken it initially on Cam's phone, with a timer, and then forwarded the photo to her phone.

Or at least, that was what Cam was alleging. Because Cam was sticking to his "I was 100% blacked out" story. Makayla, however, was insisting Cam took the picture, that *she* was blacked out, that *he* was blackmailing *her*.

PRINCIPAL PITT

I didn't know what to think. Every day now at Dobson High was turning into its own episode of *90210*. Or *Gossip Girl*. Or whatever relevant teen soap opera type show is popular right now. It was exhausting. Dealing with all their dramas. I needed an Alka-Seltzer by nine thirty every morning.

Here it was supposed to be Spirit Week—fun, laid back, rah-rah, go Mustangs!—and I'd been praying there'd be no more copycat suicides, and now I was having to deal with a teen dick pic on someone's phone.

I was supposed to know the legal ramifications. But I didn't know. I didn't have a clue.

Shocker: I didn't go to school to be a lawyer. I didn't know anything about the law. These cellphones were making my life hell. It was hard enough before cellphones. There were still teen dramas then, of course, but at least they weren't *documented*. They were rumors. Unsubstantiated. Unprovable. In a court of law.

I had Mrs. Stone get the school attorney on the line. Then I remember the school attorney was Jessica Spencer, Cam's mom.

COACH W

I didn't envy Mike (Principal Pitt). Who can keep up with all these new technologies and the rules, or, laws, that go along with them and seemed to change every five seconds.

Every time I turned on *The Today Show*, Matt Lauer seemed to have a different attorney on making different claims regarding the legalities of teen texting.

CAM SPENCER

The picture *was* on my phone. I hadn't even noticed it until we were in Principal Pitt's office and Makayla accused me of having taken it. It seemed obvious to me in the photo I'm passed out but Makayla insisted my eyes were closed because at the moment the photo was taken I was ejaculating into her mouth.

I had to hand over my phone at that point and Principal Pitt and both Makayla's parents and my parents got to look at it.

It didn't look good.

I was being fucking set up.

I was eighteen and Makayla was fifteen.

And to top off the whole fucking nightmare, they also found photos of Taylor and me on my phone. Dick pics I'd actually taken and sent my *girl-friend*. Pics of Taylor's tits. Other shit. Shit you'd find on any teen's phone these days.

I was terrified they were going to call Taylor's mom, get her involved in this shit, too. The last thing I needed was Anabel against me. Anabel was the one person always on my side.

And everything was extra awkward because my mom was the lawyer Principal Pitt normally consulted on shit like this. But now it was a... what do they call it... conflict of interest or something. Since it was *my* dick pic that was in question.

ANISSA GRANT

Taylor was inconsolable. I couldn't tell if she believed Cam or not. If she believed Makayla or not. As much as I didn't like Cam, as much as I kind of hated Cam, I had the feeling he was telling the truth this time. But I didn't say anything. I kept my mouth shut. For one, Taylor hadn't asked me what I thought... yet.

And I wasn't sure if it was that the whole school knew or that now Cam was possibly facing legal trouble, could possibly be kicked out of school or worse, why she was so upset. He'd already been suspended from the foot-ball team, "until further notice, until we have time to investigate," or if it was because her parents were freaking out or because she loved Cam and still planned on marrying him.

I just sat with her in silence, staring at the lake. We sat there a long time, that day. I knew she was prolonging going home, the inevitable fight with her mom.

Of course I wanted to offer her comfort, to rub her back or hold her hand or something, but I refrained. I let her have her space. I could tell she was going through so much.

MAKAYLA RICHEY

I had no idea it would blow up like this, that the whole school would find out and our parents would be called and all of that shit. I mean, do you think I wanted that kind of attention? It fucking sucked for me too. Not as much as for Cam, maybe, but my parents were freaking the fuck out. Because then I had to turn over my phone and because I hadn't thought any of this through, because I'd naively thought this would remain a drama just amongst us teens, I hadn't thought to delete the photos of Matt and me on my phone either.

My parents still thought I was a virgin, for Christ's sake. They thought Matt and I were "waiting for marriage." Our families went to the same church. We were Pro-life. Republicans. *Christians*.

I didn't tell anyone, of course, that Matt and I had come up with this plan together. That we'd staged a fight, that he'd purposely left me there alone. He hated Cam Spencer. A lot of people did. It was worth it to him to see Cam's dick in my mouth if it would ruin Cam.

We just never thought it would blow up like *this*.

We thought we could keep it contained.

But it only took one day. Four hours. And *everyone knew*. And all our worlds were fucked. Not just Cam's and Taylor's.

My life was *fucked*.

COACH W

Everyone at school was freaked out now that Cam was potentially going to be charged with child pornography. I was freaked out too. It could have been me. Tatum could have taken a photo of us. Or even just told anyone what had happened. Even without photographic proof I'd be fucked.

Hell, she could have texted me a photograph of herself I didn't request.

The most logical thing for me to do have done at this point would have been to become a total hermit, to be 100% rigid in my dealings with any teenager. Not to let any lines get crossed, any ambiguity... keep my dick in my pants.

That would have been logical. Given the situation at school.

But humans rarely act logically, do they?

Instead, what happened was, the most illogical thing you could think of: Tatum and I had sex again.

ANISSA GRANT

I don't know why I ran to Colton—Coach W—for comfort. Maybe I felt alone since Taylor's mom wouldn't let her see anyone and wouldn't let her have her phone either. I could hardly stand it. Being apart from her. She wasn't in school Tuesday or Wednesday. Neither were Cam, Makayla or Matt. Spirit Week was a bust. I didn't think anyone was dressed up that day for Freaks or Geeks but then again, it was hard to really tell. Chase and I ate lunch together but we were both pretty quiet. I guess we are both introverts. The whole cafeteria was eerily quiet, actually. A weird white noise of whisperings.

So, Wednesday after school, I went to talk to Colton. Innocently, I swear. I didn't have a plan to seduce him again. I just genuinely wanted to talk to someone and he was the only person other than Chase I felt I could trust and while I trusted Chase, I couldn't really *talk* to him. If that makes sense.

I'd gone and gotten us both coffees from the new Starbucks they put in the Kroger's across from the school the week before.

I'd gotten Colton a standard venti coffee because I didn't know what he liked but he seemed like a standard coffee kind of guy.

I got myself an iced soy latte. Hey, I was from California. What do you expect.

We sat down on the floor of the theater. No one else was around. Everything at school had been cancelled. No one was letting their kids go anywhere those first couple days after news of the photograph broke.

Maybe it was because of how much we both knew we shouldn't do it again. Of how risky it was. Because we'd seen what could happen. Maybe the excitement of the inherent risk was too much, too exciting. I don't know. You do the math.

But we ended up in the back closet of the theater, with forty years of high school musical costumes, fornicating like dogs in heat. No, like, literally doggy-style.

As soon as it was over, Colton said to me, "If you want to tell someone, I understand."

Maybe that was his way of ensuring I didn't tell anyone. Reverse psychology or whatever. Maybe it was his way of not wanting to kill himself for fucking a student.

I did feel kind of bad, allowing him to believe he was committing some sort of crime. A *felony*. Not to mention a possible ethical infringement. Depending, I guess, on what he really thought of those Ancient Greek pederasts he'd told us about.

Of course I wasn't going to tell anyone because telling someone would reveal my own crimes, my own ethical infringements.

TAYLOR RAGNER

I couldn't believe I was missing Spirit Week of all weeks. I couldn't believe Makayla had pulled this shit just in time for Homecoming. It was probably all a stupid high school plan to get Cam kicked off the team and out of school so Matt had a shot at quarterback and Homecoming King. The stupidest thing was I knew Chase would get both roles. Matt was lucky he was on the team. But he wasn't a good player, he wasn't going to be recruited by any university officials like Chase and Cam. Or, like Cam *would have been.*

By Wednesday, I no longer gave a shit about the pic. I don't know why I'd reacted the way I had in the first place. I guess even when you don't really want something anymore, you don't want someone else trying to sneak around and steal it out from under you either. It's still yours. Until *you* decide it's not.

By Wednesday I was just pissed off that Makayla and her stupid loser boyfriend had gotten Cam suspended from school.

Even if I no longer wanted to marry Cam or have his babies, I still didn't want his life ruined. Over some basic bitch with a conniving, basic boyfriend.

My mom wouldn't give me back my phone. She'd taken it Monday after school. So I waited until she went to take Jolie to ballet, got the keys to the Jeep out of her desk drawer, and drove over to Cam's.

CHASE WHITING

My dad had called his attorney, too. Just to be on the safe side, since the photo was taken at our house. And everyone knew I'd thrown a party with liquor and underage drinkers. He was worried he'd somehow be held responsible. Or that I would. Luckily I hadn't yet turned eighteen. That's what my dad said, anyway.

Coach W said we were still going to play the Homecoming game on Friday, with or without Cam. He moved me into quarterback position. Matt was still allowed to play for some reason. I couldn't stand to look at him so I looked at the ground if I had to address him. I knew somehow he was part of it. If only because he and Makayla didn't break up.

I wasn't an aggressive person. That was Cam's role. I'd never fought anyone. But something in me wanted to fight Matt.

I was ready to fight anyone, actually, who talked shit about Cam in front of me.

COACH W

It was the week from hell. *Spirit Week*. There was so much shit happening at school, so much shit to deal with, think about, and now I'd just added fucking Tatum again to the whole mess in my brain. I probably should have started doing drugs, too, that week. I mean, why the fuck not? Get good and high and fuck everything, you know?

But I didn't do drugs. For some reason I believed I still had lines I wouldn't cross, if you can believe that. The guy, the *teacher*, fucking the student, having principles. What the fuck was I thinking? How delusional can you get?

CAM SPENCER

I was pacing my house like a lion. Or a tiger. My dad was in the basement pumping iron to Rage and my mom was talking to fellow attorneys in Indianapolis who had more experience in these kinds of things. She had texted me not to worry, that she'd get everything figured out. She didn't bother my dad and brother and me about her work too much. We were all proud of her but we didn't really get it. She was gone a lot. Sometimes she stayed at a hotel in Indianapolis in winter when the roads were bad and she had a night class she taught at Indiana State. I guess she was really independent. My parents said that's what kept them together, the time they spent apart. I didn't think too much about it. Anyway, she said she'd fix everything and I believed her. She was a really smart, strong woman. I used to think Taylor was a lot like her. But I was starting to doubt that now. I was starting to think Taylor was the exact opposite of my mother. Like, I was starting to question if she even had any principles, anymore.

TAYLOR RAGNER

I didn't like Makayla but I felt sorry for her, having the whole school, the whole town, find out. I think pretty much everyone had seen the photo in question by now. Rumor was, her parents weren't going to let her go to Homecoming. She'd brought it all on herself, of course, by not thinking things through, but even I didn't think she or Cam should have any legal charges pressed against them or that either one should have to be put on the sex offenders' list. That was just stupid. You can't child abuse yourself. That didn't make any sense. And for that matter, half the school would be child abusers based on that criteria. Because we all sent naked photos of ourselves to our boyfriends or girlfriends or guys or girls we liked. Jesus.

MAKAYLA RICHEY

My parents hired a lawyer from Indianapolis. He said there were other cases like mine around the country—teen boys and girls brought up on child abuse charges for sending or receiving nude photos. The good thing was, my lawyer said usually the girls only ended up with community service. I didn't want Cam to go to the penitentiary, either, though. That's what our town was known for. There were two in town, actually. The old prison was used to film a bunch of famous movies. One, a Stephen King. But the new one would be where Cam would go, instead of juvie, since he was eighteen. I knew people who had older brothers or dads or uncles who worked there. Horror stories, of what they did to the inmates, how they fucked with them. I was starting to hate Matt for instigating me to do this, for coming up with the idea. I mean, sure, Cam was an asshole, but he didn't deserve to go to prison over this. And I was pissed my parents might not let me go to prom now. I was pissed everyone had seen a picture of me with a dick in my mouth. I just wanted to move, change towns, go to a whole new school, get a whole new set of friends, a new boyfriend, a new life.

COACH W

Thursday night I couldn't stop thinking of Tatum, of what we were doing, of how stupid and lame I was. So I drove two towns over to Fredericktown which is where I go sometimes when I don't want anyone else to know my business.

There's a small corner bar there that looks like it's straight out of 1947. Straight out of a Steinbeck novel. I don't know why I just picked that random year. I could have said 1885 or 1919. None of us has very specific knowledge of that far back so it all sort of runs together in our minds, even if you teach high school history for a living.

Anyway, I go there once a month. Sometimes twice a month.

Drink a beer and a shot of whiskey. Then do it all over again thirty minutes later.

The place really isn't much more than a single long bar. A booth or two along the wall. Not even darts or a pool table. Not even a jukebox. There's a small TV always turned to news up over the bar and Gary the bartender leans on the bar watching it when he's not pouring shots.

I'd never seen anyone from Dobson or Elkheart in Gary's.

ANISSA GRANT

Thursday after cheer practice I went home alone because Taylor's mom insisted Taylor spend the evening with the family since she'd been out so much lately and was going to be out again the next night. I think she probably wanted to have "the talk" with her since so many girls lose their virginity on Homecoming night and her mom seemed kind of clueless.

I got online and looked first at the social medias of Cam and Taylor and Chase and other people at our high school. I'd gotten 19 more followers...

Then I went to look at Tate's. Something within me changed—only a feeling, maybe—whenever I switched from looking at the social medias of Dobson High people to looking at Tate's. Maybe it was some sort of maternal feeling. I don't know. My mother robbed me of most of those. It was hard to recognize.

She still hadn't posted anything in three days. This wasn't like her. It wasn't like any fifteen-year-old who regularly uses social media. I couldn't remember a 24 hour period in which she hadn't made a post.

I was starting to let myself worry... like a mother, a maternal feeling of panic was swirling inside me. Before, when it'd only been one day, then two,

I'd told myself I was being ridiculous. Now I was sure something bad had happened. Bad things were always happening to young women in Hollywood. One of the actresses I'd worked with in the 80s had been shot by her boyfriend, and another actress I didn't work with but knew of was strangled by a stalker. And then there were all the cocaine/rape stories and cocaine/sex tape stories and cocaine/snuff film rumors, and the od's and suicides. My mother didn't get it. Or she pretended not to get it. She was so fame hungry and living vicariously through us.

I had to get out of the apartment. I couldn't tell Taylor or anyone else what was wrong, why I felt like my heart was being ripped out of my chest.

I put on a pair of pin-striped pants and a blouse, a pair of high-heeled shoes I'd brought for meeting the leasing agent when I was signing for the apartment. For going to the bank. For any adult meeting I might have to have. I applied different makeup than I wore to Dobson High: darker shadows and lipstick, no mascara. I put on a pearl choker my mother had bought me years ago. Pulled my hair into a chignon. I wasn't sure what role I was playing. Maybe I was playing myself. Maybe I was playing Catherine Tramell. I couldn't be sure. I didn't have an ice pick, but I was never really sure.

I got in the car and started driving, at first just out of Elkheart. I didn't know where I was going. Maybe I was following Colton. I can't remember. I ended up in a town with one stop light and one bar on the corner. I think it was called Barry's or Gary's. Something like that.

TAYLOR RAGNER

My mom finally agreed I could leave the house for two hours so I drove over to Chase's. I wanted to talk to him in private, just the two of us. I wanted to hear from him firsthand what had happened that night after Tatum and I left.

Chase's dad answered the door and called Chase down to meet me. Chase's dad had lost weight, since Chase's mom had died. He looked thin, waifish. Maybe he was worried about Chase's involvement in this school phone scandal. On top of everything else.

"How are you doing, Taylor?" his dad asked me.

"I'm alright, Mr. Whiting, thank you," I said. I knew I should be polite and ask how he was doing too but I was afraid to ask. I was afraid he might answer honestly. And then I wouldn't know what to say.

"Hey," Chase said, meeting us in the foyer. "Come on upstairs."

I smiled at Chase's dad and followed Chase upstairs to his room.

"Why didn't you just bring Cam up here with you?" I said. I was sitting on his bed.

"I don't know," Chase said. "That's what I keep asking myself."

I had the sense he was lying, though. That there was a reason but one he would never share with anyone.

COACH W

I didn't notice her at first. I was actively avoiding people, avoiding making eye contact. I heard someone else come in but it wasn't until I'd finished my second beer and shot and was looking up to signal Gary that I needed another that I saw the woman seated at the other end of the bar. It took me a full minute to figure out who she was. My first thought was how do I know this woman. She was attractive. Younger than I am but not so much younger. She was wearing a silk blouse and pearls. No one around here owned a silk blouse or pearls. I guarantee it. I subtly studied her, taking careful glances with every sip of my whiskey. Finally, it came to me. In a confusing surreal realization. Like seeing someone in such an out of place setting. Like in a dream.

She must not have noticed me yet. I think if she had noticed me first she might have left. I was trying to put together the puzzle pieces in my mind but my mind was soaked with bourbon which made it an even harder task. Nothing fit.

Which was when I saw her look up, saw her face change, out of the corner of my eye, out of the periphery. I waited to see what she would do next, if she'd come over and say something or leave.

CHASE WHITING

I'd known Taylor since we were kids. We lived in the same neighborhood. Our moms had been friends and I'd been friends with her brother before he went off to college. I liked Taylor but she made me nervous. I used to think she had a crush on me or that maybe I had one on her. There was some sort of unspoken tension between us once she went through puberty that hadn't been there before when we were younger. But my sexuality felt as much a mystery to me then as it seemed to be to everyone else.

I'd only known Cam since sixth grade but very quickly we'd become inseparable so it felt like I'd known him longer. It felt like he was my brother, though I wasn't as close to my actual brothers as I was to Cam. I knew Cam rubbed people the wrong way, that he could be a dick, a total douchebag sometimes. But with me he let his guard down a little. Maybe in a way he didn't even with Taylor. He was always afraid Taylor was going to hurt him, going to leave him. I used to think he was paranoid. I'd told him a hundred times he was worrying over nothing. Maybe it was him making his fears come true. I don't know. But I did have the feeling lately that Taylor wanted out of the relationship, that maybe she'd outgrown it, which only made Cam cling more tightly. It was a little hard to watch.

Maybe I was trying to rip the Band-Aid off, putting Cam and Makayla in a room together. But I certainly wasn't going to tell Taylor that.

"Do you even want to be in a relationship with Cam anymore, Taylor?" I said.

I couldn't believe I was asking her that question.

She looked as surprised as I was.

"I don't know, Chase."

"Because I guess the photo is irrelevant if you don't," I said.

Man, I was really going for it, for some reason. I don't know why.

"Yeah," she said, quietly, biting her cuticles and spitting one on the floor absentmindedly.

ANISSA GRANT

Of course I ran into the very last person I wanted to see in that hole in the wall two towns over. Well, not the very last person. The very last person would have been Taylor's mom. Or Taylor's dad, I guess, except I didn't really know what Taylor's dad looked like because he was never around. I only knew what he looked like from the family photographs around the house and they were all ten years old or older. So I guess I should be glad I didn't meet and accidentally fuck Taylor's dad. Phew. I wasn't sure what to do about Coach W, though, now that I'd seen him. Colton. Colt 45. I knew he'd noticed me. he was doing a bad job of pretending he hadn't.

It seemed stupid to go along with his pretending we didn't know or see each other so I picked up my purse and my glass of wine and walked around the bar and took the seat next to him.

"Hey," I said. I knew I was carrying myself differently, that I was almost a different person from the one he was used to. I felt like that British actress in *The Verdict*, a Paul Newman movie from the 80s. Charlotte Rampling, I think her name is. The first thirteen years of my life were spent watching old movies, first on VHS and later on DVD, with my mother. Charlotte

Rampling, at least in that film, is a calm, cool customer who dresses in silk blouses and slacks. She's sensual and elegant but chilly. Very chilly.

"What are you doing here, Tatum?" Coach W said and I wasn't sure if he meant this bar or this state or Dobson High.

"Having a drink, same as you," I said, holding his stare. Charlotte Rampling him.

"Right, but, you're a high school student, you're sixteen, right?" he said.

"That's right," I said. "Cheers," I said, holding up my glass toward him and swigging down the last of the wine in it.

TAYLOR RAGNER

On the way home from Chase's, I tried calling Tatum but she didn't pick up. I drove by her apartment but her car wasn't there. I sat in the parking lot, texting her. I didn't know where she was. I figured maybe something had come up with her aunt, that maybe she was with her mom, helping out. I sat and lit the bowl I'd shoved in my purse. I listened to a new song by a DJ Chase had told me about. I sat and waited. I was way too high now to drive home. I knew my mom would be waiting up. While I was waiting, a text finally came through from Tatum.

COACH W

When we had sex that night at my house it was different than the sex we'd had at school.

I wouldn't say passionate but maybe heavier, darker, with more layers.

It was hard to tell which of us was or should be more worried about our affair becoming public knowledge now.

We seemed on more equal footing, I guess you could say. So maybe it was a draw.

Tatum was sexier in a way she hadn't been when I thought she was sixteen. More sensual, alluring.

I was worried I'd fall in love with her now.

I was less worried now that she'd fall in love with me.

We took a shower together, after, in my bathroom. I was embarrassed by the pubic hair on the bar of soap, by the cobwebs on the ceiling, the dust balls on the floor. It'd been a while since I cared what my house looked like, or, for that matter, what I looked like.

I hadn't looked like a football player in a while, years, for one thing.

I worried about Tatum comparing me to whatever boys she had recently seen unclothed. The six packs. The youthful testicles. The round buttocks. The teenage stamina.

I kept forgetting she wasn't a teenager either. Even now that I knew. Or kind of knew. She wasn't. She hadn't fully or even partially explained her story to me. And that was maybe the most alluring part of all, what made me so horny for her now. Having no fucking idea who she was or what she was or why she was here and when she would leave and where she would go…

We did it again in the shower. Took turns down on our knees, before I finally entered her from behind, up again the back wall of my shower, one hand grabbing her tit, the other holding tightly to her pelvis, pulling her in close.

It felt good to be fucking another adult, even one who was clearly deranged in some way, sick in the head, posing as a high school student where I taught.

I grabbed hold of her hair and yanked back her head to kiss her wet mouth.

I don't know where that side of me came from. I'd never been the grab-a-woman-during-sex sort of guy. NEVER. I'd always been either the sad, pathetic missionary type, over in a jiffy so as not to annoy the woman too much, or the do whatever I could to please her, ask before I did anything, gentle, gentle, almost invisible lover.

Now suddenly I was grabbing a woman by the hair in my shower while fucking her from behind. I'd never even had sex in the shower.

I had the sense after she dried off and left—after all, it was a school night, we both had to be up early—that this couldn't last. That we might have sex another one or two times and then she'd be gone. Back to wherever she'd come from. Back to whatever life she'd lived before she'd lived the life of a sixteen-year-old sophomore fucking her high school history teacher.

Talk about roleplaying during sex.

I had to masturbate before bed again just thinking about it.

The whole thing was turning me into a sex addict.

Or maybe it was just that it'd been so long since I'd had sex. Or since I'd had sex that felt like sex instead of masturbation.

All of a sudden my dick wouldn't stop getting hard.

I couldn't stop thinking of Tatum. Or whatever her actual name was.

I jerked my dick thinking of what she might be doing with Taylor Ragner and Cam Spencer and Chase Whiting. What teen sex games they might be playing. I got out my laptop and looked at their faces online and came all over myself just like I'd come on Tatum's back in the shower. And then I got up and took another shower and fell fast asleep. I hadn't slept that hard in a long time either. And then I woke up with another hard on. And then I had to jack off all over again before school.

ANISSA GRANT

I don't know what I was doing with Coach W. I guess it'd started out as part of my whole high school fantasy: fucking the football coach, the acting teacher, the history teacher. All in one. It was like I was doing research for a role. Everything could be justified that way.

Then I sort of started to like him. Not love him. Just feel fondly toward him, I guess. like, he was someone I could always count on to be there. Because he was a sad loner like I used to be, like I still was, outside of this situation, outside of this acting role I was playing, this teeny tiny fictional world I had created for myself. Eventually it would all go bust and when it did I'd be all alone again. Just like Coach W. We were alike like that. I didn't know what he'd done to earn his loneliness. To deserve his isolation. Maybe he just liked it that way. Maybe I did too.

It's so hard to tell in life, if you're pushing people away or if they aren't even trying to get in.

Anyway, he was someone I could hang with when Taylor wasn't allowed out of the house. Or when Taylor was busy with Cam. Or, later, when Taylor wouldn't talk to me.

I saw Taylor's car when I pulled in the apartment parking lot.

I said the word "Fuck" out loud.

I was still dressed in my heels and blouse and slacks. I was disheveled. It was probably obvious I'd just gotten laid. That I wasn't a high school sophomore. That I was some sort of demented sociopath.

I made a quick U-turn and drove out by the lake. I had a pack of cigarettes in the glove box and I rolled the window down and lit one. I checked my phone. There were a couple missed calls from Taylor, four or five texts.

I held the cigarette between my lips and started texting. "oh, sorry, didn't see these. am with my mom. my aunt's real sick. see you tom, tho, bae."

I'd promised myself I wouldn't lie to Taylor and now I was breaking a promise and telling a lie all at the same time.

I blew smoke out the window, turned on the radio.

Nirvana was playing.

For some reason Nirvana always reminded me of Quinn.

Maybe because he had Kurt's name tattooed on his arm. Maybe because he was going to play Kurt in a movie. But then he died. Quinn, I mean. Kurt was already dead.

It was the live version of "All Apologies."

I started to cry. I cried every time that song came on the radio. The live version was the worst. Quinn and I used to cry together. Even though I was only ten when Kurt did it, when he killed himself. Quinn was seventeen. He didn't leave his house for three days, he told me. Didn't eat either. Just sat around doing heroin and smoking cigarettes and watching MTV. Another sad loner. Kurt Cobain. Quinn James. Coach W. Me.

I ran out of cigarettes. I would have to stop for some on the way home. I smoked the same kind as Kurt. At least, that's what Quinn had told me when I smoked his. They came in a gold box that said Park Avenue New York on them back then. They didn't say anything about Park Avenue anymore. But they still came in a gold box.

TAYLOR RAGNER

After the texts came through from Tatum I waited to get my shit together so I could leave. I stopped at the 7-Eleven across the street for a shitty hazelnut machine cappuccino to sober me up.

I was waiting to pull out of the 7-Eleven parking lot when Tatum pulled in. She didn't notice me. She parked right up next to the building and got out of her car. I recognized the car or I might not have known it was her. She was dressed like a teacher or a young working mom. She was wearing heels and her hair was up in some kind of messy bun.

Or maybe I was imagining it. I was still pretty high. Maybe it wasn't her or it *was* her but she wasn't wearing heels and her hair wasn't in a bun. Maybe it was her mom. I'd never seen her. I wasn't 100% sure what I'd seen. So I waited. Then she came back out with a pack of the gold box cigarettes she liked in her hand. It was definitely Tatum and she was definitely dressed like a teacher or an attorney, a professional woman of some kind.

I just sat there staring because it didn't make sense. Why she was dressed like that. Why her hair was like that. Would she dress like that to go help her mom with a sick dying aunt? I didn't get it. She didn't notice me, she just drove right out of the parking lot and turned into the apartment complex where I'd been sitting half an hour.

I opened my phone and typed out a text. "Are you still with your mom?" I hit send and waited. I could see her car parked now in front of her apartment. I saw her get out of her car as the text came through. "Yeah, sorry, I'm not going to be home for another hour or so, things are pretty bad." She put a sad faced emoji.

I stared at my phone. At her text. At the lie she'd written me.

Something about it had sobered me up.

I drove back home. Surprisingly, my mother wasn't waiting up for me. I went straight to my room and got in bed.

ANISSA GRANT

It felt so shitty lying to Taylor but once I'd done it the first time there was less hesitation the second. I guess that's what they mean by one lie begets another. Duh.

I opened the sliding glass door and hung the clothes I'd worn to the bar in front of it. They smelled like smoke. And like Coach W.

I got in bed and there was still no update from Tate.

I went to Taylor's Instagram account and there was a photo of her with Chase in what looked like Chase's bedroom. I figured that was going to cause trouble for Chase, as far as Cam went. Or maybe for Taylor.

I felt so bad lying to her. I wanted to tell her everything, eventually, if I stuck around that long. But how long was "that long"?

COACH W

I thought about texting Tatum "goodnight" but then I realized I didn't have her number, that we'd never exchanged phone numbers. And anyway, would that be weird? Could I potentially get in trouble? For texting a student a goodnight? Even if there was no way said student was under eighteen? And how long was she going to keep up this charade, anyway? And what was the point of said charade?

CAM SPENCER

My mom was acting as my attorney and had been in talks with the school board 24/7 for three days. It seemed like everyone in town was behind me, or the majority of people anyway. Everyone except Makayla's parents, basically. No one had wanted me to miss the Homecoming game and in order to play in the Homecoming game I had to be at school Friday so Principal Pitt had called my parents Thursday, late, to tell them I could come back.

It was unclear if I was still going to be prosecuted later but the school wanted me in that game so I went to CVS and got some bleach for my hair. Friday was the last day of Spirit Week and the theme was rock or hip hop.

If I was going back to school I was *going back*. Full force. Fuck those fuckers. Fuck the haters.

I didn't even care that the dance was the next night and that Taylor was probably going to bitch about my hair.

I got out a white t-shirt and a necklace with dog tags. I had one hoop earring for my right ear. I had a pair of baggy grey sweats.

I got a magic marker and wrote "Rot in Pieces" on my abdomen and above it I wrote "Taylor."

It was going to be so sick when I walked into school since no one expected me to be there and no one expected me to come back as Slim Shady.

TAYLOR RAGNER

I wasn't going to let Cam's suspension from school ruin the last day of Spirit Week. I'd already missed two days and I'd had my Avril Lavigne costume planned out for weeks. There was no way I wasn't going.

Cam had never gotten his shit together long enough to figure out how he was going to dress for it anyway.

He always did everything last minute.

I saw Chase in the hall first. I wasn't sure who he was supposed to be. He was wearing red skinny jeans and a black blazer and his hair was gelled and he had on multiple fake gold chains. I couldn't even figure out honestly if he was supposed to be rock or hip hop.

I guess he couldn't figure out who I was supposed to be either because he looked at me and said, "Who are you supposed to be, Miley Cyrus?"

Miley Cyrus! As if.

ANISSA GRANT

I didn't know if anyone would know who I was supposed to be, if Courtney Love was even a recognizable figure anymore. I was wearing an old baby-doll dress from a Halloween party I'd gone to with Quinn and ripped tights and I'd ratted my hair and over-applied and smeared red lipstick. I'd written "witch" and "slut" on my forearms.

Of course Coach W got it immediately. He was dressed like Axl Rose: bandana over wig, sunglasses over bandana, jeans, Guns N Roses tee under a fake leather vest. He looked ridiculous. And I couldn't help smiling. Which ruined my Courtney Love tough rocker chick pose.

"Is this where I say to Kurt, 'control your bitch'?" Coach W said.

"Yeah except there isn't a Kurt. Look around, Kurt's dead," I said.

"Do you think Axl and Courtney ever slept together?" Coach said.

"No, but I think part of both of them probably wanted to, which is why they hated each other so much," I said.

"Interesting," Coach said.

"Well," I said. "Gotta go to class. See ya!"

"See ya, bitch," he said.

CHASE WHITING

Taylor said she was supposed to be Avril Lavigne. I barely knew who that was.

"You know," she said. "Sk8tr boi."

"Oh yeah," I said, even though that didn't mean anything to me.

"Who are you supposed to be?" she said, squinting up at me through layers of black eye makeup and bangs covering one eye under a sideways ballcap.

"The Bieb," I said.

"Who?" she said.

"Justin Bieber," I said, pushing my fake glasses up my nose.

"Oh right, I get that now," she said. Her pants were low and when she walked away I could make out the tops of her underwear.

She had just turned the corner at the end of the hall when I saw Cam slouching toward me, holding his crotch, smirking.

COACH W

If you didn't want to sleep with high school girls on any other day of the year, you probably still wanted to have sex them during Spirit Week when they came to school dressed in sexy pajamas and sexy rock girl poses.

If I hadn't been into Tatum before, and I definitely was, I couldn't think of anything else now that she was walking the halls done up like my early 20s crush in a babydoll dress and the words "witch" and "slut" written on her arms in marker.

I wanted to push her into a bathroom stall, bend her over my knee, pull up her dress and spank her.

Maybe it was the Axl testosterone coursing through my veins.

Maybe it was the fact that if I pushed my finger upside my nose and inhaled real deep, I could still smell her pussy on my cuticles.

I'd already done it twice that morning, alone in the classroom with no one looking.

Everyone was acting kind of strange that Friday. It was like the whole school had been woke, sexually, by the blowjob allegations, and the suicides, and the fact it was Homecoming weekend.

Even Principal Pitt was dressed up. I couldn't tell if he was supposed to be Mick Jagger or Steven Tyler or Tom Petty. It didn't matter. Ms. Corwin was a later in life, mid-career, post cocaine rehab, slightly chubby Stevie Nicks, in a twirly skirt and peasant top she must have gotten at Chico's, a store my ex-girlfriend used to drag me into at the mall.

CAM SPENCER

You should have seen everyone's faces. It was priceless. I felt like the real Marshall Mathers, the way people reacted to me when they passed me in the hall. Especially when I yanked up my shirt to reveal the fake tattoo with Taylor's name on it.

"Oh my god, dude, you're going to be in so much trouble when she sees that," this guy Nathan in my Physics class said.

"Nah," I said. "She'll get it. It's actually a tribute to her. I mean, if I'd written Makayla's name, which I actually considered before I realized how Taylor would take it, that would have been fucked, you know?"

I grinned and grabbed at my crotch.

ANISSA GRANT

I passed Cam in the hall after first hour. I couldn't believe he'd bleached his hair just for today to look more like Eminem. Now he was going to have bleached hair for Homecoming, too. Taylor wasn't going to like that. Add it to the list of shit Taylor didn't like.

CAM SPENCER

I didn't know who either Tatum or Taylor were 'sposed to be. No one was dressed hip hop but me and some ninth grader whose dad was black and whose mom was white and who'd come as the Fresh Prince in a Malcolm X tee and an African beaded necklace.

Taylor was wearing a green t-shirt with one of her dad's striped ties and a black pair of pants and a pair of Converse that must have belonged to her brother. And Tatum was wearing an old dress that looked like it belonged on a doll or a ghost and her hair was ratty and she had little girl plastic barrettes clipped into the mess.

I couldn't stop staring at them and finally they came over and Taylor said, "What?"

And I said, "What?"

And she said, "What are you looking at?"

And I said, "I don't know. That's why I'm looking."

And she said, "I hope you're planning on dying your hair back for tomorrow night."

And I said, "I wasn't, actually. I kind of like it bleached now."

And she rolled her eyes and huffed off.

CHASE WHITING

At lunch, Cam kept riding me about my costume. He said, "Dude, if half the people here already think you're a fag, maybe coming to school dressed as Bieber wasn't the best move to make them think otherwise, you know?" I guess it had never occurred to him I might actually be a homosexual. I didn't know if I was or wasn't but it would have been nice to have felt supported either way. I already had my dad making coded or not so coded negative comments about famous gay people in front of me every chance he got.

He'd told me this story about one of his best friends in the Army one night trying to give him a hand job about a hundred times. He told me he never talked to the guy after that, except when he had to out of professionalism.

I wasn't sure if he was trying to tell me he'd never talk to me again if I ended up being gay as he must have feared I would.

I wasn't sure if I was 100% gay. Like I said, there was some weird tension between Taylor and me. But I also felt a weird tension between Cam and me. I think maybe only I felt the tension in each of those relationships, though. So maybe it wasn't sexual but something "other." Or maybe I was trying to sexualize both of my close friendships. Which was odd since I couldn't seem to sexualize any other relationship.

I just looked at Cam and laughed, though, because in his Slim Shady "costume," he couldn't have looked "gayer."

ANISSA GRANT

Coach W kept trying to corner me. I could feel it. I could practically feel his big boner from across the cafeteria digging into me.

I turned my back to him, concentrated instead on Taylor, who, in her black pants, father's tie, and chain wallet, had never looked more badass or sexier. She'd even painted her nails black. She had a habit of biting them and the cuticles around them, which I found sexy, as well.

"I'm staying at your place tomorrow night," she said. "I just decided. I'm sick of staying at my house. My mom is such a fucking freak."

"Okay," I said. "I don't know if my mom will be there because my aunt is really sick right now, though, so I don't know if that's a problem for your mom or what."

"Fuck my mom," she said. "We'll figure something out. It's fucking Homecoming for fuck's sake."

"Right," I said. I hoped I didn't look too eager. Taylor and me all alone in my apartment for an entire night...

TAYLOR RAGNER

I couldn't even look at Cam, he looked so stupid. And I knew now that Tatum was lying, at least partially, about her mom and her aunt and that whole weird story, since I'd caught her lying the night before.

I was excited to spend the night at her place, which, for *some reason*, we'd never done. We'd always stayed at mine.

My mom was probably going to want to talk to her mom, though, which seemed like it might be a problem. But, whatever, it was Homecoming so it was worth getting in trouble over. It was worth whatever freak out grounding my mom did.

I just wanted to get fucked up Saturday night, after the week I'd had. I was tired of trying to be Miss Perfect. Miss Perfect Daughter and Miss Perfect Cheerleader and Miss Perfect Girlfriend. I wanted to kill off all of them, bury them on the football field tomorrow night. I never wanted to be any of them again. I didn't know what I wanted to be I just knew what I didn't. I was done being Taylor Ragner. I was finito being Cam's girlfriend.

COACH W

The cheerleaders had never looked hotter at a pep rally. Taylor still had her thick Avril Lavigne eye pencil on and her drawn on tattoos and Tatum still had her ratted hair and smeared lipstick and "witch" written on her arm. They both had a new attitude I'd never seen before. Apathy, maybe. Like the cheerleaders in the Nirvana video. Apathy, it turns out, can be sexy.

I should have been concentrating on the upcoming/impending game, the plays we would run, but all I could think of was Tatum in my shower, the water smearing her makeup, running the letters on her arm down the drain.

I was going to have to get a hold of myself. I was turning into a sex addict, just because I'd had sex three or four times in one month. That's how repressed and pathetic my life had become. Before Tatum. Before this mysterious girl/woman had entered Dobson High, entered my life. But who the fuck *was she*. I'd spent the morning googling her name and nothing came up, just a fairly new social media profile it looked like she'd made when she moved to Elkheart.

I watched her, between Taylor and Keisha, moving her hips side to side, raising her arms up over head, the perfect American Midwestern cheerleader as played by Courtney Love.

Which was when I realized the smile on my face was a little too wide. My interest a little too public. I toned it down a notch. Cleared my throat. Wiped my face with my hands, wiping away the I-fucked-her-last-night grin.

CAM SPENCER

I stood beside Chase, watching Taylor at the pep rally like I'd watched her a hundred times. Normally, I felt a mix of pride and horniness watching my girlfriend cheer. Normally, I'd look around, notice other guys watching her, too, and that would turn me on even more, knowing they wanted to fuck my girlfriend, knowing she was probably who they fantasized about while choking the monkey before and after school. Today, though, when I looked around and looked back at Taylor, I felt something different. An urge to possess her, to break something about her. I wanted to blindfold and gag her, turn her over on her stomach, and fuck the shit out of her. I needed to humble her. Humiliate her. To wipe that cocky smirk off her face. To make her remember me, who she's dealing with. For some fucked up reason, I felt the same way when I looked at Tatum. Which is when I started thinking about gang-banging them both. Tying them up together in my basement in front of the mirrored wall. Seeing their naked bodies helpless and vulnerable on my basement carpet. Waiting for me to fuck the shit out of both of them...

I shook my head and body, like the piss shivers, tried to shake these images out of me. They were fucked up. Even I knew that. I was fucked up.

I looked around the gym. At Chase. At Coach W. At fucking fuckface Matt. No one seemed to care anymore. Whether we won this game or not. I could feel that. I still wanted to win, though. I thought: *fuck these pussies*. I *always* want to fucking win.

CHASE WHITING

I think Cam had been dipping into his brother's 'roids again because he was acting a little nuttier than usual. Maybe it was the Slim Shady get up working him up. He was acting a little like Eminem. More misogynistic than normal. More aggressive. More homophobic. He kept laughing manically at shit *he* said, which seemed directed more at himself than at me.

The night before I'd watched gay porn and stuck my fingers up my ass, just to see what it felt like. I'd come hard. Part of me wished I could get Cam to direct some of his aggression in a sexual manner toward me.

The only problem my fantasy solved was the one in which I asked myself if I was bisexual or asexual.

I felt an overwhelming drive now, suddenly, to get out.

To get the hell out of this town.

Somewhere men could date and fuck each other without getting bullied or killed. I realized now that in watching Cam get his dick sucked by Makayla I was putting myself in Cam's body, but imagining it was Cam's mouth around my dick, not hers. Maybe I'd unconsciously orchestrated the whole thing because I wanted to witness it, to see Cam's dick. Not that I'd *never* seen it. But I'd never seen it hard. I'd never seen it in someone's mouth. I wanted it in mine. I wanted Cam to shoot his load in my mouth. Even if he hated me and himself, even if he hated both of us, afterward, for liking it.

ANISSA GRANT

No one seemed that into the game that night. I'd never been to a Homecoming game before but I sensed it wasn't normally this chill. We girls still cheered and the boys still played, seemingly with the intent of winning, but the crowd was subdued, the atmosphere overwhelmingly chill. Only Cam still seemed to have that killer vibe. That true sociopath energy. Maybe even more so, now that his girlfriend was pissed and he was Marshall Mathers.

The latest suicide had left the rest of us with an overriding feeling of doom, of apocalyptic dread. I guess Cam hadn't noticed. Or didn't give a shit. We won the game.

Even the parade and subsequent naming of King and Queen felt lackluster. Cam was named King, of course, and Mallory Swindell, a senior and our cheer captain, was Queen. They'd ridden around in some dad's convertible on loan from his car dealership, waving in what seemed like slow motion, plastic, invasion of the body snatchers smiles plastered on their faces, like a scene out of an 80s teen horror movie. In the midst of it all I felt Taylor grab my hand. It was cold and I brought it to my mouth and blew on it to warm it up.

COACH W

It was the weirdest Homecoming game I'd witnessed in the decade I'd been coaching. It was like the whole town had ingested some of that Kool-Aid. Not enough to kill them, but enough to make them not care about the game's outcome or who was named King or Queen or if Cam was guilty of sexual assault or the victim of a blackmailing scheme.

The school hadn't announced it yet—in honor of it being Homecoming weekend—but it'd come to the administration and then the student body's attention midway through the day, right before the pep rally, that there had been another suicide over night: Joby Crenshaw, a quiet junior involved in choir and 4-H. Another train. People were saying we were going to have to find a way to divert the tracks, or hire people to sit in folding chairs and guard them.

Principal Pitt said we would officially announce Joby's passing on Monday at an assembly, have psychologists on hand for students to talk to. We were going to have a faculty meeting about how best to look for warning signs in students, how to address the warning signs, when to tell the principal and call parents, etc.

Other school systems around the state were experiencing similar outbreaks.

We'd heard one school in Ohio had had eight suicides since school started. That was the most I'd heard of.

It took me back to '94, the immediate days and weeks following Kurt Cobain's suicide, the handful of copycatters, but also the universal fear that there'd be more, before they eventually petered out.

The internet was making it impossible to control. Social media fed off the frenzy.

The first suicide had been sad but easily forgotten. Maybe too easily. The second had felt a little coincidental, but also pushed aside, written off as two separately depressed kids; sad but understandable. You were always going to have a couple depressed teenagers, it was unavoidable. But by the third, it felt like something was happening we adults didn't understand and couldn't stop or control. Like it was all out of our hands. It felt like an epidemic. I think the whole town felt a bit numb about it, in hindsight. Which is how you tend to feel about things you can't control, I guess.

Or, maybe, in hindsight, it was the calm before the storm.

TAYLOR RAGNER

Of course Cam was named Homecoming King. That was a given. I watched him ride around in that car with Mallory, waving like some about-to-be-assassinated politician. He looked so stupid with his bleached hair and earring. I only felt something when he put his arm around Mallory, when she gazed up at him with her stupid blank smile.

I don't know why I hadn't seen it before, how fake he was. I don't think even Cam knew who the real Cam Spencer was. I think he thought he wanted me because I was his idea of the perfect high school girlfriend and playing football was his idea of being the perfect high school boyfriend, the perfect son.

But I didn't know who he really was or who I really was. I didn't know who any of us were.

All of a sudden my boyfriend looked like a mannequin to me. A soulless talking head. I grabbed Tatum's hand to feel something real. I just wanted to fast forward to the next night, to the end of the night, to the dance and to spending the night at Tatum's. I wanted to get drunk and ask her questions. The questions I couldn't ask her sober or in front of others.

I'd been too afraid to pry before but now I felt *unafraid*. Like Eminem. LOL. Like my artificial mannequin boyfriend pretended to be even though I could tell he was a terrified baby inside. Or already dead inside. One of the two.

CAM SPENCER

Taylor was being a bitch, *again*. Still. Still punishing me. She said she wanted to go home early after the game. She didn't even congratulate me on the win. She said she was tired from the whole week and from getting up early to get in costume and from practice and "all of the drama" and she wanted to just sleep twelve hours so she'd have energy for tomorrow, for Homecoming night. I was tired too but I still missed her. I still wanted to fucking *see her*, see my fucking girlfriend, even if only for an hour or two after the game.

But she just stopped answering her phone so Chase and me and the guys went to Denny's, got Grand Slams and Lumberjack specials. Loaded up on protein and carbs and Cokes.

Then Joe got his brother to buy us some beers and a fifth of Jack and we went out to Jake's house to celebrate. Jake's parents were older—Jake was the baby of the family—and they'd built an addition on to the side of the house for Jake and his brother, Robbie. It had a bar and one of those big L-shaped couches and a hot tub in the middle of the room. It had its own back staircase up to their bedrooms also. We never saw their parents. They had their own living room in the original side of the house. Jake and Robbie could sneak girls up to their rooms any time they wanted, or just have sex with them in the hot tub right in the middle of the room. Their parents never came to that side of the house. It was like an unwritten rule or something. It was weird but what the fuck did we care, as long as we got to party!

Chase was acting weird, weirder than usual, quieter, keeping even more to himself than normal. He was also getting way drunker than normal.

Chase didn't normally get that drunk. He looked blacked out to me when I went and sat down beside him around one in the morning.

"What's up?' I said, nudging him on the shoulder. "Why you over here moping?"

He didn't say anything. Just looked at me.

"You didn't know that girl, did ya? The one who died?" I thought maybe that was why he seemed so... out of it.

"She killed herself," he said.

"Yeah, I know she killed herself, stupid," I said.

"She didn't *die*, she ended her life."

"Right, I got that. We all got it, champ."

Then it hit me that maybe Chase was thinking about it, was feeling suicidal, on account of his mom or on account of what happened at his house between me and Makayla or on account of something else I didn't know about, something he wouldn't tell me.

"You'd never do something like that, right, Chase?" I said. I put my arm around him; patted his shoulder.

"I don't know, Cam, would you?" he said, looking up at me through that drunken gaze.

"Of course I wouldn't. It's not Christian. It's a sin," I said. "I don't want to go to Hell. Why would you ask me that?"

"I don't know," Chase said, and shrugged his shoulders. "I don't know. Sorry, man."

"It's okay, buddy, just don't ever ask me a dumb question like that again, okay? Jesus. Fuck."

I took a sip of the Jack bottle. There was only a little bit left.

The next thing I knew Chase was throwing up on the carpet in front of the couch.

"Aw, shit, man," I said. "Here, let me help you to the bathroom, bud."

But it was too late. Chase vomited a trail all the way around the hot tub to the bathroom. We were just lucky we weren't in the hot tub, I guess.

CHASE WHITING

I woke up on Jake's bathroom floor. I barely remembered anything about the night. I remembered eight of us getting in the hot tub in our underwear. I remembered Cam sitting across from me, me trying not to stare. I remember someone passing me the bottle of Jack. I remember a wad of chaw in my gums. I remember needing to get out of the hot tub, away from Cam. I remembered sitting by myself on the couch playing video games while everyone else was at the bar talking about football and guns and girls. I didn't remember anything else. After that my memory went blank.

ANISSA GRANT

The Saturday after Homecoming I woke up late. I'd slept ten hours and I could have slept more. I'd barely slept all week. I woke up with my Courtney Love lipstick smeared on my pillowcase.

I got up and got my laptop and googled Tate's name. A photo from a party at the Chateau Marmont came up. Finally. Some evidence she was alive, at least, if not well. In the photo she was wearing what looked like a Dolce & Gabanna dress. I'd seen a similar one in a fashion magazine earlier that summer. Both dresses had cherries on them, though the one Tate was wearing was cut different, strapless. She'd died her hair darker, almost black, and she was wearing more makeup than normal and she looked older, more mature, than I remembered, more filled out, almost a woman. I stared at her face a long time while drinking my instant Starbucks coffee. I could see more of Quinn in it this time than I ever had in the past. And that both endeared me and scared the shit out of me.

TAYLOR RAGNER

I couldn't wait for it to be four o'clock, the time we'd agreed upon for Tatum to come over, so we could get dressed and do our makeup and hair together. I'd promised my mom she could take pictures of us before the dance since I wasn't coming home after.

At five till four Tatum rang the bell. Jolie ran to the door. She was almost more excited than I was to see her. She was wearing the dress Tatum and I had bought her last time we took her shopping.

Tatum had brought Jolie a corsage to wear. I could have cried when I saw it. You have no idea how excited it made Jolie. I took a pic on my phone as Tatum pinned it on.

"There," she announced. "Now you're perfect. Now you're *beyond* beautiful!"

Of course Jolie had to be in the bathroom with us the whole time we were getting ready, watching us putting on eye shadow and lipstick, demanding us to put some on her, too.

It was the only thing I worried about, when I thought about leaving town: Jolie. How could I leave her? I wanted to take her with me wherever I went because wherever I went would be bigger than Elkheart and a better place for Jolie.

I couldn't bear the thought of her being picked on or bullied, or worse.

I hoped things would get better real quick, even in a small town like Elkheart, but I couldn't count on it. I didn't know why my mom didn't see this, why she wasn't planning to move soon as I graduated, for Jolie's sake. If not her own.

ANISSA GRANT

Taylor was wearing sweats and a tank top and her hair was in a ponytail when I got there and she was already beautiful. I know that's a cliché, that, like, Drake and some country singer dude and a million other people wrote songs about girls who looked sexier without makeup or their hair done or fancy clothes, but it was especially true of Taylor. I thought she always looked sexiest first thing in the morning or after we'd worked out, her face all flush and sweaty, not a stitch of makeup on it. I didn't look good at all without makeup. I looked like a plain Jane. Perfectly boring and overlookable. I only remotely looked interesting when I was "in costume" which was how I thought of myself at school or in my cheer uniform or anywhere I was outside my apartment. It'd always been that way, though, going back far as I could remember. Even besides the hair and makeup, there was just something I had to *do* to become *a person*—a person who isn't invisible. And a lot of the time I didn't care to expend that energy. I was perfectly fine blending in. I didn't feel the need to become someone, someone worth noticing.

I always tried around Taylor, though. I didn't want her to pick up on how boring I could be, on what a loser I *actually* was.

I focused all my energy on being charismatic in Taylor's presence. Because Taylor was naturally charismatic. She didn't have to put forth any energy. She didn't even have to try. She was just this force of nature, someone you'd gladly risk jail time, prison time, to spend a weekend with. To be the only one in her presence.

CAM SPENCER

I picked up Chase and the two of us drove over to Taylor's for pictures. Taylor had promised Anabel we'd all sit for them. Or stand. Or whatever. I didn't mind that much. Taylor's mom and I had a slightly flirtatious relation-ship. Friendly. She liked that I was dating her daughter, I could tell that. Just like my parents liked that I was dating Taylor. Everyone always assumed we were going to get married some day; made jokes about it that didn't feel like jokes. Even Taylor. Until recently. I'd noticed she'd stopped making those jokes lately. I tried not to think about it, but it was hard not to. Every time I looked at her I wanted to get down on one knee. I wanted to make her belong to me, forever. No more of this high school boyfriend/girlfriend bull-shit. Just make her *my wife*.

Taylor's mom posed us in the backyard and in front of the fireplace in the living room. Taylor looked gorgeous, of course. And she didn't seem that pissed anymore about my hair. *Or* the photo. [smirk] Chase and I were each in a tux. Taylor in a full-length ivory gown and Tatum in a black mini dress. They were like the ying and yang or whatever that hippie shit is of each other. And I was happy I had the girl in white. Or ivory. Close enough.

Of course, we had to take a couple photos with Jolie, too. Tatum held him in her arms and Chase stood him in front of him. I hated using the female pronoun when it came to Jolie. It was bad enough they'd allowed him to change his name. He was only in first grade, for chrissake! In Elkheart! It wasn't that I cared, it was that I didn't want him to get killed, dragged behind some redneck's truck when he's thirteen and wearing a skirt to school. Taylor always got mad at me for saying "him" and "his" and "he," but I was just trying to treat the kid normally. Like this was real life, cuz that's what Elkheart *is*. This isn't some reality TV show in New York or L.A. You'll get the brains kicked out of you here for standing out like that. And *I'm* the insensitive one. Or so Taylor says.

Taylor and I got in my truck and Chase and Tatum followed in Tatum's Taurus.

We had dinner reservations at this place in Millington—Rocky's, which was downtown and reminded me of a place mafia types would go to if this was New York instead of Indiana. Rocky's was dark. There were no windows. A bar up front and red leather booths in the back. The place hadn't changed in forty years. We slid into a booth: me and Taylor on one side and Tatum and Chase on the other. Chase and I ordered steaks and Taylor and Tatum each ordered the special, which was a shrimp and pasta dish.

Everything for once was perfect again, even if I had to stare across the table at Tatum all fucking night.

CHASE WHITING

There were a lot of other Dobson High couples at Rocky's since there were only a couple places in the area considered "fine dining" or that weren't a chain restaurant like TGIF's or Outback or Red Lobster. To be honest, I hadn't really wanted to go to Homecoming but my *father* really wanted me to. He'd kept reminding me it was my senior year and telling me I'd regret it if I didn't. It was hard to say no to him now that Mom wasn't here. I felt this pressure to be happy or to appear happy. Just so my dad wouldn't have to worry about me on top of everything else he had to worry about.

Tatum looked pretty and she was easy to talk to. We'd had a nice conversation on the drive over, mostly making fun of Cam and of Cam and Taylor as the cliché high school couple who break up and get back together constantly. But I wasn't "into" Tatum and, thankfully, I didn't think Tatum was "into" me.

At one point she even said, "You know, you and I..." she pointed between us. "We don't have to *be* anything or *do* anything..."

I laughed. "I know," I said.

"Just, cuz, I know it seems like Taylor and especially Cam want us to..."

"Yeah, I know. I'm on the same page... I think... as you, I mean."

"No disrespect," she said. "Cuz you're gorgeous."

"Same," I said.

"I just..."

"I know," I said. "Me, too."

ANISSA GRANT

The school year was going by so fast, like a movie shoot where everyone feels the excitement of the movie building during filming.

This was one of *the* days I'd always dreamed of, while attending movie premiers and film festivals and being interviewed on TV talk shows: Homecoming, the way some girls grow up dreaming of their wedding day, I'd dreamed of attending Homecoming and prom, even if it was turning out a little different than I'd planned it years ago back when I pictured myself swooning over a football player instead of another cheerleader. I didn't know how long I could keep my secret crush secret or if it would be reciprocated. Taylor was flirtatious with me but Taylor was flirtatious with *everybody*. She was extremely physically touchy and always so complimentary, always commenting on your makeup or a top you were wearing. It was just her nature. Sometimes I wondered if she was an extrovert or manic. It was why everyone was drawn to her, the same way they'd been drawn to Quinn. Maybe the way they were now drawn to Tate, judging by her social media posts. It seemed like she'd changed a lot in the few months I'd been gone. For the better, I mean. I didn't want her to be like me, or like I was at her age, socially awkward, isolated, friendless.

During dinner Taylor kept kicking me under the table and rolling her eyes whenever Cam said something fucked up or stupid which was pretty much all of the time.

Everyone seemed to have forgotten, at least temporarily, the video Makayla took, and Taylor didn't seem to give a shit about it anymore, at least for the weekend, which I hope meant she was going to break up with Cam soon and that was why she didn't care.

When we were done with our main courses, before we ordered dessert, Taylor kicked me under the table again and nodded toward the restrooms.

"Come with me," she said. "I gotta go."

So I got up and followed her across the room and down the hall. As soon as we got to the bathroom she opened her purse and pulled out a pint of vodka.

"Jesus," I said. "Don't go anywhere without it?"

"Not if I can help it," she said, twisting off the cap and taking a swig. "Not when I'm with Cam, that's for sure."

"I hope Chase won't mind driving my car," I said, taking a sip.

"He won't care," Taylor said. "Chase is so chill. He never cares about anything."

Then she walked into a stall, lifted her dress, and squatted to pee. Without closing the stall door. Smiling at me the whole time.

CAM SPENCER

Somehow Taylor and Tatum were both drunk by the time we got to the school for the dance. Sloppy drunk and hanging all over each other. Which was fucking annoying. I felt like a third wheel with my own girlfriend, at my own goddamn senior year fucking Homecoming dance. So I started dancing with this other girl whose boyfriend was in the bathroom puking his guts out. I think her name was Tracy but it might have been Lacey. I don't know. Who fucking cares. I didn't give a shit about her. Tracy, Lacey. I was just trying to get my girlfriend to pay attention to me for once. But it didn't work. She barely noticed. She didn't seem to care either. She was too busy tryin to get up in Tatum's bush, which, as I recalled, was a real fucking forest. Real woodsy. Dark.

ANISSA GRANT

We'd been drinking on the drive to the dance, too. Both of us squished together in the front cab of Cam's truck. Taking shots of vodka when Cam wasn't looking. When he stopped for gas. When he spat out the window. I knew he hated me now but what did I care. I had Taylor's attention. The world was my oyster, so to speak. Nothing bad could ever happen to me again, now that I had Taylor's attention.

A song by that girl who used to be on Barney came on (I had some vague memory of doing a movie with her but maybe it was the other girl from Barney, I honestly couldn't remember) and Taylor turned it up and we both started singing and dancing, which I could tell really annoyed Cam, but who the fuck cared, fuck him, FUCK CAM SPENCER UP THE ASS, this was *our night* now. I could feel it.

COACH W

Taylor and Tatum were both obviously intoxicated and dancing together and making a spectacle of themselves. By which I mean, everyone was watching them in the way you'd watch a celebrity couple at a restaurant. Or the only openly bisexual females at a small town Homecoming dance. T&T, I think I'd heard other kids call them.

Except Cam who seemed to be beside himself, grabbing whatever other free girl he could find to make out with on the dance floor even if it didn't result in Taylor batting an eyelash because Taylor was practically making out with Tatum.

I have to admit, it was hot. Lesbian porn watching hot. Barely legal hot. Except one of the two "girls" literally wasn't legal. And the other one I'd developed feelings for. The sort of feelings that make you want to go home, drink a lot of beer, and cry your eyes out because you know it's never going to work out for you, because you're old and washed up and a loser and even if she's not sixteen, she's still a lot younger than you and clearly in love with this other hot young girl and clearly not going to give a fuck about you anymore now that *this* is happening. Now that *her* dreams are coming true. Now that you're nowhere in her mind. Nowhere on her radar. You don't exist anymore. you might as well not even exist.

Which was how I felt before Tatum but it was harder going back now that I'd been seen, by her, even if only for a moment.

MALLORY SWINDELL (Homecoming Queen)

Everyone was staring or trying to watch without seeming like they were staring. Everyone was very *aware*, let's say that, of what was going on with Taylor and Tatum at Homecoming. And aware that their dates, Cam and Chase, were being left out, excluded. Two of the hottest, most popular, desirable guys at school, and Taylor and Tatum were treating them like they could *not* have cared less.

It was pretty shocking. No one had ever seen two cheerleaders hooking up before at Dobson High. You might hear about two goth chicks making out at a party but that was different. That was two goth chicks. No one cared. This was *Taylor Ragner—Cam Spencer's girlfriend—*and "the new girl." The girl from California. The mystery girl. Who knew what *she* was into. What she'd done. Back in California. How she'd tricked Taylor into leaving Cam for her. What lesbian voodoo she was into. Witchy shit. She didn't seem to have a social media history or past. Her life seemed to start here in Elkheart. Which was weird. Super weird. Like someone should warn Taylor weird. But now it maybe was too late. Now Taylor was tonguing her on the Dobson High dance floor for everyone to see.

CHASE WHITING

Cam was pissed, to say the least. I had to take him in the bathroom to calm him down. At first he kept trying to cut in on Tatum but Taylor was belligerently drunk and kept yelling at him to go away, to "get your own girlfriend." Which didn't sit too well with him, as you can imagine. He was really confused and sort of bouncing off the bathroom walls. If Tatum had been a guy, he could have fought him. Taylor wouldn't have liked it and it wouldn't have ultimately done anything except push her farther away, but it would have felt good to Cam in the moment. He could have gotten his rage out, exerted his adrenaline. But because Tatum was another girl, he couldn't hit her or challenge her to a fight. He couldn't do anything. His hands were figuratively but also almost literally tied. I didn't know what to do with him either. I kept trying to calm him down by saying it was just a drunken experimentation. High school girls playing with being "bi." That sort of thing. "Nothing to worry about." "It'll all be over in the morning." "You'll have Taylor back tomorrow." All that shit that I didn't actually believe either. Shit I didn't think was true. But what the hell can you tell your best friend when his girl's getting down with another girl right in front of him? Right in front of everyone. A part of me was jealous, of course, that Tatum was getting what she wanted. I think I'd wanted something similar for a long time, but I wasn't going to get it. It wasn't going to work out for me.

I think I realized in that moment, alone with Cam in the high school bathroom, trying to talk him off the ledge, him out of his mind over Taylor, that I was in love with my best friend, too.

But now wasn't the best time to let him know that. I think he would have killed me if I'd told him in that moment, in that bathroom, him out of his mind over losing Taylor. I think he would have laid me out. Just a knee-jerk reaction. No thought involved. Just more rage.

So I didn't say anything. I never said anything. I just stayed with him. I just kept trying to calm him down.

TAYLOR RAGNER

I honestly wasn't aware of everyone staring. People told me later. Mallory. Keisha. Whitney. I wasn't aware of other people or of Cam. I mean, hell, I knew Cam was pissed. I would have had to have been dead not to know *that*. What I mean is, I didn't care. I didn't give a fuck. About Cam or about anyone at school watching. I was so sick and fucking tired of worrying about what *they*, what Cam, what my mother thought.

I was drunk and at Homecoming and dancing with Tatum and I was happy. I was so happy. The kind of happy I hope Jolie will be someday. The kind of happy where you feel free from all bad thoughts and free from the past and the future and just in the moment. I was in the moment with Tatum.

I didn't know or care where Cam had gone. I was just happy he was out of my periphery, out of my way, leaving us alone. He could have any girl he wanted at school so why did he have to want me.

I didn't know how we were going to get back to Tatum's apartment. I just remember wanting to leave. I just remember all of a sudden needing to go.

CHASE WHITING

An hour after we got to the dance, Taylor wanted to leave. She came up to me, super sweaty, wasted, hanging on my arm, telling me I had to drive them, had to drive her and Tatum back to Tatum's apartment *right now*. Cam was on the dance floor with Ivy Wilkins. Someone had given him some whiskey. Someone else, I think, maybe had given him some molly. I asked our friend Jake to watch him. Told Jake I'd be right back, just had to run Taylor home, that Taylor wasn't feeling well, but not to tell Cam that. I didn't need Cam knowing I was driving Taylor anywhere. I didn't want to be on the receiving end of Cam's rage. I was trying to get through the night without getting the shit beat out of me. I was just trying to survive this night. To survive Homecoming. Like it'd turned very quickly into a Stephen King horror novel. And my best friend was Jack Nicholson, wielding a fucking axe.

ANISSA GRANT

We left the dance with Chase. Got in the backseat of his car. I remember curling up on the seat, putting my head in Taylor's lap, her petting my head, smoothing my hair off my face. I remember looking up at her but she was looking out the window. She was so beautiful. Like an actress in the back of a limo on Oscar night. That's what I remember thinking. In her beautiful ivory satin gown. Her hair up. even sweaty and makeup smeared and hair a mess, she was beautiful. Gorgeous. Unbelievably gorgeous.

CHASE WHITING

I parked outside Tatum's apartment and the girls insisted I walk them to the door and then insisted I come inside. I hadn't had anything to drink. I was DD'ing it for the night. I needed to get back to the high school to check on Cam. He was blowing up my phone. *Where the fuck ru? Where the fuck is my girl?* He'd already tried to call me four times. I didn't think the girls needed an audience, anyhow. They seemed pretty intent on what was going to happen next. They were both smoking cigarettes, still sipping from the bottle of vodka in Taylor's purse.

"Goodnight," I told them. "Don't drink too much more. I don't want either of you getting alcohol poisoning."

"We won't, Chase'y," Taylor said. "Thank you, Chase'y!"

She threw her arms around my neck, cigarette still burning in her hand.

Tatum came up behind her and stretched her arms out around the both of us so we were all in this big hug sandwich.

"I love you, Chase'y," Taylor said.

"We love you," Tatum said.

I didn't stop to look around the place, to wonder where Tatum's mom was, why no one had ever met her mom. I only thought of that later, hours later, home alone in bed. The last glimpse I caught of the girls was of them dancing in the moonlight coming in the sliding glass door. Dancing and smoking cigarettes. Like they were in an Aerosmith video from the 80s. Like one of them was Steven Tyler's daughter and the other one was that girl from *Clueless*. (My dad *loves* Aerosmith.)

I got in my car and just sat there a minute. I didn't want to go back to the school but I couldn't leave Cam. I knew he needed me. I drove across the street to the 7-Eleven for a Slurpee and a Moonpie. I needed something to get me through this night and I couldn't drink so sugar was going to have to be it. Sugar was going to have to be my Homecoming vice.

ANISSA GRANT

After Chase left, Taylor and I danced in the living room for a bit. Smoked cigarettes. Drank some vodka and then I drank a big glass of water out of the sink in the kitchen. Taylor stuck her whole head under the faucet. She had water running down her chin and she wouldn't stop grinning.

"What the fuck are you grinning at?" I said.

"You," she said. "I'm fucking grinning at you, Tatum Grant."

Then we went into the bedroom, unzipped each other's dresses and fell on my bed. Taylor was wearing only her thong and bra and I was in a pair of boxer briefs and a strapless bra. We were both drunk.

Taylor said, "Why are you wearing so many clothes? You're always wearing so many clothes, when you sleepover. Stop it. Stop wearing so many goddamn clothes."

She was tugging at my bra. I laughed and reached around to unhook it. Her hands were all over me, my face, my tits. She leaned forward on her knees to mouth them, to slide my nipples in her wet, hot mouth. I moaned and reached around to unhook her bra. I barely got a look, her tits were everywhere. I wanted them in my mouth but before I could get to them she sat up and pulled the back of my head down toward hers. Her tongue was finally in my mouth. I could feel myself growing wetter, my legs weakening. We laid back on the bed, side by side, our tits pressing together. I reached down and felt between her legs without pulling away from her mouth. The only porn I watched was girl on girl, but the kind made for hetero couples to watch. I didn't know if this was what "real lesbian sex" was like. I didn't know anything. I just knew it felt good to finally be naked in my bed with Taylor. I didn't care what we did. I wanted her to sit on my face and I wanted to make her come with my fingers inside her. I wanted to make her come again and again and then smoke more weed and fuck her with my wet fingers again. Her face was so beautiful, sweaty and flushed, like after running. Her mouth was so warm and wet, like her pussy.

She got on top of me and I felt her hair all around my face like a dark curtain. I felt her soft mouth again on mine. Her bare chest pushed on top of me. Her thighs wrapped around. I closed my eyes. I didn't want to open them again. I wanted to wake up with her still wrapped around me, naked on top of me. I wanted to sleep this way every night.

But when I woke up later at three or four in the morning she was wrapped around me, big spoon. And I remember laughing softly to myself because if you'd asked me when we first met that day waiting in line to get our school ID photo taken who would be big spoon and who would be little, I 100% would have said she'd be little. Which just goes to show, you never know till it happens what you'll do in any given situation.

Walk a mile.

Walk two.

You don't know what it's like to be face to face with Taylor Ragner.

You forget your age.

You forget where you came from.

What your name is.

That you were ever nominated for an Oscar.

That you're a mother.

That you were once in love with Quinn James before he died, tragically, before he became an icon, when you were both still young and hopeless and dead inside.

With Taylor I felt alive. I *was* alive.

These moments, in her arms, my fingers smelling of her pussy, my fingers in her mouth, were enough to go to prison for, enough even to die for. These moments were a Lana del Rey song, a Lana del Rey video, an Amy Winehouse lyric, an Amy Winehouse tattoo, under my hair, on my inner wrist, along my thigh.

COACH W

I couldn't believe I'd spent all these years resisting temptation, even when temptation was doing a really fucking proactive job of testing me, only to end up fucking a student who wasn't even a student.

I was a fuck up even when I thought I was fucking up.

I couldn't even fuck up right.

Up was down. Down was up.

Fuck was up. Up was fucked.

I drove out to Quinn's grave that night with a fifth of Jaeger, our old favorite black-out drink. Someone had left kiss marks on his grave. Someone was always leaving something. Cigarettes. Bottles of booze. Needles.

It was kinda fucked up.

But so was Quinn. So was I.

So who was I to judge?

How anyone mourned or honored my dead best friend.

I got really drunk out there, sitting on top of Quinn, leaning back on his headstone.

I said hi to his grandma next door.

Tipped my hat to her.

She was the sweetest old lady.

She made the best candy buckeyes.

You know those chocolate peanut butter balls?

She made them every Christmas for Quinn.

Lined a coffee can with wax paper and stuck them inside.

Someone in her family was from Ohio. The buckeye state.

Brutus and all that shit.

Sometimes she made me a tin, too. Normally, I didn't care much for the chocolate peanut butter combo, Reese's and shit. But I ate the hell out of Mamah's buckeyes.

Quinn and I sure as fuck did.

CAM SPENCER

I don't remember Taylor leaving the dance. I don't remember Chase taking me home.

I woke up the next morning with a killer headache, parched, so dehydrated, in my briefs and tie and socks, looking around my room, going WHAT THE FUCK, DUDE?

I had no idea what'd happened.

I texted Taylor but she didn't text back.

I texted Chase like WHAT THE FUCK.

Half an hour later he replied, "I know, right?"

But I didn't know. I still didn't have any fucking clue.

I texted him back, "Come over. We'll lift."

My parents were away visiting my brother at his university.

I needed all the blanks filled in. I needed to know how pissed I was going to be.

"Bring Gatorade and Advil," I told Chase.

Then I got dressed and went for a run. I vomited twice. I had to get this shit out of my system, the same way I needed to get rid of Taylor. But it wasn't that easy with Taylor. I couldn't just vomit her out. I couldn't kill her either.

TAYLOR RAGNER

In the morning Tatum made us iced coffees from a jar of cold brew she had in the fridge and we drank them in bed while watching *Chaotic*, the Britney Spears/Kevin Federline reality show. There were only five episodes and we watched all five while smoking cigarettes and making out and eating each other out.

Tatum had a thing for Britney which I "got" but I liked K-Fed, he looked and acted like a white Snoop Dogg. And who doesn't like Snoop Dogg?

It was like the best Sunday I'd ever had in my life. I wasn't checking my phone and Tatum wasn't checking hers. We'd made a promise not to check until 5 pm.

At 5 pm the shit would hit the fan. My mom, Cam, *everyone*.

But until 5 we were living our own version of *Chaotic*, in Tatum's apartment in Elkheart, Indiana instead of on the road in fancy hotel rooms in Europe.

At one point we even made our own video.

ANISSA GRANT

Taylor was wearing a pair of Guess underwear she'd bought at the fancy mall we'd gone to in Indianapolis, the kind designed to look like sexy men's briefs.

I was down between her legs, pushing her sexy underwear to the side so I could shove my tongue in. Britney was asking K-Fed how he felt about marriage. "I don't believe in it," he was saying but we all knew how that turned out.

"I like that you don't shave your pussy," Taylor said. "I'm going to stop getting mine waxed."

"Okay," I said, looking up from my vantage point between her thighs. "Either way. I don't care."

She said, "I'm not shaving my armpits anymore either!"

And I said, "That's hot," because I'd always thought—like cigarette smoking—it was hot when done by a hot chick (or man). Like, I'd seen old photographs of Madonna with hairy armpits and I found it attractive, sexy, something to push your face into. Instead of an absence. A place for pheromones to thrive. Another sex mound. It made no sense, when you thought about it, to shave it off.

I couldn't wait for the hair to grow in under Taylor's arms.

I was in denial about how long this could last. I was pretending we were normal high school girls in love. Like we could go on hanging out watching reality TV and banging forever if we wanted. Like we had parental shit and boyfriend shit and teacher shit to deal with but nothing that could keep us apart, nothing major to get in our way.

CHASE WHITING

I texted Taylor on my way to Cam's but she didn't respond. I was worried about the blow up. I couldn't keep Cam in the dark forever. I couldn't lie to him about dropping Taylor off at Tatum's the night before.

I was going to have to tell him the truth eventually and once I did he was going to lose his fucking mind. He was going to lose his shit and all of us were going to pay.

I stopped for Gatorade and Advil and took two of the latter. I bought another Moonpie, and ate it on the drive. I felt like I was going to throw up even though I wasn't hung over.

I wanted to get on the highway and keep driving in any direction. I wanted Cam to see me the way I saw him. Then maybe he could let all this shit with Taylor go. He didn't *need* her, but he'd never see it that way. I didn't *need* him either, but I wanted him.

I kept thinking back now to this time when he and I were twelve or thirteen, home alone at my house during a sleepover. We'd gotten into my parents' liquor cabinet, mixed together all these different liquors we didn't know: rums and whiskeys and vodkas and sweet liqueurs. Of course, we both ended up puking our guts out but before that, in that sweet spot between sobriety and vomiting, that may have lasted all of thirty minutes the way we were pounding down this wicked concoction, there was some experimentation, some kissing and touching. I remember Cam came in my hand. It was so unexpected. Seeing his semen there in my palm. We both just laughed. But a part of me felt sad washing it away, watching it go down the drain in the basement bathroom.

But we never talked about it the next day. We never talked about what happened that night, ever again.

But I couldn't stop thinking about it. I never stopped thinking about it over the years. What it might have meant, for Cam and for me.

And lately I'd been obsessing over it. Reliving it while I masturbate every morning and most nights. I kept wondering if Cam ever thought about it. I wanted to ask him but I was too scared of how he would react if I did. Maybe he'd pushed that night far out of his mind, had no memory of it at all anymore.

I pulled the car to the side of the road, opened my door, and threw up the Moonpie. It was chocolate, anyway. Banana was the only good one but they were out of banana. I guess everyone liked banana.

COACH W

I'd been sober ten years and then all of a sudden—like that [snaps fingers]—I was a drunk again. I could blame it on Tatum, which I definitely did for a while, blame her for my unraveling, my undoing, but ultimately it was my own fault. All of it. I'd started messing around with her when I still thought she was a student. I'd started drinking, just a beer or two, to try and deal with that, with the idea I was sleeping with a student, that I could lose my job, wipe out my career. I'd started drinking more once I realized she wasn't sixteen, wasn't a student, was something else entirely, I didn't know what. And I'd started drinking to the point of blacking out when I realized she'd forgotten me for Taylor. Taylor Ragner. Who wouldn't forget me for Taylor Ragner. I was no competition. I was a pathetic middle-aged high school acting teacher and Taylor was an almost sixteen-year-old drop-dead-gorgeous, charisma-of-a-serial-killer cheerleader. I'm sure she had the pussy of a Greek goddess, too. I had the semi-flaccid penis of a guy ordering pharmaceuticals off the internet.

I was no competition for anyone

I never had been, though, that's the thing

You'd have thought I would have been used to it by now.

I don't know what my fucking problem was.

Why I ever thought this would go any different; why I was so fucking pissed off.

ANABEL RAGNER

It was noon on the Sunday after Homecoming and I couldn't get a hold of Taylor. I'd been texting her since 9 a.m.

Finally, I texted Cam. I figured he'd know where Taylor was. I didn't have Tatum's phone number, which was a mistake. I should have gotten it a long time ago. I should have insisted she give it to me the first day she came to my house, wiggling her little ass, shaking her pom poms. I should have seen then what kind of person she was, what effect she was having on my daughter, on *my* baby.

Cam replied right away, said he thought she was with Tatum, at Tatum's apartment. He didn't explicitly say he couldn't get a hold of her either, that he hadn't heard from her either. He was still probably trying to cover for her to some extent. I was still a mom and he was still Taylor's boyfriend. He still had the instinctive loyalty to Taylor that Taylor apparently no longer had for him.

I said, "Okay, thanks, Cam."

I didn't tell him I was giving her another couple hours, and then I was going over there, over to Tatum's. I didn't care if I embarrassed her. Or if she didn't like it. At some point you have to stop trying to be your child's best friend, you have to get over caring if they're mad at you, if they like you or not. For their own best interest. For their own safety and mental health and welfare. For the sake of their vagina, if nothing else.

CAM SPENCER

I tried to warn Taylor. I texted her that her mom was looking for her, that she'd texted me, but she still didn't reply. Maybe she wasn't looking at her phone. She was probably too tied up eating Tatum's ass to check her messages.

Chase had come over and brought me my meds: the Gatorade and Advil, and we'd gone down to the basement to work out. I'd had to fish it out of him, ask him 20 questions, the whole nine yards, but he finally confessed it all: driving the girls to Tatum's, how they were both drunk and high as fuck, dancing and making out, all over each other, both at the high school and in the middle of Tatum's apartment.

I'd known for a while Taylor wasn't all that happy, that she wanted "to explore the world" and "have new experiences." That Oprah bullshit.

I figured she'd wanted to see what it was like to eat pussy, to be with a girl, and now she knew and maybe now we could move on with our lives.

I saw it as a one-time thing. A once in a lifetime experience.

Taylor didn't read gay. She liked dick. She sure as hell had liked *my dick*. She sure as fuck had *begged for it* on a number of occasions.

I didn't think overnight she would totally lez out.

That she'd no longer need me, or my dick. That she'd do a complete sexual 180. That she'd fall for a girl. Especially not Tatum Grant. *I'd* had Tatum. She wasn't all that. Which was something Taylor didn't know, of course. Which was something maybe Taylor needed to know, something maybe Taylor was going to find out.

ANISSA GRANT

Of course Taylor's mom came looking for her. We should have been expecting it. We shouldn't have still been naked in bed at four on Sunday watching *Chaotic*, stoned out of our minds. It wasn't like everyone didn't know where I lived, like we were hiding out at an unknown location, the Chateau Marmont or wherever. We just were not thinking at all. We were in total La La Land. Total denial that anyone cared, that anyone would come looking.

But at four on the dot, Anabel Ragner came knocking.

I got up and looked through the peephole with Taylor standing in her underwear behind me.

"Just a minute," I yelled through the door.

"One minute," Taylor echoed me and then we both went running back to the bedroom, throwing on clothes. I gave Taylor a pair of sweats to borrow and a tank top and threw on a pair of shorts and t-shirt.

Anabel wasn't too happy when we finally opened the door. The apartment was a mess and Taylor and I were a mess and the place probably reeked of cigarette and pot smoke.

"Where's your mom?" Anabel said.

"She's already at my aunt's," I said. "She's been there since early this morning. She hardly ever gets a break anymore."

"Come on Taylor. Get your stuff, let's go," she said.

"Ok, one sec. I'll be right there. Wait for me in the car," Taylor said and pushed her mom back out the door and grabbed me to kiss me. We were just like every disgusting high school couple now. We couldn't keep our hands off each other, couldn't keep our tongues out of each other's mouths.

Soon as she left I checked my phone and there was a text from Cam, "You gna tell her or should I?"

He didn't have to elaborate. I knew exactly what he meant.

TAYLOR RAGNER

Soon as I got in the car my mom started in on me.

"What is going on, Taylor? Why couldn't I or *your boyfriend* get a hold of you?"

"He's not my boyfriend anymore, Mom," I said.

"Oh really?" she said. "Does he know that? Have you bothered to tell Cam that?"

"I'll tell him!" I said. Jesus. Like he couldn't figure it out. Like why did my mom care so much what Cam thought, what Cam felt. *I* was her daughter, not Cam.

She never seemed to care that much about my thoughts or feelings.

Sometimes I thought she'd be happier with Cam as a son than with me as her daughter.

Then she started in on Tatum.

"And what about Tatum? What's going on there that I need to know about, huh, Taylor?"

"Jesus, Mom," I said. "What do you care? It's not like I can get *pregnant*. So you can stop worrying."

That shut her up, for a second, anyway. Long enough for me to stare out the window, remembering the way Tatum's tongue felt on me, *in* me.

I just wanted to be eighteen, already, an adult. Capable of making my own decisions. Without running them by Anabel Ragner or Cam fucking Whiting. Without clearing it with everyfuckingone before I engaged in cunnilingus with my fucking girlfriend.

I sent a text to Tatum, "SMW."

Tatum replied, "Totally. 100%. <3."

CAM SPENCER

I drove over to Taylor's house at seven p.m. on Sunday night. Her mom said she had to take Jolie to Target, that she'd be back in an hour. She didn't need to be gone that long. It only took five minutes after her mom pulled out of the drive for Taylor to tell me we were done.

"I just can't do this anymore, Cam, I'm sorry," she said.

But she didn't look sorry. She looked fucking elated, like she was trying to hide how goddamn happy she was now that she'd traded me in for Tatum. Now that she'd traded in *my* dick for *her* pussy.

"What are you talking about, Taylor?" I said. I was trying not to lose it, trying not to bitch out and cry. "You can't do *what* anymore? Us? This? What happened? What the fuck is going on with you?"

"I don't know," she said. "I don't know what you want from me. I just want to be fifteen, to live my life, to not have so much pressure on it and on me, from my mom and you, I can't take it."

"Oh, now *I'm* in the same category as your mom? I'm the bad guy?"

"You're not the bad guy, Cam. But I don't want to be the bad guy, either. Why can't you just let us be friends? Why does it have to be this huge drama?"

"Um, it's this 'huge drama' because we were supposed to get married and spend the rest of our lives together, Taylor, remember that?" I said. "Because you said you loved me forever."

"I know," she said. "But I was thirteen, Cam. People change. People grow up and want different things."

"I see," I said. "So, now, let me get this straight: when you were thirteen you liked dick but then you grew up and now, now that you're a grown ass woman at age fifteen, now, now you like pussy? So are you gay now, Taylor? Are you a lesbian? A fucking dyke? Have you been a dyke this whole fucking time? Was my girlfriend secretly a fucking dyke bitch this whole fucking time? Is that what you're telling me, Taylor? Because you could have fooled me. You did fool me, actually. I guess I was just a fool this whole fucking time. Because, I don't know, I'm no fucking expert, but it seemed, it seemed, Taylor, like you liked fucking dick! You seemed to like sucking it and you really seemed, seemed to me, anyway, to like fucking it!"

"No, you weren't a fool, Cam. I did want you. I don't know what I am. But, yeah, I want Tatum. I want to get to know Tatum and to be with Tatum. And I want my independence. I want my freedom. I want to be allowed to *not know* what I want. At fifteen. I think that's okay. I think that should be alright."

That's when I'd had enough. I saw the look on her face. She didn't want to talk to me anymore. She was hoping I'd leave. So she could text Tatum. So she could shit talk me with her new girlfriend. So I left.

"Okay, Taylor," I said. "Good luck with all that. Good luck with this journey you're on, having fish for dinner, whatever the fuck it is you're on."

And I got in my truck and pulled out the drive and didn't look back. I turned off her road onto the main road into town and I pulled the truck over to the side of the road. I was bawling my fucking eyes out. I couldn't believe this was fucking happening, that it was all over, all my dreams for our future, it was all falling apart in my lap, and all because some new girl had moved to town, all because of Tatum Grant, whoever the fuck she was, some *bitch*. I couldn't help thinking if she'd never moved here, Taylor and I would still be together. This would all still be okay. Taylor wouldn't be a dyke and we'd still be in love and heading toward marriage. Toward our life together. We'd still be fucking okay. Everything would be fucking fine. If it wasn't for Tatum. If Tatum had never moved to our fucking town.

TAYLOR RAGNER

I was so relieved when Cam finally left. It felt like a thousand years we were standing there, arguing about this. Or him lecturing me about this. Him calling me a dyke like a zillion times. I ran back up the stairs to my room to text Tatum and then it hit me. And then I was on my knees on my floor. I was terrified Cam would kill me. Like OJ killed Nicole and that guy. Kill *us*. Me *and* Tatum. He wasn't going to let this be this easy. That wasn't the Cam way. Neither was killing himself. Like Lance or Chen or Joby. He was way too selfish for that. But he wasn't going to just let this go. I didn't know if he'd ever let me go. I knew in his mind I belonged to him. Like a goddamn slave or doll. Like Rihanna and Chris Brown.

But just as quickly I pushed the thoughts out of my mind. "Fuck you, Cam Spencer! You're done fucking with my mind. I'm not going to let you manipulate me anymore. I'm *not*."

I wasn't going to let him ruin this moment for me. My freedom. My liberation. I wasn't going to let him ruin me falling in love with Tatum. I wasn't going to allow him any more time or space in my life. In my head. In my vagina.

I didn't care how much Adderall he was taking, how many steroids he was on!

CAM SPENCER

I don't know why I didn't tell Taylor then, about Tatum and me. Honestly, I think I forgot. I was too caught up in losing Taylor to remember Tatum.

It was only after I got home and stopped crying and calmed down that I remembered I still had that.

I was going to hold onto it a bit longer.

See how it played out.

Maybe I wasn't done fucking with Tatum. Maybe now that Taylor had dumped me I was more into hurting Tatum than I was into trying to get Taylor back.

Maybe I wanted to see what I could get Tatum to do for me, to keep me quiet.

Maybe I wanted to see if she would fuck me again. See how much she really liked Taylor. What it was worth to her for Taylor not to find out what a little slut she was, what a liar. What a backstabber and betrayer. A fucking dyke whore.

I was going fucking crazy. I was drinking a bottle of Jack I'd stashed in my room. I was eating the Adderalls I'd stole from Jake's.

I texted Chase, "There's something else no one knows. Something about Tatum."

I took another swig from the bottle while waiting for him to text back.

CHASE WHITING

If Taylor and Tatum thought this whole thing was going to blow over any time soon, they were really stupid. If they thought Cam was going to let this go, they were fucking insane. I knew Taylor wasn't that naïve; that she'd seen Cam get crazy before; but still, it was nothing like that, nothing like in the past. He was texting me nonstop, all this shit about revenge and getting what's coming to you and something about his "ace in the hole." About having something "up my sleeve."

I think he was taking more and more 'roids and they were fucking with his head. Working out nonstop.

I kept trying to talk him down off the ledge, kept trying to talk some sense into him, point him in the direction of a dozen girls who were dying to go out with Cam Spencer. Fuck Homecoming King Cam Spencer. But he didn't want to be distracted. He was a man on a mission. Like a boxer before a fight. He was obsessed with Taylor and Tatum, with making their lives miserable, with making them "pay." For whatever injustice they'd caused him. For whatever pain he wasn't dealing with.

On top of it there was still the legal issues with the video Makayla had made. Which he also wasn't dealing with. Which he was also ignoring.

To cope with it all I started beating off more. Beating off and eating Moonpies. I was constantly at 7-Eleven.

ANISSA GRANT

Everything was happening so fast. I didn't have time to think about Coach W, to worry about his jealousies and pettiness like I should have. Like I would have had I had another couple days to come out of this euphoria I was feeling after having sex with Taylor. After falling 100% in mad love with her, in a way I hadn't even fallen for Quinn.

I never should have taken my eye off Coach W, though. I totally underestimated his nice guy persona / façade.

Never underestimate a woman scorned or a man forgotten.

I'd never seen *Fatal Attraction* but I should have.

Maybe I would have seen it coming if I had, what happened next.

I just thank God I didn't have a rabbit. Or a pot to put it in.

TAYLOR RAGNER

Those first couple days after Homecoming, Tatum and I were just in a blissed out daze. We were obsessed with each other and obsessed with Britney and K-Fed. We watched those five episodes over and over in Tatum's bed, smoking weed and cigarettes after school or after cheer practice.

We went around talkin' with Britney Spears' accents. Or mostly I did because Tatum loved it; she *begged* me to do it. She thought it was so sexy. So I played it up. I made grits with slices of Velveeta cheese and brought them to her in bed and said, "Hey, y'all, whatcha know about my fav-rit home-style grits?" I said, "Who wants to go to the eye-full tao-er?" I said, "Some-then's up."

And sometimes Tate'd put on a hat and low-slung sweats or jeans and do a K-Fed impersonation. Squint her eyes up real tight, take a long drag on a cigarette, smile real Cheshire Cat like, say, "There was a couple times when she threw me off and I was just like… whoa."

Which made me laugh and made me wet. Her lookin' all masculine / feminine. It was hot.

We even made some videos of us as Britney and K-Fed.

In them my hair's pulled back under a trucker hat and I'm wearing a white tank and no bra like Britney and I'm sayin', "Huh? Huh?" a lot and "I don't know why I just said that *werd*."

And Tatum as K-Fed would say all low voiced and sexy, "I don't know why she was so nervous, I guess cuz she had *feelings*."

Britney was so happy and carefree then, in the *Chaotic* episodes. So charismatic and funny. It's sad to think what happens after that, after things fell apart with Kevin and she went apeshit and shaved her head and got an umbrella. Tatum had *Britney: for the record* too but it was too sad to watch. We only watched the first few minutes. Britney was biting her nails the whole time, twitching her feet and legs. She wasn't happy Britney anymore. She wasn't carefree and spontaneous. She was sad-eyed and anxious; broken.

Tatum turned it off, said it was too sad to watch.

I made my best Britney pouty face and she kissed me. Kissed my big fat pouty bottom lip. We were still blissed out, still in our *Chaotic* phase. Still carefree.

PRINCIPAL PITT

Nowadays, with the phone technology the way it is, you had underage kids sending photos of themselves naked or of *their* genitals, their genitalia, and that was a sex crime, because they were underage. Didn't matter that it was a picture of themselves, of their own genitals, because they couldn't legally consent, because they weren't legal adults, they weren't eighteen, in the eyes of the courts.

So now a photograph of yourself, a "selfie," was problematic, was a crime, in the eyes of the law.

Let alone receiving a photograph of your underage teen girlfriend or boyfriend.

Any one of these "crimes" could end you up on the sex offenders' list with a charge or charges of child pornography.

Even if you hadn't asked for the photo in question, even if you had no part in it being sent to you.

Ostensibly a whole student body could be brought up on child pornography charges for a single photo being forwarded around on the kids' phones.

It was a bit of a nightmare for us, for those of us overseeing the student body, those of us in the school administration.

Cam was going to be made an example. We were going to have to sacrifice Cam and maybe Makayla to save the others.

TAYLOR RAGNER

It only took five days for the hair under my arms to cause a minor uproar. I'm really hairy on account of my Latina heritage. It's like, have you ever seen early photos of Madonna? Like the really old b&w ones? Some amateur photographer took? Back when she was at the University of Michigan? She's hairy as fuck. Unibrow. Hairy pits. Hairy arms. That's me. So much hair!

My pits looked like Frida Kahlo's eyebrows in no time.

My mom was the first to notice.

"Taylor," she said. "What's up with your lack of self-care, your lack of grooming, lately? You've always been so meticulous about how you look, about your hair and body. Are you *trying* to turn Cam away?"

I said, "Mom, I keep telling you, Cam and I are *done*. We're broken up. We're not getting back together."

She refused to believe me.

"You're just going through a phase," she said. Just like Cam. Cam kept saying, "I'll still be here when you're done with this… *journey*… or whatever it is you're going through."

I kept telling them both, "I'm gay! I'm in love with a Tatum."

But neither one of them would listen, neither of them would hear me.

Then the other cheerleaders noticed.

Mallory and Keisha and then Ms. Harden.

Ms. Harden said, "Look, Taylor, I honestly don't care. I really don't. But the school… the student body… your fellow cheer team… Principal Pitt, they're all complaining, they're all riding my ass about it. So just do me a favor, do me a solid, and shave?"

But I refused. On feminist grounds. On my rights as a woman.

So they cut me from the team.

Apparently, I didn't have any rights, after all.

If you can believe that shit.

2016 and you can't let the hair under your arms grow if you're female without it being a huge school fucking drama. Like, what?

I said to my mom, "Mom, what kind of example is this to Jolie? That I can't have hair under my arms because I'm *female*?"

She didn't say anything to that.

Tatum just laughed.

"People are stupid, Taylor," she said.

Little did we know the hair under my arms would soon be the least of our problems. That we'd yearn for the day that my unshaved pits were the most important topic of conversation.

COACH HARDEN

I'd been a silent witness to this whole Taylor/Tatum/Cam business all fall and into winter.

As a gay, but newly "out," woman myself—it'd only really been "safe" for me to "come out" a couple years earlier, and the kind of "coming out" that wasn't too in the town's face, if you know what I mean, like, "You can be gay but just, be gay *quietly*, like, over there, in the corner," you know? ike I think they were afraid if I was too openly gay and working with teen girls, some parents would have a problem with it, you know? And god forbid any of the teen girls I worked with "go gay", which was exactly what was happening. Not that they… I mean, you and I know they didn't *go gay*… but for all the town knows, for all the school board thinks…

So, anyway, yeah. I was sort of watching the whole thing unfold from the cheer team side of things. Which was where Tatum and Taylor really bonded, really became close. They were so cute together. Always joking around together at practices. Acting goofy, playing practical jokes on each other and the other girls, on me. Before everything blew up in their faces, I mean.

Which was when I sort of had to step up and say something, help them. Try and guide them through the chaos, because I'd been through it myself, years earlier, with my family and school and stuff, back in Texas. And I figured if I could survive coming out in Texas, they could do it in Elkheart, Indiana.

Boy, was I wrong.

The Midwest is a whole 'nother apple.

You'd think it would be way more open-minded, way more accepting, but you'd be wrong. I'm sorry to say.

These girls didn't stand a chance, as it turns out. And maybe it was in part because they were so classically, traditionally "pretty" or mainstream. Maybe if they'd looked more "bulldyke" like me, more masculine, or been less popular, people wouldn't have cared, would have left them alone. But the community or student body felt like the girls owed them something more because of how they looked, like "them." Because of what they represented. Because they were "popular." I honestly think Taylor's age was much less an issue than how they looked, than who they *were*. This was: *Taylor. Ragner.* Girl next door, town sweetheart. Jennifer Aniston back in her *Friends* days.

It was the same problem Miley Cyrus had when she no longer wanted to be Hannah Montana, when she dared to cut her hair, to be her own person, with her own very in your face wants and opinions and desires, especially the sexual ones.

People aren't ready for the liberated sexuality of young women.

Miley Cyrus couldn't show her bared back in a magazine without people losing their shit, losing their minds.

I had to cut Taylor. My hands were tied. Principal Pitt made me cut her over the underarm hair, which was ridiculous, yes, but maybe not being on the team would bring her and Tatum less eyes, less criticism. Maybe it was for the best. That's how I rationalized it anyway. That's how I lived with myself. After I told Taylor I was cutting her.

Of course Tatum immediately quit in solidarity.

I knew she would. I expected nothing less.

MAKAYLA RICHEY

Chase didn't know that night I could see him, there on the stairs in the dark. He saw what was happening and he didn't go back up to his room. He just stood there on the staircase the entire time I was giving Cam head. I could even see his hard-on through the thin nylon of his basketball shorts. He probably went up and jacked off after. The thing is I'm pretty sure he wasn't turned on by me but by seeing his buddy Cam. Everyone at school suspected he was gay and in love with his best friend, except, maybe, Cam.

It finally made sense to me that night, why Chase had rejected me. Politely, nicely, but still: rejected me. He didn't want me, he wanted Cam. Or maybe Matt. Or maybe Coach W. But he sure as fuck didn't want me and my *vagina*.

And he didn't want Taylor. And he didn't want Tatum, either.

TAYLOR RAGNER

Coach W was always going on about truth and how the truth changes and how truths are subject to fads, like everything else in history. Yesterday he'd gone on about Oscar Wilde. He was going on today about how it used to be a "fact" that the earth was flat and a fact that homosexuality was a mental illness and a fact that rock 'n' roll was going to rot the brains of the youth.

I wished he could have talked to my mother.

She seemed intent on supporting my little brother's transformation to being my little sister in first grade and just as intent on ruining my life for being in love with a girl!

I mean, hello! Hypocrisy!!

I wanted to take Jolie with Tatum and me and run away, raise her in California or Portland or Key West, somewhere *progressive*. Jolie was never going to be treated the way I thought she should be treated in this town. The town wanted Jolie to reflect them the way my mother wanted me to reflect her.

COACH HARDEN

Another thing that was happening at that time was a succession of popular nonfiction books about adolescent/teen female sexuality were being published and publicized.

Every time I turned on NPR that year there was another woman promoting her book about teen girls and sex.

How sexist is *that*?

Where were the books about male adolescent sexuality?

Oh, right, there weren't any.

Because, news flash, male sexuality is accepted, expected, OKAY, taken for granted.

But female sexuality, that's where all the problems lie. All religion. All politics.

No one, including women, maybe, *especially women*, want to allow that a female is inherently sexual, especially a "young" adolescent female.

I kept hearing parents, mothers especially, say: "I'm okay with her having sex as long as she's in a committed, loving relationship." [holds hand out open-palmed] You think they said that about their boys? [guffaws]

Well, news alert: we are. We *are* sexual beings.

We don't *need* to be "sexualized", Terri Gross. (Have you *seen* Sixteen & Pregnant, Terri Gross?)

We are sexual beings, *just like boys*, just like men.

Just like horny perverted high school male teachers. Just like them.

COACH W

We were reading the ancient Greeks and talking about pederasty and pedagogy. I'd been teaching these concepts for ten years and only in the last twelve months or so had it become "sensitive material," controversial to teach.

I wasn't *advocating* anything, you see, merely teaching *history*. But some parents thought teaching history was advocating what in our current time and culture was viewed by some, perhaps the majority, as sexual abuse or statutory rape.

But the students were almost always interested, with the exception of one or two homophobic males who were probably, in reality, the most interested of all.

We also read about Sappho, read some of her poetry, talked about why she was important.

We read about the Greek gods who chose younger men or boys to fight for and to love.

"The ancient Greeks, as we learn, very rarely if ever participated in what we today would refer to as 'oral sex,'" I said. "Perhaps the most common form of 'sex' if we want to label what occurred between adolescent males, aged 12-18, and older males, was intercrural sex, meaning, the penis between the thighs. They would also distinguish between pederasty—sex with the aforementioned 12-18 year olds—and androphilia—homosexual sex between two adult males, which was actually frowned upon, as men acting 'feminine' as they would view it, was frowned upon, and adult men were also supposed to take a wife and procreate heterosexually."

"Often what transpired in these courtships between an older or adult male and an adolescent male was gift-giving from the older to the younger, wrestling, reading of poetry, talk of politics and philosophy, and at the symposiums, feasting and drinking and light petting, and kissing. Often-times, what we consider sex, *anal sex*, never occurred."

After that last lesson I received five complaints from parents. Up three from the previous school year. I was waiting on Principal Pitt to call me down to his office, tell me I had to stop talking about the ancient Greeks and their kinky sex practices.

COACH HARDEN

I got complaints from parents all the time. It's part of the territory, when you teach sex ed in public schools. They don't want you to teach girls it feels *good* or it's okay to *feel good* or that you *should* feel good. They want you to teach girls abstinence and that losing their virginity is something to think about, something to make special.

But it doesn't have to be. Nor should it be, *necessarily…*

And god forbid you talk about orgasms, with high school females. God forbid you talk about masturbation, *with high school females.*

God forbid you encourage either or both.

You just might be a pervert, getting off on thinking about a young woman orgasming. Instead of trying to encourage healthy sexuality. Independent pleasure-seeking. Self-love and self-care. An awareness of one's body and how it works.

Just stick to the negative sides of female sexuality, like pregnancy and STDs and rape culture and never mind teaching the girls anything positive about their bodies and sex. Leave that to the boys, to the men. To Coach W and Cam and Chase.

We're *women.* We're not supposed to bother ourselves with feeling good.

We're just to concentrate on preventing unwanted pregnancies and STDs and sex outside of a "committed relationship." A committed *hetero* relationship, to be specific.

I was not to talk about gay sex in any "explicit" manner. Meaning, I wasn't supposed to talk about it at all.

And I sure as hell wasn't supposed to mention Hillary Clinton. [grins]

CHASE WHITING

I wished Cam was in our class so he could hear all this shit about the Ancient Greeks, so maybe his curiosity would be peaked just a little. So maybe he'd have something else to think about for two seconds besides Taylor and getting even with her and Tatum.

My sister told me, recently, when she came home for a weekend, she thought she and Coach W were going to have sex when she was a senior, like four years ago. "And I think I would have been okay with it," she told me. "I wanted it to happen. I told my friends we were going to, that it was just a matter of time, an inevitability. He was so hot, especially after he got his braces off."

Yeah, apparently Coach W had had braces. As a thirty-something-year-old man.

"I was pretty disappointed, to be honest, when it didn't happen," Shailey said. "It would have been better than the sex I had with Ryan, that's for sure."

Ryan was her high school boyfriend. He's *out* now. Living in Chicago. Going to Northwestern. Majoring in Theater. Go figure.

ANISSA GRANT

I could feel Colton, Coach W, throwing me shade in the halls. I could feel him watching me. Watching Taylor and me. I knew he was branching from normal interest level into psycho obsession. But I wasn't worried about it because what was he going to say? What was he going to do? He'd fucked a student (me). He couldn't do shit.

Taylor and I were pretending to be in this untouchable bubble. She'd text me to meet her in the bathroom during classes. We'd both get a hall pass, and she'd be waiting for me, pull me into a stall, sit on my lap, facing me, her tongue instantly in my mouth.

But the thing was, *everyone* was able to touch us. Sooner or later.

First Coach Harden, throwing us off the cheer team. Then Taylor's mom, trying to come between us. Then Cam, and Coach W, and Principal Pitt and even Chase. You name a person, they tried to stop us.

COACH W

I couldn't figure out my next move. If I even had one.

I called Tatum over at the end of class, told her we needed to talk after school.

"Okay," she said. "But can we talk tomorrow? I'm really busy today. We have practice and everything."

"Okay," I said, even though I knew she'd already quit the cheer team. Coach Harden and I talked all the time. But I didn't feel like calling Tatum on it. I had other stuff to call her on. "But right after school tomorrow. Don't forget."

"Alright, alright, alright," she said. She was standing, feet shoulder width apart, both hands shoved deep down in her pockets. She had that Matthew McConaughey/Cara Delevingne lesbian swagger now. For about a minute. Before it all came crashing down. She was really enjoying it there for a moment.

ANISSA GRANT

I had stopped caring about anything except Tay. I didn't know if I was gay or a lesbian, I just knew I was in love with a girl. I didn't think about things like legalities or that I was "passing" as a teenager and that I might at any moment be caught or found out.

I had stopped caring about that, too.

I was fully immersed in this method acting I'd started back in the fall, back the first day I met Taylor, the first day I set foot in this school as Tatum Grant.

I didn't feel like Anissa anymore. Or Rachel.

I finally felt just like me. Which was ironic, I guess. That the only time in my life when I felt like myself was the time in which I was pretending to be someone else.

But none of that mattered now. Later, it would all matter. But right now nothing did. Just me and Tay.

eleven

. . .

ROBIN GRANT

Anissa had been gone six months and we hadn't heard a word. Not one word. Not a postcard or an email. Nothing.

We'd stopped talking about her. Tate and I. I think it was too painful. I was trying not to think of the holidays—Thanksgiving and Christmas. I'd not been without her during them for thirty years. It'd been just she and I— the first fifteen of those years, and then Tate had come along. And then there'd been the three of us for another fifteen. We had our routines, our traditions; making pies while we watched the Macy's parade on a small kitchen television, watching *Miracle on 34th Street* while we ate our Thanksgiving dinner on snack trays in front of the TV. For a long time, Anissa had idolized Natalie Wood. She'd even wanted to change her name to Natalie. After I'd shown her *Splendor in the Grass* and *Rebel Without a Cause*. She collected books about her, which made it easy to buy for her for Christmas. Christmas was another holiday bookended by classic movies. Christmas Eve we'd watch *My Man Godfrey* and Christmas morning *The Philadelphia Story* and in the evening, on Christmas, we'd put a couple ice cubes and a little Bailey's in a glass or in a cup of cocoa and watch *It Happened One Night* and *The Thin Man*.

The holidays, Christmas especially, were always about movies for us. Especially for Anissa and me. Tate was less into them. Tate always argued for more modern films. *Home Alone. Planes, Trains and Automobiles. Gremlins.* 80s movies, mostly.

I didn't have any other family. I'd long ago renounced any relations back home. Long, long ago. I never received letters anymore. For a while I did. A great aunt or cousin would write to tell me the goings on in the family. I never wrote back.

I liked it being just me and my girls.

Me and my gals and our movies.

But now one of us was gone and the other was barely home anymore.

Tate was busy, busy, busy.

And unlike Anissa when Anissa was young and acting in movies and on TV, Tate made friends, had a thriving social circle, other actresses and actors, musicians, fashion designers. Anissa had rarely befriended anyone. Excluding the short period of time with Quinn, at the end of the day, it was always back to Anissa and me, at home together.

More and more now it was me, home alone with a glass of Grand Marnier and an old film. Lately it'd been Montgomery Clift movies. What a sad, beautiful, lonely actor. Perfect company for my sad, beautiful, lonely life.

ANISSA GRANT

After school we'd head straight back to my apartment and get naked. Taylor stopped asking where my mom was and I didn't acknowledge anything. It was like we both knew she knew now, but neither of us gave a shit to talk about it.

Instead, we drove back to Indianapolis, to one of those Lovers Lanes stores. We giggled our way around the walls, fingering all the dildos and vibrators while the middle-aged cashier woman watched. I bought a strap-on and made Taylor come three times with it as soon as we got home. We were both wearing our cheer uniforms and after she was lying there all flushed and sexy looking, her hair in tangles. And if I hadn't known I was in love before that moment, I knew now.

Later, after we'd smoked a couple cigarettes, drank a Diet Coke, she put the strap-on on herself and pushed me down on the bed. She could be very aggressive, too. I think she was enjoying how aggressive she could be.

Taylor never did ask how come the woman had let me buy it with my ID seeing as how you had to be over 18. It was like we both knew she knew but neither of us said anything aloud, acknowledged anything aloud. Neither of us wanted to break the role-playing, ruin the fantasy.

COACH W

Of course, what I didn't know then was that Tatum and I had something larger in common. Tatum and I shared a special friend.

I wouldn't find that out until later.

That she'd picked this town specifically.

That it was no accident she ended up in Elkheart.

Which makes this whole story even more odd. We couldn't have known that. Either one of us.

Maybe someone else knew.

ANABEL RAGNER

I just felt something wasn't right. I'd felt that way a long time, pretty much since Taylor had introduced me to Tatum. Something was off. I could just feel it.

And then when Taylor and Cam broke up and Taylor started wanting to spend all her free time with Tatum, at Tatum's apartment, and Tatum's mom never being there, me not able to meet her mom... I could only imagine what was going on over there. The two of them unsupervised, doing whatever they wanted. Drugs, sex, what have you.

I just started letting go of certain ethical dilemmas I'd had up until then, about privacy—my daughter's and Tatum's.

Other ethics seemed to trump the privacy one. Like my daughter's safety. Like my responsibility as a parent.

So I got out my computer one day, while everyone was out of the house, Jolie and Taylor both at school, and started doing searches, started googling.

I don't remember how exactly I came upon *the information*. But it didn't take me that long, really. A couple days of intense researching. I paid for a couple extra research helpers they have online. Stayed up until three in the morning a handful of nights. What else did I have to do? Taylor's father was a ghost, at this point. I wouldn't have been at all surprised to find out he had a whole 'nother family in another state. I think this one was making him uncomfortable now, what with an out of control teen daughter and a trans child, a sad, disappointed wife.

I wouldn't have come home either, if a better option had presented itself.

Of course, that's not true.

I loved my kids too much.

Which was exactly why I was doing this, to protect Taylor, to save my baby girl.

Somebody had to, and it wasn't going to be her father. That was for goddamned sure.

CAM SPENCER

Anabel, Taylor's mom, texted me. We'd been texting here and there, anyway. She'd texted me the day of the break up, actually, to say she was sorry. To say she was crying, too. We'd gotten super close over the years. I did so much with Taylor's family. All the holidays. Vacations. I went with them to Mexico and to Florida. I was real tight with her mom, especially, since her dad was usually away working somewhere, in another city for days at a time. Sometimes, Taylor made a sarcastic comment about how she thought I wanted to hang out with her mom more than with her. That wasn't true, but I did like feeling included; I did like the attention her mom paid me, making me an Easter basket for Easter, cookies on my birthday, that sort of thing. My own mom was always so busy being a professor down in Indianapolis, a *feminist*. My own mom was rarely home.

So her mom texted me. Maybe a week or ten days after Homecoming. Said she wanted to meet me in person, to talk.

I said, okay, of course.

I had no ill will toward Anabel. In fact, I knew if Taylor and I were ever going to get back together, my best bet was to stay on good terms with Anabel, even if I was on no terms with Taylor.

As much as Taylor shit-talked and belly-ached about her mom, they were super close, best friends, probably—at least until Tatum came along.

She asked if we could meet somewhere out of town. We both knew Taylor would be pissed if she found out we were talking behind her back. So we decided to meet at the Outback in Millington on a Wednesday at 3:30, right after school. Jolie was going to be on a playdate. Taylor was going to be with Tatum. No one had to know.

I didn't know what she had to tell me, what she wanted to talk about.

I figured it might just be the normal, I hope you guys get back together kind of talk or the let's shit-talk Tatum together talk.

I wasn't sure. I was just happy to meet her. She was a second mom to me, for sure. I thought she was going to be my actual mom, meaning, when Taylor and I married someday. I thought it'd call her "Mom" the rest of my life after that. "Grandma," even, one day.

TAYLOR RAGNER

Tatum and I were really getting to know each other, spending every minute we could together. We talked about leaving Elkheart together. We both wanted to leave as soon as possible. I'd been wanting to get the eff out of this town since I could remember.

I could talk to Tatum in a way I could never talk to Cam.

And Tatum *listened*.

I mean, I didn't even know if I wanted to go to college. Maybe I wanted to take a year or two off. And that kind of thing, even trying to mention that to my mom, she would, like, freak the fuck out, rip her vagina in half. She'd say, "People who take a year off, only 50% end up going back," Eyeroll. Okay, whatever, Anabel. I'm not people. I'm *your daughter*. I mean, why couldn't she have a little more faith in me?

I started to feel like I could only really relax, like I was only "safe," with Tatum.

I could be 100% myself with her.

And she was real cute. And the sex was amazing. By the way. Lol. Just in case you were wondering. The sex was UH-MAY-ZING.

No comparison—sorry, Cam. Not that I'm comparing... just... yeah, amazing.

COACH W

I didn't know what I wanted to say to Tatum.

I'd been a mess, lately; since Homecoming. Or even before.

I was going through a fifth of gin, now, every two days.

I went to school, did my job, and came home and started drinking. I drank through dinner and drank after dinner and passed out on the toilet or on the couch or on the floor.

I'd wake up in these places around my apartment. Eat off the floor like David Hasselhoff in that video his daughter made to publicly humiliate him and get him to stop drinking. Except, I didn't have a daughter or anyone else around who gave a shit to humiliate me into stopping drinking. So I didn't. I kept drinking.

I didn't want to have to blackmail Tatum into having sex with me, but I didn't want her to stop having sex with me, either, and that seemed maybe the only way. As fucked up as that sounds. As dark and depressing as I know that is.

ANISSA GRANT

Colton looked worse for wear. He looked bloated and bloodshot and generally "not good." I kept my backpack on my shoulder. Remained standing. I didn't want to send the wrong signals. This wasn't going to be a fuck-fest, like before. I had someone now. As ridiculous as that sounds, in hindsight. I, me, thirty-year-old Anissa, posing as sixteen-year-old Tatum, *had someone*, had a fifteen, almost sixteen, year old *girlfriend*.

I looked at Colton and I saw a man with nothing left to lose. I wasn't even sure he'd had anything to lose, really, when we met. His job, I guess. His "career," if you could call it that. But in some sense, I knew he'd given up on life way before he met me.

I think, in retrospect, I'd made him think for a second he hadn't given up.

And when that turned out to not be true, that's when he fully embraced the IDGAF model of living.

Which was when I knew I was fucked, too.

If he wanted to fuck me, in that non-literal sense of fucking, now that we'd fucked in the *very*-literal sense, I mean, he most definitely *could*, fuck me.

Fuck.

I was fucked.

That's what I was thinking, looking at Colton.

ANABEL RAGNER

I met Cam at Outback. I ordered a blooming onion and a Long Island iced tea. I didn't normally drink and before we left I had two cups of coffee, but I needed that alcohol to get this conversation started, to overcome my fear of Cam walking out, shaming me as a bad mother; going to Taylor to tell her.

But of course that's not what happened.

Of course he said he was "on your side, Anabel."

This was part of what I'd always loved so much about Cam. He backed me up when it came to Taylor. No one else sure as fuck did. Not her father. Not her. Sometimes I really needed that. Cam would say, "Come on, Taylor. I think your mom is right. She just wants what's best for you." And Taylor would have to listen then, because someone her age was making the case, was saying it. She couldn't just wave it off as "my crazy mom making some crazy claim."

I smiled across the booth at Cam. Maybe it was the Long Island ice tea but I felt better already. I felt better than I'd felt in weeks. I felt like maybe things would be okay. With the two of us working as a team. With the two of us on the same page with regard to Taylor and, more specifically, with regard to Tatum. "Tatum."

CAM SPENCER

I told Anabel, I told Taylor's mom, I wanted what she wanted: Taylor back. Taylor safe and sound, at home. I told her I'd read some stuff online and I thought Taylor might be manic, or have one of those personality disorders or something.

I said, "I don't think she's herself. I don't think she's thinking in her right mind."

Her mom nodded.

"And not just cause we broke up, not just because she broke up with me."

Anabel nodded again, patted my hand. "I know, Cam," she said. "I know, hon. I've been trying to get her back to seeing her therapist since school started but she refuses to go. I think she probably needs to be medicated. After last year, after what happened."

I still didn't like to think about it.

It was so fucked up, Taylor trying to kill herself and shit. Or Taylor making a good play at wanting to kill herself.

You think she told Tatum that shit?

Tatum didn't know; Tatum didn't have a clue.

She didn't know Taylor like me and her mom knew her, how vulnerable she was, how fucked up she could be.

Tatum didn't know shit.

COACH W

I tried to be as diplomatic as I could, under the circumstances, given that I was three shots into my Wednesday night brown out or black out or whatever.

I said, "Look, Tatum, I'm not trying to be a dick here."

And she interrupted me. Said, "Then don't be, Colt."

Touché.

Okay, so I *was* trying to be a dick.

First to admit! Got me there!

I said, "It's just that, well, I don't want to make this easy on you. In fact, I want to make it as hard as possible. To stop fucking me, I mean. To stop sucking my dick."

"Okay," she said. "Well, I hate to break it to you, but that's not gonna happen. I'm done fucking you. I've got someone now. I don't want to fuck that up. And I'm *officially*: done. Sucking. Dicks. I'm retired on the dick-suck-ing, Colt."

"Right," I said. "Which is how I'm going to make this hard."

"Uh huh," she said.

"Don't you want to know what I mean?" I said.

"I know what you mean," she said.

And then she lit a cigarette, just got up and walked out. Just like that. Like what I said had no meaning at all to her, like I wasn't the threat I thought I was or wanted to be.

She was calling my bluff.

And, honestly, I wasn't sure she wasn't right.

I'd really just been counting on her being scared and fucking me.

I hadn't counted on this, on her calling my bluff, on her *not* fucking me.

I was an idiot. An idiot alone with his boner. Yet again.

ANABEL RAGNER

We traded information: He told me he'd slept with Tatum, once, before school started. He started to tear up when he said it, when he admitted it, and I patted his hand again, told him it was okay. I felt bad for him. I really did. I knew Taylor had pushed him away at that point; was already wanting to break up with him. She'd hinted at it all summer. I didn't blame him for having sex with the new girl. I blamed Tatum. For everything. For all of this. "Tatum." That bitch trying to steal my daughter.

CAM SPENCER

Taylor's mom told me she'd been reading Taylor's diary, logging into her social media, reading her messages.

At first I was shocked. To be honest, I was scared. Because that meant she'd seen whatever fucked up messages Taylor and I'd sent each other. Not to mention photos and shit. And, shocker: Things hadn't been great between us the last year or so. Understatement. We'd fought a lot. Especially when we were both shit-faced. I knew there was a time or two I'd crossed a line. Definitely crossed some lines. When I'd shoved her a little. It was hard to say if she'd fallen from being drunk or from me shoving her. She'd had a bruise, on her hip. She said she didn't remember how she got it and I'd told her she'd fallen over the bed when she was blacked out but part of me thought she was lying about not remembering, that she remembered our fight, me pushing her...

So I didn't know what was in her diary. What she wrote in that thing.

But apparently she hadn't mentioned any of that, or if she did, Anabel hadn't read that far back, or Anabel was only looking to get shit on Tatum.

Anabel said Taylor had written about how they'd had sex Homecoming night. Her and Tatum. Fucking gross. Fucking disgusting. I wanted to throw up the blooming fucking onion right fucking there but Anabel said that was enough for her.

She said now that we knew Tatum was lying about her identity, about her age, that that was rape. Statutory rape. Sex with a minor.

I didn't know how you proved it with two females. Like, if it was still rape if a penis didn't enter a vagina. But I figured I didn't need to worry about all that because Anabel was worrying about it.

I figured I could just sit back and enjoy the show.

Sit back and watch Tatum get her ass handed to her.

ANISSA GRANT

Honestly, I thought Colton was all talk. I felt sorry for him. He was a weak-willed, lonely man who never got what he wanted because he'd never fought for anything in his life.

I wasn't worried about him because it seemed unlikely he'd start (fighting) now. *Especially over me.* I mean, we'd fucked a couple of times. It wasn't a love story. We weren't affectionate or romantic. It was purely sex. Illicit, teacher/student sex.

And wouldn't he look as bad as me, anyway, if people found out? Even if I wasn't technically sixteen, I was still a "student" and he was still a "teacher."

Did he think people wouldn't care?

That their logic wouldn't be: well, sure, *she* isn't underage, but he didn't know that, and if he fucked her, he's probably fucked other students in the past or will again if we don't stop him.

Did he think *he* wouldn't be the biggest loser of all if he told?

I felt like I should have been the one trying to blackmail him, not the other way around.

I wasn't too worried. I drove back to my apartment. Taylor was already there, smoking a bowl in bed, waiting on me. I guess Chase had dropped her off or something. I'd stopped on my way for Taco Bell. It was like Christmas morning every time you brought Taylor Taco Bell when she was high.

She leaped up on the bed in her boxers and my t-shirt, cute as fucking hell, screaming, "Taco Bell! Taco Bell!" and running in mini circles on my mattress.

I wanted to die from how fucking cute she was.

I wanted to kill her and myself in that one perfect moment but that's when she grabbed the bag from me and sat cross-legged on the bed and started unwrapping wrappers like a hungry raccoon, her little hands so busy, and she was too cute to kill.

So I just sat on the bed watching her eat instead; smoking the bowl.

Her underarm hair and pubic hair were grown out now. After she finished eating I got a healthy noseful of each. Inhaling deeply like Dennis Hopper in *Blue Velvet*. Like a creepy pervert. Like Taylor liked. She wiggled underneath me and whimpered. I had to pin her arms down with my knees to hold her still. Cover her mouth with my palm. Cover her breasts with my mouth.

She was emitting the rank smell of refried beans and beef and marijuana, which on Taylor was the sexiest smell. The most base aphrodisiac.

TAYLOR RAGNER

It was like two hours later my mom texted me.

"Fuck," I said to Tatum. "Fuck my life. My mom is outside in her car. She says I have to come home right now. That she needs to talk to me *right now*."

"Fuck," Tatum said. "That doesn't sound good."

"Tell me about it," I said. "This bitch is going to make me slit my wrists for real."

"Don't do that, babe," Tatum said, grabbing my arm, pulling my hand toward her mouth. "You have such beautiful, delicate wrists." Then, one at a time, she pressed her mouth to each, gave each the tiniest kiss.

"Ugh," I said. "I have to go, babe. I can feel my mom's vagina drying up right now. We need to get her some lube or something. Maybe if she actually got laid or something, she wouldn't be in our business every two seconds."

"We'll make her a Tinder profile," Tatum said.

"El oh el," I said.

I leaned in for a kiss and next thing I knew another three minutes had gone by and my mom was honking the horn like a goddamn crazy person. I swear to fucking god, every mom in this town just needed to get laid. It was like an epidemic or something. All the dry vaginas, all the moms who needed to get fucked.

ANISSA GRANT

I waited for Taylor to leave and then immediately started packing. Just enough for a weekend. I didn't know what was going on, what was happening, but I sensed it wasn't good. I wanted to be ready in case I had to leave town at a moment's notice.

I threw my bag in the trunk and drove over to Taylor's. She'd only been gone five minutes. I wanted to make sure she was okay. That everything was okay. That nothing bad was happening, nothing bad was going down.

ANABEL RAGNER

I said to Taylor, Cam standing beside me, "Taylor, you were *raped*. You are a *victim* here. You were sexually *assaulted*, honey."

I said, "I think you should report it. I think you should report *her*."

Which was when she started freaking out, screaming at both of us that she was never going to report *it* because *it* never happened.

"Everything Tatum and I have ever done has been consensual!" she screamed.

"I'm not a baby. I can make my own decisions. Whether you or Cam like them or not! Just because you don't like the choices I'm making *now*, doesn't make them non-consensual. Doesn't mean I was raped!" she said. "If anyone did any raping here, it was Cam, not Tatum, Jesus. I was thirteen, for chrissake, Mom! And you were perfectly fine with that! Remember?"

Which was when Tatum walked into the house. I guess she'd been waiting for Taylor this whole time out in her car, out on the lawn, hovering somewhere, like the stalker we now know she is.

"Is everything okay?" she said, looking at Taylor. "What's going on, are you okay, babe?"

Babe. I wanted to throw up. I could barely look at her. It was like looking at a photo of a sexual predator online. I didn't want her in my house. I didn't want her anywhere near Jolie.

I looked at Cam like, *do something*. Like, *get this bitch out of my house.*

TAYLOR RAGNER

My mom had set me up, had Cam waiting at the house to ambush me. They were both acting like complete psychos. Gaslighting me, trying to manipulate me and control me. Threatening me. "Maybe you just need to take some time to relax in the hospital again," my mom was saying. "Yeah, Taylor, maybe you need medication or something to help you feel better," Cam said, nodding. I just stared at them. They were using my past against me. They were using my mental illness to question me, to make me question *myself*.

And they were acting like it was some huge fucking revelation they'd uncovered.

I already *knew* Tatum wasn't sixteen. I'd figured it out a long time ago. I *didn't care*. That's what Cam and my mom didn't get. I didn't give two shits if Tatum was sixteen or twenty-five or thirty. I didn't FUCKING CARE. Maybe she was *trans-age*. Later we joked about that. "Yeah, baby, I'm thirty on paper but inside I'm your age, I'm sixteen," Tatum would say.

"Or maybe *I'm thirty* inside," I would say. "Baby, I was born this way: old AF."

Then Tatum had walked into the house. I guess she'd followed us over.

"No, babe, I'm not okay," I said to her. "I'm *not* okay." I'd been crying and I was trying not to cry again and I think she could see that. I think it was pretty fucking obvious.

CAM SPENCER

I walked over to Tatum, asked her to wait outside the house, please, polite and shit, but she refused. The bitch refused. The bitch pretended she hadn't heard me. Pretended I wasn't a physical threat. That I couldn't make her ass wait outside if I fucking wanted to. That I couldn't pick her fucking bitch ass up and *put* her outside. If I wanted to.

An image of her with my dick in her mouth by the lake flashed through my mind.

I felt the bile in the back of my throat, tasted the rage.

Another image flashed through my mind: the one of Chase and me, twelve years old in a basement, shit-faced, my dick in his hand.

I didn't know what the fuck that was doing there. What had made me think of that.

Then an image of Taylor naked in my bed, that sweet smile she got after we'd had sex, after she'd come. Then, next thing I knew, I was seeing Taylor, that same sweet smile, but in Tatum's fucking bed, Tatum fucking next to her instead of me, her whole fucking man hand up inside her, up inside my girlfriend.

I felt sick to my fucking stomach, like I was actually going to puke.

But I held it in.

And that bitch just stood there in front of me, that dumb fucking look on her face. Thinking she was better than me. Thinking she knew Taylor better than me. That dumb fucking bitch.

ANISSA GRANT

I didn't know what my role was here, what I should do. Everyone was freaking out, screaming at each other, threatening each other. Taylor's mom and Cam were both threatening me. Saying they were going to go to the school board—lol, go to the police.

I looked to Taylor, to see what she wanted. I would do whatever she wanted me to do.

Her mom had her phone in her hand. I don't know who she was trying to call. Taylor's dad, the school, 911…

Taylor said, "Tatum, stop her!"

I had the gun with me. One of Quinn's gun. The one he had given me after *The Westerners*. I had brought it as a deterrent. I hesitated with my hand wrapped around it inside my jacket.

ANABEL RAGNER

When Tatum pulled the gun out, I screamed. I screamed and dropped my phone.

I screamed, "Don't do it, Tatum! Think of Jolie. Think of Taylor's little brother. He's only six!"

In the heat of the moment I didn't think politically.

I just saw my little Jimmy, age six, without a mom. I just saw my little boy, the day I brought him home from the hospital, the day he turned one, two, three… all the days of his short life ran through my mind.

Taylor ran and stood behind Tatum.

I looked over at Cam and he was staring at the gun. It looked like he was contemplating his options. Trying to pick the smartest one. It was like I could see the wheels turning in his head, like in an old Warner Brothers cartoon.

Finally, he looked at Tatum and said, "Come on, Tatum, don't be stupid. You don't know how to shoot a gun. Give me the gun."

Cam was a hunter; went hunting with his dad and brothers and grandpa.

We didn't know then that Tatum had shot guns in movies, had been trained to ride horses, to shoot semi-automatic weapons. Who knows what the hell else they taught her to do out in Hollywood.

CAM SPENCER

I couldn't believe the bitch had a gun. I couldn't believe she wasn't some diehard anti-gun enthusiast. I pictured California people being all lovey dovey hippie'd out, anti-gun, anti-American, anti-Libertarian, anti-everything except muff-diving and spilling tears for Mother Earth and killing fetuses.

I had that split second thought of should I try and grab it from her?

TAYLOR RAGNER

Tatum held the gun real cool, real calm, like she knew what she was doing… it was honestly super hot. I mean, I didn't have the composure or time to think that then, but later, when we were driving off into the sunset together, and I had a moment to think back, I definitely thought it, definitely told her, "Babe, that was so fucking hot when you pulled the gun out. That was fucking fire, babe."

ANISSA GRANT

I'd brought the gun with me just in case. I'd actually started carrying it because of Coach W, because of him acting so funny, so obsessive, lately. I just wanted to be able to scare him, if I needed to. There weren't even any bullets in it. I'd taken them out before driving over. The bullets were in the glove box of my car.

I told Taylor to go pack a bag…

TAYLOR RAGNER

I ran up to my room as fast as I could to grab my purse and to throw a few things into my cheer bag: my hairbrush, my toothbrush, my pajamas…

Which was when I heard Tatum peel out of the drive.

I looked out the bathroom window.

I couldn't believe it.

She'd left without me.

I tried calling her, frantic, but she wouldn't pick up.

So I called Chase. I didn't know who else to call.

He said he'd be right there. He said he was already in his car on the way to the high school gym and he'd be right over.

ANABEL RAGNER

I didn't know what to think. I was just glad she'd left, that Tatum was out of my house. Gone. I prayed I'd never see her again, that we'd never see her again.

Cam had run out of the house after her. Got in his truck and tried to follow her.

I started to call the cops again but Taylor came down right then and pulled my phone out of my hand.

ANISSA GRANT

It just suddenly occurred to me, I was about to fuck up Taylor's life.

And I'd already fucked up Tate's.

I didn't want to be responsible for fucking up anyone else's.

I didn't know what I was doing in my own life. Let alone with someone else in someone else's life.

Taylor went upstairs and it just clicked in me. I ran out of the house and got in my car and never looked back. I figured Cam would try and follow me so I made a few turns out of my way and finally lost him at a stoplight.

CAM WHITING

I tried to follow her. Soon as Tatum ran out of the house I ran after her. I would have caught her too but a light turned with a car in between us and there was a cop on the opposite side of the road at the light, waiting.

I was already facing jail time because of the photo scandal. I couldn't afford to get in any more trouble with the law. My dad woulda killed me.

So instead I sat at the light bashing my fists on the steering wheel and then when that didn't work, bashing my head against it too.

I was so fucking sick of this bitch.

I didn't know why she'd had to come to this town, ruin all our lives.

CHASE WHITING

The night before I'd hung out at Tatum's with her and Taylor.

We'd smoked some pot and sat in a circle in the dark listening to music and smoking cigarettes and talking.

I wasn't used to smoking marijuana and the conversation had gotten kind of heavy, kind of philosophical. We were talking about the LGBTQ community. About Elkheart being so behind the times of other towns, of other cities.

They made such a cute couple, Tatum and Taylor. We were all sitting on the floor and Taylor was sitting in Tatum's lap. They were inspiring to me. I wanted that kind of love, that sort of affection, in my life.

I ended up telling the girls I thought I might be queer, too. I told them about the time with Cam when he and I were twelve, how I'd thought of it ever since, how I thought maybe I was in love with him.

I thought that might be weird for Taylor to hear. I told her I was sorry. That I never would have acted on my feelings, not only because I was afraid of Cam's reaction, of his probably homophobia and denial, but because of my respect for them as a couple.

Taylor had come and sat in my lap, told me to forget about it, that she understood, 100%, that she wasn't mad, that she just wanted me to be happy, too. That she wanted me to find someone, too. Someone like Tatum but for me.

I said, "So you don't think that someone could ever be Cam?"

And she said, "Honey, honestly? No, I don't. I'm sorry, honey. I know that you think you're in love with him, but I just really don't think that would ever work out. I think you need to move on, out of this town, out of here, and meet new people. More open-minded people. And then you'll find somebody, honey."

I don't know why but I was crying. I knew she was right.

I needed to leave, to go to a university in a big city, far from here.

But I was afraid to leave Cam. I didn't want to leave my best friend.

TAYLOR RAGNER

When I came back downstairs, Tatum was gone and Cam was gone and my mom had her phone in her hand and was dialing. I figured she was calling the cops so I grabbed her phone, shut it off, and threw it in the tank part of the hall toilet.

"You're not calling the cops!" I yelled. "She hasn't done anything. Just leave her alone!"

"She's thirty years old, Taylor!" my mom screamed back.

"I know that!" I said. "I don't care! I don't care how old she is. I don't care if she's forty-two or sixty-five. I. *DON'T. CARE.*"

"Well, *I* do and the law does, Taylor," she said.

"Yeah, and the law doesn't want Jolie to use the bathroom she wants to use, so…"

"This isn't about Jolie," my mom said.

"But it is, Mom," I said. "It's about personal freedoms and there are people in this country who think a child, a teenager, can make a choice about his or her own gender so why can't I make a choice about who I want to love? I'm going to be sixteen next week, for chrissake! The coal miner's daughter was thirteen when she got married and that turned out perfectly fine!"

"You're not getting married. You're not the coal miner's daughter, Taylor. You're my daughter and so help me, you're not going to keep seeing her. You're fifteen years old and you're not going to date a thirty-year-old woman, Taylor!"

Which was when I saw Chase pull in the drive. Thank God.

"Chase is here," I yelled, as I maneuvered through the front door. "I'll be right back," I said, hoping she wouldn't follow me, lying through my teeth.

ANISSA GRANT

I was five seconds from pulling out, from getting the hell out of Elkheart, I was fastening my seatbelt at a light of all things when Chase and Taylor pulled up next to me in Chase's car.

Taylor immediately jumped out ran around to mine, screamed at me to open my door. She was holding her purple Dobson high cheer bag.

"What are you doing? Where are you going? You're not leaving without me!" she was yelling. She was frantic. She was standing there shaking and tears were in her eyes. "You're not leaving me!"

"I'm sorry," I said. I got out of the car, stood there in front of her. "I didn't want to fuck up your life any more than I already have."

"You haven't fucked up my life, Tatum, you've made it survivable. I hate this town. I hate my life here. I want to leave. I want to go with you. Don't leave me here. Don't leave me," she was sobbing with her face pushed to my chest and I was holding her. I was rubbing her back. I was saying, "Okay, okay, I won't leave you. It's okay. Don't cry."

Chase got out of his car then and walked over. "If you're trying to leave town, you better go now," he said. "Cam just texted me asking if I know where you are. He said Taylor's mom is looking for her. One or both of them will probably be here any second."

"Okay," I said. "Shit. Thanks, Chase."

"Yeah, Chase, thank you so much for coming to get me. I wish we could take you with us," Taylor said.

"No, I have to stay here," he said. "I have things to figure out."

"Okay, Chase, we love you," Taylor said, and threw her arms around his neck.

"Bye, Chase," I said, and hugged him before getting in the car. Taylor got in next to me, threw her cheer bag in the back.

We waved goodbye to Chase. Taylor put her window down and leaned out, "Love you, Chasey!" she yelled.

"I wish he could come with us," she said, rolling her window back up.

"Me, too," I said.

I looked over at her and she was sitting up with one foot on the seat and one on the floor and she had wiped away her tears and she was smiling.

I turned toward the freeway, toward freedom. Hopefully. Fingers crossed. Knock wood. All that shit. *Freedom.*

This is where in a movie the George Michael song would start to play. "I won't let you down, I will not give you up. Gotta have some faith in the sound. It's the one good thing that I've got. I won't let you down, so please don't give me up. Cuz I would really, really love to stick around, oh, yeah!"

CHASE WHITING

I texted Cam back and told him everything was fine, that I was hanging out with Tatum and Taylor right now and to let Taylor's mom know everything was okay, that I'd bring Taylor home in a little bit. I'd driven over to Tatum's apartment building, was just sitting in my car outside.

I wanted to give the girls at least an hour lead time.

I knew it was kind of a shitty thing to do to Taylor's mom, lying and all, but I felt even more that it was a shitty thing to try to separate Tatum and Taylor, to try to get Tatum in trouble with the cops, who would maybe take her to jail.

They'd told me everything the night before, her and Taylor. Told me she was thirty, that she'd gotten pregnant when she was fifteen, that she'd been a child actress, that she'd never really had a childhood, never gotten to be a teenager, never got to live that life.

I guessed now she wasn't going to live that life anymore, either, but at least she had gotten to for a little bit, for a couple months, at least. She'd made the cheerleading squad and gone to Homecoming and gotten a girlfriend.

In some ways, Tatum had gotten more of what she wanted than I had. I was still living in the closet, still afraid to tell my family and friends, to tell Cam, that I thought I was gay.

I sort of admired Tatum's bravery, her determination to live the life she wanted to live, even if it was going to cost her greatly. Even if she might lose everything in the end, pay great consequences.

At least she could say she'd lived her life free, for a moment, the way she wanted, which was more than most of us could say.

I made a vow to myself standing in that parking lot, staring at Tatum's apartment where the night before I'd sat with her and Taylor, admitting for the first time to anyone I was gay. I made a vow to tell my father and Cam, before the week was over.

I wanted the whole school to know, somehow, without me having to make a huge announcement. I didn't want to carry this secret around with me anymore.

I didn't want to hide anymore.

I was inspired by Tatum. I owed a lot to her, actually.

TAYLOR RAGNER

Soon as we were on the highway we both chucked our phones out the window.

Tatum said we would get another car, too, soon as we were far enough away from Elkheart to stop somewhere.

"Like, what, Tatum," I said. "Steal one?

"No," she said. "Buy one. Just another used car. I have cash on me. We can get an older car pretty cheap."

It felt like we were both holding our breath until we made it to the border, to the state line, till we crossed into Kentucky.

I didn't know how much cash Tatum had. I had about four hundred dollars. Tatum said we couldn't use credit cards but I didn't have a credit card, anyway. I just had the cash my dad had given me the last time he'd come home. Guilt money. A payoff.

We drove another two hours after that and by then it was pretty late. Pitch dark. We took an exit with plenty of signs for hotels and got a room at the one furthest from the freeway, a Red Roof Inn. Taylor parked the car back-end in.

"Tomorrow we'll get a new car and new clothes," she said.

"I want to dye my hair and cut it, too," I said.

By now we were inside the hotel room. "Let's get ice and some chips," I said.

"Let's order a pizza," Tatum said.

"Okay," I said. "Our first outlaw pizza," I said, and jumped up and down on the bed until it sounded like it was about to break.

Tatum was on the phone, ordering a Hawaiian pizza and a two liter of Diet Coke.

I went and sat on the bed beside her. I got down on my knees and pushed her knees apart so I could fit in between them.

"How long till the pizza gets here?" I said, after she'd hung up.

"Twenty minutes," Tatum said, rubbing my hair with her hand.

"Just long enough," I said, and started pulling down Tatum's pants.

I watched as Tatum lay back on the bed, stretching her arms way up over her head. I rested my cheek against the soft hair below her belly for a second and then inched my face downward, my mouth open, tongue extended.

ANABEL RAGNER

I never should have believed Cam. Or Cam never should have believed Chase. Or I never should have believed what Cam believed.

Chase was a nice kid but we should have known he'd lie for the girls. Or for Taylor and *that woman.*

I'd waited an hour like Cam said and then I'd gotten Chase's number from Cam. The first time I called he didn't pick up so I left a voicemail. I was crying and pleading, begging for any information about my baby. I waited ten minutes and called back. This time he answered. This time he apologized, told me he was sorry but that the girls had left town an hour earlier. Maybe an hour and a half, by now, he'd said.

I hung up on him. I don't hold it against him now but at that moment I was furious, like this was all his fault: that I didn't know where my baby was, that my baby was on the run in a car with some woman none of us knew anything about, who could have been an escaped felon, or on the sex offenders list. Sure, I'd looked for her on it and couldn't find her but that didn't mean she wasn't, under another name, maybe, in another state. Who knew how many pseudonyms this person had. How many aliases. How many other girls she'd lured away from their families, from their mothers.

I hung up and called Taylor's father and then I called the police.

Taylor's father wasn't answering either.

Taylor's father was on his own run from his family.

The police said they'd be right over.

I went to freshen up in my bathroom; washed my face, brushed my hair, changed my clothes. Jolie was still at my friend Shelly's house. I'd called and asked if she could stay the night, told her it was a family emergency, told her I'd fill her in in the morning.

twelve

. . .

ANISSA GRANT

Of course I had doubts in my head, lying there next to Taylor in a Red Roof Inn in B.F.E., Kentucky. My teen-aged sweetheart under my arm. The two of us on the run from the law and her mom and the whole town too, Cam and Coach W and everyone. The two of us dumb and in love and in denial of the inevitable ending.

I guess we were just trying to make it last as long as we could.

That's what we were thinking.

We were dumb but we weren't stupid.

We knew eventually we'd be caught. But we wanted to see how long we could last, how long we could outsmart everyone. Two days, two weeks, a month?

I mean, it's not that different from life in general, right? You know you're going to die. You're not going to outsmart death. But you try to make it last as long as possible. Most people try to, anyway. That's the general instinct. To hold on.

The TV was on, turned to some channel that plays classic movies. Taylor was asleep on my chest. I was eating Pringles out of a can, drinking Diet Mountain Dew from a plastic bottle. One of Quinn's old movies was playing, one of the ones from when he was really young, eleven or twelve, one of the first ones he ever made.

In it his little face is cherubic, his body pretty cherubic, also; he's not fat but he's a little husky.

A couple years after Quinn died, when Tate was just a toddler, I was watching a movie he'd made a couple years before I met him. The movie was directed by a woman and after I'd rewatched the movie, I watched it again with the director's commentary. Quinn's not the lead or anything so every time he appears on screen the director almost makes an *aww* sound and then says something sweet about him, how good-looking he is, how cool, how crazy. And this commentary was made well before he died. At one point, the part that always chokes me up when I think about it, the director pleads with any other director working with Quinn to watch out for him, to not "mess him up." I think the movie he made after he made her movie was with this older male director famous for encouraging his actors to "method act" or his version of method acting which meant unsimulated sex, unsimulated drug use. I think rumor was already getting out—when that female director made that commentary—that Quinn was using drugs to play a druggie in his next film.

I wondered if there was a chance Tate was somewhere watching her father's film right now, too. I wanted to be able to text her to ask her, or to tell her to put on whatever channel this was, but I didn't have my phone and I didn't know her number by heart and I wouldn't have texted it even if I did. I was too afraid of her at this point, afraid of rejection, afraid of her (well-deserved) anger, afraid she didn't love me, that she blamed me the way I'd blamed Mom. So I stayed gone.

Dermot Ellis
(front desk clerk at the Red Roof Inn, BFE, Kentucky)

I'm surprised I remember anything about them at all. I think the only reason I do is because when they checked in one of them had sort of mousy blond hair and the other was a pretty brunette and by the time they left, the one that had been blond now had jet black hair and the pretty brunette was a bleach blonde.

They seemed like nice girls, nice young women, I mean. Affectionate. More PDA than we're used to seeing from the gay community around here, I'd say. But I didn't mind it. I thought they were cute. They said they were heading south. Didn't specify where but I heard one of them, the one who had been brunette and who was now blonde talking about Mickey Mouse so I figured they were headed for Disney World. Epcot Center. Animal Kingdom. [laughs] I just took my family down last year. Drove, too.

ANABEL RAGNER

I finally got a hold of Taylor's father and of course his first reaction was to be nonplussed, as usual, and his second reaction, once I'd told him I'd talked to the police and that now the police wanted to talk to him, was to blame me.

But he flew home that evening. Forget where he said he was. Omaha. Or Salt Lake. One of those Mormon cities. Probably had a Mormon wife and kids out there. At the very least a little Mormon whore. Or is that an oxymoron? Oxymormon. Ha.

Jolie was excited when I told her. She loved her dad, even if he slighted her. Maybe only I picked up on the slights. I saw the hesitation, the stiffness in his body language, whenever he first saw her, after a long trip. As though he'd forgotten she was a girl now. As if he'd hoped it was just a fad and now she was back to being his son.

I was trying to hold it together for Jolie. I went into the bathroom if I felt like crying. Cried into a towel so Jolie couldn't hear me. She kept asking where "big sis" was and I told her big sis was away on a school trip for a few days; that she'd be back soon.

Scott seemed more worried about talking to the police than he seemed about his own daughter. Taylor, I mean. He kept asking me to go over what they'd asked me. He wanted to know every thing they'd said. Every question they'd asked. He was acting like a guilty person. A suspect. Instead of like a concerned parent, instead of a loving, caring father. Forget about husband. He hadn't been a *husband* in a long, long time.

TAYLOR RAGNER

Right at the start we had so much fun on the road. Just like I'd always imagined a road trip would be, with gas station snacks and coffees, drive-thrus and cheap motels and the radio playing and waving at truck drivers, making signs to hold up to the window as we passed them and other cars. We'd never taken a road trip as a child. My father insisted on flying anywhere further than two hours. He said being in the car was a waste of time, especially if you could afford to fly. I think what he meant was he didn't want to spend any more time with his family than he had to; get where you're going and get home. Or, in his case, get home so you can get the hell out again.

The next morning we left our room at the Red Roof Inn and drove to the Walmart and bought hair dye and bleach and scissors and a razor and picked out a couple outfits each, real incognito clothes. Tatum got a shirt that said "Mr. Happy" on it with a big smiley face and I got a red, white and blue t-shirt with an eagle on it. We each got a pair of thin black leggings and big hooded black sweatshirts. Tatum bought a pair of boxers and a three-pack of men's white undershirts and a pack of white socks. I bought a tube of dark purple lipstick and some black liquid eyeliner and a three-pack of dark eye shadows. On the way to check out there was a twirly thing of sunglasses so we each got a cheap pair of those too. Tatum's had mirrors and mine was neon-colored. Then we drove to Wendy's and got Frostys and fries and jr. bacon cheeseburgers and took them back to the room to eat them.

We were watching Dr. Phil talk about recovered memories and Tatum said, "We need to buy a new car, but we need to get rid of this one first. Destroy the plate or something."

"How do you know how to do all this?" I said. "You been on the run with someone before me?"

I was pretending to be hurt. Jealous.

"No, I just read books, dum-dum," she said. "Also, I played a gangster's doll in a movie, based on actual people. You learn shit that way—shit about crime, playing out history in real life."

Right, I was just getting used to the idea my girlfriend was a famous actress who had worked with a bunch of famous directors, famous actresses and actors, even if no one remembered her.

"Well, how much money do we have to buy a new car, cuz I have like three hundred dollars."

"Don't worry about it," she said. "I have enough."

I had no clue how rich she was. I knew a lot of child actors were supposed to be bankrupt, victims of bad managers or bad parents. Tatum didn't like to talk about it, family or money or her past, so I let it go, the way I let everything else go, *my* family, *my* money, all of it. It felt freeing, letting go, becoming somebody new, somebody else, *anyone else*.

SCOTT RAGNER

I knew I wanted a divorce. I'd been planning on asking for one the next time I came home, but now that Taylor was missing, that was going to have to be put on hold.

Still, I slept in the guest room downstairs in the basement. I could barely stand to be in the same room as Anabel for thirty minutes.

I was looking forward to being interrogated by the police just so it would get me away from Anabel for an hour or two. I couldn't stand the way she scratched her head nonstop with her nails. How she always had a sinus infection or stomach ache or headache. How gluten was always the culprit in either situation. Instead of her own raging hypochondria. I was actually surprised she wasn't one of those Munchausen by proxy moms.

This family was falling apart: missing teenage daughter, missing six-year-old son.

I know that's mean to say, but you don't know what it's like until it's your son. It's a lot easier to be supportive when it's not your six-year-old with gender dysmorphia.

Of course I blamed Anabel, for everything, for Taylor and for... *Jimmy/Jolie.*

I knew I was partially to blame for being an absentee parent, but I also thought blaming me for what was going on with the kids was like blaming a sea captain who's been away on land for six months on a typhoon that capsized a boat.

I don't know. Maybe that doesn't make sense.

Not much made sense, anymore.

I wanted to cut my losses and get out.

Remove myself from this family. Maybe that's awful to say, but sometimes in life you just need to know when to fold your cards. Know when to walk away. Know when to run. Whatever that Kenny Rogers song says. "The Gambler?" That one.

ANISSA GRANT

Taylor was manic; joyful. She was running everywhere we went: gas stations, Walmart, the motel hallway.

"BABY!" she'd screamed in the middle of Walmart. "I found the perfect shade of hair color for you!" I'd walked over and it was black. Jet black. Blue black.

"You'll look like Elvis!" she yelled. "Or Elvis's daughter, what's her name? Priscilla?"

"No," I said. "That's Elvis's wife. Lisa Marie is his daughter."

"Right," she said. "You'll look like Lisa Marie, baby! And I'll look like Marilyn! Have you ever had black hair, for a movie role or whatever?"

"Yeah," I said. "One of my first movies as a teenager they dyed my hair black and cut it short with bangs."

"We should cut it like that tonight!" she said. "I've never been a blonde. My mom would never let me even get highlights. She'd say, 'Taylor, you have beautiful virginal hair. I'm not going to let you ruin it.' I think she just liked that *something* about me was still *virginal*."

I don't know why, but her talking about virginity made me think of Tate. I had no way of knowing if she was or wasn't. I was missing that too. I was no longer her confidant, no longer the person she confided in. That hurt me so I pushed it aside, stopped thinking about it, her. Compartmentalize!

"What's the matter, baby?" Taylor had said, coming over and putting her arm around my shoulder. "Are you sad about my missing virginity?"

Which made me snap out of it. "Yes," I said. "I'm very upset and sad about your virginity that is no longer. We should have a funeral tonight, to honor it."

Taylor got really excited about that idea. We had to go to the party store across the street and buy black plates and black balloons and black candles and then we got ding dongs because they were the closest thing to a black cake we could find at the gas station.

TAYLOR RAGNER

Back at the motel I got out the new razor we'd bought, draped a towel around my neck, and told Tatum to "go for it!"

She said, "How much and how close to the scalp?"

We were standing in the bathroom with bad lighting. We were shaving and cutting my hair first, and then we were gonna bleach it. She'd already cut a good six inches off. I'd tied it in a rubber band first and she'd cut through the ponytail straight across. I'd wrapped the ponytail in a plastic Walmart bag, stuffed it in my duffel.

Tatum's hair was dripping black beads onto the floor and onto the towel around her neck. The sink was still black from her dye. There were dirty blond clips of her hair in the wastebasket. We'd cut maybe three inches off hers. Hers wasn't as long as mine. There wasn't as much to cut. We still had to cut her bangs. But first we were shaving my head, one side of it, the left.

"Ouch!" I yelled. "What the fuck!?"

"Sorry," she said. "I'm not used to these kind of clippers. I've never used them before, baby."

"Well be careful," I said. I inhaled on my cigarette, watching in the mirror.

"If old Anabel Ragner could see me now, she'd shit her pants!"

"So would Cam," Tatum said.

"Fuck Cam. Fuck Cam Spencer!" I said.

"Fuck him," she said.

I watched as the hair on half my head fell in a pile at our feet.

I watched as the perfect cheerleader and the perfect daughter and the perfect girlfriend all died a grisly death on the bathroom floor of the Red Roof Inn in I-don't-know-where-the-fuck-we-are, Kentucky.

ANISSA GRANT

Tatum was sitting in a chair in the middle of the hotel room with a towel still around her head watching TV in my old t-shirt and her underwear, waiting for the bleach to take effect. I said I'd be right back.

"No!" she shouted.

She didn't want me to go without her. But it seemed safer to go by myself. If anyone was looking, they were probably looking for two girls. Two runaways. Kidnapper and kidnapee.

"What if something happens?" she said.

"I'll be right back," I said. "It'll be fine. I'm 'Mr. Happy,' remember?"

I pointed to my t-shirt, gave the thumbs up sign.

"Hurry!" she said. "Don't be late for the funeral. And get me a pack of smokes, please, babe!"

"Okay," I said, and kissed her mouth, which was wet and tasted like Twizzlers. She'd bought a giant pack of them at Walmart and it was already half gone.

I got in the car, glanced in the rearview mirror. Taylor had cut my bangs short and straight across. With the new black dye job I looked pretty Goth. I looked less like Elvis's daughter than Marilyn Manson's.

I drove off the main road until I came to a dirt road and then I unbolted the license plate and walked it into a wooded area, dug a tiny ditch in the dirt and buried it best I could. I wiped my hands on a towel in the backseat. Drove back toward town close enough I could walk but far enough it'd be a day or two, hopefully, before the car was found.

It took me about an hour and fifteen minutes to walk to the used car lot.

It's always suspicious when a woman has a wad of cash.

No one questions a man's use of cash.

I'd spent most of my walk trying to come up with a good lie about why I was buying a used car but then right before I got to the lot I decided, fuck it, I didn't need a lie. A man didn't need a lie. It was none of their goddamn business why I was buying a car. Did they want my money or didn't they? Did they want to do business or did they want my life story?

I lit a cigarette to cover my nerves as I walked onto the lot. (Like a man.) I stood there a good thirty seconds, walking around the cars, before this large man in an ill-fitting suit exited the trailer-like building to greet me.

"Hello, Welcome to Dodd's Cars, I'm Mike Dodd, how can I help you?"

He was grinning like John Candy in *Planes, Trains and Automobiles*.

I felt like Steve Martin. Like I didn't really like him.

"Just looking at cars," I said.

"Well I can see that," Mike Dodd said. "What sort are you looking for, or, what are you looking to spend?"

I had done some quick math in my head on the long walk and come up with a number: two thousand. I figured two thousand could get us to Florida. I don't know why Taylor and I had picked Florida as our final destination. Maybe because it was as far south as you could go and for whatever reason, we had picked south. Maybe it was because growing up on the West Coast, I'd never been to Florida. All I ever heard about Florida was how the people there were crazy, ex-convicts, perverts, sex offenders, child molesters, drug addicts, homeless. People who didn't fit into the rest of society, into the other forty-nine states. Outlaws. Derelicts. Rednecks. White trash. Gangstas. Criminals. Criminal minds. Grandparents. Alzheimer patients. The mentally handicapped.

"About two grand," I said.

"Okay," he said. "Well…"

He made a big production of scanning the lot for cars that cheap.

"Let's see," he said, walking backwards across the lot. "We have this pretty nice Ford Escort here. Owned by a nice older woman. She kept it in pretty nice shape."

"How much?" I said, thinking, *drink every time he says* nice.

"It's listed at $2,500 but I can give it to you for 2,300."

"What if I have cash and I only have $2,000?" I said.

"If you have $2,000 you probably have $2,300," he said, same John Candy smile.

I walked around the car, pretended I knew what I was looking for, looked inside the hood, kicked the tires.

I just wanted to be done looking, done talking to Mike Dodd, back in the room with Taylor, plotting our next move.

"I have $2,100," I said.

"Where are you headed?" he said, walking back toward the trailer-like office.

"Vegas," I said. I was standing and he was sitting and I was watching him fill out papers.

"You're going to need more cash for Vegas, sweetheart," he said.

"Yeah, I'm going there to work, not to gamble," I said, like it was any of his goddamn business.

"Gotcha," he said, making the gun of his forefinger and thumb and cocking it at me. "Well, try to resist the lure."

"Mmmhmmm," I said. How fucking long was this transaction going to take? How many minutes of my life were given over to not telling men to fuck off?

The car smelled like someone had spilled orange juice in it and it'd sat in the sun with the windows up for three days. It wasn't the worst smell in the world.

When I got back to the room, Taylor was asleep on the bed, curled into a little kitten ball. I almost didn't recognize her for a second until I remembered how we'd bleached her hair before I left. For a couple seconds I thought maybe I'd opened the wrong room. She looked like a literal angel. Like a 30s screen goddess. Someone who would rub a grapefruit in your face. Someone who should be kept in silk and pearls and ermine furs. But she also looked like an extra in *Sid and Nancy*, like a baby-faced Courtney Love. Like a kitten-faced Courtney.

I set down the keys and climbed on the bed behind her. She smelled like bleach and cigarettes. The scent reminded me of Quinn's semen. I fell asleep beside her, the TV still on, some asshole talking about the election, badmouthing Hillary. I thought, "fuck you," and then I kissed my girlfriend's neck, and then I fell asleep, thinking of Florida, thinking of Quinn's come in my hand. He never wanted to come anywhere else. He was very concerned with disrespecting me. With not doing that, I mean. He was a very sensitive poet baby. Maybe I had a thing for angels. Quinn's hair was bleached when I met him. White blonde. Halo. Fine baby hairs. He slept curled into a tight ball on the bed also. Heroin. Cigarettes. He weighed less than I did when he died. He smelled like cigarettes and bleach. He smelled like heaven. So did Taylor. I leaned into her, my nose pressed to her back. Heaven-sent. Heaven scent. Dirty angels. La-di-da. La-di-da.

ANABEL RAGNER

Scott was here a day and gone the next. He met with the police officers, answered their questions, and caught a red-eye the next morning. He must have really hated me. Must have really hated his family. At that point. Or he must have really loved someone else.

Of course, I found out later the *someone else* was a young woman three years older than our daughter, three years older than Taylor. Younger than Taylor's *girlfriend*. Barely legal. And who knew how long they'd been dating. How long he'd been fucking her. Or, more accurately, how long he'd been *paying* her. I found out later he, or, *we*, were paying for her condo, paying for her car, paying for god knows what else. Probably her fucking groceries and birth control pills.

I was beginning to understand that nothing is ever as it seems, that everything we think we believe in is disproved, at some point. That I was wasting my life believing in people and things that didn't give a fuck about me.

I was becoming my own detective, spending every waking second I wasn't with Jolie online, trying to find my daughter, looking for clues.

I had help from Cam, at least. He was coming over a lot after school. God bless him. I don't know what I would have done without him. I couldn't get my own son, Taylor's older brother, to call me back.

But Cam was a good kid. At least with me he was. And he really loved Taylor. We both really loved Taylor. And we both hated Tatum. She'd essentially ruined both of our lives. She'd fucked both of us over. It was clear she didn't give a fuck who she hurt. We were just trying to keep her from hurting our Taylor. We just wanted our Taylor home in one piece.

CHASE WHITING

I didn't have a way of contacting Taylor or Tatum to tell them what was going on back in Elkheart. The police had found their cellphones by the side of the highway. Cam told me that. Cam told me everything. He was more aggro than I'd ever seen him. I don't think he was sleeping. Someone said he was on Adderall. He was texting me 24/7, telling me everything he and Anabel were doing to try to find Taylor.

He kept asking me to go with him to Taylor's mom's house but I didn't want to go. It felt disloyal to Taylor. I wanted her and Tatum to be safe, of course, but part of me was rooting for them to stay gone as long as possible. I was scared for them to be found, for what might happen to them, especially to Tatum, now that we all knew she wasn't sixteen. I didn't know the laws but I was pretty sure she'd go to jail, prison, for taking a "minor" over state lines.

Cam was facing jail time for the photo, for what the courts were calling "child pornography" on account of Makayla being underage. But he didn't seem too worried about it. Or he was way too obsessed with finding Taylor to care. Whenever I asked he said his mom was handling it.

Also, I was trying to distance myself from Cam. For my own well-being. For my own emotional state.

CAM SPENCER

Chase was acting fuckin' weird again, weird for even Chase. Which I didn't need right then, you know? I needed him to have my fucking *back*. To be there when I called or texted him. But he never texted me back. Or he texted me back eight hours later. I didn't know what his fucking problem was. Why he was being such a total dick.

I was spending a lot of time with Anabel, with Taylor's mom. So much time my dad started riding me about it.

"I know you want to help, Cam," he said. "But don't you think you're spending a little too much time at her house? She's a grown woman with a husband, Cam."

"But Taylor's dad's not really in the picture," I said. "She doesn't really have anyone else…"

"Even more reason to distance yourself, Cam, to not get too involved."

I think my dad would have felt better if Chase had been with us. If it wasn't just me and Anabel on our own. Or if Anabel had been "Caucasian." He was kind of racist like that. Like, *oh, all Latina women are seductresses with fat asses like J-Lo*. Maybe he had a thing for Anabel himself and was, what'd you call it? Projecting or some shit? Who the fuck knows with my pops, man.

I was over there after school most days. With Taylor gone, I barely cared about school or sports or anything. I felt agitated and restless whenever I wasn't lifting, running, or with Anabel trying to find Taylor.

ANABEL RAGNER

I'd looked into what could happen to Tatum online. I didn't think she was well. I told the cops I didn't think she was well. I thought she must have a genuine mental disorder, doing what she did. Posing as a sixteen-year-old, stealing her own daughter's identification. Cuz we figured out, that's what she did. I thought maybe she was schizophrenic or bipolar or even a sociopath. I mean, who would do something like that? Who would go back to high school when they're thirty years old and try out for the cheerleading team? I'm sorry, but only a fucking crazy person would do something like that. A fucking psychopath, child actor.

Look, I just wanted her to get the *professional help* she clearly needed. After they charged her with whatever crime or crimes she'd committed. Kidnapping, for one. And posing as a teenager, two. Whatever that's called. Whatever that is. Who the fuck knows what it's called because it's never done. No one ever does it. It's fucking insane someone came to our town and did it. Came to our town and conned our daughters, *my daughter*, into believing it, into believing she was a sixteen-year-old *girl*.

I didn't even want to think of what they may have done… what they might be doing… what other kinds of perverse things she might be into.

I know we're supposed to be progressive right now and I am, for Jolie, but Jolie's not trying to con anyone. Jolie's not trying to run off with someone else's child. Jolie's right here safe and sound with me not hurting anyone. Jolie just wants to wear pretty dresses, put bows in her hair, paint her nails.

God only knows what this "Tatum" person is into.

CAM SPENCER

I finally had my day in court. My dad had ordered me a suit from Brooks Brothers and my mom had someone she knew, this thirty-year-old dude who looked like a cross between Charlie Sheen in *Wall Street* and Christian Bale in *American Psycho*, represent me. The judge was cool. He gave me a year's probation. As long as I didn't get in any further trouble, he said, it would be wiped from my record at the end of the year. Which meant I wouldn't be on the sex offender's list. That was the bottom line. My dad was fucking stoked, took me to some fancy restaurant in Indianapolis for lunch. Ordered us steaks and a couple Old Fashioneds which he shared with me.

I could barely eat. I didn't have much appetite. I was so stressed out. And the Adderall probably didn't help.

My dad said, "You're not still hung up on Taylor, are you, Cameron?"

I said, "Of course I'm still hung up on Taylor, Dad. We've been dating three years, I planned on marrying her, and she's who the fuck knows where doing who the fuck knows what with some thirty-year-old woman we know nothing about. So, yeah, Dad, I'm a little 'hung up' on Taylor still. Jesus Christ."

"I know you're worried about her, we all are," he said, in a not very believable voice. "But you also need to move on. They're going to find her. The police are going to find her and bring her back here very soon. But for your own sake, you need to let Taylor go, get your head straight, go to college, and not look back. Do you understand what I'm saying? She's not worth it. You can't let a girl mess with your head like this. I can see how it's affecting you. Your mother and I are worried, to be honest. You're not your-self, Cam. We want the old Cam back. We want to see you flourish at college. Flourish in life. We *believe in you*, Cameron."

I sat there silently nodding. Yep. Yep. I got it. He didn't understand. He would never understand. He'd never lost anything he wanted in his life. He'd been high school quarterback, frat boy, college grad, Mr. Fucking Right. He'd never lost my mom. And they'd been high school sweethearts. So what the fuck was he even talking about? So what the fuck did he know about anything, anyway?

TAYLOR RAGNER

I didn't recognize myself in the side mirror on our new car. The girl I saw looked like a girl in a John Hughes film. One of the lesser known ones. I liked the way she looked. Edgy. Badass. Like she could be a lesbian but you weren't sure, she might like dick, too.

I said that to Tatum, "With my new look, you can't tell if I like dick or pussy."

"*I* can tell," she said, grabbing my ass and pulling me to her—"V to V," as she says.

I laughed, but I liked the androgyny.

Tatum looked androgynous too but less so. Her features were too fine, too delicate. She acted tougher on account of it. She dragged on her cigarette like James Dean. Like Nicolas Cage. Like Johnny Depp.

I turned my body so that my feet rested in her lap.

"What the fuck are you doing?" she said, pretending to be mad at me. "You're going to make me wreck our brand new car!"

She'd made us leave the motel before breakfast. Made me wait two hours down the freeway before she'd stop at a Waffle House. I'd wanted French toast but they didn't have French toast, apparently, which I thought was bullshit.

"But IHOP has waffles," I'd said to the waitress, who was about fifty-five and uninterested in my wants or reasoning. She was probably jonesing for her cigarette break. So she could text her abusive alcoholic boyfriend. Maybe I'm generalizing. Profiling. Anyway, she didn't seem too happy. Maybe it was me but I didn't think so.

"Well, this isn't IHOP," she said.

"Clearly," I said.

"Okay," Tatum had said. "Let's go."

She handed the waitress our menus and grabbed my hand.

"What?" I said.

"Let's find you some French toast, princess," she said.

"I'm sorry that I think it's bullshit that every pancake place has waffles and French toast but Waffle House only has waffles."

"No," Tatum said. "You're right. It *is* bullshit. Which is why we're going to that Denny's across the street, to get you French toast or pancakes or whatever it is you want. But just FYI, maybe *don't be* a Kid Rock asshole at Waffle House, since we're trying to blend in. Since we're *trying* not to be noticed. Just a thought, hotshot."

Then at Denny's I'd ordered waffles—just to be a dick. Just to make Tatum laugh, just to piss her off, which sometimes meant the same thing.

ANISSA GRANT

There was no way of knowing how hard the police were looking for us. We had to assume they'd alerted the police in other states, the highway patrol. I had to be careful not to speed. I didn't want them catching us just because I'd gone five mph over the goddamn speed limit.

I told Taylor to watch for cops, too, but she was almost never paying attention. She was fiddling with the radio or playing a Hank Williams or Loretta Lynn CD we'd bought at a truck stop or Cracker Barrel.

I told her I wanted to try driving straight through for one night, to try to get ahead of the police if we could.

She said, "Does that mean we can use one of those showers at a truck stop then? Because I'm all about that!"

"Don't get so excited," I said. "I'm sure they're super shitty. I'm sure you'll be complaining thirty seconds in."

"Fuck off," she said. "I will not! You don't even know me, Tatum Grant, if that's what you think of me. If that's how you see me!"

"Mmmm hmmm," I said. "We'll see. But either way, I'm going to need some more energy drinks. Since you can't fucking drive. No offense."

"Oh, sorry I'm not sixteen till next week. Sorry you picked a fucking teenager to fall in love with," she said, staring out her window, turning her head away from me.

"Who said anything about love?" I said.

"*I* did," she said.

"Mmmhmmm," I said.

"That's right: mmmhmmm," she said.

She had me there. I was in love with her. That wasn't a question. The only question was: now what?

TAYLOR RAGNER

The showers weren't as awful as Tatum said they'd be.

And they were cheaper than a motel room.

And there was no one in the women's.

You had to buy your own shampoo and soap, though, which, like Waffle House, seemed like bullshit. I was finding out more and more stuff about the south was bullshit, but whatever, we were having fun.

I asked Tatum to shampoo my hair for me.

"Come on," I said. "It'll feel a lot better if *you* do it. Pah-leeeeese?"

I was standing under the water, naked, soapy underarms, soapy pubic hair.

Tatum was washing her own hair in the shower next to mine.

"Alright," she said. "If it'll keep you quiet."

She came over and stood behind me. "Bend down," she said.

I squatted a little, bent my knees. It felt like we'd been in the car for days. I waited until she'd massaged my head half a minute, then turned to kiss her.

"Do you think there's cameras in here?" I said.

"I don't know. Wouldn't that be illegal?" Tatum said.

"I don't know," I said. "But I also guess I don't care. Give me the soap."

I lathered her tits and stomach and under her arms and down her thighs. I kneeled in front of her, feeling the water stream off her body onto my head, onto my face and tits. I slid open her legs with my hand, slid my tongue up between them. She took a step or two back and I followed on my knees a step forward. She leaned against the wall, pressing her palms flat and wide, like Spiderman, like she was climbing. Which was how she acted a minute or two later.

After, we toweled our hair, and I stuck my head down under the hand dryer on the wall.

I got dressed and walked back out into the gas station. Tatum was already there, her arms full of Hostess products and energy drinks. I got two bananas, two oranges and a jar of dry-roasted peanuts. I looked up at the clock behind the register: 2:33 a.m.

"We can't just eat junk," I said, setting my pile on the counter next to her Twinkies and Suzy-Qs and Doritos.

"And a pack of Marlboro Reds," she told the cashier.

She carried the bags to the car, loaded them onto the backseat floor behind her.

"Slim Jim?" she said as she got back into the driver's seat.

I turned and she was holding a Slim Jim in one hand and a single red rose in the other.

"Awww, for me?" I said, batting my eyelashes.

"For you," she said.

And I reached for the Slim Jim, smiling, bit off a big bite, packaging and all; spit the cellophane onto the ground.

"Fine," she said, and threw the rose out the window.

"What the fuck did you do that for?" I said. "I was kidding! I wanted it."

"Too bad. Love isn't for jokesters," she said.

"Love is for losers," I said.

"Cheers to that," she said. And opened her third energy drink of the day.

"We're going to have to stop somewhere soon," I said. "You're going to crash hard in about an hour.

"We'll see," she said.

I put my feet back up on the dash, bit off another section of Slim Jim and turned on the radio. Nirvana was playing. "Heart-Shaped Box."

I pulled the trucker hat I'd taken from the gas station out from my purse, unsquished it, and put it on my head.

"Where the hell did you get that?" Tatum said.

"I stole it," I said. "It says, 'I don't want a great love affair, I just want a good blowjob.'"

"Oh my god, no you did not," Tatum said.

"Don't worry," I said. "I got one for you, too."

I pulled another hat from my purse. This one said, "If you're wearing this hat, you might be a redneck."

"Put it on," I said.

"No way, man," Tatum said.

"Oh, you think just cuz you're from California, from *Hollywood*, you aren't redneck?" I said.

"Yeah," she said, lighting a cigarette, rolling down her window and sticking her arm out. "That's exactly what I think."

"Okay, Little Miss Hollywood," I said, and I stuck the hat on my head on top of the other one.

"Well, *I'm* a redneck *puta* and proud of it," I said.

"Yeah," she said, taking another long drag from her cigarette. "I can see that."

"Good," I said. "I don't want you to be disillusioned."

Tatum laughed. "I'm not disillusioned," she said.

"Okay," I said. "Just making sure."

ANISSA GRANT

I drove another hour or two, till one or two in the morning. I was beat. I didn't know where the fuck we were. Georgia somewhere. There were peaches on all the signs. Boiled peanuts for sale on the side of the freeway. I'd drunk so many energy drinks, I was pissing neon green. Or neon yellow. Maybe I was color blind from so much energy.

I told Taylor we were going to have to stop for a few hours. We both wanted to get to Florida as quick as possible. As though it were its own country. A land of freedom in which we didn't have to worry about things like "consent." Lol. Consent for us was Taylor deciding—or, *demanding*—to come with me. Her birthday was in a week, which in some states made her legally capable of making decisions for herself and in others it still wouldn't matter.

"The coal miner's daughter was thirteen when she got married," Taylor said.

"Coal *minor* daughter," I said.

"Haha. Dad joke," Taylor said.

"Anyway," I said. "Loretta was fifteen. She lied about her age. Shaved two years off."

"Fifteen, whatever. I'm fifteen. I'm almost sixteen. Anthony Kiedis was eleven when he fucked his daddy's eighteen-year-old girlfriend. You don't see him complaining about PTSD or whatever it is people think you get from sleeping with someone older."

"Nope, you don't. You see Anthony Kiedis struggling with addiction issues and haircuts, but you *do not* see him complainin' about fucking his dad's teenaged girlfriend when he was eleven; that you *do not* see."

"People just like to get in other people's business."

"Yup. Yup, they do."

We were parked outside a non-denominational church in "north central Georgia." Whatever that meant. I think it meant we were a good ways from Florida still.

"Give me a kiss goodnight," Taylor said, after she'd peed behind the church.

"You smell like urine," I said.

"Fine!" she said. "*Don't* kiss me." And she turned on her side, away from me, facing the car door.

I waited a minute or two, like I was already sleeping, then opened my door.

"What are you doin?" she said.

It was pitch black out, though, so she couldn't see. They really needed a street light or two in that parking lot. To keep out the riff raff.

I crouched around the back of the car to Taylor's door and opened it real fast.

"Hey!" she said. She about fell out of the car onto the pavement.

"I'm here for my kiss," I said. I was on my knees and the pavement under them hurt.

"Hurry up," I said. "I can't kneel here on the ground forever."

"Or can you?" she said, grabbing hold of my shoulders, pulling me to her.

I never thought a church parking lot in Georgia could be so romantic.

I got back in the car beside her. We fell asleep holding hands, singing "Malibu". Which was a place I wanted to take her someday.

State Patrolman Andy Kirk, Georgia State Police

I found their car parked in the church parking lot off the highway near Macon. It was 4:45 in the morning, according to my record, on a Thursday. I tapped on the half of the window that was up. It was pretty warm, still, for December. Shined my flashlight into the car. There were two young women inside, sleeping. One had on a shirt with Daffy Duck on the front, I remember because I've always loved Daffy since I was a kid. I mean, who doesn't love Daffy, right?

The other, the driver, or the one in the driver's seat, had on a black hoodie, the hood pulled up over her head, so at first I couldn't see if this was a man or a woman, black or white. I just didn't know. You get a surprising number of people parking in church lots overnight. I guess they think churches are exempt from laws because they don't pay taxes. Wrong! Churches themselves may be a refuge of sort, but the parking lots are not. The parking lots are subject to all the same laws as a Target lot or any Main Street in Any city, U.S.A.

"Evening," I said, shining my flashlight on each of their faces in turn.

The one with the hood shielded her eyes with her hand, which was when I saw the chipped nail polish and rings. Female. At least, that was my knee-jerk inner thought. I know that's not always the case now; that you can't always tell based on things like that now. But that was my assumption and it turned out to be a correct one, far as I know. I haven't been told otherwise.

The passenger's eyes were crammed shut tight. A ring of dark makeup under them. She had on a pair of what looked like sweats or what my daughter sometimes calls "leggings," with her Daffy Duck tee. And hair bleached white blonde like Rebel Yell or White Wedding era Billy Idol—if you're old enough for that reference to mean something to you.

Honestly, they looked harmless, a pair of teenage runaways, maybe, but probably from good homes—middle class to upper middle class, even. It looked like they were "dressing down." I don't know why I say that. You just get a sense for these sorts of things, I guess. Who is *actually* poor and who's pretending to be for street cred.

I figured I'd radio them in, return them to their concerned parents.

I figured this would be a cakewalk of a stop.

Then the bitch Tased me.

ANISSA GRANT

I didn't know what happened, exactly. It was all a series of knee jerk decisions and reactions —one after the other—starting with me handing him my fake ID and ending with me hitting him with the Taser when he returned to the car with it to tell me it was a fake ID—"No shit, Sherlock," I said as he lay on the ground, sort of convulsing and shit—Taylor screaming bloody murder beside me—and then we were on a series of back roads that the compass on the car told us was south.

I was full of adrenaline. I'd never actually Tased anyone before. My only example of how one worked was watching *The Hangover* over and over with Tate a few years back when she bought the DVD and insisted on playing it every night for two weeks.

The Taser scene was her favorite scene. But it didn't work exactly like that in real life. In real life… [coughs]

TAYLOR RAGNER

Apparently the Taser was something Tatum had bought for her road trip east, last summer, before leaving L.A.

"Would have been nice to have been warned about it," I said, once we were an hour further south and it felt okay again to talk.

"We need to get another car," Tatum said.

"Another used car," I said. That seemed risky. But so did keeping the one we were in now that we'd Tased a Georgia cop. Also, I didn't know where we were going to find a used car lot out in the middle of nowhere, which we were.

"Nah," she said. "Steal one."

"Don't most people out here—*rural people* —have guns?" I said. I was looking around; there were a lot of pink and green houses, a lot of dogs on chains. A couple Confederate flags. A mammoth Trump sign.

"Well, so do we," Tatum said. I didn't know how many hours we'd slept. One. Two. Not enough. Definitely not enough.

Matty Johnson
(BFE, Georgia resident)

I don't know, man. they told me it was Tatum and Taylor who stole my car. I hadn't heard of any chicks by those names before. I didn't read about it on the internet till later.

And honestly, I didn't give a fuck who stole it.

I'm not one to care about celebrities.

I don't even know who Brajolita or whoever or whatever that is. I promise you. I don't care. I don't pay any attention to that shit. That's "girl shit." Celebrity gossip TMZ shit. Bitch shit.

I just wanted my goddamn car back.

I'd had to work three jobs for six months just to buy it.

And now—two months later—she was gone. My baby. My one true love. My Ford F 1- 50.

Injun red. Pretty as a cherry. Smooth as a virgin. Tight, tight, tight.

ANISSA GRANT

Hotwiring cars was something else Quinn taught me. He and a buddy back where he grew up hotwired cars, boats, dirt bikes, you name it. He was an award-winning actor and a little criminal. A juvenile delinquent. The James Dean James Dean only pretended to be in movies.

That was the most interesting thing about Quinn. He had the sweetest baby face, the gentlest aura about him at all times, never raised his voice, never acted macho or tough. At least not around me. But he had this dark side. This criminal side. Inherited from his father.

He couldn't escape it. It made him a better actor, but it also took his life.

Anyway, I hotwired that truck in about two minutes and we threw our stuff in it and got the hell out of there.

Then about twenty minutes down the road, Taylor said, "What are these?" and held up a set of keys that'd been sitting in the car console.

The goddamn keys to the car had been there the whole fucking time.

ANABEL RAGNER

By mid-week, the cops told us they were getting closer to catching them. They were following them south, had talked to a motel clerk who recognized them—Red Roof Inn, I think they said, a Waffle House waitress. Both in Kentucky.

Cam said he wanted to drive down south himself, that he could probably do a better job than the cops. I don't know what he was basing that on. It was sweet of him to want to try, but I told him he had to stay in school. He was too close to graduating.

It was two weeks before Christmas and I hadn't put up a tree. Jolie was beside herself, missing her sister. I'd lied and told her she was away at a cheerleading camp. Luckily, a six-year-old doesn't know better, doesn't realize cheerleaders don't go to camp in mid-December.

She kept asking about Christmas too. Normally, I have the whole house decorated by Thanksgiving. It had seemed like bad luck to put up a tree until Taylor was found. But then I decided it was good luck. To have the whole house decorated and ready for her homecoming. Positive thinking. Almost like a dream board in our house. Like we knew she would be home in time for the holidays. So I went all out. I went above and beyond. Jolie was thrilled. We had Santa's train in our front yard. Santa's sleigh on our roof. A zillion reindeer inside and out: on the front yard and on the roof and on the second floor landing overlooking the living room.

I hired Cam and Chase to help me decorate: to hang lights in all the trees, to get on the roof, to do all the chores Scott and Tyler should have been helping with. If I hadn't somehow pushed both my husband and son away.

I tried not to think about how now I'd pushed my eldest daughter away.

Instead, I focused on Jolie and Cam. I made the three of us pot roasts and ham dinners.

I didn't know what Taylor would say when she came back about all the time I'd been spending with Cam, but I couldn't worry about that now. Cam was the only person who kept me from total bed-taking, crippling depression. Besides, it was pretty clear my daughter didn't give two shits about Cam anymore. It was pretty obvious who she cared about and it wasn't Cam or me.

CHASE WHITING

I went over to Taylor's mom's house with Cam a couple times to help hang lights and all the other decorations she'd ordered for the house, inside and out. She was acting sort of crazy. Every time we went over, there was more to hang. More lights to put up, on the roof or on the back balcony.

I thought about suggesting she see someone—a therapist or professional of some kind. But I didn't think I should be the one to make such suggestions. It wasn't my place. After my mom died, we had people we barely knew texting and emailing us tips on dealing with death. It was nice of people to think about us, but what I really needed was someone to talk to. When someone close to you like a parent dies, your closest friends, at least in my experience, maybe because I'm a guy, tend to avoid the topic. Maybe they are afraid of making you emotional. But the thing is, they end up encouraging your sense of isolation and loneliness. My mom used to be the person I talked to most and now I didn't talk to anyone, really. At least now that Tatum and Taylor were gone.

Hanging Christmas decorations for Taylor's mom was a good distraction from my own house where my dad seemed in denial it was Christmas. Plus, it meant a reason to spend time with Cam. I had barely seen him outside of school since Taylor and Tatum left. He was always with Anabel, I guess. They had this way of interacting with each other now, very husband and wife. It was weird. They talked in codes and whispers. I felt like a third wheel. Which sort of defeated the point of spending time with Cam.

I was heartsick, now, whenever I looked at him.

Maybe I was channeling the grief from losing my mom into my want for Cam.

Maybe both emotions were happening simultaneously.

I didn't know if Cam and I would end up at the same college, or if we even should.

Part of me thought I should go to a school out of state, out of the Midwest, where no one else I knew would go. Start over. Become a new Chase.

Get a new life. Where I wasn't the "in love w his best friend, mother dead, weirdo perv." Where I wasn't a series of labels. A clean slate.

California. That was where people went to start over. To be someone new. Well, everyone but Tatum. Tatum had to do everything backwards. Tatum had to leave California, come to the Midwest.

TAYLOR RAGNER

We were crossing into Florida, finally. But I was feeling uneasy again. I said to Tatum, "I think we should change our hair again. I bet by now they have descriptions of us like this." I was staring into the tiny mirror on the back of my window visor. I was thinking of buzzing most of my hair off. Or of shaving it.

"Yeah," Tatum said. "Or we could just wear our hats. Wear our sunglasses. Be less conspicuous."

I guess that eliminated shaving my head.

I didn't know what our plan was after Disney. Disney was all we'd ever talked about. Maybe Tatum thought we could get jobs there. We'd need fake IDs, but we could be Cinderella and Snow White. Or Tigger and Mickey Mouse. What the fuck did we care as long as we could stay at the Magic Kingdom. As long as we didn't have to go back home.

"I don't want to go back home," I said to Tatum. She was chewing nicotine gum in between cigarettes. Anything for a buzz. To keep us awake. To stay ahead of whoever might be onto us.

"We're not going back," she said, grabbing my hand and kissing it.

I felt taller in the truck. Less fragile. I felt like a truck driver's girlfriend. Sassy and bold and sexual. I wanted to lean over and give Tatum a blowjob. It was harder to be spontaneous in a moving car if you were lesbians, dykes, whatever we were. I had to settle for rubbing her clit through her leggings, putting my mouth on it and tonguing it through the fabric. It had the same effect, anyway. We almost ran off the road on a highway near Panama City.

After, I looked at myself in the mirror again. Ran my fingers through my hair, a cigarette burning in one of them. I still wanted to buzz my head. Not shave it all off, but clip it pretty frickin' short.

CAM SPENCER

Anabel sent me a link to a news article on the internet that was about them buying some used car somewhere down in Kentucky. Some dude down there who owned a used car lot said he recognized Tatum from the photos he saw online. I was three seconds away from getting in my truck and driving down there, but my dad was home and stopped me. Took my keys till he said I'd settled down. He even made me drink a beer and do a shot of Daniels with him.

It was hard to sit still up here in Indiana when I could *feel* the path they were taking, could *see* the route they were on, headed south, in my head.

Like they were on their way to Mexico. But I didn't think they'd end up in Mexico. They'd be caught at the border, unless they went through illegally. And did anyone go *into* Mexico illegally? [laughs] They tried to act tough, like real *independent women*, feminazis, but neither of them was tough like that. They weren't going to spend ten years living in Mexico. Even if Taylor did speak Spanish. Her mom was from Puerto Rico, not Mexico. It wasn't like they had family down there or something.

After that, Anabel begged me just like my dad not to go looking for them. She said, "I need you here with me. I don't need you out there lost somewhere I can't reach you too."

I guess we'd grown really close in the last few days; bonded over losing Taylor. We'd gone to Office Depot and bought a whiteboard and sticky notes and made a map of the United States and pinned notes where Taylor and Tatum were known to have stopped. We were following them on the map. We told Jolie it was Santa's sleigh we were tracking. I'd gotten so used to Jolie being a girl by now I usually forgot she was born a boy, that I'd known her first as a boy, for two and a half years. I mean, whatever, right? Who fucking cares if she's a boy or girl. It used to bother me. I'll be the first to admit: it used to bother me a lot. When Taylor first told me about it, about *him* becoming a *her*. I was really against it. I didn't fucking get it. How could a boy *feel* like a girl inside? But since I'd been spending so much time with them, with Anabel and Jolie, and since Taylor was gone... I just realized it didn't fucking matter. The only fucking thing I cared about was finding Taylor and getting her home. The *only* thing. Jolie could tell me she felt like a frog inside. Want us to call her Kermit. I'd be like, fine, hello, Kermit! Nice to meet you, Froggie. Now, where the fuck is Taylor? Let's find Taylor! Let's find Taylor and pray she doesn't feel like a boy inside and we'll all be good.

Sometimes Chase came over for dinner or to help out or whatever, but he was just so fucking weird. Quiet. Fucking quiet as hell. He didn't fucking talk. It was awkward as fuck. I figured maybe it was hard on him being Christmas and his mom being gone and all, but I didn't know what the fuck to say. We'd never talked much about personal shit like that. I don't know why. It's just not what men do. You don't talk about your fucking feelings. Unless you're a fag, maybe. Otherwise, you talk about video games and girls and football and getting loaded and who's going to buy beer and whose house you're going to party at, whose parents are out of town, what bitch you're banging or going to bang or want to bang, shit like that. You don't talk about your fucking feelings.

To be honest, it was kind of a fucking downer being around him. You'd think that's how it would have been being around Anabel but it wasn't. She and I tried to be upbeat, to stay focused and positive. Chase just had this cloud of sadness around him. You'd think it was *his girlfriend* got kidnapped!

His girlfriend who took off with some old lesbian dyke! And to be honest, he didn't seem all that worried about Taylor. I kinda got the feeling he thought they were perfectly fine out there on the road together. It was like he was in denial about Tatum being a fucking thirty-year-old criminal pedophile sociopath. Like she was just another cool teenager like us. It was fucking weird, man. It was like I didn't know him anymore. Like I didn't know my own best friend. Like, who the fuck was he?

To be honest, part of me thought he'd never wanted Taylor and me to be together. That he'd always secretly hoped we'd break up. But I couldn't figure out why. It wasn't like he didn't like Taylor. I knew she counted him as one of her closest friends. I knew they talked all the time, not just when I was around. All I could think was maybe he was in love with Taylor. That he secretly wanted her for himself. And that's why he never dated anyone this year, why he was still a virgin, why he was so weird. Such a fucking loner. I don't know. It was the only thing that seemed to make any sense.

ROBIN GRANT

Ever since Anissa left, things had been crazy with Tate. She and I had a very different sort of relationship than the one I'd had with Anissa. I won't say better or worse, just truly different. In some ways we got along better and in other ways we weren't as close. But maybe that's not such a bad thing. Being as close as Anissa and I were… well, you can see how that ended.

With Anissa, neither of us really had other friends or anyone else we were close to. Just each other. I guess today it's popular to refer to close relationships like that, like ours, as "codependent." I don't know if we were or weren't. "Codependent." We were just super close, best friends, mother and daughter.

And I'm fully aware what Anissa has said about having to parent me, on account of my drinking and blah blah blah. It was never that bad, I don't think. Kids exaggerate everything, you know. Even adult kids. Trust me. Wait.

But with Tate, I'm more of a traditional mom. As well as her manager. It helps that I *am* sober now, too. I get that.

But she keeps me in the dark about a lot of things. She is definitely independent and private. She's fifteen but she acts forty sometimes. The things she says to me. Or the way she says them. The looks she gives me.

Anissa never challenged me or my rules. With the exception of the few months she was seeing Quinn. Tate does what she wants. I can't enforce anything with Tate. She just laughs and walks away. She realizes the power she has. She understands that she's making a lot of money and therefore has a lot to say about her life, and the choices she's making. With her I have more of a secretarial role. Less of an authority figure. Forget disciplinarian.

Anissa never realized she had any power. Or she didn't want it. Maybe she liked being passive. Having her decisions made for her. Maybe she didn't know how to make decisions or what decisions to make. She let me make them and then for a brief time she let Quinn make them and then she let me make them again.

Tate's been out every night this week. School nights. Weekends. God knows where she goes. She'll tell me one thing, something that's clearly not the whole truth. Or clearly a starting point for the evening. Not the final destination by any means. I'm not stupid.

She comes home one, two in the morning.

If I say anything the next day she threatens me with the emancipated minor stuff.

She says, "Reese did it. Drew did it. I can do it."

She says, "I can do it like that." and she snaps her fingers.

She says, "I've already talked to my attorney about it."

She adds, "Just out of curiosity." To soften the blow. But I get it. I'm one minute from being 100% replaced.

So I do what I'm asked to do, book her gigs, remind her of her appointments. Drive her when she needs a ride, which is less and less often. Mostly she Ubers. Soon she'll have a license. She keeps telling me that, too.

"I can't wait to get my own car," she says.

Even without the emancipated minor business, I only have another year or two with her, tops. Unless she keeps me on as manager after she moves out. And let's face it, most child actors don't keep their moms on much after they turn eighteen.

I don't know what I'm going to do when both girls are out of the house. It'll have been thirty years of living with my babies and then nothingness. And then no one. And then just me and the cat. Maybe I'll get a dog. Or one of those potbelly pigs.

I don't know what I ever did to make neither girl want to hang around, to want to leave me the second they get the chance.

Other than love them unconditionally. I just loved them both so much. I just love them both with all of my heart.

ANISSA GRANT

I had been used to playing a role for so long, to inhabiting the body of a character, it was hard for me to know who I really was or *what* I was. I felt most comfortable being told the background of my character, the backstory of her, taking on her identity. As a small child, even if I wasn't at the moment working on a film or play, my mother would have me role-play at home, as exercise, enforce the Method acting rules of 24/7 submergence, a different classic role each week, beginning on Sundays, when we would map out my character's personality traits, her histories, her antagonists and love interest.

My mother was more Stella Adler than Mom. More Stanislavski than parent.

In retrospect, I was growing up inside the actor's studio.

Without much if any knowledge of our own family history, of my own backstory. Questions regarding that were unwelcomed, were quickly given a backseat to whatever character study we were engaged in. As though my mother were distracting me from some horrific knowledge, some horrible secret history.

My mother kept me playing one role after the other—Helen Keller, Juliet, Annie, the child in *Paper Moon*—

It'd been a decade since I'd worked formerly and I still couldn't shake the feeling of being dissociated from myself. Of an absence of identity. Of feeling a blank slate.

"Maybe you're just having an identity crisis," Taylor said.

We'd been driving eight hours straight, only stopping for drive-thrus and gas station breaks.

Yeah, duh. "Do you ever feel like that, though?" I asked, lighting a cigarette, cracking open another can of Monster.

"Feel like, what?" she said.

"Like you have no idea who you are," I said.

"Sort of, I guess. Mostly I feel like I know but it's not who my mother or other people want me to be," she said.

"I guess that's why I left California, why I came to Elkheart," I said.

"To play another role?"

"To find myself by returning to a time before adulthood, before the self is fully formed."

"Oh, I thought you said you came to Elkheart to try out for cheerleading and to go to Prom or Homecoming," Taylor said, spitting her nicotine gum out the window and lighting a cigarette.

"That too, smartass," I said.

"I thought you came to Elkheart to fall in love," she said, smiling.

"Yeah, but I pictured myself with a football player, not the football player's girlfriend," I said, running my hand over Taylor's newly shorn white-blonde locks. Her whole head of hair now was about an inch long. Half an inch, maybe. It was sexy as hell. It was like being with a boy and a girl at the same time. I wondered if this made me pansexual. Maybe I didn't see gender anymore. I only saw Taylor now so gender didn't matter.

Age ain't nuthin but a number and gender ain't nuthin but a letter of the alphabet on your driver's license. SMW. LOL.

COACH W

Everyone at school was talking about Taylor and Tatum, T&T, of course. The rumor mill was working overtime: Tatum wasn't sixteen, Tatum wasn't female, Tatum was an undercover cop like Johnny Depp on *21 Jump Street*, Tatum was a Scientologist, Tatum was into witchcraft and had put a spell on Taylor, Tatum was researching a role and fell in love with her subject.

Tatum had kidnapped Taylor was the main point of every rumor, no matter which other way it went.

Tatum was going to do time when they got caught.

Or go to an asylum. That was the other main rumor: Tatum was crazy, certifiably insane.

I was surprised there weren't rumors about or calls to burn her at the stake. Yet.

I was trying to keep my head low. I went to work, I went home. I drank till I passed out. Watched TV till I passed out. Got up and did it again.

Groundhog's Day, 2016: the final chapter.

TATE GRANT

My mom, or, *grandma*, was acting different toward me now. Now that I was Quinn James's daughter. Now that I was a working actor, bringing in money, bringing home a paycheck. She'd stopped trying to control me. Which was weird. Of course I liked it. What teenager wouldn't like more freedom? But it felt weird, too. Like she was afraid of me or something. Like she was intimidated by me all of a sudden just because other people were treating me different.

Like I actually was eighteen, now, an adult.

You know how sometimes you're friends with someone or dating someone who caters almost too much to your wants and needs, to the point you actually sort of hope they'll stop? Like, sometimes you're thinking to yourself, *why are they doing this? why didn't they just tell me no?* Like you almost kind of lose some respect for them because they did what you asked for the zillionth time? Or because they *always* do what you ask?

That's how things were getting with my grandma now.

The more she didn't say no, the more I tested the line.

And apparently there wasn't one. Or I hadn't found it yet.

It was fine for me, but it was weird, too.

It sort of made me never want to go home, to be honest.

I stayed out later and later, was gone way more than I would have been, I think.

I just started to feel uncomfortable around her, around this person I thought was my mom for fifteen years.

That was another thing. I didn't know what to call her anymore. So most of the time I didn't call her anything.

It was all getting so awkward. With Anissa gone. At first it was great, things were way better. I got so much more freedom. Now it felt like I had almost too much freedom. Like no one really cared. Or cared enough. I don't know. I tried not to stop and think about it. I tried to just keep going. Signing on for more and more movies, in addition to my TV role. In addition to all the partying I was doing.

What was there to stop me? Who was there?

Just me. And I wasn't going to stop me.

I mean, duh, obviously.

TAYLOR RAGNER

We were so close to Disney! So close to Orlando! A couple hours.

The day before we'd stopped to go to the ocean. To the Gulf, or whatever it's called. Got a room at one of those tiny motels in Clearwater Beach. They were everywhere and they were so cheap.

The motel we picked was called By the Sea and it had a teeny tiny swimming pool right there in the parking lot!

It looked like an old rundown Motel Six inside, like the ones Cam and Chase got to party in for a night back home.

The carpet was stiff and crunchy and the bed cover felt damp. It smelled like mold or mildew and the air conditioning was loud and barely worked. But we didn't care. We didn't give a fuck! We were only staying a night. We just wanted to swim in the ocean. I'd never stepped foot in an ocean—any ocean!—and Tatum had only ever been in the Pacific.

We'd each bought a cheap bathing suit at one of those beach shops near our motel. Mine had stars and stripes on it. Very patriotic! Tatum's was neon green and said "Clearwater Beach" on the ass. Tres sexy! We ran down the beach into the water holding hands and laughing and then we made out in the water, salt water all up in our noses and mouths and vajay-jays, Tatum's fingers all up inside me. I opened my eyes at some point and all these fish, a school or whatever, were swimming by our ankles. It was so romantic!

ANISSA GRANT

Disney World was all decorated for Christmas—it was honestly so beautiful —and it felt like Taylor and I were on our Honeymoon there.

We were staying at a Disney hotel—The Contemporary, riding the monorail to and from the parks every day. We'd had lunch at Cinderella's Castle, held hands going through It's a Small World and the Haunted Mansion and on Splash Mountain. We even bought a disposable camera and had strangers take our pictures in front of the castle and the big silver ball at Epcot.

It was the perfect couple days. Disney felt safe. Like there were so many tourists and people, we could slide right in. We didn't feel in danger of being noticed. We bought Mickey and Minnie shirts and wore them just like everyone else. Bought mouse ears and wore those too.

And the nights were just as perfect—the perfect honeymoon nights, wrapped around Taylor's naked body in bed, staring out the window at Cinderella's Castle, at the fireworks, as I kissed her neck, as I felt my fingers push into her warm wetness between her legs. I never wanted to be anywhere else but there in bed with her. For the rest of my life, our lives. I knew then I wanted to marry her. Even though I didn't believe in marriage. I just wanted to be with this beautiful girl the rest of my life.

I didn't allow myself to think of Tate. If her face or a thought of her ever popped into my brain I immediately pushed it back out. Maybe that sounds cruel, but I just couldn't think of her then. What good did it do to think of her? When she was so far away and she wasn't mine anymore?

TAYLOR RAGNER

Tatum was in the shower when a special news bulletin came on the TV. I can't remember if I was watching something like CNN or E News or what, but suddenly there was a photo of the actress Kaylin Jennings-James on the screen with the headline that she'd just been rushed to an L.A. hospital... I remember I gasped. I'd just started following her on Instagram like a month before or something. She was in some TV show and was dating someone famous, not Justin Bieber but... or was it Bieber? And then another photo flashed on the screen, one of Quinn James and a young woman who looked familiar but who I couldn't right away place. The woman on the screen, the newswoman said, "It was recently revealed that Kaylin Jennings-James is the daughter of the deceased Oscar-winning actor Quinn James and the former child actress Rachel Grant..." I about shit my pants. I bit my lip so hard it started to bleed.

I lit a cigarette and waited for Tatum to come out of the bathroom. I felt numb with all this new information. Like my brain wasn't sure whether to feel pissed off at Tatum or sad for her. I was worried for her daughter; *daughter*. Tatum had a fucking *daughter*. My age! What was I going to find out next? She was a he? If so, *he* had a really authentic vagina. *He* had a really good pair of tits.

The craziest thing was, outside our sliding glass door was the Magic Kingdom. I could see Cinderella's Castle from where I was sitting.

This was supposed to be the happiest place on earth. But suddenly I didn't feel so happy. Suddenly, I felt like I was going to be sick.

My brain was spinning with famous people's names and faces and my girlfriend being somewhere mixed up in all of them. My girlfriend I didn't really know. At all.

I hadn't cared that much that she was older, that she *wasn't sixteen*, but all this, everything else, was harder to take in, was confusing and disorienting... I honestly didn't know what the fuck to think.

I didn't know who I was in love with or who claimed she was in love with me.

What if this was all a secret project, research for a role? I'd seen an old movie like that once. A guy comes to find out this girl was only dating him as an art project for school. For college. He'd been in love with her and she'd been just faking it, for the project, for her art.

I didn't want to be anyone's art project.

I sure as shit wasn't going to be broken up with out of nowhere, when the research period was over.

COACH W

It was Coach Harden who texted me. She said, "Yr not gna believe this. turn on cnn." It was eleven in the morning on a Sunday and I'd just made myself a second Bloody Mary. I was in a brown terrycloth robe over a pair of shorts and feeling very *Big Lebowski* which was how my days felt generally now. Coach Harden was pretty much the only person I talked to outside of school. Sometimes, she and I met for a drink, to shoot the shit about everything that had happened and was happening. Neither of us could believe it, how our lives had turned out. I joked we should move in together so we'd at least have someone to watch TV with while we drank but I knew we were both too introverted for that.

I grabbed my phone and Bloody Mary and went down into the basement and turned on the TV. I had to wait a while to see what she was talking about. I didn't think she wanted me to see some story about a beached whale being pushed back into the ocean by a team of scientists. What was with these whales, anyway? Did they have a death wish too? Like the kids on the railroad tracks? Were they like, why the fuck are you saving me? Please, leave me alone!

Then I saw it. The photo Coach Harden, Jen, wanted me to see. It was a photo of Tatum with Quinn, from sixteen years ago. From right before he died. How can I explain to you... It was like a bucket of ice cold water being poured over my head. Like I'd just coached a team that won the Super Bowl and the Gatorade being poured over my head was green. Or yellow-green. Gatorade green. Gatorade yellow. Whatever. Point is, I was in shock.

I couldn't believe I hadn't seen it all those weeks. That I hadn't recognized her from photos I'd seen sixteen years earlier. From movies and magazine clippings. Sixteen years was a long time. What had she been doing in the interim? Apparently raising this child, Quinn's daughter, no one knew about. Who was now in critical condition in an L.A. hospital. Familiar story.

I don't know what to say, what to tell you, except it was like a life changing moment for me. I put down my Bloody Mary. Put out my cigarette. It's not like I never drank again, never had a smoke after that. Of course, I did. But suddenly I felt a responsibility. To Quinn. To try to help. To stop being an asshole creep. To get my shit together. It seemed like Tatum and Taylor might need me. And if there was ever any way in the world I could help his daughter... I just knew I had to be ready. I had to stop fucking around wasting my life.

ANISSA GRANT

I was towel-drying my hair as I came out of the bathroom.

"I can't believe how sunburned I got," I was saying. "My whole chest is red. I look like a farmer."

The room was weirdly silent except for the TV. Normally, Taylor was flitting about, smoking on the balcony, painting her toenails, blow-drying her hair, running up to hug or kiss me.

"What's the matter?" I said. Taylor was just sitting there, watching TV, but her face was weird. She was staring zombielike at the screen. I felt like she was avoiding me for some reason. "What? What the fuck is it?" I said.

I sat down on the edge of the bed with the towel in my hands. My initial thought was that there'd been some sort of terrorist attack. Or some sort of natural disaster.

The TV was on a commercial when I sat down. "Will you please tell me?" I said to Taylor. "Just tell me what happened."

But she was silent. Like a person in shock. She wasn't moving. Taylor was never not moving. Taylor was as restless as they come.

"You're freaking me out!" I said. I was practically crying even though I didn't know why, what was happening.

Which was when the commercial break was over and the news came back on. A pretty blonde with too much makeup and too much Botox was talking. I watched her lips move. Her hair was stiff, her facial muscles frozen. I couldn't hear what she was saying or what she was saying wasn't making any sense to me. I still didn't know what was happening.

Then a photo of Tate appeared onscreen. One I recognized from her social media accounts. I knew it was the one from a dinner she'd gone to at the Chateau. But they'd closed in on her face and blurred out the faces of those around her. Tate looked so beautiful in the photo. Young and alive and vivacious.

My stomach turned and my mouth went dry. I couldn't speak but I felt like I was going to throw up.

Then there was a photo of me, with Quinn. I didn't know how they got it. I'd never seen it before. But I remembered the moment it was taken as soon as I saw it. We were in someone's kitchen, at someone's house party. Quinn looks pissed or stoned and his arm is around me and in the hand around my shoulder he's holding a glass. Both my arms are around his waist and there's a can of something in one of my hands. A beer or a pop. I don't remember which. Quinn's hair is long in the photo, like Johnny Depp's used to be. I look young. Younger than I ever remember looking. I must have been fourteen, fifteen but I look younger. Quinn was twenty-one, maybe twenty-two.

The newscaster woman was speaking again but I still couldn't make sense of what she was saying. I just heard "daughter of" and then I heard Quinn's and my names.

"Oh my god," I heard myself suddenly say, as much to myself as to Taylor. "What's happened? What happened to her?"

I no longer had the instinct to lie or to cover up. I didn't care what Taylor knew or didn't know. I just needed to know what was happening to Tate, what was happening to my daughter. I needed to know Tate was alive, that she was okay.

"She's at an L.A. hospital," Taylor said. "That's all they're saying. That she was rushed to the hospital early this morning, which, remember, is three hours behind us. She must be alive, because they haven't said…"

I put my face in my hands. I tried to remember my mother's phone number. I tried to remember Tate's. My mind was blank. I couldn't remember anything. I couldn't even remember Tate's other name, the one she used now for acting.

And then the frozen woman said it. Said my daughter's name. Our daughter's name. Quinn James' daughter's name. Suddenly he and I were parents again. Parents for the first time…

This wasn't how I wanted the world to know.

Tate had only known a few months, for chrissake.

The newscaster woman seemed more focused on this revelation than on getting any information on Tate, on how she was doing, on IF SHE WAS EVEN ALIVE!

They just kept alternating between the photo of Tate at the Chateau and the photo of Quinn and me at that party.

It all felt so intimate and I felt so exposed, so vulnerable. Our little family we never got to be. All the sadness I still hadn't grieved after Quinn died because I'd been too busy denying it.

It just all came rushing out, rushing through me.

I got up from the bed, went into the bathroom, and was sick.

TAYLOR RAGNER

As soon as Tatum came out of the bathroom, as soon as I saw her face change, as she watched the news, as she took in what was happening, what had happened, any anger I had turned immediately to concern and anxiousness and worry for Tatum, and for her daughter, for Kaylin.

I couldn't be angry with Tatum when she was so clearly and genuinely distraught. I couldn't imagine what she was going through, seeing her daughter being talked about on TV in that manner, like that. It was a major news network but they were talking about the whole thing—about everyone involved—in a very tabloidish fashion. Like TMZ or E news. They just kept showing photos of Tatum with Quinn James, who I guess she had dated before he died.

She looked so different: young and blonde and innocent.

I didn't know anything about Quinn James except that he'd died. I couldn't even remember if it was suicide or a drug overdose or what.

I'd only seen one of his movies. The one he won an Oscar for. The one where he's a cowboy. But I couldn't remember it.

Now I didn't know if I'd ever seen a movie with Tatum in it. I would have had to bring up her IMDB page, looked at her Wikipedia. And we didn't have phones; I would have had to have gone down to the hotel computers. It felt too creepy doing that, now that her daughter was in the hospital, a possible drug overdose or suicide attempt, they weren't saying or they weren't sure which.

COACH W

I hadn't looked at a photograph of Quinn in a long time. I went into the storage room in the basement, dragged out the coffin-sized plastic bin I used in place of a hope chest, to keep all my depressing memories. Photos of Quinn and me from grade school. A few from middle school, before he became too successful, before he moved to L.A., away from his grandma and me.

I'd only met his mom once. I'd never met Quinn's father. He was in prison by the time Quinn and I met. His mother was always off on a drug bender, according to Quinn. In and out of jail, herself. He was raised by his grandmother. Grandma Betty, the nicest woman you could ever meet. She died ten days after Quinn. They're buried together, side by side, in a cemetery on the other side of town.

I wonder if Tatum knew that.

That must be why she came here, why she chose this town. I mean, you don't accidentally end up in your dead ex's backyard, in the town he grew up in, the town he was laid to rest in, by chance.

You don't end up fucking his best childhood friend by some random force.

That shit has to be premeditated. You have to have planned that shit out.

Not that I thought she fucked me to get back at Quinn for dying. That's not what I'm saying. I don't think.

ANISSA GRANT

Coach W asked me later if I'd known he was friends with Quinn, when I initiated our affair. But the funny thing is, I didn't. Quinn had never talked about him directly or shown me pictures. He'd once, maybe twice, mentioned a childhood friend back home, but he never said his name. And I never asked. Quinn was a very private person, and we didn't really know each other that long. Before he died.

It's true I picked Elkheart to feel closer to him. But I didn't know anyone in that town by name before I moved there. Quinn's grandma had been dead a long time. She was the only person he really ever talked about. She was the only one I knew from him.

Maybe Colton and I were drawn together by our subconscious love of Quinn. I know that sounds crazy, but crazier things have happened. I fell in love with a fifteen-year-old cheerleader, for one. Or no, she fell in love with me. *That*'s the crazy part.

Then again, how old was Lisa Marie when she fell in love with Elvis? Fourteen? Fifteen? Then they *allegedly* waited until she was eighteen to have sex, but, in the meantime, he provided her with a home in Memphis. He relocated her to be near him. Housed her and her parents in one of his properties. Kept her real close. Kept an eye on her. At the very least. Made sure she stayed pure. At the very least. How old was Elvis? Twenty-four? Twenty-five?

Age ain't nuthin but a number. Aaliyah sang. She was fourteen or fifteen when she allegedly married R. Kelly, though the marriage was illegal so it didn't count and before she died at age twenty-two she'd already started refusing to talk about R. Kelly or answer any questions about him. It's hard to tell in those situations if it's just like any bad break up or if the age was the primary reason for the bad blood.

If things didn't work out with me and Taylor, would it because of the hundreds of reasons relationships don't work out or because she was sixteen and I was thirty?

Would we ever know?

ROBIN GRANT

I kept waiting for Anissa to call. I was sure she must have seen the news by now. It was all over the place. On CNN and TMZ, hashtagged on Twitter. Whatevered on Instagram.

I was inundated with texts and emails and voicemails but none of them were from Anissa. None of them were from my daughter, from Tate's *mom*. They were all casting agents and producers and directors and people I'd worked with over the years. We didn't have any actual friends, or family. Or, *I* didn't have any actual friends or family, to call and share their concern.

It looked like she was going to be okay, but that she was going to have to go to a psychiatric hospital and then rehab. It was uncertain if she'd intentionally tried to kill herself or if the overdose was accidental.

She'd been at the Chateau, staying with friends—"friends," no one I'd ever met—in a bungalow. She had Adderall, Norco, Klonopin, and marijuana in her system. Traces of cocaine. And alcohol. Plenty of alcohol.

I guess we're just lucky she didn't go the way of Whitney. Or Whitney's daughter. What was her name? Bobby Jr? Something like that… so sad…

Just lucky that she didn't take a bath.

I'd been home…

She'd been fighting me for legal emancipation.

She'd hired a lawyer, was taking me to court.

You could do that at fifteen in Hollywood, if you were successful enough, if you made enough money. You could divorce your parent (or grandparent, your legal guardian, as I was). It was one of the traps of helping your child—or grandchild—find success as an actor. It led them to shutting the door in your face. It gave them the power to shut you out of their life, to go off and do all the drugs they want.

CHATEAU MARMONT MANAGER

I'm sorry but I cannot comment on any of our guests. The Chateau is a refuge for many celebrities and we hold their privacy with the utmost respect and care. I cannot confirm anyone's stay at the hotel, past or present. You'll please forgive me, I have to take this call.

TAYLOR RAGNER

I couldn't believe Kaylin was Tatum's daughter. I tried to remember if her name had ever come up when we'd been talking. She was such a big name now, like, just, all of a sudden. She had like a zillion social media followers. Not as many as Selena Gomez or anything, but *a lot*. I mean, I was following her!

She was more popular for her social media presence than for her acting.

For the teen show she was on, which I still hadn't seen, other than a few clips on the internet.

She was beautiful. My age. Thick dark brown hair down to her waist. Gorgeous face. Always perfectly contoured. A body to die for. Thick hips, tiny waist. It was weird, she'd always looked so healthy, compared to the other young actresses who clearly had eating disorders and probably drug addictions. Kaylin always posted selfies of herself working out or going for a hike or making smoothies.

The headline on *US Weekly* that Monday was, "Young Actress's Secret Pain." It almost killed Tatum when we saw it.

We were in a gas station, filling up before we left the Orlando area.

"Turn that around, will you?" Tatum said when she saw it.

So I did, of course. I turned over the *People* and the *Enquirer* too. They all had Kaylin's photos on the cover. Just some were smaller than others. In some she was a small picture in the corner. Only *US Weekly* had her face blown up, taking up the whole cover, the photo of Quinn and Tatum a small pic in the corner.

Then, just as we were leaving the store, Tatum turned to me and said, "Actually, do you mind buying them for me? All of them? Please?"

I went back inside and piled four of the magazines into my arms and carried them to the cashier. Tatum was waiting in the car. I set them on the backseat. She said she'd look at them later.

COMMENTS POSTED ON KAYLIN JENNINGS-JAMES INSTAGRAM

feeling for and sending love to kaylin jennings-james. This is really scary and lonely. hollywood is such a dark place and she clearly needs a new team and some people that actually give a f–k about her.

Something is seriously up with kaylin jennings-james and I'm actually worried for her. I hope everything is okay fr.

CAM SPENCER

I couldn't believe Tatum was Kaylin Jennings-James' mother. I couldn't stop laughing when I heard that shit. Anabel was the one who told me. She texted me early Sunday morning.

I tried imagining Taylor's face when she found out that Tatum was a *mom*. That she had a kid *her age*. A famous kid. An "influencer." Like, what the fuck, bitch? WHAT. THE. FUCK.

Like, how are you going to come to our town, pretend to be sixteen, fuck my girlfriend, take off with her, when you've got a daughter *the exact same age*? Bitch!

It was sick. It was disgusting.

And I couldn't imagine that Taylor was going to want to keep hanging with Tatum now that she knew.

I texted Chase immediately to tell him. Maybe *now* he'd fucking *get it*. That Tatum was a fucking pedophile. That she was going to bring Taylor down into whatever dark shit, this fucking sick game, whatever this was she was living. Illuminati shit. I don't fucking know. Sick fucking shit.

I didn't want to see Taylor on the TV next, in a hospital, on account of whatever fucked up shit Tatum, or, Rachel, or whatever the fuck name she wanted to call herself, did to her. Like she did to her own daughter. Telling her lies all those years. Hiding the truth from her like she did Taylor. Fucking with her head.

And Taylor accused *me* of playing mind games! Jesus effing Christ!

Anabel and I had read all about it online and in magazines: how Tatum and her mom had lied to Kaylin about Tatum being her mom, told her she was her sister instead. For fifteen years. No wonder Tatum was so good at lying. So good at manipulation. She'd had fifteen years practice.

It was pathetic. Tatum was pathetic. And now Taylor was pathetic by extension or—what is that they say—you are the company you keep? By association, I guess it is.

Yeah, they were both gonna end up pathetic. I should have been feeling like I dodged a bullet at this point.

But I wasn't feeling anything, really, for some fucking reason.

ANISSA GRANT

I just didn't have the will to fight anymore. Not now that Tate was in the hospital. I couldn't go on running, not knowing if she was okay. I was ready to turn myself in, if it meant a phone call from my mother, if it meant finding out what was going on, maybe even getting to talk to Tate.

I was terrified what had started happening to her father was happening now to her. That she was using drugs and alcohol to cope with other issues. Manic-depression or bipolar disorder. Something like that. An absentee parent. A feeling of loss and abandonment. I couldn't believe how selfish I'd been to run off and leave Tate like that. I'd left because she told me to leave but now I saw that it was a teenager's job to try to push her parent away and the parent's job to stay.

And I shouldn't have left her alone with my mother. It was like leaving a teenager alone with Joan Crawford. I'd survived it but I was a different person than Tate. And to be honest, I didn't know that I had survived. I was alive, yes, but I wasn't a whole person.

But I loved Taylor. I didn't want to lose Taylor. I was so afraid if I left, if I turned myself in or tried to go back to L.A., I'd never see Taylor again.

It was a Catch-22 situation.

I'd never read the book or seen the movie but it felt like that. I felt like that.

I couldn't win. I could only lose. Lose/Lose.

TAYLOR RAGNER

Tatum was freaking out. We'd gotten another hotel room in Orlando proper, off Disney grounds. Just a small one. Days Inn or whatever. Nothing fancy.

We stayed in the room with the blinds pulled, reading the magazines, going out on the balcony to smoke every half hour or so. Maybe it was her way of telling me everything. About how Kaylin had thought she was her sister and about her and Quinn falling in love on his last movie shoot, him dying six months later, her going into a semi-retirement, only taking a couple tiny roles in tiny movies for the next fifteen years after that. Her weird relationship with her mom. Her mom being an alcoholic, emotionally abusive. The dad she never met.

"They get a lot wrong, but they get the overall picture right," Tatum said.

It was a lot to take in, I'm not going to lie. But none of it made me stop loving her. Maybe it kind of made me love her more. In a different kind of way.

I didn't really understand it all but I understood how you could wake up one day wondering how you got where you were, questioning the choices you'd made up until that point. Like, one day you wake up a new person in an old body with the person-you-were-before's choices.

That's what happened to me last summer. I woke up one day and my whole life felt so surreal, like someone else's. I didn't want to be with Cam or to be a cheerleader or even to be in high school. I didn't feel fifteen. I didn't feel any age. I didn't feel like I belonged in the life I was in but I didn't feel like I would belong in any other life either.

Which I guess is how I ended up in a hospital. Why my mom says I tried to kill myself. I don't even know if I was trying to do that.

I was just trying to change something. To change me. In some way I can't explain.

I wondered if that was how Kaylin felt.

I didn't want Tatum to feel that way.

I got up and walked over to where Tatum was sitting on the balcony in her boxers and tank top. I sat down on her lap and took the cigarette from her, took a drag and handed it back.

"I'll never stop loving you," I said. My arms were around her neck and I closed my eyes and pushed my chin over her collarbone. "I don't care if they try to separate us. I'll wait. I'm going to be sixteen tomorrow. Then seventeen. Then eighteen."

"Just like Priscilla," Tatum said.

"What?" I said.

"Nothing," Tatum said.

"Are you ever going to stop loving me?" I said. I was sitting up, but my arms were still around her neck. I was staring into her eyes. her bangs were in them. I pushed them away, kissed her on the temple, and smiled.

"No," she said. "I'm not."

"Okay, then," I said. "That's all we need to know."

"Yeah," she said. She was leaned back in the chair with her arms over her head, her legs wide, and I pushed my knees aside her hips, pushed my mouth against hers. I was in my red white and blue bikini even though we hadn't been swimming. She picked me up and carried me inside to the bed, untied my bikini. It felt like we kissed all night. Her mouth was so warm and tasted like Diet Cherry Coke. When we fell asleep, her head was on my stomach, my hand in her hair, and I wanted to fall asleep that way always, holding onto her hair.

JUSTIN BIEBER

I reached out to Kaylin. Or my people did. I didn't know her that well. We'd only hung a couple times when I stopped by to film my cameo on the show. But she was tight, a cool kid. Reminded me of me at that age. A bright star but just sort of lost, ya know? Lost in new celebrity and youth. I offered her my oxygen chamber. And my pastor's #. They'd both really helped me through my bad times. Everyone thinks celebrities don't suffer, don't have depression. But we have it as bad as anyone. Just because you're in a Drake video doesn't mean you're not suffering. The public doesn't see what goes on behind closed doors. It's not all partying and Rolexes and fucking other celebrities. Well, it's some of those things, but then there's the depression too.

You can be fucking the most famous model in the world and still depressed. You can be best homies with Drake, real tight, and still be suffering internally. Shit, even Drake gets depressed, right? We talk about it, pray on it. For real. We really do.

ANISSA GRANT

When I was thirteen, another thirteen-year-old model and I spent a day at the house of an older model we knew who was trying to make the transition to photographer. She dressed us up in designer women's clothes, put makeup on us, and blew dry and curled our hair. She told us she was shooting a spread for a fashion magazine and the theme of the spread was friendship. Me and the other girl were in all of the photographs together. We didn't take any independently. I remember it feeling slightly awkward and ironic, taking these photos in which we pretended to be best friends and then at the end of the day leaving and not talking and seeing each other at castings after that, but not talking beyond a polite and forced hello or goodbye.

The photos were controversial at the time because we were said to be taking on womanly, sexualized poses when we were thirteen. I think the fact there were two of us, posing together, made the photos seem more provocative than if it had been either one of us alone in a photograph.

Now that Tate's face was everywhere—on TV and magazine covers and all over social media—her photos—both professional and personal—were being scrutinized in a similar fashion.

"I don't see why they're doing it," Taylor said. "They don't do that to One Direction guys or to Justin Bieber. The press never used the word 'sexualizing' in the same byline with the name of a young male actor or musician."

"Right," I said. "But I'm a bad parent or my mother is a bad parent for 'allowing' Tate or me to take roles in which a female character has sexual feelings or expresses any sensuality. I mean, Jesus Christ. Grow up. Jodie Foster was thirteen when she was in *Taxi Driver*."

We were sitting out on the beach at sunset, smoking and watching the water come closer and closer to our feet.

"And they wonder why so many young female celebrities 'go crazy,'" I said.

"It's the same thing for non-famous teenage girls, too, though," Taylor said. "You think my brother faced the kind of scrutiny I have to go through on a daily basis? What I'm wearing, what I'm doing, how late I'm out, who I'm with, what I've been drinking, if I've been having sex... I never heard my parents ask Tyler *once* what he was wearing and they barely ever asked or cared where he was going or what he was doing, when he'd be home, as long as he didn't date anyone seriously, because no girl was ever good enough for Tyler, meaning, according to *my mom*, which, now that I think about it, was just more of their sexist bullshit misogyny."

"I wish they'd just leave Tate alone," I said, staring at a photograph of her walking on the beach in a bathing suit and jean shorts. "I tried to tell her. I tried to warn her."

"She shouldn't have to stop doing what she loves doing, though," Taylor said. "And she shouldn't have to hide her sexuality from the public like it's something to be ashamed of."

"Come on," I said, suddenly, standing up and wiping the sand off. "Let's go inside."

"Why, what's wrong?" Taylor said.

"I just wanna go inside. I'm hungry," I said, trying to act normal. So Taylor would act normal. So anyone watching would act normal in reaction.

I pulled the curtains soon as we got inside the room.

"What is it?" Taylor said.

I was peeking around the edge of the curtain, waving her back behind me with my hand.

Tomorrow was Taylor's sixteenth birthday. I hadn't planned on spending it running again. I'd wanted to take her to get tattoos as a surprise. To commemorate our time on the road together, before I turned myself in.

Now that I'd seen the cop hovering around us, I didn't feel like turning myself in just yet.

I didn't like feeling like the decision had been made for me. I wanted to spend my girlfriend's birthday with her. I didn't want her birthday to be spent with her crying over some police shit drama I'd caused.

So I went for a gun. I wasn't sure if I should get my stun gun or the actual gun.

I wasn't sure if the cop was alone or if she had a partner.

ANABEL RAGNER

I don't know how it happened. I wish to god it hadn't happened. That Tatum hadn't moved here, that Taylor and Cam had never broken up, that my husband hadn't left his family, that my eldest son hadn't left his family, that my daughter hadn't run away with a thirty-year-old woman and that I hadn't found myself in such a vulnerable state, in such a compromised... position.

CAM SPENCER

How do you go from feeling so happy you think you could die of happiness to so shitty you want to die to so numb you don't care if you live or die to so afraid of your own instincts and desires that you find yourself sleeping with —okay, *fucking*—your ex-girlfriend's mom?

Wait. When did I start thinking of Taylor as my ex? When she started fucking Tatum? Or when I started fucking her mom? Cuz I'm pretty sure I never thought of her like that, as my "ex," until just this minute... fuuuuu-uck. Fuck me.

CHASE WHITING

Cam didn't tell me, I caught him. I don't think they were planning on telling anyone. They probably thought it would be a one and done or a two time thing and no one would ever know and maybe that's how it should have been. Who knows if anyone would have ever found out if I hadn't walked in on them that afternoon.

I was looking for Cam because Coach W wanted to talk to us. He wasn't answering my texts so I drove to his house and he wasn't there so I drove to Taylor's house and his truck was there in the drive. I didn't think anything of it. The front door was open. The screen door was unlocked. I yelled, "hello?" a couple times, and then I went in, thinking they'd be right there in the kitchen or with Jolie in the living room. But Jolie wasn't there, apparently. Jolie was on a playdate at a friend's and Cam and Anabel were on their own playdate in the middle of the living room. It was a split level so the living room was just down the stairs off the kitchen. I saw them as soon as I turned toward the stairs. Taylor's mom was bent over the ottoman on her knees and Cam was bent over Taylor's mom on his knees behind her.

I didn't know whether to back out of the house, slowly, or to say something...

Partly my heart was in my mouth again, my stomach on the floor.

I didn't know why I was the last person Cam seemed to think of like this.

What was wrong with me, was I *so* disgusting...

I felt myself getting hard and the realization of that, that I was turned on at the same time I was disgusted and sad and angered by finding my best friend fucking our friend's mom, made me want to vomit.

It also made me, more surprisingly, want to fight Cam.

I think, in retrospect, I had all this sexual repression energy pent up inside me from the last five years and I just couldn't hold it in any more.

I couldn't keep pretending and swallowing my feelings anymore.

So I did the unthinkable, the unimaginable.

I said Cam's name. I walked down those stairs. He was startled, in shock, standing there with his cock out. And I punched him in the face. And then I punched him again. I kept punching him until Taylor's mom pulled me off.

ANABEL RAGNER

You tell me what you'd do when you haven't had sex in five years and your husband's off with another woman in another state and never comes home and your daughter's run away somewhere and you're worried sick about her and you're under the most stress of your life and the only person you can talk to, the only person who's been kind to you and listened to you and made you laugh in a very long time is eighteen and your daughter's ex boyfriend.

Tell me.

What would you do?

Good for you. I didn't do that. I didn't do nothing.

CAM SPENCER

I didn't know what the fuck Chase's problem was. Why the fuck did he care if Anabel and I had sex? Again, all I could think was he was in love with Taylor and somehow by punching me, he was defending Taylor's honor, her mom's honor. It didn't make much sense, my theory, but neither did Chase punching me.

And then he was sobbing, soon as Anabel pulled him off of me.

We were all three sitting there on Anabel's living room floor, two of us naked, Chase sobbing.

I asked him, I said, "Chase, what the fuck is the matter with you? Why are you fucking acting like this?"

He didn't say anything, he just kept sobbing. So I said, "Chase, are you in love with Taylor? That's what this is about, isn't it? You're in love with my girlfriend."

Chase didn't say anything. I looked at Anabel. I guess it was kind of fucked up to refer to Taylor as my girlfriend, right after fucking her mom.

POLICE OFFICER MARIE CRUZ

We'd gotten a bulletin, mistakenly, about a pair of "teenage girls" on the run from Indiana. Jayden and I were on the beach, patrolling, when I saw a couple of girls I thought might fit the descriptions. They were the right heights and weights but their hair wasn't right. The shorter one was supposed to be a brunette and she had shaved, platinum blonde hair and the taller one was supposed to be a blonde and she had jet black hair. I figured they could have dyed it, cut it, done what they could to disguise themselves. So I radio'd Jayden I was walking down to the beach to get a closer look. He was still at the Waffle House finishing up, shooting the shit with Max, the manager there, paying the bill.

I walked a little closer to where the two of them were sitting down on the beach. There weren't too many other people around. Right before Christmas, believe it or not, is a little slow. Everyone piles in the day after round here. The locals were being quiet too. Which was why Jayden was taking his time, hanging back. Also, to be honest, I wanted to check this scene out myself. There's still a lot of gender stereotyping on the force, believe it or not. If I radio'd Jayden about the suspects, I'd just be following behind him taking a passive role.

I got a little too close a little too quick, though. I guess I was over-eager. I was probably worried Jayden would get there and steal my thunder.

It seemed like the dark haired one took notice of me. They started getting their things together, headed up the beach toward the motel.

I hung back a bit before following. Acted like I didn't notice. Like I was just doing my rounds.

POLICE OFFICER JAYDEN MORRIS

I was finishing my dinner when I got the radio call for backup. Marie... Officer Cruz, had only been gone a few minutes. Maybe ten. I guess records indicate twelve. I got the call and ran right over to the Days Inn.

When I got there the motel room door was open and Officer Cruz was on the ground, blood gushing from her head. Turned out not to be from a bullet but I didn't know that at the time. My first thought was she'd been shot dead. There was quite a bit of blood and she wasn't moving.

I did a quick search of the room even though it appeared to be vacated. No suitcases or duffel bags. No personal belongings other than a bikini hanging in the bathroom. Red white and blue. American flag type. Also a pair of hair clippers. Some bleached fuzz still in them. And in the sink.

I ran back out to where Officer Cruz was lying. On closer inspection I could see it had probably been a blunt force to the back of her head rather than a bullet. Also, she appeared—by the looks of it—to have been Tazed.

I heard the ambulance coming. I stood and looked around for any more clues. By now, the people in the neighboring rooms were milling about, trying to see what was happening. There was a considerable amount of commotion. Backup pulled in at the same time as the ambulance. Two more officers. Which meant I could take off on pursuit. The night manager said he thought they were in a pickup with Georgia plates. So I set off looking for my favorite license mascot: the Georgia peach.

TAYLOR RAGNER

"There's blood on my shirt, Tatum," I said.

Tatum was driving like crazy out of there. Everything had happened so fast and so slow at the same time. I saw it all unfolding in scenes like on a DVD I could select and replay at will.

"I know," she said. "There's blood on my shoe. We'll change them here in a sec, once we're a little farther out."

I looked down at her feet.

"I forgot my bathing suit, my favorite one," I said.

"I'll buy you another," she said.

I looked down at my hands; they were shaking. I was still so full of adrenaline.

"Actually, just throw it out," she said.

"Out the window?" I said.

"Yeah, just take it off."

I pulled the shirt over my head, balled it up in my fist and chucked it far as I could. I watched it open like a flower in mid air, float back to the ground.

I didn't have a bra or bathing suit top on under it. I glanced in the side mirror. I looked like River Phoenix in *Stand by Me*. My hair was short like his. I ran my hair over it, lit a cigarette to finish the characterization.

"I look like a twelve-year-old boy," I said, turning my head side to side in the mirror.

"With that hair you do," Tatum said, glancing over. "But not with those tits, sunshine."

She was wearing her Mr. Happy T-shirt again. Everything memorable always happened when she was wearing her Mr. Happy T-shirt.

"I want to stop the truck right here," she said, taking my wrist and bringing the cigarette still in my fingers to her mouth. "Make sure you still have a pussy in those jean shorts."

"I don't know," I said. "Maybe I have a dick now."

I stuck my hand down my shorts, made a dick out of it, stuck it through.

"I'm gonna have to pull over the truck so I can have a lick," Tatum said.

I put a bare foot up on the seat beside me, my arm around my knee. I couldn't stop staring in the side mirror at my hair.

"What if Jolie isn't the only trans kid in the house," I said, blowing smoke through my nostrils, blowing smoke rings after that.

"Yeah," Tatum said. "What if."

Which was when I remembered tomorrow was my birthday. I could finally get my license. I was finally the age of consent. At least in some states. I didn't know what Florida's age of consent was. Indiana's was 16.

ANISSA GRANT

My goal was to make it one more twenty-four hours with Taylor and then if they caught us, they caught us. I wasn't turning myself in, but I wouldn't run anymore after that.

I just wanted to spend one more night alone with my girlfriend, usher in her birthday with her, get matching tattoos together. I didn't know what, exactly, but something unifying. Something representative. To remind us when we were a part of what we were. Of what we had.

I drove as far off course as I could manage. Off the main highways. Onto little back roads.

We ended up near Lakeland, Florida.

A boring city in the middle of the state, far from beaches and the Atlantic.

TAYLOR RAGNER

Tatum took me to Bennigan's, a chain restaurant in the south. She told me I had to order steak for my birthday so I ordered the filet mignon which was the only cut I knew. Medium. With a potato and onion rings.

Tatum got a buffalo burger with an egg on top. A side of fries. A glass of milk.

I know she ordered the milk just to gross me out.

She knew I couldn't stand it.

She drank it all sloppy on purpose too. It was running down both corners of her mouth. People were staring. She was chugging it like someone had dared her. Then she wiped her mouth with the back of her hand.

It was quite the scene. Mr. Happy in a Got Milk? Commercial in a Bennigan's in central Florida. Home of the Miss America pageant.

Then she tried to kiss me, with the milk still on her breath like a baby cow. Like a disgusting baby animal.

Everyone was watching.

I let her slip her tongue in once and then made a show of pushing her away.

"It's her birthday, guys," Tatum said. Standing now at her seat, clapping. She was getting everyone riled up. She was starting everybody singing.

"Happy birthday, dear Taylor... Happy Birthday to you!"

Great, I thought, now everyone knows my name.

"Come on," she said, pulling me up out of my chair by the back of my neck, gentle but firm, the way I liked.

She'd left enough cash on the table to cover the bill and the tip by forty percent.

I guess she was feeling generous.

Of course, I didn't know then she was planning on us getting picked up the next day. For all I knew, we were driving across country westward next. I had no interest in going home, myself. Not til I was eighteen, at least. Not til I was a legal adult, capable of making all my own decisions.

ANABEL RAGNER

I didn't do anything but cry all day on Taylor's birthday. It was her sixteenth. Sweet Sixteen. I sat in her bedroom, sat on her bed and sobbed, staring at the posters on her wall: Demi Lovato, Kylie Jenner, the Weeknd; and all the photographs of Taylor in her cheer costume, competing and at games, and selfies she'd taken with other cheerleaders and with Cam.

I'd always pictured that day. My only little girl. Well, now I have Jolie, too. But I'd been picturing Taylor's Sweet Sixteen party since she was just a little baby, a sweet little baby girl in my arms. Everything was always pink for Taylor. Just like it is now for Jolie.

I'd always imagined having her Sweet Sixteen party at a fancy restaurant in South Bend, all the girls in fancy dresses. Taylor's the fanciest of all. Her hair done up, her makeup perfect. Steaks and dancing and fancy gourmet desserts.

I wanted my baby home with me on her birthday. I kept staring at my phone, thinking she might call or the police might.

I was avoiding Cam now. Seemed like he was avoiding me as well.

Neither of us texted or called one another anymore, now that Chase knew.

I think we were both terrified, or ashamed, or both.

I didn't know what Chase was capable of, how vindictive he could be. He was clearly in love with Cam, though, and that was what worried me most.

I didn't want anything to come between me and my daughter.

I'd had a weak moment, that was all. For once in the sixteen years of Taylor's life, I'd been weak.

I knew I should have a talk with Chase, ask to meet him, but I didn't know what to say.

Before I left Taylor's room I saw a new picture pinned in the upper corner of her desk. I hadn't noticed it before. It was of her and Tatum, both in their cheer costumes, after a game, at McDonald's. They were sitting in a booth, their arms around each other, smiling. I took the photo down, stared at it closer, and ripped it into pieces.

ANISSA GRANT

We found a tattoo parlor open down the street. Neither of us had ever gotten a tattoo before. I'd stopped for a small bottle of Beam. We'd each taken a couple swigs in the truck before going inside.

The man inside was eating a Hot Pocket and drinking a giant Mountain Dew. He was in his forties, fat and covered in ink.

We looked around at all the examples on the walls. Animals, celebrities, mythologies, symbols, bodies of water, pieces of land, cartoon characters, roman numerals.

"What about a yin and a yang?" Taylor said. "Like I could get one and you could get the other."

"Maybe," I said. "Isn't one more female and one more male, though? I wouldn't know which one to get."

"Yeah," she said. "Good point."

I knew it was bad luck to get your girlfriend's name or portrait tattooed on your body—that doing so would ensure you broke up—but I wanted something hugely significant. I didn't understand the point of getting a tattoo, otherwise.

"What if we each get the same word on the same part of our body?" Taylor said.

"Like, what word?" I said.

"I don't know," she said. "Like, Absolutely!"

"Absolutely?" I said.

"With an exclamation point," she said. "Like, ABSOLUTELY!"

"I don't know," I said. "Let me think about it."

I went outside the store to smoke a cigarette, and to take another swig from the bottle of Beam. I thought about getting Tate and Taylor's birthdates on my arm. Or their names.

"What if we get today's date?" Taylor said. She'd come out for a cigarette and a swig, too.

"Your birthday?" I said, squinting up at her through the sun.

"The day I turned sixteen," she said. "The day I can legally give myself to you, in the eyes of Indiana, anyway."

I sat down on the curb to think about it. Taylor sat next to me.

"You just don't want me to ever forget your birthday," I said, smiling.

"You better never," she said, flicking her ash on the ground.

"I don't know," I said.

CAM SPENCER

I remember back when Taylor and I were dating, we'd always looked forward to her sixteenth birthday as this special day we'd have together. I don't know why, really. It was just this All American birthday, I guess.

Sweet sixteen and never been kissed. Haha. What a joke, right?

Sweet sixteen and muff-diving her way through America! More like it.

I wanted so bad to text her a happy birthday but I knew she didn't have her phone.

I hadn't been texting Anabel anymore. I wanted to erase everything that had happened between us from my memory, and from Chase's. It was a fucked up mistake. I didn't mean it. I didn't love anyone but Taylor. I didn't fucking *want* anyone but Taylor. Taylor has always been *the only one* I have ever loved. The only one I ever really wanted.

I wanted to kill myself without her. But I don't believe in suicide. So I just kept working out, running and lifting, lifting and running. I didn't know what else to fucking do. Without her. Without my Taylor.

TAYLOR RAGNER

It hurt both more and less than I thought it would.

I went first. Tatum stood next to me, holding my right hand.

I watched as the man etched "Mr. Happy" into the flesh on my left forearm, a few inches up from my wrist. It took maybe half an hour. It took longer than you'd think.

Before we left, Tatum got the same tattoo in the same place.

"My mother will love this," I said, holding my arm out so I could look at it. It was wrapped in Cellophane and tape. We weren't supposed to let it get sun.

We stopped at a drugstore for the specific kind of lotion we were supposed to use.

I looked at Tatum. We were both Mr. Happy now. Wherever we went, whatever we did. Mr. Happy came with us for the rest of our lives.

I walked up to where Tatum was standing in front of the refrigerated cases and wrapped my arms around her hips. She grabbed my hands from around the front, pulled me close.

"I love you," I said.

"I love you, too," she said.

It was the first time either of us had said those words to each other. It felt like the first time in my life I meant them.

CLEARWATER POLICE OFFICER NATHAN TUCKER

We'd gotten bulletins, seen pictures of both the girls.

Someone in a Bennigan's in Lakeland had reported seeing them.

We knew they were close, that we almost had them.

I was doing my nightly patrol of the beach.

It was almost like they wanted to be caught.

They were asleep in the bed of the last truck they'd stolen. It still had Georgia plates.

ANISSA GRANT

I'd driven us back to Clearwater because Taylor loved the water there, loved the beach.

I didn't want to get a room. I wanted to walk the beach, stand in the ocean, and fall asleep in the back of the truck, in the open night air, staring up at the stars next to Taylor.

I didn't know if it'd be my last night of freedom but I knew it'd be close.

We'd laid down back there on a blanket, smoking cigarettes and sipping more Beam, just talking and making out and holding hands. It was perfect, and the thing about perfect is, it can't last. Perfect has to end or it wouldn't be perfect.

CLEARWATER POLICE OFFICER NATHAN TUCKER

It was 4:45 in the morning. Neither of the girls put up a fight. Just let us cuff them, put them in the back of the car.

We took them down to the station, called up to the Indiana state police, where they were wanted, or where Anissa Grant was wanted for kidnapping and a host of other crimes. Where Taylor's mom was waiting for her.

The girls were very polite. Asked if they could have their lotion for their tattoos. Apparently, they'd just gotten them the day before and they were still fresh.

They said, "Mr. Happy."

I didn't get the significance of that. I figured it was an inside joke. Maybe something to do with being young lesbians. I don't know.

Other than that they just wanted coffee. Lots and lots of black coffee.

thirteen

. . .

ANABEL RAGNER

I got the call at six in the morning that the girls had been picked up in the back of a truck in Clearwater Beach. I was so happy. So relieved. I'd fallen asleep sobbing the night before, Taylor's birthday. It was December 23rd. Two days before Christmas. Tomorrow was Christmas Eve. I'd have my baby back for Christmas. I was just so happy.

I immediately got up and showered. Picked up the house and started making Taylor's favorite homemade cinnamon rolls.

They said it'd be a while before they got her home. I didn't know if they were flying her or driving her. I offered to buy her a plane ticket. I would have offered to buy her a first class seat on the next flight out of Tampa. Anything to have her home with me. Me and Jolie.

I woke Jolie up telling her Sissy would be home soon.

She was so happy.

We made a big sign to hang inside the front door, "Welcome home, Taylor!" Jolie drew hearts and flowers and snowmen and Santa all over it.

She was so excited. She wanted to wear her new pink velvet dress I'd bought her for Christmas. I told her we'd wait and see if Taylor would be home tonight. I told her soon as we knew when she'd be home, she could put it on and we'd do her hair, too. Put it in rollers or braids. Something special.

I wondered if Cam knew but I didn't text him. I didn't tell anybody. I figured they'd all know soon enough. I wanted a few hours, one night, alone with my baby, before the whole town broke into chaos.

I was worried there'd be reporters and people like that outside our house once they knew Taylor was back. I didn't see how she was going to go to school again like a normal person. I figured maybe we'd have to get her a tutor, have her home schooled for a while.

COACH W

The whole town knew within a couple hours. I don't know how. Someone at the police station told someone and that person told another someone and pretty soon we all knew Taylor and Tatum had been picked up down in Clearwater, Florida.

Nothing was secret long now that everyone was on social media. It was a giant game of telephone and that giant game was called THE INTERNET.

Certain specifics and details were always wrong but the general sense of things was usually right.

I was just waiting for everyone to find out about Tatum and me. I didn't know if she'd told anyone. Taylor or whoever. I didn't know if my job was in jeopardy. If I was going to have to move towns soon.

Maybe this was my silver lining opportunity.

My burn the forest down rebirth in another city. Another state.

My second go around at California.

Or Phoenix, like Ellen Burstyn in *Alice Doesn't Live Here Anymore*.

Except I'm not a single mom and I don't sing. So I don't even have that going for me. I just play guitar, badly. And teach acting to teenagers in BFE, Indiana. Go, me!

CAM SPENCER

I wanted to go down to the police station, to be there waiting when they brought them back into town. I wanted to beat the shit out of her. I didn't care if she was a woman. That was the point. She was thirty years old messing with a sixteen-year-old girl! She was a fucking pervert! A fucking child abuser. She deserved worse than she was going to get in jail, worse than she was going to get in court.

I thought about texting Anabel to see if she knew anything about what they were going to charge her with or when they were going to be back in

Indiana but then I thought maybe that would be a bad move, that it'd been good we hadn't been talking.

I was worried Chase would tell Taylor what he saw. Or what he *thought* he saw.

I thought there was still a chance for Taylor and me. Not right now. Not even this year, maybe. But in the near future. In a year or so, after she realized what sort of monster Tatum really was. After she realized it'd all been a big joke, a big disgusting fantasy. That it wasn't real, whatever they had, whatever had happened between them on the road.

Maybe then she'd see that what she and I had *was* real. That I wasn't going anywhere. That *this*—what she and I had—was normal. That she could be normal again too. That the life we'd dreamed of could be ours again. College. Marriage. Kids. All of it. No one would blame her. She was the innocent victim of a deranged fucking mind. Taylor was innocent. I had already forgiven her for everything that had happened. I forgave my angel for everything.

But Chase could ruin it all. Chase and his big fucked up hard on for me. His own deranged sick fantasy of he and I being together.

I wasn't going to let him come between Taylor and me the way I'd let Tatum come between us.

I was going to proactively stop it. Stop him.

TAYLOR RAGNER

I was terrified of going back, of going "home." Home wasn't home anymore. Not for me. You can't go back to being caged up once you've tasted freedom. Once you know what it feels like to have the wind on your face, you can't be kept in an airtight room anymore.

(Isn't that the premise of *The Bell Jar*? We'd just started reading it in AP English before all this. I was pretty sure it was about something like that. A girl going crazy because she isn't allowed to breathe or something, isn't allowed her freedom.)

Anyway, I was terrified of seeing Cam. Of him showing up, thinking I still belonged to him. I was worried my mom would have him at the house waiting for me. She never listened to me when it came to Cam. When it came to much of anything, really, but especially Cam once I didn't want to be with him anymore.

I was terrified she wouldn't let me see Tatum.

I was sixteen and she treated me like I was eleven. It was so fucking unfair. She'd never treated my older brother like this! She'd let him do pretty much whatever he wanted.

But with me, it was like I couldn't make up my own mind about *anything*, about who I was friends with, who I loved.

Wasn't this why Juliet died? Because they didn't trust her to know what was best for her? Because she wasn't allowed to love Romeo? She was younger than I was. She was like a couple weeks shy of fourteen! Romeo was a few years older. Eighteen or nineteen.

How old was Joan of Arc? When they burned her at the stake!

I mean, cheese & rice, people. What the fuck. Can a person with a vagina make any decisions for herself? Can we elect Hillary? Can we break some glass ceilings? Please?

This was all so fucking stupid.

Arresting us, arresting Tatum, just because we wanted to be together and I was *only* sixteen.

People always talk about wanting to be on the right side of history but I didn't know what history this was the right side of.

ANISSA GRANT

I wasn't sure where they'd put me. In jail or the mental ward. Maybe they'd put me one place first and then another.

The cops told me I'd probably be charged with grand theft auto and kidnapping and sexual misconduct with a minor, but they didn't know for sure, the specific laws of Indiana.

They said if I had a good attorney, he could probably go with the insanity defense. Get me off that way, in a hospital rather than a prison.

But I didn't want to go that way. I *wasn't* insane. I'm *not* crazy.

I wasn't mentally unwell. I was in love.

We were in love.

I knew they'd say she was brainwashed. That she had Stockholm Syndrome. It was part of the undermining of a young woman's mind. The distrust of it.

I knew if Taylor was a sixteen-year-old boy in any time period before now, he wouldn't be questioned. Or if I were a man in any time period before now…

I just wanted to be able to make a call back to California, back to my mom in L.A. I just wanted to know how Tate was. If she was going to be okay.

ROBIN GRANT

I was shocked when I first heard. When I first found out. Tate was still in the hospital—I was still dealing with the shock of that—of her accusations about me—when I got the news Anissa was being held in jail in Indiana, of all places.

What was she doing in Indiana? But of course. It made perfect sense once I realized that was where Quinn was from. Where Quinn was born and where he was buried.

I got a call from a police officer. He explained Anissa was being held on multiple charges, the primary one being the kidnapping of a fifteen-year-old girl.

Then they said I could speak with Anissa. I cried before she even got on the line and then I made myself stop. It'd been seven months since I'd heard from her. I didn't want to waste our time with my tears. I didn't want her to feel guilty or to feel I was trying to manipulate her with my emotions.

I never thought consciously she was dead but once I heard her voice I realized I hadn't known, that it must have been a thought in the back of my mind. That I'd actually been terrified all along of that possibility, of losing my baby girl forever.

CHASE WHITING

There were reporters waiting outside the police station with cameras and microphones and behind them a couple protesters. I drove by quick so I only saw one sign. It said, "Lock her up!" and on it was a picture of Tatum in her cheer uniform at a game just a couple weeks before.

It was crazy to think back to then, to fall, to the four of us hanging out and all our little mini dramas, compared to today's dramas, they felt like nothing at all, like pebbles in a shoe.

I don't know why I'm talking like a Buddhist.

Maybe because I've been standing in the self help section of Barnes & Noble all morning, looking at books by the Dalai Lama and Deepak Chopra and people like that, trying to find some way of dealing with all this, some sort of alternative to the online social media madness that surrounded Tatum and Taylor even if they weren't online to see it. There were a million tweets with the hashtag "T&T" and half were in support of them and half thought Tatum should be locked up forever.

I was wrestling with my feelings for Cam and with the dilemma of whether to tell Taylor about her mom and him. Part of me thought it was none of my business, and that she wouldn't care anyway and that Cam might kill me if I told her, and the other part of me thought I would want to know.

I didn't know which part of me was in denial. Which part was lying.

Maybe I wanted everyone involved to feel as miserable as I did.

I drove by hoping to catch a glimpse of Taylor.

I needed to see her face. To see if she was okay.

I knew they weren't going to let Tatum out, that it'd be a long time before I saw her face. And when I did, it might be on TV or inside a courtroom. Unless I could somehow get permission to visit her. I didn't know what that would entail. I figured my father would know.

ANISSA GRANT

They'd separated us as soon as we'd left Florida. Put Taylor in one car and me in another. Like they were afraid we'd escape again together. Or like they were punishing us, punishing me already.

I felt numb as soon as I was without her.

I immediately gave up, surrendered whatever fight I'd had in me.

I focused on thoughts of Tate, of praying she was okay, of hoping to be able to talk to her or my mom. I said little prayers to Quinn to watch over our baby, to make sure our daughter was okay.

TAYLOR RAGNER

I'd fought them at first. Made my body rigid so they'd have a hard time getting me in the car. Refused to answer any questions. Refused to look at anyone, even the "good cop"—the woman who tried to offer me McDonald's. I hated them. Each and every one of them. For taking me away from Tatum. For taking me back to Elkheart. South Bend. Back to my mother. Back to my miserable life where I had no rights. Where I was still *a child*.

I wanted to hire a lawyer, get emancipated minor status. But you had to show proof you could pay your own bills, support yourself, to get that. Which was why mostly only actors and actresses could afford it. To live like adults when they were fifteen, sixteen. Edward Furlong, Tatum had told me about him. She'd made a movie with him a long time ago. I guess he and that Quinn guy were friends.

I thought I could drop out of school, get a job. There were strip clubs in South Bend. I knew girls who worked there. Or I knew of a girl who *had* worked there. Briefly.

My great-great grandmother had dropped out of school in the seventh grade, used a fake ID to get a job in a maraschino cherry factory. She told my mom her hands were stained red for two years, until she switched to working at a factory rolling cigars.

My grandfather had gotten his high school girlfriend pregnant when he was fifteen, dropped out and used a fake ID to get a job at a Kmart Little Caesars, which he ended up managing.

I didn't want to strip but I didn't want to be held hostage by my own mother, by my own age, unable to see Tatum, unable to make my own decisions.

But I'd have to get a fake ID. And since my name and face was probably all over the news now, it didn't seem likely I'd be able to get away with that.

I didn't have the anonymity my great-great grandmother or grandfather had.

I don't know why if I was the alleged victim, it felt like I was being punished, too.

I couldn't even think about Tatum. I was beyond terrified of what they were going to do to Tatum.

CHASE WHITING

The more I thought about it, the more I decided I had to tell Taylor. Not right away—she would probably be in an emotionally fraught or vulnerable state —but after she'd had time to acclimate again. After she was in a safe place. I didn't want to cause drama, but I'd decided I would want to know, if my dad was having sex with my girlfriend. Or *boyfriend*. If I were ever so lucky.

COACH W

I drove by the station that morning. Christmas Eve. I wanted to see the scene for myself.

I'd gotten a text from Chase Whiting, saying he needed to talk to me. He didn't say about what and I felt anxious, like maybe somehow he knew.

I'd started smoking cigarettes again, after fifteen years of quitting. After fifteen years of nicotine gum and lozenges. I'd even started chewing on occasion. Most of the high school guys chewed. Cam. Matt. Not Chase, of course. But most of the other football players and school athletes. Smoking cigarettes seemed to be out but chewing was once again in, because you could do it indoors. You couldn't legally smoke anywhere, not even in your car. I remembered when Quinn and I were young, he'd chewed, so I'd tried it. Started dipping with him. I did everything he did. I wanted to be exactly like him. Until he started in on the hard stuff; crack cocaine and heroin. I tried a little coke with him but I could never go in for the real hard stuff. I guess I was a pussy like that. I was scared. Quinn was fearless. Or Quinn had a death wish. Is there a difference? I was terrified of death, of dying. I still am.

I passed Coach Harden driving by the station. Waved awkwardly. Like we'd both been caught doing something we were embarrassed to be doing. Being nosy teachers. Gawking at our troubled students because our own lives were so uneventful, so boring. Quiet lives of desperation and all that shit, all that jazz. HAHA. Lame.

TAYLOR RAGNER

I didn't want to go with her. I didn't want to be released into my mother's custody.

I could barely stand to look at her.

I just wanted to get home, to get to my room, to close and lock the door.

The *only person* I wanted to see, that I cared about seeing, was Jolie.

I somehow knew my father wouldn't be with her, wouldn't give two shits about me. Which, to be honest, was preferable to my mother pretending to.

If she actually cared about me, she would listen to me, to what I wanted, to what I had to say.

But she never fucking listened. She knew best. Why should she ask me my thoughts? My feelings?

ANABEL RAGNER

I took Jolie with me to pick up Taylor. I was afraid of fighting with Taylor right off the bat. I just wanted there to be a quiet period. I figured she wouldn't yell at me if Jolie was there with us. That we could focus on being a family and on Christmas for a minute with Jolie.

I had her all dressed up in her velvet dress with her ribbons and curls.

I hadn't anticipated the crowd, the reporters, the onlookers, the protesters. If I had, I probably would have left Jolie with a friend. She kept asking me why all the people were there, if it was because of Taylor, if they were having a parade for Taylor coming home. I said, yes, that's what it was, that was why all the people were here, waiting.

I was prepared for a shock when I saw Taylor. They'd told me she'd cut and dyed her hair. But they hadn't told me she was practically bald, that she looked almost nothing like my daughter, the fifteen-year-old high school cheerleader who'd left my house fourteen days earlier.

She looked like a punk in a documentary from England in the 80s.

I was surprised she didn't have a big nose ring on top of everything else. A gang or frat sign burned into her flesh.

I couldn't help crying when they walked her out to me.

I didn't notice the tattoo until later, in the car, on the drive home.

She looked like she'd been on drugs. Doing meth. She looked "strung out," like she'd lost weight, like she hadn't slept in days. Like she'd been crying.

I just wanted to hold her, wrap her in my arms, tell her everything would be okay.

But she wouldn't look me in the eye. She only looked at Jolie. Only talked to her.

I thought about making her take a drug test. I'd read about kits you could buy, that parents bought, made their kids take. It'd always seemed a little over the top for me. But now I wasn't so sure. I didn't know if that was something the police had already done, already administered. I made a mental note to speak about it with my attorney on the 26th, the day after Christmas, soon as the holidays were over.

Taylor had never been the type to do drugs. I was pretty sure. But she'd never been the type to have an affair with a girl, a *woman*, or to run away either.

I know it sounds cliché to say I felt like I didn't know my daughter anymore, but I didn't.

I caught glimpses of this new creature in the backseat via the rearview mirror.

Half of me wanted to fight for her, for my daughter that was still in there, somewhere, and the other half of me wanted to let go, to stop trying to control things, to stop trying to make things right. To just give up.

I was exhausted.

I didn't know if it was time for tough love or time to surrender.

But it was still Christmas Eve, as the town greenery and lights reminded me, and I put on the radio, turned it to a station that played Christmas songs. It was that one where the man is trying to convince the woman to stay. Because it's cold out. I used to find the song charming. It was one of my all time favorites. Now it just sounded like an anthem for date rape. Even Christmas music was exhausting now. In 2015.

TAYLOR RAGNER

It was a fucking shit show outside the police station. Every local amateur newsperson was there. It was a sea of hair plugs and lip enhancements, bad contouring jobs and spray tans and fillers.

I would come to know them—Roger and Michelle and Janelle and Willis —the way you know the other kids in your classes. Without ever speaking to them. You notice when they've cut their hair or lost weight or bought a new outfit. I would see them every time I had to go to court or go to meet with my attorney or go back to the police station.

I knew Mom would bring Jolie with her. I knew she was scared of me. So I only talked to Jolie. I only looked at Jolie. She looked so pretty. Like a little Christmas angel.

She was scared of me at first. She didn't recognize me. She started to cry and I said, "Jolie, it's me, Tay-Tay. I got a makeover. I got a new hairdo. Don't you like it?" I picked her up and hugged her and Eskimo kissed her like we always did and then she smiled and nodded.

"It's pretty different, isn't it?" I said. "I'm pretty cool now, tho, huh? Do I look like a cool chick? Maybe we should cut your hair and dye it like mine."

And my mom about had a shit fit. As though I would actually do that. Like I would really cut my six-year-old sister's hair. Or shave her head. Jesus. Get a grip, Anabel. Jolie would die without her long hair. I knew her hair was her identity now. Just as the tattoo on my arm was my identity. Just as my shaved head was my identity. My love for Tatum.

I got in the back of the car with Jolie. I didn't want to leave the station, to leave Tatum. I wanted to wait for her. Physically wait—not metaphorically— outside the building for her.

I didn't know how I was going to deal with my mom, with being back at the house. With being without Tatum.

It was back to feeling like a prisoner.

In some ways, I would rather have been in jail or prison than at home. Even if I wasn't with Tatum. At least I wouldn't be subjected to 24/7 questioning and artificial concern that had more to do with my mother than with me. At least I would have my own headspace in prison. My mom was already on my nerves and she hadn't even said anything yet. It was just the way she held her face. The look she had. It was so fucking annoying and so fucking disingenuous.

She didn't see the real me at all. She never had. She saw a projection of herself.

She saw what she could tell her "friends," the neighbors, people at the grocery store.

I wished I could text Chase. He was the only person other than Jolie I wanted to see. But since Tatum and I had ditched our phones, I didn't have one. I had no way of contacting him. Except with my mind. so I tried mental telepathy'ing him. I tried shining him. I closed my eyes and said his name over and over in my head. I wouldn't know if it worked for a while. In the meantime, I kept trying.

ANISSA GRANT

I knew Taylor was going home. That they'd called her mom to come pick her up. That they were releasing her into her mother's custody. I knew if I let myself shed a tear I'd never stop bawling so I held it all in. I chose to feel nothing at all, except sorry for Taylor, having to go "home" again. Having to face her mom and the crowd alone. You can never go home again. Ain't that the truth.

When I finally got to talk to *my* mom, it was like no time at all had passed. She sounded exactly the same. Neither of us cried or showed emotion. It was a very matter of fact phone call. We spent 90% of the time talking about Tate, who had secretly been released from the hospital that morning.

"She's staying with her agent, Felicity," my mom said. "She's not speaking to me right now. Even though it's Christmas. She's filed for emancipation. Couldn't even wait for the new year."

"Oh, okay," I said. "I guess everyone just wants their freedom."

"What?" my mother said. "I couldn't hear you. Someone is using a leaf blower of all things, in L.A."

"Nothing, Mom," I said. "Well, as long as she's okay."

"I mean, I assume she is or they wouldn't have released her but I don't really know."

"Right," I said. "Well, my time is almost up."

"Should I fly there? I think I could fly out tonight or tomorrow morning."

"If you want to," I said.

I didn't know how I felt about my mother flying to Elkheart.

"I could probably use a lawyer," I said.

"I just want to get you out of there," my mother said.

"They're setting my bail at like a million dollars or half a million dollars, Mom," I said. "I'm not getting out."

I wondered if they sent a chaplain to speak with you if you weren't on death row. If you were only receiving death threats but not actually scheduled by the state to die. I don't think they were supposed to, but one of the police officers slipped the local paper to me. I was front page headline news. I was "a pedophile." A "statutory rapist." "Someone with probable personality disorder." "A likely sociopath." "A mental defective." "A social pariah." Only one person mentioned me with regard to my movies. "And only a so-so actress, anyway; forgettable."

Those were all the local tweets on the matter the newspaper had decided to print.

TATE GRANT

Felicity took me to her house, let me sleep in her kid's room. Her kid was away at college. There were Taylor Swift and Joe Jonas posters everywhere. It was comforting, being surrounded by so many smiling, wholesome faces. Like a Mormon fucking tabernacle. Even if I'd heard rumors about Taylor and Joe and Nick. Whatever. They were still nice to look at. After you've been hospitalized, after you've had your Britney meltdown at age fifteen, before you are really even famous. *Barely famous*. Is that the movie title? Something like that.

It was almost my sixteenth birthday. I tried to imagine Anissa pregnant with me sixteen years ago. I'd never seen a picture of her pregnant. It was hard to imagine it; her in maternity clothes, her giving birth.

I tried imagining Anissa holding me in the hospital. I wondered if she'd considered adoption. Considered abortion.

Quinn would have been dead five months by then. Quinn died knowing I was in utero. What an asshole. What a lazy motherfucker.

I hadn't turned my phone on yet. I couldn't bring myself to do it. I just wanted to hide out a little longer. One more day. One more lifetime.

I was terrified of what I would find out if I started googling my name, or looking at social media or receiving texts.

I didn't even know if I still had a job. I just wanted a cigarette. I kept forgetting it was Christmas.

I didn't even know about Anissa yet. The whole kidnapping thing. I wouldn't find out for another twenty-four hours. Felicity was cool like that, not telling me. I was blissfully in the dark. Thinking I was the only crazy one. I had no idea Anissa was making headlines, too. And not just in entertainment news. That our family was suddenly as famous as the Kardashians. The Presleys. The Jacksons.

We were a national fucking media circus.

But I still had one more day of thinking this was all about *me*. That I was the star of this show. That this was my Amanda Bynes moment. My time in the crazy girl spotlight.

I was shining.

Bright like a diamond.

Like Scatman Crothers talking to Danny in his mind at the end of the movie, Jack Nicholson wielding an axe in the snow.

Jack Nicholson was the paparazzi. TMZ. Anyone who got $$$ for info about me, for a photo.

TAYLOR RAGNER

And then my mom turned on the goddamn Christmas music station. Like this was a perfectly normal Christmas Eve and we were all one perfectly normal, happy family on our way home to trim the tree.

And then, as though the whole thing, the whole reunion moment, had been choreographed by God or my mom, it started to snow. Large, fat flakes.

And then—for the real topper, the real grand finale of the whole mother/daughter jail cell reunion—Jolie asked about Tatum. She wanted to know where she was, when she was coming over, if she'd got a makeover too.

And I started to cry. I couldn't help it anymore. Couldn't hold it in.

And since I couldn't talk and Jolie looked confused, my mother butted in, took the opportunity to say some bullshit about Tatum going away for a while, how we wouldn't see her for a little bit. But how she was okay and we'd see her again *eventually*.

Which was when I wiped my eyes and cleared my throat and said, "Is that when dad is coming back? *Eventually*? Does 'eventually' mean never, Mom?"

And I guess she didn't like that question because she didn't answer it. She just turned the goddamn Christmas music louder. So I smiled at Jolie, scooted over closer to her, took her hand, kissed it.

"Don't cry, sissy," she said. "It's Christmas."

And she wiped my tears with her little hands and it was all I could do not to bawl. It was all I could do to say, "Okay, I won't anymore." And pull my face together, suck in the tears. Merry fucking Christmas. All I wanted for Christmas was a cigarette. Think Santa could manage that?

TATE GRANT

Before all this, before I was taken to the hospital, a suspected overdose or suicide attempt, and honestly, even I'm not sure what it was. Desperation. That's what it was. Fear. Loneliness. Isolation. Alienation.

Fuck, I sound like an emo girl in a really bad YA novel.

Anyway, I'd just started seeing this new person. We'd just started hanging out all the time. Me and this person. Okay, this girl, woman. Model. She was super cool. Australian. So she had *that accent*. She'd already dated a famous rock musician and a pop star. I didn't know what she saw in me. Why she wanted to spend so much time with me. She modeled lingerie on TV. She was a fucking famous lingerie model and she'd sought me out on social media, started liking all my shit, then asked to hang out.

It wasn't the first time I'd done cocaine. A couple of the actors on the teen show I was on did coke on breaks in their trailers. Everyone knew and sometimes I joined them. But once I started hanging out with the lingerie model, things just sort of escalated. There was just always a party to be at, the Chateau to meet up at later in the night, in the early morning hours.

I stopped sleeping. I only slept an hour or two. Georgia always seemed to have a little pharmacy, a virtual drugstore, in her purse: bars of Xanax, Adderall, Roxies, Ambien. Whatever.

Georgia kept texting me now. Asking if I was okay. Asking when I was going to get out of the hospital. Asking when we could hang out again. Telling me what great shit she had. What great parties were coming up. That she missed me. That she wanted to come see me. That she was dying without me. That she had more Roxies.

I don't know why but I couldn't respond. I didn't tell her it was my sixteenth birthday the next day.

I hadn't made up my mind what I wanted to do. Felicity kept asking me if I wanted to go to Malibu, which meant rehab. It was all very Courtney Love song coded, the way Felicity spoke. Except I wouldn't have known, wouldn't have *gotten* it, if Felicity hadn't spelled it out for me, hadn't said explicitly, "Malibu means rehab, like in the song 'Malibu' by Hole." Oh, okay, gotcha, Felicity.

CHASE WHITING

I decided to go over to Taylor's house on Christmas evening.

I knew she didn't have a phone and even though I had Anabel's number, I didn't want to use it. It felt dirty. I felt dirty. I deleted it and Cam's numbers from my phone, even though I had Cam's number memorized. So I definitely would know if he called or texted me. I didn't block him.

Anabel answered the door looking frazzled. She hadn't had time to get her hair done in a while. The grey was starting to show.

There was a news van parked on the curb. A guy sleeping inside.

"Oh, Chase, what are you doing here?" she said. The look on her face was fear or shock. Maybe she thought I was here to tell Taylor about her and Cam. Maybe I was. But probably I wasn't. Probably it was too soon to bring that whole thing up with Tay. I just wanted to see her, see how she was doing. Offer my support.

"Merry Christmas," I said.

"Merry Christmas, Chase," she said.

"I just wanted to stop and say Merry Christmas to Taylor," I said.

She just sort of stood there looking at me a second, processing what I was telling her, I guess.

"Okay, Chase," she said. "But Taylor's in a very fragile state. I don't want her getting all emotional. I'm trying to keep her calm. Peaceful. I don't want you asking her a bunch of questions that will get her all excited. I don't want her reliving the last two weeks. Even I haven't asked her about it yet."

"I won't," I said. "I just want to see her, give her a hug, let her know I'm here for her."

"Okay, then," she said. And she led me up the stairs to Taylor's room.

I stood behind her as she knocked on the door. It was a familiar view.

"It's Chase," she said, through the door. "Chase is here, Taylor."

The door opened and a person I'd never seen before was standing behind it.

I tried not to look shocked. I tried to keep my face normal.

"Come on in," she said, grabbing my arm and pulling me in.

Then she shut the door and Anabel was back on the other side and I was alone with this creature. I was alone with what used to be Taylor Ragner.

ANISSA GRANT

The first thing they had to determine was if I was fit to stand trial. If I was insane or not. I thought about the possibility of faking it for them. Of really giving them some *One Flew Over the Cuckoo's Nest*, Jack Nicholson shit. But I didn't want to do that to Taylor. Or to Tate. Tate already had one parent who'd flaked out on her. And playing insane would delegitimatize what Taylor and I had. Make it one big phony sociopath story. So I resolved myself to playing it "straight," LOL, if you will.

They brought in multiple psychiatrists to ask me questions. I don't even know where they got them all. Flew them in, I guess, from Harvard and Stanford, Berkley and shit. Real academics. To evaluate me. They kept asking me questions about my childhood, about being a child actor and growing up in Hollywood, like they'd already worked out the reasons for my psychosis or psychopathness. I think they were actually disappointed when they couldn't label me crazy. When they couldn't give me an official label or diagnosis.

In the end they all said I was fit to stand trial. I was, they reluctantly admitted, "sane." Which was both a relief and a challenge. Being sane was a lot more work.

TAYLOR RAGNER

I was going crazy locked up in that room without Tatum.

I just kept screaming at my mom through the door. "You can't regulate love! You can't put laws on a heart! Look at what happened to Juliet! You can't regulate suicide, either, Mom!"

A girl at our school, a freshman, was pregnant. Chase told me. She was fourteen and her boyfriend was nineteen and in college. You can make all these laws for statutory rape or whatever you want to label it but you can't keep a girl from getting pregnant. You can't keep a girl from killing herself, either.

At the end of the day, we girls have more power than you think.

I had the power to break my mother's heart, permanently. I knew that. But I also knew at the same time it would break Tatum's, and Jolie's, and I couldn't live with myself, I couldn't kill myself, knowing that.

ANABEL RAGNER

I spent all day calling around, trying to find a therapist for Taylor.

I didn't know if she'd been brainwashed. Or if she was a victim of that Stockholm thing. Where you fall in love with your captor. Where you think you want to be with them.

When I told Taylor about the therapist I found she said, "*Mom*, you can't de-gay me. This isn't the 1980s. And we're barely even religious. Lapsed Catholic or whatever. So I don't know why you're doing this."

"I'm not trying to de-gay you, Taylor," I said. "I just want you to have someone you feel safe talking to, confiding in."

"Well I'm not going," she said. "I don't need to talk to anyone. I just need to see Tatum. I feel *safe* with Tatum. I want to *talk with* Tatum. When are you going to let me go see her? I'll fucking burn this house down, Mom, if you don't let me go see her, I swear to fucking god!"

Well, I'll tell you, that scared me. That scared the hell out of me.

I called the therapist back, asked if she made house calls, asked her to meet me at the house as soon as possible.

CHASE WHITING

I was worried about Taylor. Really worried.

She was distraught. Agitated. Terrified. She said she was afraid they were going to lock Tatum up for years. In prison or in a mental ward. She said she didn't know which would be worse and I wasn't sure, either.

She said she wanted to be in with her. That she would commit a crime if it meant she could be in prison with Tatum but since she was only sixteen, they'd just send her to juvie anyway.

She said she had contemplated suicide, but she didn't want to leave Tatum on this planet alone. But she didn't know how much longer she could take it: being separated from her, being victimized by her mother and everyone else who wanted Tatum locked up, who thought they knew what was best for her, who didn't believe she could make her own decisions for herself because she was only sixteen.

I just sat on her bed beside her listening and nodding, holding her hand.

I knew what it was like to not be heard, to not be taken seriously, to be told how your life will go, the type of person you will be.

I told Taylor I would try and see what I could do about getting in to see Tatum. I didn't turn eighteen for another two months and I didn't know if you had to be eighteen to visit someone in jail.

Taylor nodded and laid her head in my lap. I touched my fingertips to the yellow stubble on her head. It felt like the side of a soft cactus. It hurt a little.

CAM SPENCER

I'd seen Chase's car outside Taylor's house Christmas night. I'd been driving by trying to decide if I should stop. I kept going to text Taylor and then remembering she didn't have her phone anymore. I even sent one text early that morning to wish her a merry Christmas before I remembered. My mom and dad kept asking me a million questions about what was going on and I kept telling them I didn't know but they wouldn't stop asking me shit, like they thought I was hiding something, hiding that I knew, to protect Taylor or something. I don't know what they thought. They both kept saying bullshit about how they'd always known she wasn't trustworthy and how they'd tried to make subtle hints but that I was just too thickheaded, that I didn't listen. I tried to go down to the basement for a while, tried to lift and listen to music and forget what they'd said but eventually my dad came down and went on about Taylor some more, made me feel stupid, like she'd really pulled one over on me. Finally, I had to get out of the house. I got in my truck and just started driving and of course I drove by Taylor's and the third time I drove by was when I saw Chase's car there.

So I drove a little ways down the road, parked my car, and got out and walked back through the snow to Chase's car. It was unlocked, so I climbed in back and laid down and waited for him to come out.

I must have waited an hour and a half. Two hours. Hell, I don't fucking know how long I waited. No matter how many times the cops and attorneys ask me, I just keep telling them I don't fucking know. I'd left my phone on the dashboard of my car. I had no idea how long I laid there. I just remember finally Chase opening the door. I remember his scent in the car. He smelled like that spray cologne Taylor bought at Victoria's Secret at the mall. Like, beachy. Even though it was mid-winter, eighteen degrees and snowing. He smelled feminine beachy. Not like the shit he wore from Hollister. Not like masculine, a man's smell.

He smelled like fucking Taylor, like the last time I'd seen her, touched her. I guess something about that smell, her smell, in the car, triggered me. I mean, I was already on fucking edge from not seeing her for two weeks and from my parents riding my ass about her and from knowing Chase was with her, behind my back. God knows what he was telling her, about me, about me and her mom…

What the fuck would you do in that situation? You think you'd do something different? The love of your life, the person you thought for three years you were going to marry, inside a house you couldn't go in anymore and your best fucking friend coming out of it? I did what any man with any fucking self-respect would do. With any sense of loyalty. Of brotherhood. Would do. When his best friend betrayed him like that.

ANABEL RAGNER

Officer Browning came by the house an hour, maybe two, after Chase left. Said there'd been an accident. Was inquiring as to the state of Chase's mind when he was here, the length of time he'd stayed, all these other questions. Asked if we'd seen Cam around, if he'd come to the house. If I'd seen him drive by, noticed his car parked nearby since I'd brought Taylor home. I told him I hadn't seen Cam in days. Weeks. Of course that was a lie. I'd seen him five days earlier. The night Chase walked in...

But I wasn't about to tell the police that.

And I prayed to god Cam didn't either.

OFFICER BROWNING

It seemed like it was just one thing after another in this town now. They say when it rains it pours. It was Christmas evening, for chrissake. We couldn't cut a break. My wife was complaining because I hadn't been home more than five consecutive hours in days. I'd missed Christmas Eve at her family's. Christmas morning with mine. Now this.

I'd been called to the scene of a car accident out by the lake. Two teenaged boys. Well, I knew right away who it was.

Chase was lying in the snow when we got there—had a pulse but wasn't moving.

Cam said he'd been thrown from the car but something told me maybe he'd been dragged. Cam said Chase had been driving the whole time but it was obvious from about a million pieces of evidence that Cam had been the one driving just before impact.

Cam was barely injured. He had a few cuts and scrapes. Some bruises. Nothing major.

Chase wasn't moving.

Cam was pacing like a lion in the snow.

ANABEL RAGNER

I didn't tell Taylor right away. She needed to rest. She'd already been through so much. I didn't want her worrying over Chase now too. And who knows what she'd do about Cam. The little we'd talked since she'd been back... well, she just seemed to have a lot of anger. Toward him. *And others*. Me. Now.

She'd talk to Jolie. Otherwise, she was either raging at me or completely mute. Wouldn't talk at all. I guess she was giving me the silent treatment. I guess she was pretty mad at me. Which I did not understand at all. I was the one trying to help her. She didn't get that, though. She thought I was against her. She didn't understand being a parent. She saw me as the enemy.

She locked herself up in that room doing god knows what. Not eating! I can tell you that much. Maybe she was on a hunger strike. She was trying to punish me. Doing whatever she could to make me worry more. To punish me, more. And it was working.

CHASE WHITING

They told me later that I was unconscious for three days. LOL I don't remember.

Apparently, while I was unconscious, Cam was spouting his usual bullshit and lies. I don't know why anyone was surprised. I don't think he's ever been truthful with himself. So how could he ever be truthful with anyone else?

That's what had kept me holding on for so many years.

I just kept thinking at some point he'd have to face the truth.

I truly believed that. I guess I was wrong, though.

He's never going to face it. He'll destroy both of us, but he won't face the truth.

OFFICER BROWNING

It appears—though it's too soon to know fully—that Chase Whiting will never walk again. I don't know what that means for Cam Spencer. It's not good, though. Especially since he was eighteen at the time of the accident. Though, to be honest, even if he'd been sixteen, they might have tried him as an adult. Hard to say. White kids usually get off easier. A black kid, they get tried as adults at fourteen. Thirteen. White kids from the suburbs have better lawyers. Or their daddies do.

Cam might have been okay. Cam's mother is a kind of big deal.

She probably knew the judges.

Normally, they'd probably cut him a good deal, keep it nice and hush hush. But now, because of Tatum and Taylor, we were all on the national stage. Too bad for Cam. He was probably going to do some time. Reckless driving resulting in serious bodily injuries, minimal—attempted murder, at maximum.

CHASE WHITING

How ironic, right? I'll never be able to fuck anyone now that the person I'd been saving myself for put me in a wheelchair. How Shakespearean is that? What a tragic comedy. Or comedic tragedy?

Course, as the doctors kept reminding me: it was too soon to tell, and I still had use of my hands. And mouth.

I still had an asshole.

COACH W

I didn't know who to go see first. Chase. Cam. Taylor or Tatum. They were all in various states of grieving and trouble. And in the meantime, we'd had another suicide. A junior softball player. She left a note saying she'd seen what they'd done to Tatum. How they'd put her in jail. The media was writing up the story like a Romeo/Juliet situation with Tatum and Taylor as the star-crossed lovers. Apparently, Darby had tried coming out to her family at the beginning of the school year, only to be taken to church more frequently. Only to be threatened with barring her from participating in sports. She wrote in her suicide note that softball and being LGBTQ were the only things worth living for and since both had been taken from her, she didn't want to live anymore.

I guess she missed the "It Gets Better" campaign. I guess that was a few years ago. Maybe it wasn't a thing anymore. Or maybe she didn't believe it. Who was I to know.

My life had a different set of problems but none of them had ever gotten better. They were still the same old shitty ones each day. Each year. Maybe a new one or two. But not less.

TAYLOR RAGNER

My mom was trying to keep me locked up with no contact with the outside world, like that would make everything okay. I didn't have a cell phone and she'd taken my laptop and iPod.

I think she wanted to pretend none of this had ever happened, wanted me to forget Tatum had ever existed.

I was so tired by the time I got back from Florida I actually slept for almost three days straight. I think I really just wanted to go to sleep and never wake up. I didn't know what else to do. My own powerlessness was like was a hard sedative. A sleeping sickness. What was the point of being awake?

When Chase came to see me, I was still so out of it. I was still like a sleep-walker, 24/7.

Finally, one day, a couple days after Christmas, I woke up and had some newfound energy, a new determination that came from the realization I had nothing to lose. I got up and got dressed and snuck out of the house without my mom ever knowing. I left a note on my desk that said I'd be back, not to call the police, even though I knew she probably would.

I went out the back, in case there were any reporters in the front.

I sort of stuck out like a sore thumb in this town now that a) I looked like a girl in a futuristic sci fi movie from the 90s and b) my face was on the front page of every paper.

I got outside the house and cut across the backs of a few houses' yards ala Ferris Bueller and just started walking toward town, toward the police station. I figured I'd ask someone if I could use their cellphone. Chase had written his number down on a piece of paper I had in my back pocket. The only number I had memorized was Cam's and I sure a shit wasn't calling him. If I wanted to forget anyone existed, it was Cam.

ROBIN GRANT

I'd booked a flight out as soon as I'd hung up with Anissa. Even though we hadn't been on great terms—or any terms—even though I hadn't heard one word from my daughter in months, I knew she needed me. And being needed by my daughters was all I lived for. I wasn't happy, of course, Anissa was in jail, but I was relieved to have finally heard from her. And I felt like I had a reason to get out of bed again, my life had purpose once more.

I booked a flight and called several attorneys, first here in California and then in Indiana. I knew Anissa had taken money out when she'd left but I knew she probably still had a good chunk remaining and I had a little money saved away too if she needed help.

A good attorney was an investment in the future like none other. My father had taught me that.

I'd never been to Elkheart, of course. I had to google what airport to fly into. I had to rent a car. Book a Holiday Inn Express. Some of the hotels were already filled completely up with journalists, I assumed.

I tried calling Tate but she still wasn't answering my calls so I left a message with her agent. I didn't say why I was going to Indiana but I figured she must have seen Anissa in the news, if she was keeping up with the world at all, in any capacity, which it was possible, but unlikely, she wasn't.

COACH W

I saw Taylor walking toward town on my way in. I wouldn't have recognized her if I hadn't seen pictures of her all over the internet with the shaved head. Both she and Tatum were famous now. National news. I stopped and pulled the car over to see if she wanted a ride. She looked like she'd lost weight. She wasn't wearing makeup and she was wearing an oversized hoodie and track pants. She was biting her nails.

She got in, made a weak attempt at a smile, asked if I had any cigarettes.

I said I did, in the glove box, and she opened it and took one from the pack, lit it and cracked her window.

"Thanks," she said. "It's been a few days."

For a second I worried about someone seeing me with a student smoking in my car and then I remembered all the shit that was happening and realized smoking was probably the least of anyone's worries now.

"Hey," she said. "Can I use your cellphone to call someone?"

"Sure," I said, and dug it out of my pocket.

I watched her dial and waited, wondering who she was trying to call since I knew Tatum was in jail.

"He's not answering," she said.

"Who's that?" I said.

"Chase."

"Oh," I said. I guess she didn't know what'd happened. I didn't want to be the one to tell her.

TAYLOR RAGNER

As soon as I said Chase's name I could tell Coach was hiding something from me.

"What?" I said. "What is it? What's wrong with Chase?"

But Coach just sat there. Just kept his eyes on the road like that would get me to forget my good friend. Maybe my *only friend*, other than Tatum.

"Coach, you have to tell me, please. Is he okay? Is he alive?"

I was instinctively worried Cam had done something.

"Was it Cam? Did Cam hurt him? Please, tell me. *Please*. It was Cam wasn't it. I'll kill him. Fuck."

I was crying now. I was convinced Cam had killed Chase. I didn't know why, but I could feel it. I just knew.

"He's not dead, Taylor," Coach W finally said. "He's going to be okay. But he's in the hospital."

I said, "Oh my god, what did he do? what did Cam do, tell me."

"There was a car accident…"

"When?" I somehow knew the answer before Coach said it.

"Christmas night…"

"That was the night Chase came to see me. He must have been leaving my house… Cam must have been stalking me!"

"I don't know," Coach said. "I only know at some point it appears both boys were in Chase's car and Chase was hurt. But we don't know any details yet. They're not releasing any details."

"I know what happened, though. I *know*. It should have been me. Cam wanted to kill *me* and since he couldn't, he tried to kill Chase," I said.

"We don't know that, Taylor. We don't even know if Cam was to blame. Maybe it was really an accident," Coach said.

"It wasn't an accident," I said "Cam's going to murder someone someday."

"Okay," Coach said. "Well, even if that's true, Cam's in jail right now."

"With Tatum?" I said. "The same fucking jail?"

"I guess," Coach said. "I hadn't thought of it like that, but I guess."

I couldn't fucking believe it. He was probably going to try to kill Tatum too.

I needed to get down there and talk to her, but I knew they weren't going to let me see her. I had no way of contacting any of the people I cared about and no one could contact me and I had no way of helping anyone.

I didn't even have a goddamn phone.

And I felt like I'd aged ten years. I felt like I was thirty but people were still treating me like I was twelve.

It fucking sucked.

"Can I have another?" I said, opening the glove box.

"Sure," Coach said. "Anyway, where am I taking you and how are you, Taylor? What is going on with you? Why don't we start there?"

COACH W

Taylor was a mess. I honestly wouldn't have even known it was the same girl if she hadn't happened to be walking by and gotten in my car. Everything about her was different, not just her hair. It was her mannerisms, her voice, her way of talking, her way of carrying herself. The fifteen-year-old cheerleader was gone. Maybe she hadn't been there in a long while and we just hadn't noticed.

I took her to Big Boy and bought her a sandwich. She looked like she needed to eat something. I got some eggs and pancakes. To keep her company.

We ordered a large pot of coffee and she told me all about her trip south with Tatum. Or she told me what she wanted me to know. I could feel the holes in the story. They were the most interesting parts.

TAYLOR RAGNER

I needed a cellphone so I had Coach Wellsley take me to the store in the strip mall on the other side of town to get one of those prepaid ones. The kind drug dealers and other criminals got. I still had a wad of cash Tatum had made me take before the police handcuffed her.

I wasn't even sure who I'd want to call or text.

Coach W?

Coach Harden, maybe?

Chase, if he ever woke up?

I didn't trust anyone from high school. I would never have tried to get in touch with Makayla or Mallory or any of the other cheerleaders.

I wasn't like one of them anymore; I hadn't been in a very long time. What would I have to talk to them about.

I thought about texting my brother but he'd never given a shit what was happening back home before so why would he now. Ditto my father.

I got back in Coach W's car and asked for his number. He looked reluctant, like all of a sudden he was worried about his job, worried about someone finding my number in his phone.

Tatum had told me what had happened with him. He didn't know that of course. Though he must have worried I knew. He must have suspected. He could have saved his worry. I didn't fucking care. Right now, he was the very least of my concerns.

"Come on," I said. "Really?"

So he gave it to me. Cool, now I had one person to text.

ANABEL RAGNER

It was so obvious to me what Tatum had done to my daughter. My daughter had never acted like this. She was beside herself. Distraught. Manic and depressive at the same time.

Tatum was like a sexual predator preying on my daughter and my daughter was suicidal because of it, because of what Tatum had done to her, what she'd put her through.

She couldn't emotionally handle it. She was only fifteen. Well, sixteen now but just barely.

Sure, she'd been dating Cam for a couple years. Three. And he was older. But not *that* much older. And that was way different. That was high school puppy love. They were always so happy, Cam and Taylor. I don't know what happened.

Tatum happened, I guess.

In my memory, everything was perfect before Tatum.

Other than that one small incident, that one tiny blip on our mother/daughter radar. But everyone had a blip. You couldn't call yourself a mother without one little blip.

TAYLOR RAGNER

After that "little escapade" as she called it, after she'd called the cops just as I knew she would and they brought me home, after I'd had Coach W drop me at the station, after I'd demanded to see Tatum, after I'd seen Cam and yelled at him to go fuck himself— after all that, my mother made go to a therapist. She sat there right in front of me and told the doctor I'd been molested and sexually assaulted by a thirty-year-old woman. She said she was going to press charges. Like, once again my opinion and what *I wanted* wasn't even a consideration.

Which was when I jumped up and rammed my head into the filing cabinet. It'd been that or the letter opener to my wrist. It'd been sitting there trying to decide which the whole time those two had been talking about me and talking about Tatum like I wasn't even in the room.

I guess I rammed it pretty hard. I didn't notice the cord to the doctor's laptop and I tripped on that and busted my front teeth out on the fall downward.

I came to in the ambulance and started screaming, which was when they stuck my arm with a needle and I don't remember anything after that.

CAM SPENCER

I wanted out of this fucking town. It was full of people who hated me for no fucking reason. No fucking reason! What the fuck had I ever done to anyone? To the cops, to Chase, to Taylor? I'd been nothing but a good citizen, a good friend, a good boyfriend. And this was how they, how fate, repaid me?

Locked up in the same fucking jail as that pedophile bitch? That sociopath kidnapper? That rapist?

What kind of justice was that?

It was disgusting, the way I was being treated.

Like *her*.

They were acting like she and I were guilty on the same fucking level, of equal fucking crimes.

She'd brainwashed and bullied and taken off with a minor child, *had sex with her*, drank with her, gotten high with her, and what had I done? Gotten into a car accident? Slid off the road in the snow? On an icy road? Pulled my best friend from the car, tried to give him CPR, administered mouth to mouth, to save him?

I'm sorry, I really am sorry, but his paralysis is not my fucking fault. I didn't do that. I barely escaped dying myself! Chase and I are both fucking lucky to be alive.

I don't know why they were trying to make it like a malevolent act.

Like something I'd premeditated.

I had *no reason*. No motive. Why would I want to do something like that? Chase Whiting was my best friend. *Is* my best friend.

And they let Taylor in here to scream profanities at me while she tried to see her sex offender girlfriend?

What was she even *doing here*? Why wasn't she at home on lockdown? It was like Anabel had zero control over her own daughter.

No one in this town had any control anymore, that was the problem, of themselves or their children. That's what my father said when he and my mother came to see me. They brought a group of the best attorneys from the tristate area along with them. They said the Spencer name would not be tarnished by this town's inept police force.

My dad literally said, "Don't worry, son. You'll be out of here in twenty-four hours."

I hoped he meant out of this town and not just out of this jail cell. I didn't want to see ninety-eight percent of these people ever again. Not in my lifetime. Not in Taylor's.

TAYLOR RAGNER

My mother blamed Tatum. It wasn't Tatum that made me suicidal! It was everyone else—my mother, Cam, the cops, the whole stupid town! All of them. Every single one of them. Except maybe Chase. Was against us. Against Tatum. Saw her as some sort of criminal and me as some sort of victim.

That's what was so fucked up.

It wasn't us, or our love, that was… bad. Our love was pure and simple and good.

It was the way everyone reacted to it, viewed it, that was dark and twisted and evil.

But that actually gave me the incentive *not* to kill myself. Because I knew how they'd spin it. How they'd twist it, write about it in the papers, on social media. How they'd make it Tatum's fault. Our age difference the reason.

No one would look at my mother, at how she'd treated me when I got home. The mental and emotional abuse I suffered. Because of her.

No one would ever look at Cam. At how fucked up and emotionally abusive and controlling he'd been. Because I'd never told anyone. I'd never told anyone but Tatum. I'd barely let myself see it. In fact, I hadn't really seen it. I'd been so in denial, until he and I broke up, until I was away from him long enough to see who he really was, how he really had treated me.

No one would write that I'd been suicidal, had been hospitalized, before

I'd ever even met Tatum. No one would write that because that would be "blaming the victim."

Well, guess what. I am not a victim!

Now my mother was trying to get the nurses to make me take Xanax and Zoloft, both of which she'd gotten the "doctor" to prescribe for me. Along with other "medicines" I couldn't pronounce or remember the names of.

But I wasn't going to take them. Either of them. *Any of them.*

I wasn't going to go around being some zonked out sixteen-year-old so she could feel better about her choices. Just so she could feel safe, with a zombie daughter at home in her bedroom.

I needed to get out of my hospital room and find Chase.

ROBIN GRANT

It seemed like the whole town of Elkheart—and everyone in it—was coming unhinged. Like in a Stephen King novel or miniseries.

There'd been the suicides I'd read about and the cell phone pornography scandal and Tatum and Taylor "on the run" and now this accident with Cam and Chase.

It was a lot, too much, and I worried how my daughter would be affected. If she could get fair treatment, a fair trial if it came to that. An unbiased judge, unbiased jury.

She spent her whole career as the actress that floats under the radar, who is unrecognized in public, off film, on the street. Hell, she dated one of the most famous young actors in Hollywood at the time, costarred in a movie with him in which her face was the only one on the poster, and still almost no one knew her name or recognized her or remembered her. And we hadn't known, but it'd been a blessing!

And now her face was everywhere. In newspapers, magazines, and online articles.

She was getting more press than Tate did when everyone thought Tate had OD'd or killed herself.

Now everyone knew both their names.

The one story fed off the other.

Tate's face was usually somewhere with Anissa's. Or Anissa's was somewhere with Tate's, depending on who was that particular article's focus.

My anxiety was through the roof. I was drinking more, again, to deal with it all. Vodka was the only thing that calmed me. Vodka and Virginia Slims.

My heart was split in half, in two different places.

For months, Tate had been the only one speaking to me and I had been heartsick over Anissa and now Anissa was talking to me and my heart was broken because Tate was, for all intents and purposes, divorcing me.

All I did was care for these girls, *my girls*, help them with their careers, and all I got for it was heartache and loneliness and accusations.

But as a mother you always had to come when called.

It was an instinct, not a choice.

ANISSA GRANT

It was maybe a day after they brought me in that they brought Cam in. I couldn't believe it when I heard his voice. I thought, "Shit, I hope he's not coming to see me, to talk to me." I didn't have anything to say to him. And I didn't have a clue what the fuck he'd be wanting to say to me.

Then I saw he was in handcuffs. I saw them take him back in the same room they'd taken me into when they first brought me in.

My heart sunk and I felt like I was going to be sick. I was terrified he'd done something to Taylor.

My mom got there a couple hours later and told me he'd been arrested following a bad car accident. She said another person had been involved but she didn't know who. Again, I was out of my mind, worried it was Taylor. That somehow Cam had gone and gotten her, even though I knew she wanted nothing to do with him, that she'd never go willingly with him. That maybe Taylor's mom had aided him somehow, thinking if Cam and Taylor got back together, Taylor would forget about me and all her problems would be solved.

I had my mom go ask one of the police officers and they wouldn't tell her the name but said it'd been another boy Cam's age so I just knew it was Chase. They said he was still alive but in the hospital. And my first thought was of Taylor, that this was just more drama Taylor didn't need to know about or deal with.

I worried what would happen to her out there on her own, surrounded by all the chaos, without me. I felt like I'd abandoned her, being in here. Being locked up. Unable to leave. Being unable to go to her, to find her and comfort her. It was the worst feeling in the world. Helplessness.

ROBIN GRANT

I'd seen photos online but of course it was different seeing Anissa in person.

Her hair was short and dyed black with bangs.

It reminded me of the hairstyle she'd had in a movie as a teenager. Right before she met Quinn. Or maybe that was the hairstyle she had when they met. I can't remember. It's been so long, so many years, so many different TV and movie roles, so many different hairstyles.

I was used to not recognizing my daughters. I was used to their various personalities, too. Like being the mother of Cybil. Remember that TV movie from the 70s about the woman with multiple personalities? I think Jane Fonda or Sally Field played Cybil. I forget now, but one of them, I'm pretty sure.

There were all these horror movies featuring women back then. Women who were crazy or murderous or possessed by the devil.

The Stepford Wives. Rosemary's Baby. The Exorcist. Cybil.

Now poor Anissa was living a real life horror movie, starring in it.

She and Tate both.

What with all the media involvement and speculation and the paparazzi following Tate and now down here in Elkheart, too.

I didn't know anything about this Taylor girl, the one Anissa ran away with, except what I read on CNN.com or saw on *The Today Show*. Someone from their high school had already done an interview with Matt Lauer. Some girl who claimed to have been on the cheerleading squad with Taylor and Anissa, who said she wasn't surprised what they'd done; who said everyone knew they'd left Homecoming together, even though they'd gone with dates. Even though Taylor allegedly wasn't a lesbian, was allegedly dating the quarterback of their high school football team.

I was afraid to ask Anissa too much about her right off the bat. She seemed on edge, and for good reason. I figured I'd let the lawyers and attorneys ask all those questions, that I'd get all the info then.

Until then I was just trying to be here for my daughter, a physical presence, here for emotional support.

She'd tell me when she wanted to tell me.

But she was a nervous wreck, and who wouldn't be.

She was smoking cigarettes and drinking coffee and biting her fingernails and not eating.

The tabloids were having a field day with using photos from her younger acting days side by side with photos from today. With her mugshot and photos from the day they walked her into jail when they got her back here from Florida.

It wasn't fair. It was like those Top Model side by side photos of past contestants who were now on drugs.

Except Anissa wasn't on drugs, she was just wrecked from the system, from being arrested and made out to be a villain by the press. A child abuser and sexual assaulter.

I tried not to show her any papers.

Tried to keep our conversations light and focused on the future. Even though secretly that's what I was terrified of the most. Anissa's future.

TAYLOR RAGNER

I hadn't looked at my social media since Tatum and I had left town. But my mother brought me an iPad from home to use while I was in the hospital even though she'd been trying to keep me offline since I'd gotten home. I guess now she was more worried about me killing myself than she was concerned with keeping me isolated from the world. Maybe the therapist had recommended it, thinking I'd reengage with my high school friends. Who the fuck knows. I was too tired to question the gesture. I just went with it.

It'd been two weeks since I'd logged into any of my accounts.

My amount of followers across the board had tripled and quadrupled and I had like a zillion notifications.

I didn't have time to look through them all. I read the first few, which ranged from support for Tatum and me to accusing Tatum of being a pedophile and rapist and calling me brainwashed and stupid and a slut.

I decided to google our names. I wanted to know what was being written about us, how we were being portrayed in the media, online.

The first headline I saw said "Runaway Teen Found, Thirty-Year-Old Girlfriend Arrested." Another said, "Former Child Star Found with Kidnapped Teen Girl." Another: "One Time Hollywood Actress Found Asleep in Bed of Stolen Pick-up Truck in Florida with Missing 15-Year-Old After Man Calls 911."

It was all a bunch of bullshit. There was barely any truth to anything I read. It was just gossip and misinformation. I couldn't stand to read any more of it. It made me sick what they were saying about Tatum. It made me want to vomit how they were portraying me, too; making me out to be some mindless victim.

I decided to make a video and put it on YouTube.

I didn't have any makeup and my hair was still buzzed and I was in a hospital gown so I knew people would draw their own crazy girl conclusions but I didn't care. Let them think what they wanted, for their own theories and conspiracies and opinions. But I was going to say what I had to say first.

MAKAYLA RICHEY

It was so weird. Taylor's video.

She posted it at like one in the morning from the hospital, apparently, and by noon the next day it already had 50k views. Everyone at school had seen it. Probably most people in town had too.

The weirdest thing was how she looked. I'd been going to school with her since kindergarten and she'd never had anything but long dark hair. In elementary school she wore it in these long spiral curls her mother must have made each morning for her. She had little red cowgirl boots back then, too.

In the video she looks like some kind of alien and there's a tattoo that says something like Mr. Happy on her arm and she doesn't have on any makeup and she has dark circles under eyes like she hasn't slept in forever or like she's on drugs or crazy and she's saying all this shit about people not listening to her and not hearing what she's saying and about how she's not a victim and how she wants to be with Tatum and is going to be with Tatum even if she has to wait ten or twenty years.

Then she makes some weird coded message that seems to be about Cam, even though she doesn't say his name. It seems like she's saying Cam was the one who brainwashed her. Or raped her. Or something. I don't know.

She says she's never known freedom until now and she can't go back to being imprisoned.

It's all super dramatic and eye-roll worthy and there's like already three hundred comments and mostly they're people arguing over what age should be the legal age of consent and about homosexuality and the state of our country and feminism and Christianity and witches.

MALLORY SWINDELL

Everyone was talking about it at school. The Mr. Happy tattoo. What did it mean? Was it code for something? Anorexia or lesbianism or feminism or witchcraft? Was it a cry for help? Did it literally mean "help"?

COACH W

Yeah, I didn't have a clue about the Mr. Happy tattoo, either. But everyone kept asking me. Other teachers, other students, Principal Pitt, Mrs. Stone. It took two more days before someone noticed Tatum had the same tattoo. But that didn't clear anything up. Everyone was still trying to figure out what Mr. Happy was code for. We still don't know.

TAYLOR RAGNER

I'd never told anyone, including Tatum, how Cam had assaulted me sexually. I don't think I'd realized it myself until I was away from him a while. Then I started seeing articles online about the signs you're in an abusive relationship. I took online quizzes. Answered all the questions "yes." Cam fit all the stereotypes, all the descriptions of an abusive boyfriend. Looking back I could barely remember a time he hadn't coerced me into sex, a time the sex hadn't been painful. I couldn't really remember a time in which I had enjoyed having sex with him. I couldn't remember a time in which we were alone that he didn't try to fuck me, even if I wasn't feeling well, if I had a headache, if I just didn't feel like it. Then after he'd berate me for not being into it, for not enjoying it enough.

I remember thinking, "I guess this is what it's like. Maybe I'm asexual. Maybe there's something wrong with me."

I didn't have anything to compare it to.

But then I had sex with Tatum and I was like, "Nope. I like sex."

I told Chase everything.

CHASE WHITING

It was kind of weird, listening to Taylor talk about Cam and about having sex with Cam and about how it was almost never consensual, was almost always forced.

It was weird because I truly felt bad for her. Her experiences sounded truly awful.

And at the same time, I was still horribly attracted to him. I still had the nauseating desire to have sex with him. It was still all I thought about. Even if it made me sick that I thought about it so much.

It was hard to wrestle with the two thoughts of Cam. Or the hundreds of thoughts of Cam.

I was more ashamed than ever of my sexual desires for him. I was filled with self-loathing and I couldn't bear to tell Taylor anything I was thinking,

It made me feel so good she felt she could confide in me.

And I wanted to confide in her.

But I just couldn't.

I couldn't bring myself to tell anyone what was going on inside of me.

I'd tried to tell Cam and he'd almost killed me. Maybe he'd tried to kill us both.

ANISSA GRANT

It was Tate's sixteenth birthday and Mom and I made a wish for her. Mom insisted we close our eyes and hold hands.

I didn't like thinking about Tate. I had too much guilt. It hurt too much.

I kept thinking now that maybe I should have given her up for adoption instead of having my mom pretend she was hers. Maybe that would have been the most selfless thing I could have done for her. But it never even occurred to us then. It was never an option.

I think I loved Quinn too much then to give away anything that was a part of him.

Thinking of Tate always led me to thinking of Quinn, too.

She had so much of him in her. For better and worse. It was probably part of why I split; the older she got, the more she reminded me of her father.

I did the math quick in my head; he would have been thirty-nine now, had he lived. Had he not taken the fucking easy way out. Like Ted Nugent said, the fucker.

I hated Ted Nugent for saying that. What did he know about Quinn?

He'd never met him. Ted Nugent didn't know shit. Ted Nugent should have kept his big redneck hunting mouth shut.

He didn't know the pain Quinn was in. No one knew.

I didn't want that fate for Tate.

When Mom and I made the wish for Tate I wished with all my heart she'd be okay.

And that gave me something to fight for. A reason to get out of here.

I needed to do right by my daughter.

And I needed to do right by Taylor.

I didn't know how I'd become the person who abandons people, like my father, like Quinn, like Taylor's dad.

But I didn't like being that person.

I saw how selfish I'd been. I didn't want to be selfish anymore.

TATE GRANT

I got a text from Anissa on my birthday. Well, the text was from my grandmother's cell number but she said the message was from both of them. I knew Anissa was in jail somewhere in Indiana. I'd read what I could find about it on the internet after Felicity told me.

I stared at the one photo they had of Anissa with that girl, Taylor.

It was weird because Taylor looked my age.

In the photo with Anissa she has a blonde buzz but in the high school yearbook photo they always seemed to put beside that pic she has long, thick brown hair like Kylie Jenner.

They always put these crazy headlines on the articles about them. Like, "the real life Bonnie and Clyde" or "the real life Thelma and Louise."

I'd never seen either of those movies but Anissa had talked about both of them.

She liked all those movies about young couples in love on the run.

They made us read *Lolita* last year in school and the part where they're driving around staying at different motels was the only part I liked.

I figured Anissa had read that too or seen the movie and molded her life after it and all the other books and movies like that. *Badlands. Kalifornia. Natural Born Killers.* All the ones she'd made me watch when I was growing up, the years we shared a bedroom because I thought we were sisters.

I spent my birthday with Felicity watching a movie of my dad's I'd never seen before. I'd been tempted to steal some liquor from her cabinet but so far I hadn't. I'd been tempted to reply to the text from my grandmother and mother but so far I hadn't.

I didn't want them to think I wasn't serious about filing for emancipated minor status because I was.

I was done working for my grandmother. I was done letting anyone other than me make decisions for me.

I got a text from Georgia too but I didn't reply to that either.

All I'd been doing was talking to hundreds of different people for six months and I didn't feel like talking to anyone anymore.

The only person I kind of trusted was Felicity. And even her I didn't trust all the way. I didn't think I'd ever trust anyone all the way ever again after everything that had happened. After all that had been revealed. Finally and fully. After almost seventeen years of lying.

But despite all that, I kinda wanted to talk to Anissa. I missed her being my big sister. And I wanted her to be okay.

FELICITY MEIJER

I tried to get Tate to watch the movie her mom and dad made together with me. I thought it'd be a fun way to celebrate her birthday—seeing her parents so young, knowing they fell in love making it—and I'd never seen it before either. But she didn't want to.

She said, "Not yet. I'm not ready to see that one yet."

I said, "Are you sure? I bought it special for you, for your birthday."

But she just really didn't want to and after that I didn't want to push it.

But I kind of couldn't wait to watch it myself. I thought about watching it later, after she went to bed, alone in my bedroom.

Her dad was so hot on the DVD cover. His face was still thin and chiseled then.

He was barely older than Tate was now. He was still practically a baby when he died. Twenty-one or twenty-two. Something like that. So young and so talented and already a two time Oscar nominee and already he didn't want to live. It was so tragic and heartbreaking. One of the most tragic stories in Hollywood history, really.

But he was still so frickin' beautiful.

He was still Quinn James. Heartthrob. At least on that DVD cover. *Damn.*

I wondered how weird it was to have such a hot dad. Even if he was dead. Especially if he was dead. And had died basically the age you were now. Eternally hot and young. *Damn.*

ROBIN GRANT

I'd talked to several attorneys to explain what was going on.

I knew what the charges were—sex with a minor, kidnapping, crossing state lines with a minor, assaulting a police officer (s), grand theft auto (s)—but to me the charges were a misrepresentation of my daughter, of what had really happened, based on what she'd told me. Well, at least the ones involving sex with a minor and kidnapping.

Anissa told me that everything that happened had been consensual and I believed her.

Anissa had never been one to force her will on others.

She had a hard enough time standing up for herself.

Also, I'd been sixteen when I married her father. And while that hadn't worked out, neither did over half the marriages in this country and I didn't believe my age had anything to do with it. I didn't believe the ability to consent began the day you turned eighteen.

Look, Tate wanted emancipated minor status at fifteen and maybe I should have granted that to her. Maybe I was wrong to fight it.

ANISSA GRANT

The attorney my mother hired was female and from the city. She kept pointing out she'd driven from South Bend to be here and she seemed ticked off about the drive. She sat across a table from me, asking me questions I'd answered hundred of times, hundreds of different ways, already, barely looking at me, with an uppity attitude like she was the shit and we were lucky to get her.

She was wearing an outfit I thought would be useable to sell real estate and her foundation wasn't rubbed in all the way. I could see the line on her jawbone.

Also, it just seemed like we rubbed each other the wrong way.

I asked to be excused. I actually wanted to go back to my cell.

That's how bad we rubbed each other.

I thought about how she'd probably call someone and complain the whole drive back to the city while I sat in my cell not driving anywhere.

I thought about what a cunt she was for not looking me in the eye, for that weak ass handshake she gave me and her fake ass gelled nails Super tacky.

CHASE WHITING

I got used to Taylor being at the hospital with me.

At night she snuck into my room and we watched TV together in my hospital bed. It was like watching TV with the sister I never had. Sometimes we even held hands and Taylor fell asleep with her head on my shoulder.

It was great to feel so intimate and affectionate with someone without the threat of sex looming overhead.

I loved the smell of Taylor's shampoo. I understood what it was Cam and Tatum loved about her, what they were drawn to.

She was the most charismatic and sweet person I knew.

She was full of contradictions. Strong yet vulnerable. Outgoing yet mysterious, like she was always reserving some small part of herself for someone that wasn't you. Traditional but reckless. Preppy but rebellious.

Her hair was growing in a little and I liked to palm it as we watched TV.

We barely talked about anything happening outside the hospital. The trials or whatever.

I think we both were worn out by real life.

TAYLOR RAGNER

I knew Cam had tried to kill Chase so I vowed never to mention his name around Chase again, unless Chase brought it up.

I was worried what I'd say.

And I didn't want to upset Chase in his delicate state.

Or make him feel bad. I didn't want to unintentionally "blame the victim."

Instead, I told Chase how I was going to wait for Tatum, even if I had to wait ten years. I told him how Tatum and I had made this long term plan to move to California and told him he could move with us.

I was worried he felt isolated and alone.

I knew the feeling.

I didn't want anything bad to happen to him. Anything like what had happened to Chen and Lance and Joby and now Darby Finefrock.

I couldn't bear the thought of that happening to Chase. I couldn't bear the thought of him seeing Cam again, either. I was terrified Cam would kill him this time. Or me.

Cam was the one person I didn't worry about killing himself. He was way too much of a narcissist for that. I almost added "unfortunately," but even I'm not that mean and hateful. I didn't want Cam to die...

Or, maybe I did. If he was really going to kill someone next time. I didn't want "next time" to be me. Or Tatum. Or Chase.

ROBIN GRANT

I could tell Anissa didn't care much for the first attorney we got so after she left I called another one. This man named Leonard who was also recommended to me.

Anissa said she wanted a lawyer like Kevin Costner in *The Client* and I told her Kevin Costner wasn't in *The Client*.

"You know what I mean. Richard Gere then," Anissa said. "I think it was Richard Gere."

I looked it up on my phone.

"Nope," I said. "It was Tommy Lee Jones in *The Client*."

"Okay, then," she said. "So get me a lawyer like Tommy Lee Jones, please. Jesus. What difference does it make who was in *The Client*. You know what I mean."

"Okay," I said. "Sorry. I'll get you a Tommy Lee."

Of course we found out later that our original attorney was representing Cam Spencer in his trial.

"Doesn't that figure," Anissa said when we found out.

I didn't know yet that it did. Come to find that out later.

ANABEL RAGNER

Taylor's father flew in while Taylor was in the hospital. And her brother Tyler drove back, too. Jolie was so excited. She hadn't seen either of them in so long. She'd drawn special pictures with their names on it. When they got here though they didn't seem to know how to talk to her. They acted sort of awkward around her like how you act around a new friend's child you've just met for the first time. Sort of fake and shit. It pissed me off and sort of broke my heart because Jolie had been so excited about their homecoming.

Now I was worried they'd both just make things worse when Taylor came home from the hospital. Scott was already interrogating me about everything that had happened. He kept saying, "How could you let her go off with that girl?" as if I'd given my approval for all this. As if I hadn't been fighting with Taylor constantly the last five months while he was god knows where with god knows who doing god knows what.

"Yeah, I don't know, Scott," I said. "Why *did* I give my consent for Taylor to go on some crazy road trip with her new thirty-year-old girlfriend? Oh wait, that's right, I *didn't*. That's right, Taylor's only been hating me nonstop since she met Tatum because I never liked her, never trusted her, and have been trying to come between whatever they have the whole time. And where were you, this whole time? Because I didn't see you fighting this? I didn't see you at all."

G Sus. What a hypocrite. What a typical male. Was here for his oldest child, his son, but once he had two daughters left in the house, he was out of here. He was bye-bye gone.

I knew he was only here now because of the press, because Taylor was like a celebrity. Because there were cameras outside our house 24/7. Because he'd seen me on TV. It was why her brother was here now, too. We hadn't seen Tyler in over a year, thanks to his lovely girlfriend. And now look who else was back. Smiling for the cameras. Offering his two cents when he didn't have a clue what had happened, what was going on.

TAYLOR RAGNER

When we got home from the hospital, there was a news van parked outside and a guy jumped out when we pulled in the drive and started yelling my name.

"Taylor! Taylor," he said. "How's Tatum? Have you seen Tatum?"

"Ignore him," my mother said.

"Duh, Mom," I said. "I wasn't planning on talking to him. I'm not stupid. Also, we've already been through this when we left the hospital. You don't have to keep telling me the same shit over and over. I got it. I'm good. Well, not good, but... you know. I'm here. I'm alive. Let's celebrate. Let's have a party."

So I was already in a shitty mood when I walked in the house and saw my dad sitting there on the couch all casual like, trying to act, I guess, like he hadn't abandoned us, like it wasn't fucking unusual as hell for him to be here.

I just looked at him like the pathetic piece of shit dad he was.

"Don't you have another family now?" I said.

I didn't give a fuck about pretending like I didn't know anymore.

"Watch your mouth, Taylor," he said.

He was so full of shit.

"Why don't *you* watch *your mouth, Scott*," I said. And I went up to my room. But I heard him say something shitty to my mom and for the first time since I'd been back, I actually felt sorry for her.

I didn't even notice my brother Sam. But I guess he was home too.

ANISSA GRANT

My new attorney said we'd try to get the charges lowered. Try to make a plea deal. He promised I wouldn't serve more than six months, wouldn't have to register as a sex offender. He said that was Mary Kay Letourneau's original deal but she botched it by sleeping with her lover right away again when out on probation. That's the word he used: "*lover.*" Got pregnant a second time. After that, they threw the book at her, he said. Locked her up seven and a half years.

I didn't believe him—that they wouldn't "throw the book at me" right away, it was a different time now, even if I wasn't a teacher—plus Mary Kay Letourneau hadn't stolen a car or Tased a cop. And she hadn't crossed state lines with a minor. I hadn't had anyone murdered like Pam Smart, but I'd done more than sleep with someone.

Sometimes I sat in my cell staring at the walls or staring at my Mr. Happy tattoo for hours, just thinking about Taylor. I know it sounds silly, but I'd never really believed in soul mates before I met her.

I never thought Quinn and I would be together forever. I was too in awe of Quinn to even really be friends with him. And he was too distant from me and everyone else around him anyway because of the drugs for any of us to get truly close to him. I think he used the drugs as a way of protecting himself from us, from me. like a wall he built. On account of his shitty childhood. Sorry for the Pop Psychology 101 bullshit.

I just missed Taylor a lot. And I couldn't see Taylor. And I couldn't get a message to her. I needed to find a way. I needed a go-between.

I wouldn't blame her if she moved on. Wouldn't blame her at all. Moving on might be the best thing for her, might be her only way of coping with all this drama, especially since we couldn't be in communication.

So maybe, I decided, I shouldn't find a go-between.

Maybe the most honorable thing to do, the most selfless, was to let Taylor go.

For now, at least.

Let her live her life, and deal with my shit on my own. With my mother.

In the end it always comes down to you and your mom. *Grey Gardens* style. Me and Robin!

I hoped one day I'd be there for Tate when she needed me like this.

I mean, I hoped she wouldn't need me "like this," but if she did, if she ever did need me, I wanted to be there for her. Like Robin is here for me now.

TAYLOR RAGNER

I still had the iPad. I couldn't believe my mother hadn't taken it away from me. I was using it to keep track of what was happening with Tatum, what was in the news about her case, and to look up legal information pertaining to it. I wanted to help as much as I could even though I wasn't allowed in the courtroom or to see Tatum. Even though I was barely ever allowed out of the house.

I was considering going into law now, of studying it in college, if I ever got my high school diploma, if I was allowed back at school.

One day, after I'd gotten out of the hospital, I looked at my Twitter and Instagram accounts and it said Kaylin Jennings-Dames was following me. At first I figured it wasn't really her, that it was a fan page or something. But when I looked closer it said "verified account" and the posts and photos seemed legit. So I followed her back. Two minutes later I had a DM on Twitter. I clicked on it and it was from Kaylin. *Fuck.*

"hey taylor, you don't know me but you know my mom. anissa. i've been following you guys online. i know my mom is in jail there. i just thought maybe we could talk. hope that's not weird. <3, kaylin."

Shit.

TATE GRANT

I didn't know if Taylor would reply to my message. I didn't blame her if she didn't. She didn't know me from shit and it was probably weird that she and I were like the same age. It was probably weird for her to think about Anissa having a daughter. It was fucking weird for me too. Not like it's *not weird* for all the children of male celebrities who date women their age or younger, but... people get used to shit, I guess.

And then all the TMZ celebrity gossip bullshit I'd been going through recently on top of it.

I'd watched her hospital room video, though, and she seemed cool. She seemed like someone I could relate to.

I guess I wanted Anissa to know I was thinking about her even if we weren't in contact right now. And I was curious about Taylor. Somewhere in the back of my head maybe I thought I might fly out, maybe go to the trial. If I could find a way to go without the media knowing and getting hold of the story. And if I could, I'd rather go to court with Taylor than with my grandmother.

I didn't know then of course that Taylor wasn't allowed in the courtroom unless she was testifying. Unless she was called in by the judge or whatever. I didn't know anything, really. It was hard to know what in the media was true and what was just gossip.

I didn't want to admit it, but I was worried for Anissa. I was worried about my *mom.*

CHASE WHITING

I didn't want to testify against Cam. I didn't want anything to do with the courts or his case or any of it.

To be honest, I was hoping it would all just be dropped, just go away. What was done, was done.

As long as my medical bills were compensated. I was trying to talk my dad out of a civil suit, but he said we might have to, to get the full compensation. He hated Cam, blamed him for everything.

But, in a way, it was all as much my fault as it was Cam's. I know that probably sounds extremely self-blaming and stupid to you but that's because you don't have all the facts, you don't know my state of mind that night, what might have happened if Cam hadn't been waiting outside Taylor's for me. Things might have been worse.

I mean, I'm still alive, aren't I? I'm still here.

ANABEL RAGNER

I made the mistake early on, when Taylor was still in the hospital and the reporters were hounding me every time I went in or out to see her, of talking to them. Just once, but it cost me. Taylor found out about it and wasn't happy about it and she let me know.

They'd asked me what I thought about Tatum.

They caught me at just the right moment. When my own anger was very much at the surface. I'm not proud of what I said, of how I reacted, but I think it's understandable, given the circumstances.

I turned to them, and I could see the look of surprise in the guy's eyes when I did, since I'd never acknowledged any of them before. I turned to him and said, "Well, at least a thirty-year-old lesbian can't get my sixteen-year-old daughter pregnant. Unlike some of those cases with female teachers and male students. So I thank god for that, for the biological unnaturalness of the union."

I don't know why I said it, and, even as the words were coming out of my mouth, I sort of regretted them.

After all, I had Jolie at home and I knew there were lots of people who would say she was biologically unnatural. And I would hate them for saying it. I would want to kill them for saying it.

But Jolie didn't have another person trying to run away with her, trying to take her from me. That was the difference, I guess. Taylor was still my child until she was eighteen. And no other person—male or female, sixteen or thirty or fifty—was going to take her from me. And I would play any card I had to keep that from happening! Even if it was the gay sex is unnatural card or the statutory rape card or the inability to consent card. I'd play any of them or all of them. To keep my daughter.

TAYLOR RAGNER

It took a while before I started feeling myself again. In the hospital I'd felt so numb. Maybe they'd given me shit when I first got there, that was still affecting me days later. All of a sudden I was feeling it all, everything that'd been bottled up inside me since I got back, and I couldn't stop crying. I couldn't stop writing letters to Tatum. Even though I had no way of getting them to her.

I needed to talk to someone I could trust since I couldn't talk to Tatum. I didn't have anyone other than Chase and he was still in the hospital. He was going through so much, both physically and emotionally. I hated to bother him with my problems. I tried to just be there for him, to listen and support him.

So I texted Coach W and asked him for Coach Harden's number. I hadn't seen her in a long time, since Tatum and I left town. But she'd always been easy to talk to. I'd felt pretty close to her the two years I'd been cheering and it seemed like she liked Tatum. Or she had when she thought she was a high school student like me. I didn't know what she'd think now.

But I texted her and she was super open and nice and we agreed to meet at her house since meeting anywhere out in public now was impossible. She said she'd pick me up in a couple hours. I didn't tell my mom. I tried to have as little contact with my mom and the rest of my family as possible.

I played with Jolie when she got home from school, before she went to whatever dance or music lesson she had that day. We watched cartoons and old episodes of *Hannah Montana* together while I painted her nails or braided her hair or let her paint or braid mine. I wished I was old enough to get a place for me and Jolie to live in together. I wanted to raise her myself. Sure, my mom was doing okay with her now, but she was only six. How would she do with her once she started puberty? Once she was thirteen, fourteen, my age? When things weren't just cute and fun anymore? When shit really hit the fan for Jolie.

CHASE WHITING

It looked like I was going to be in the hospital and then after that a rehab facility a long time. No one really knew, not even the doctors, what my ultimate prognosis was, what to expect from rehab, what to expect in my life now going forward.

The funny thing was, before the accident, before Cam almost killed me, or us, I don't know what he was trying to do, honestly, I *was* suicidal. I was thinking about dying a lot. About how I'd do it. And when. It seemed like the easiest thing to do. The easiest answer to my problems. Just fucking end it all and be done with it. Problem solved.

But after the accident, I woke up in the hospital and I had no idea what had happened to me. And I should have been suicidal then, when they told me, when it was not directly stated but definitely implied I might never walk again, thanks to my best friend's hatred of me... Well, that's when you'd think a normal person would want to kill himself.

But, instead, it had the opposite effect on me.

I don't know why, but after that I just felt like I was going to survive this and get out of this town and I was going to have this new life I'd never thought of. I didn't know yet what it was. But I felt a sense of purpose. Like I had survived the accident for some reason I didn't even know about yet.

I wasn't religious, but it was hard not to feel something spiritual, some sort of divine intervention, after that.

I actually started reading books by the Dalai Lama and books about Buddhism and stuff like that while I was in the hospital all those weeks.

I felt way calmer and more peaceful for the first time in a long time. Which is crazy, I know. I guess before the accident I felt like my emotions were out of control and I had no meaning or direction in my life. I missed my mom and sort of wanted to follow her, to be with her. Which is really dark, I guess, saying it out loud. And now my path was very clear to me. Now I had meaning if only in that I had to work really hard, physically, to get back to an independent lifestyle and after that I had to work really hard emotionally and mentally in order to be able to help other kids deal with feelings of teenaged isolation and loneliness and suicidal feelings and accepting your homosexuality, which I was still doing, too. Which was going to be another long process.

CAM SPENCER

My attorney said we were going to get all the big charges against me dropped. That she was going to prove the whole thing was accidental. I hadn't been drinking, so I had that in my favor. And even though I'd lied initially to the police about being the driver of the car, she said that was understandable being that I was naturally fearful of the police, of being held responsible for the accident.

They let Matt come in to see me since he was eighteen now and he told me about Taylor's YouTube videos. Apparently, she'd been posting them a lot, lately. Saying shit indirectly about me, insinuating I'd been a "bad boyfriend," when what I think she meant was that I was an alpha male and what she apparently wanted was a beta male. Or, beta female, as the case may and seems to be. I was too much for her, I guess. Too strong a presence. Too fucking masculine. "Toxic masculinity" or whatever bullshit.

Obviously, because she's with a woman now. Because I guess she's a lesbian. Dyke. Whatever.

So why did she have to blame me for anything?

Was she trying to say I was the reason she was gay now? Because I thought you were *born that way*. That's what Lady Gaga said, right?

So how could I make Taylor like women, want to fuck women, by being an alpha male?

Liberals didn't make sense. They'd find a way to blame you and to take credit at the same time.

The only thing I'd ever done to Taylor was treat her like a princess and ask her to marry me.

And I told Matt that.

I said, "Maybe that was what turned her off, the fact I actually wanted to be with her forever. That I was ready to commit my life to her."

"She's sort of a flaky person, I'm seeing now," I said.

"Watch, I promise you, tomorrow she'll be back to liking men," I said.

"Not tomorrow tomorrow, but, you know, figuratively tomorrow."

"She'll like dick again soon enough. Soon as she realizes this journey isn't taking her where she wants to go. Soon as she realizes everything about Tatum is fake, is a con. Starting with whatever dick she's using to fuck her with."

"She may even want to come back to me," I said. "I won't blame her. I won't hold all this against her. I'll be here for her. And you can tell her that. You can tell everyone that. Cam Spencer is a stand up guy. Tell them that. Tell them I'm in it for the long run. I'm here to stay."

I knew this was a change from how I'd felt when they first arrested me, when they first brought me in. I'd been in a dark place then. A real dark place. I was in a better place now. I was back to feeling like Cam Spencer. I was back to being me.

COACH HARDEN

I drove over and picked up Taylor from the park down the street from her house.

I knew she was having problems at home.

Coach W had filled me in on some and said she wanted my number, that she needed someone to talk to, a mentor or whatever. A female mentor.

So I said, sure! Of course!

I'd known Taylor since the summer before her freshman year. She'd always been such a sweet girl, outgoing and flirtatious, but genuine and hardworking.

She was always the first girl to learn a cheer. Always the one to rally the troupes. Always the one with a smile on her face.

Even when it turned out later we knew she was going through stuff like depression... she never let on at games or practices.

She always just had this sunny disposition.

And then we found out later what was really going on...

But when I picked her up that day, at the park, it was like I was meeting the real Taylor for the first time.

She got in the van and closed the door and looked at me and she wasn't smiling.

I think that was an important step.

That she longer felt she *had* to smile. That she had to be this perfect teenaged girl.

CHASE WHITING

I wasn't going to tell her, I swear. I'd made a promise to myself. But then Taylor came to see me and asked me if anything fishy had gone on while she was out of town, like between her mom and Cam specifically, like she actually directly asked me that.

I don't know why she asked, how she knew something was up.

Maybe she'd found evidence or overheard a conversation... I don't know. But I couldn't lie to her. I'd never planned to tell her but I'd never planned on her asking me either.

So I said, "Yeah, Taylor, I actually walked in on them one day, in the living room."

I remember she was sitting on the edge of my hospital bed, looking directly at me, and I waited for her face to change, for her to cry or be angry, but nothing happened.

Her face just stayed exactly the same, which was almost worse, because I didn't know how to read her, what she was thinking. Maybe I should have lied. Maybe I should have told her, "No, Taylor, nothing happened that I know of."

I don't know, but then she just quickly changed the subject to me, to my rehabilitation plan and to my plans for college and to my dad.

My dad had all of a sudden done a one eighty.

Me almost dying seemed to have gotten him out of his funk, I guess, because all of a sudden he was the kind of supportive parent only my mom had been for seventeen years. It was nice to have him so interested, so supportive, to feel like he and I were really friends for the first time in my life since I was a young boy. Since I was like four, maybe five, and I would sit in my dad's lap watching basketball games and eating cold hot dogs on Saturday afternoons. Those were always the best days. Before he got too busy with work and was no longer home on Saturday afternoons.

I think all the sports I played growing up, especially football, was all for him. So he'd notice me again. So he wouldn't worry he had a fag for a son. Because I know he worried about that. I could sense it. And that was another reason it seemed like he was so busy, like he was never home.

TAYLOR RAGNER

I just could not stay in that house of lies one more minute. Not one more day.

I didn't know what I was going to do long term, but short term, in the immediate future, I had to get the fuck out.

The day before I'd been to see Chase and he'd confirmed for me what I weirdly already suspected: that my mom and Cam had had an affair when I was on the road with Tatum.

Big fucking deal. I was over Cam anyway, but it was still so fucked up for them to sleep with each other. Like, SO FUCKED UP! Like, what had I been gone at that point, five days? And my mom claimed to be SO WORRIED ABOUT ME. Yeah, right. So worried she dropped her pants in front of my boyfriend, ex-boyfriend, whatever. I mean, I know she was desperate, god knows my dad hadn't had sex with her in years. Probably not since Jolie was born and now Jolie was almost seven. So I get that she was in need. I get that she was lonely. But, like, anyone else, Mom. ANYONE FUCKING ELSE. Coach W or Coach Harden. Or Chase's dad. Or any other fucking person in town. Or out of town. Or on Tinder. Or Match.com. or fucking Myspace or Facebook or wherever old people or moms hang out and meet people to sleep with.

I just couldn't even look at her anymore. Not after she was the one who basically landed Tatum in prison, who'd accused her of rape on my behalf, and then fucked my ex-boyfriend? How was I supposed to look at a person who would do all that and then proclaim to love me? Proclaim to want to protect me?

She was sick. Like the mom in *Carrie*. Like Farrah's mom on *Teen Mom*.

She didn't live in reality.

She lived in some Anabel Ragner Land where she was this saint and all the rest of us were sinners she was trying to save us. Except what she couldn't see was she was the biggest sinner of all. And she wasn't saving anybody. Least of all herself.

She was the one who needed the shrink!

fourteen

. . .

ROBIN GRANT

I was worried about Anissa. She was so thin and frail. She didn't have an appetite.

She kept asking me if there was any way she could see Taylor or Tate.

We were about to have the bail hearing. I didn't know what to expect. How high the judge would make it. Or if he'd hold her without bail.

I know that was what was killing her, the waiting.

But even if they let her out on bail, I knew there was no way she could see Taylor. Not until the trial was over. And even then…

No one was blaming Taylor for anything. Not that they should. But I remember reading about Charlie Starkweather and his girlfriend... you know, the couple all those movies—*Badlands* and *Kalifornia* and *Natural Born Killers*—were based on? They electrified him, but they also threw her in prison. She was thirteen when she started dating Charlie and fourteen when they were on the road, killing people. I don't even know if she actually killed anyone. But they put her in prison for something like twenty, thirty years.

Back then, in the 40s, it wasn't uncommon to get married at sixteen. Bonnie of Bonnie and Clyde dropped out of school to marry her husband at sixteen. It wasn't Clyde, her husband. Her husband was some other guy who went to prison. But she was still legally married to him when she died. When she and Clyde were shot dead by the police. I know all this because Anissa played Bonnie in a made for TV movie years ago, and we did all this research together for her role. Even though almost no one saw it. That's how things go in Hollywood. If anyone ends up seeing your movie it's a little miracle. But Anissa made a good Bonnie, I thought. Good as Faye Dunaway even. Hell, maybe all those roles she played at such a young age prepared her for what's happening now. Maybe they made it so it didn't feel like that big a leap, to take off on the road with a teenage girlfriend. You know? I don't know how the mind works. I'm not a psychiatrist. But it makes you wonder, doesn't it? It definitely makes you think about things a little differently. That's for sure.

COACH HARDEN

Over winter break my girlfriend Stacy and I had moved in together. We'd been dating seven years. I'd never introduced anyone from school to her because I was so protective of our relationship but also because I didn't need any flack for being gay. It seemed like, in my experience, people were cool with you being gay, most of them, in theory, but as soon as they saw it in actuality, they had a tendency to get weird.

So Taylor had never met Stacy.

But soon as we got home the three of us sat in the kitchen having coffee and bagels and talking and Taylor and Stacy got along great.

I'd told Stacy all about what was happening of course before I went to get Taylor. Stacy had been kicked out of her house as a teen for being gay and being in trouble so she knew what it was like and Taylor, I think, could relate to her even more than she related to me in that way.

I'd asked Stacy the day before if it'd be okay if Taylor stayed with us a while. I had no idea how long that would be. I figured maybe we'd need to call a lawyer and ask some questions, on Taylor's behalf. But Stacy said of course Taylor could stay as long as she wanted and she helped me make up the guest room for her real sweet with flowers and special little soaps and mini bottles of shower gel and shampoo and lavender room spray which Stacy said is supposed to be calming.

CAM SPENCER

They finally had to let me go. After three days, the judge told the prosecutors they didn't have any evidence to hold me on. Or enough evidence. Or evidence that amounted to anything. I mean, sure, I was going to have to come back, face the civil suit, but far as the rest of it, I was out of there.

I walked out of the courthouse thirty minutes later a free fucking man.

And you bet I talked to those reporters!

You bet I told them how I felt.

I told them justice had prevailed again. That it would keep on prevailing.

I was so fucking stoked at that moment, someone in the crowd held up his hand to high five me and I high fived him back.

It was a great fucking feeling.

And then that bitch reporter from L.A. or NYC or wherever the fuck city she came from asked me how it felt to read about my ex-girlfriend on the run with Tatum and just like that I wasn't smiling anymore. Just like that the alpha male, the toxic masculinity Cam came out. And I turned to her and I said, right into the microphone, "Honey, I broke up *with her*."

Which, I don't know if that's the full truth. But it ain't a lie. If you know what I mean.

And then I yelled out, "Hashtag 'free Cam!'" and gave the victory sign.

And then I just got in the car with my parents and went to get some food. It'd been so long since I'd had a good steak. I was ready to fucking celebrate!

TATE GRANT

I don't know when the hashtags first started happening but I saw them on social media all the time now. There seemed to be two opposing main ones. Or three, actually.

First I noticed the #T&T.

Then I started noticing the #lockTatumup.

And then #freeTatum started showing up.

Me and Taylor were texting a lot by then. We'd traded numbers on Instagram messaging one night and immediately we were texting for hours. Mostly about Anissa, obviously, but also about ourselves, what was happening in both our lives. But mostly we were worried about Anissa, about getting her out.

I told Taylor I had *issues* with Anissa, with how I'd been raised to believe she was my sister, about how she'd taken off, left California without a word, but ultimately, she was my family, sister or mother or whatever. You know? So of course I loved her and of course I didn't want her to go to prison. And Taylor didn't want her to, either. Taylor said it was an insult to her that they'd locked Tatum up.

TAYLOR RAGNER

I was texting with Tatum's daughter Tate a lot now. She wanted to fly out. To try and see Tatum, and so the two of us could finally meet. We just wanted to hang out and talk.

But it would be hard with all the paparazzi and media on her 24/7.

Not to mention the media on me now.

They were treating me like some sort of B list celebrity. Like a *Teen Mom*. And Cam was acting like one of the *Teen Mom* exes, annoying and undermining me at every turn. Shit-talking me to reporters. I tried to ignore it but he was all over social media. He was like the horror villain that just won't die, no matter how many times you shoot or stab it, no matter how many times you think he's dead. He just keeps coming back to life, back at you. He just keeps coming.

ANISSA GRANT

One day my mom came in and handed me a folded up piece of paper. She said Taylor had given it to her, that she'd been waiting outside the building when she walked by with all the reporters and bystanders. She recognized her right away from the photos she'd seen online. My mom hadn't made one comment one way or the other about Taylor and me. How could she? I'd been well underage when she allowed me to go spend weekends with Quinn. People made exceptions for big movie stars: exceptions like about serving drinks to minors and allowing their virgin daughters to sleep with them.

Anyway, I waited until my mom had left to read it. I needed to be alone with Taylor and this was the closest I would get for a long time. I don't want to reveal here what the letter said. I want to keep some things private. But it was enough to keep me going for the next ten years. I kept the folded piece of paper on me, took it out and opened it and read it five, six, seven times a day. More if I needed it.

COACH W

I was reading all this shit in the magazines now, again, about Quinn. He was on the front page again. Now that the media had uncovered the fact that Kaylin Jennings-James was Quinn's biological daughter. I couldn't believe he didn't tell me. I mean, we hadn't really been talking in the months leading up to his death, but still. I would have thought he'd have made a point to call me once he found out he was going to be a father. I would have thought he might even have asked me to be the baby's godfather. I didn't think he was that close to any of his Hollywood "friends." I guess he wasn't exactly turning his life around, then, though.

TATE GRANT

I wanted to do what I could to clear Anissa's name. I'd seen what Paris Jackson had done for her dad. People couldn't be as mean about him now that he had a pretty, nice daughter saying in interviews what a great daddy he'd been. Plus, she had tattoos in tribute to him and his music all over her body.

We followed each other on Instagram and Snapchat now, so I was always looking at them in the photos she posted.

She was actually the person who inspired me to get my first tattoo. Now that I knew who my actual parents were. I got their initials inside of a heart on my arm. Like on a tree. I wanted to have it before I went to Elkheart. So when I went, the media and reporters and shit would know where I stood without me having to answer questions.

I didn't say this to Taylor but another part of why I wanted to fly to Elkheart was to see where my dad was buried, to go to his grave. I'd read online he was buried next to his grandma, my great-grandma. I thought it was so sad and so sweet how she'd died less than a week after him.

I wanted to get a tattoo of his face on my other arm, but I didn't know how Anissa would feel about it. I couldn't wait to talk to her about him. I actually really couldn't wait to see her. She may have kept a secret from me for sixteen years and yeah, that was super fucked up, but I was beginning to realize she was also always there for me. Like, physically but also emotionally. She was an amazing older sister. She didn't abandon me like Quinn's mom. She was still there. She was always there, even if I thought my grandma was my mom.

ANISSA GRANT

They had the bail hearing and the bail was set at 200k and somehow my mom paid it. She had a hotel room for me in her name and I told her I just needed some time to myself, a bath and a good night's sleep. I knew Taylor was staying with Coach Harden from the notes she'd been passing me through my mom. I found Coach Harden's number in the phone book—luckily she still had a landline. Most adults still did in Elkheart then. Especially teachers. So I called and asked to speak to Taylor and half an hour later Taylor was knocking on my hotel room door. We both knew it was stupid, that someone was bound to see us. But we couldn't stop ourselves. It'd been weeks since I'd held her face in my hands, felt her bare chest against mine. I needed more than anything to tell her how sorry I was and how much I loved her. I needed to tell her that over and over for hours, alone in the dark, alone with her body under mine, so she never forgot it.

TAYLOR RAGNER

It's hard for me to say it was worth it. I'm not the one in prison. But I'll say, *for me*, that night was worth it. A thousand percent. I'd do it a thousand times over. There are things we talked about that night I'll remember every day for the rest of my life. Things we *did* I'll always remember. [grins] And I'm so ready to wait for Tatum. For her to get out. No matter how many years they give her. No matter how many times she tells me not to, to move on, to live my life.

I can live my life fully and still stay true to Tatum. Coach Harden and Stacy said I can live with them until I graduate or even after, if I want to. I might go to community college here a year or two and then transfer to the state school in Bloomington later. I want to be a lawyer. Or a politician. Either way, I'll need to study law.

Anyway, women are better at waiting than men. Women are better at being alone. Both my great-grandmas lived twenty-five, thirty years, after their husbands passed, and never remarried, never dated.

But I know she'll get out. Sooner than later. Even if I have to fight for changes in the law first, I'll do it. Then Tatum and I can get married and get a house and be together, like a normal couple.

ROBIN GRANT

After they got wind of Taylor visiting Anissa at the hotel, they took Anissa right back to prison. This time the judge wasn't so nice about it. And this time Anissa didn't want to fight anything. She pled guilty on all charges.

She said she just wanted to do her time, take her punishment, so she could hopefully get back out and move on with her life. And even though she didn't say it, I knew she meant her life with Taylor. I wasn't going to worry about that part of the equation now. So much can happen in seven years.

PRINCIPAL PITT

Once Chase started posting his YouTube videos from rehab, the suicides stopped. At least for now. At least for this current group of kids. You can't control the future. Everything recycles. Circles back. But right now Chase is a role model for them. An example of what can happen when you stop blaming yourself for everything and start looking at all the positives in your life. Start loving yourself for who you are.

I don't know if I believed in it all but it was nice not to have to deal with suicides every other week. It was nice to see kids smiling in the halls. Helping each other instead of beating each other up, instead of bullying each other.

Sure made my life easier.

CHASE WHITING

I about died when Oprah called and said she wanted to interview me for a new show on positivity she was doing for her TV channel. After Kaylin started following me and reposting my tweets and YouTube videos, that's when my social media presence went through the roof. Suddenly, I was a social media star. I had like a million followers on Instagram and Twitter both. The Jenner and Hadid sisters all followed me. And Selena and Miley. It was crazy. It was insane. I had offers from New York publishers to do a book. Offers from publicists to do high school speaking engagements.

People in both the LGBTQ community and the physically-challenged community wanted me to be a spokesman for their causes.

Of course, I have to finish rehabilitation first. I have to build up my strength, physically, before I can go on tour. But it certainly gives me something to strive for. A reason to keep challenging myself. I could tell my dad was happy about it, too. He kept telling me how proud he was of me and how proud my mom would be. Funny, he never asked about Cam. We just never discussed him after the accident. Not once.

TATE GRANT

I was already friends with Paris Jackson and then Frances Bean Cobain started following me, too, and then she private messaged me. She said she'd read about my hospitalization and rehab. She told me she'd been sober two years now and asked if I needed a sponsor. She lived in L.A. She posted a pic of our dads hanging out together. They both looked drugged out as fuck. We decided they'd be happy to see the two of us hanging out together, sober. Break the motherfucking chain.

I'd blocked Georgia on all my social media accounts and my phone.

I'd told Felicity I wanted written off of the show. I needed time. I got my own apartment. Now that I was an emancipated minor I could live on my own. Another two years and I'd be eighteen. No more of this court bullshit. Just a normal young adult.

Sixteen and already through rehab, already sober.

I started hanging out with Frances and Paris. We joked we should contact Hailie Mathers and Madonna's daughter, Lourdes; made bets on who would be more fucked up: Jay Z and Beyonce's kids or Kanye's and Kim's. All three of us had made suicide attempts at least once. Two of our fathers had OD'd, pretty much, the other killed himself outright. We'd all three done drugs, gotten fucked up as shit. The one thing we had going for us was there hadn't been social media when we were growing up. The thing I had going for me was no one knew I existed for sixteen years.

I bought a ticket to Elkheart. I'd been messaging with Chase and Taylor, writing letters to Anissa, texting with Robin.

I'd also gotten a DM from some coach there who said he'd been child-hood friends with my dad.

TAYLOR RAGNER

I heard this female politician saying on some female talk show yesterday something like, "just because our daughters are going through changes, getting hips and... doesn't mean..." Like, she meant now that they were menstruating and getting tits and shit, they weren't women. But what are they then? What am I? I'm not a child. I'm not a girl. What are all the teen moms with children? With multiple babies? You 100% cannot be a child if you can procreate and give birth to a child. You just can't be, aren't, whatever.

It's like wishful thinking. Or like delusional thinking. It's denying nature. It's like being a climate change denier. You're just flat out denying science, denying biology, when you say a female who's gone through menstruation and can conceive a baby is a *child*.

I'm a fucking woman and I'll make decisions, choices, about my own body, thank you very much. I mean, I can have an abortion, for fuck's sake.

And no one gave a fuck when I was fucking an eighteen-year-old sociopath. But now all of a sudden everyone has an opinion about me being with the woman I love.

Flat-earthers. That's what they remind me of.

What happened to MY BODY, MY CHOICE, PEOPLE?!

COACH W

I'd been messaging with Quinn and Anissa's daughter, Kaylin. Tate. Whatever. She looked just like him. It's scary, actually, how much she looks like him. Same piercing blue eyes, same delicate hands, same sly smile.

She flew in from L.A. for Anissa's sentencing. The whole town except Taylor was practically there in the courtroom. Taylor wasn't allowed, for obvious reasons. And Chase was still in rehab. But Cam was there, smirking in the back with Matt, who he'd somehow, inexplicably, become best friends with.

I couldn't stop staring at Kaylin. She only slightly younger than Quinn had been the last time I'd seen him. His hair had been dyed black for a movie then too.

Before the sentencing I took her out to the cemetery, showed her where Quinn and his grandma were buried. She asked me where his parents where and I said I didn't know but that I thought they were both in prison somewhere. Hadn't thought about it but I guess there's a possibility Anissa will run into Quinn's mom in prison. How weird would that be? Of course they never met back when Quinn was alive. His parents both abandoned him when he was really young. Neither of them could be bothered with taking care of a kid when there were drugs to do and laws to break. Guess the apple didn't fall far from the tree.

ANISSA GRANT

They gave me seven years. Which isn't too bad, I guess. I'm already trying to think positively. Honestly, being in jail awaiting trial for two months gives you a lot of time to think. I'd already decided I want to study and get a degree while I'm in here. Robin found something online about how they sometimes run writing workshops in the women's state prison where I'm going; bring in famous authors like Eve Ensler who wrote *The Vagina Monologues*.

I figure I'll study Literature and writing maybe I can write a screenplay or two for Tate. Maybe a play, even. I think she'd be good on stage. That was something I always wanted to do but never had the opportunity. Or Robin never presented it as a possibility, I guess, since we were living in L.A., and TV and film were all centered in L.A. Plus she was from somewhere around there, somewhere near New York City, and I think it freaked her out, the idea of ever going back there. She'd never told me much about her parents or my father. Just that she'd split, left them all, right after she had me. And that my dad was older and unavailable. I got the feeling he was married or a politician or both.

I just want to be a good role model for Tate now. If such a thing is even possible in prison. I want to help other women, too; tutor them or whatever. Join N.O.W., fight for women's rights in prison.

Who knows, maybe one day Tate and I can be in a movie together. Or a play on Broadway. Like Laura Dern and her mom. Or Jane Fonda and her dad. I'd swore years ago that I'd never act again but now I felt like maybe I'd want to. Like it'd be different now because it'd be on my own terms. And I had something to prove, to the world, to my daughter, to myself.

I just have to think of anything else but Taylor right now. [sigh] I just can't… even deal with thinking about her now. Seven years is a longass time to be without that girl.

TATE GRANT

It was awesome to hear stories about my dad from Colton, Coach W. He'd gone through his stuff and pulled a bunch of photos, and yearbooks, and we'd sat in his kitchen going through them all. There were pictures of my dad on his eleventh birthday, blowing out candles on the cake his grandma made him, and pictures of my dad and Colton riding bikes and fishing and shooting guns and drinking beer. There were even a couple pictures of Quinn with a girl he dated back then, back in high school. I think Colton said her name was Rhonda. Or Ronelle. Or Ronette. Some bleached-blonde with heavy eyeliner and a mullet. He let me take some of the pictures and take photos on my phone of the others.

We talked about maybe doing a book together, about my dad, once he moved out to L.A. I wanted to do an oral history, interview people who had worked with him—other actors and directors—Colton and Anissa and maybe other people in Elkheart who knew him. Rhonda. Combine that with Colton's photos and hopefully photos from the other people I interview.

Colton said he'd finally decided to quit his job in Elkheart and move back out to L.A. He said he wanted to teach acting, audition for small roles in TV and film. I figured I could help him. He said he wanted to get sober, too. Getting sober was the new getting wasted.

TAYLOR RAGNER

They wouldn't let me go to Tatum's sentencing. They'd made me testify, made me get on the witness stand, but wouldn't let me visit her. Instead, I hung out with Tate when she was here. The paparazzi had a real media frenzy with that, with taking photos of the two of us walking into Applebee's, going to Starbucks.

She told me how the very first day she was here, before the media caught wind of it, she went with Coach W to see where Quinn was buried. It's funny, because I'd never gone. I'd heard of high school students going out there, drinking beer late at night on his grave. I'm pretty sure Cam and Chase and Matt had done it, a couple times, maybe. I'd only seen one Quinn James movie. The one where he's like fourteen and skinny as hell and playing a vampire or a werewolf, I forget which. I think I lost my virginity to that movie, in Cam's basement, when I was thirteen. I can't believe I lost my virginity to that sociopath at thirteen and Tatum's the one in prison. Go figure. Go figure, America. These laws don't make any sense. They don't make no goddamn sense, y'all.

ANABEL RAGNER

I was relieved when the trial was finally over, so we could all move on with our lives. Taylor and I have been going to weekly counseling. For Jolie's sake, she says. She's been living with Ms. Harden and her girlfriend, after she filed for emancipation. I'm done fighting her anymore on that stuff. Let her live where she wants! That woman's locked up now, anyway, so fine by me.

She says she's going to finish high school and go to college in Bloomington to study law or poli sci. I don't know where she's planning to live. Maybe her father will help her out, financially, by then. We finally filed for divorce. Scott and I. I don't know why I didn't file years ago. Denial, I guess. I've been going to yoga, too. Every day. I might get certified to teach this summer. Jolie does yoga with me at home sometimes in the evenings.

I never see Cam anymore. I hear he's going to go to school out of state in the fall. Duke. A golf scholarship, if you can believe that. Do golf pros take steroids? I guess maybe Tiger does. He looks it, anyway.

I'm about to make a profile on OK Cupid. But I hope I don't have to use my last name. I feel like everyone in this town, hell, in this country, already knows everything about me on account of the media trying to cover everyone remotely connected to the trial.

Someone from *The Today Show* tried to call me last week, get me to go on the show, but I turned them down. Taylor would have murdered me. She'd made me promise I wouldn't talk to any more reporters. She'd made all her social medias private and stays mostly inside Ms. Harden's house. She's sort of a recluse, I guess. Of course, she doesn't blame that woman, she blames *society*. She blames *the media*. I just let it all go in one ear and out the other like the therapist advises me to do. Some day when she's older she'll look back on all this and realize who was at fault, who's to blame. I just hope she realizes it before the seven years are up, before that woman gets let out, back into society. But that's all stuff I can't control and I have to let go of what I can't control and focus on what I can. Which is why yoga is so good for me right now. It's very meditative.

ROBIN GRANT

When I took Tate to see Anissa I was pretty nervous. The three of us hadn't been in the same room together since the whole big blowout fight. It'd been almost a year since they'd seen each other. And now Tate knew all this stuff about her mom and I knew Anissa was worried what she thought about her. I already knew Tate was mad at me, of course, for keeping the secret all those years. But she'd been being a little nicer in Elkheart than she had been last I'd seen her in L.A. I knew she'd been through rehab so maybe one of those steps had opened her up a little, made her a little more empathetic to the complications of other people's lives, how they don't always go the way you want them to and you end up doing things you never thought you would and hurting people you never wanted to hurt. I knew all this from personal experience, you see.

Anyway, I took her down to the women's prison. This was after sentencing, so she'd already seen Anissa in the courtroom. But they hadn't had a chance to talk. We went through all the steps they make you go through when you visit a prisoner, and then we waited a while, and then out came Anissa. It about broke my heart when I saw the way those two looked at each other. I didn't say anything, just gave them their space. They were both saying so much with their eyes. Then Tate showed Anissa the tattoo she'd gotten with Quinn and her initials in the heart on her arm. I could tell Anissa was surprised but really liked it. It meant Tate was proud of who her parents were. And that meant a lot to Anissa, I know. She'd been really worried, that Tate would never want to see her again, never talk to her. Both on account of the secret we'd kept and on account of Taylor. Then the two of them started talking about Quinn and I got up and got some coffee and walked around for a while. I just let them be, let them talk. Until time was up.

I knew Tate would be back to visit a lot now. Every other month or so, she said. At least every three, she said.

I'd taken over the lease at Anissa's apartment. I'm going to stay in Elkheart for the foreseeable future. For the time being. We lived in Hollywood thirty years. Hard to believe. I guess I can use a little break. I haven't lived alone in that many years, either. Who knows. Maybe I'll meet someone.

Maybe I'll help Taylor.

TATE GRANT

I thought it would be weird seeing Anissa in prison but it wasn't really. I mean, it was *sad*. I hated that she was there. But at least she was alive. At least I *could* go see her and talk to her. Unlike Quinn. Unlike my dad, who I could only see at a cemetery. But seeing Anissa, it was like no time had passed since we'd shared a bedroom. I just still thought of her as my sister. I couldn't help it. Maybe she'd always feel like my big sister. Maybe that's why it wasn't really that weird meeting Taylor, either.

Before I left Elkheart, Taylor went with me to the rehab hospital to meet Chase. I'd watched his videos and followed him on Instagram and was really into his story. I knew he wanted to move to California someday, too. I just wanted to help as many people as possible now. I don't know. Now that I was emancipated, I wanted everyone else to feel emancipated too. Also, I knew a bunch of hot gay guys who would all fall all over themselves to date Chase. He blushed when I told him that.

"It's true, Chase," I told him. "You're already like a celebrity out there. All my friends know who you are and we all talk about you. You're an inspiration to so many people."

"That's insane," he said, and he was smiling.

We took a photo together, the three of us, and I posted it on my Instagram and immediately it got so many likes. More likes than any other photo I'd ever posted.

CAM SPENCER

It was just so fucked up. Tatum's daughter coming to Elkheart and befriending all our people. Coach W. And Chase. And Taylor. They were all so fucking brainwashed. I don't know how she did it, but Tatum managed to brainwash half the town. Of course, the other half still hated her, like I did, still thought she was a pariah, a sexual predator. We were fucking thankful she was locked up.

I saw the photo of Taylor and Chase with Kaylin. It was all over my social media and it made me want to throw up. I don't care how many followers they all have now, they're still garbage people, in my book. Trash. Even Chase. Chase has changed so much now. Just like Taylor changed. I don't know either one of them anymore. And I wouldn't want to, honestly. It's like, good on Chase for coming out, for being his "true self" or whatever, but does he have to become such an arrogant fucking asshole? I could see how in love with himself he was now, in all his videos and photos. It was really gross. Disgusting. He'd become just like *her*, just like Taylor. Fake. 100% fake. I don't know why the rest of the world couldn't see it, but I could. I could see right through all of them. That's why they didn't like me. I called them on their bullshit. No, they didn't like that too much. Being called on their shit.

ANABEL RAGNER

Taylor brought Tate or Kaylin or whatever the girl's name is over to meet Jolie. She'd wanted to pick her up, take her out with them to dinner, but I wouldn't let her. I told her if they wanted to see Jolie, they were going to have to come to my house.

Of course the girl was very nice and of course Jolie loved her immediately. Jolie loves everybody and she knew Kaylin from seeing her on TV, even though I wouldn't let her watch the show she was on, she still saw the commercials. She saw her in the magazines I bought, too—*People* and *US Weekly*.

I'd set out stuff to make sundaes and they made them and took them down to the basement to watch *Hannah Montana*, which I didn't really like Jolie watching but since her sister was here I allowed it, for a special occasion. Taylor looked a little better, by the way. Her hair had grown out a little and she'd put back on some of the weight she'd lost during the whole traumatic time we'd all just lived through on account of that girl's mom. I couldn't believe she had a daughter the same age as mine. That just blew my mind.

CHASE WHITING

I couldn't believe it when I opened the envelope. My dad had brought it from home. He must have filled out the application on my behalf. I hadn't even thought about college since the accident. It'd been December and now it was April and here I was opening an envelope with my name on it and the return address said UCLA. And the next thing I knew I had tears in my eyes and my dad was hugging me and the nurses were clapping. I couldn't believe I'd made it out of Elkheart. I'd made it to California. All my dreams were coming true in ways I never could have imagined. Taylor was the first person I texted, and Coach W was the second. I wanted so badly to tell Tatum. Once I turned eighteen, in a month, I would be able to go see her. I knew she'd be so excited for me. She'd been the one who said I could do it, move to California, if I wanted to badly enough.

FRANCES BEAN COBAIN

The thing about Tate is, she's super open to the world. Some people, given her history, her background, how she was lied to all those years, would be real closed off. Would build a fortress around themselves from the world. Not trust anyone or let anyone in. That's sort of what I did when I was younger, in my early twenties. But Tate's not like that. She's just super laid back and chill. We're going to go to Hawaii together next month. My mom keeps telling me to tell her how hot her dad was. It's so weird. People say that to me about my dad, too. I get it, but… he's *my dad*, you know? He's an angel. Just like Quinn. Tate and I joke that they're probably up there, together, in heaven, singing and playing guitar and whining about something. Something isn't right in heaven and they're writing songs about it. Like that horrible Eric Clapton song. Tears in Heaven or whatever. I bet my dad hates that song. That's okay, I don't like listening to Nirvana, either. It's too weird. The three of us—Paris and Tate and me—we usually end up listening to Michael. Or Janet. Or Hole. Paris made a mash up of all our parents, with Quinn talking in movies over all the mashed up music. It was pretty dope. Sort of had a *Pulp Fiction* soundtrack feel. We have to celebrate the now, the here, us. We're like these weird orphaned three musketeers. No one else understands what it's like. Daddy's girls. We're going to have a séance in Hawaii. Try to talk to them, try to conjure our fathers. We just want them to know we forgive them for leaving us, and that we love them, and that we're okay.

TAYLOR RAGNER

Whenever Coach W went to see Anissa he took a note from me and brought one back from her. We weren't supposed to have any contact, you see. Not even letters. But he managed to get them through, once a month. I lived for those notes. I bought a special keepsake box for them and lined it with rose petals.

Sometimes it seems like a whole lifetime has happened in the last year. How much I've gone through and grown up. I've started taking online classes and I'm thinking of going back to school for real in the fall, once Cam's no longer in this town.

I dream of going to see Anissa. Tate and I joked that maybe I could go undercover as her, use her ID [laughs] Is that fucked up? I don't know, sometimes you just have to laugh at how absurd life can be. Acknowledge the absurdity. Jesus, I sound like Coach W. I'm talking like a goddamn philosophy major. Which, by the way, who would have thought Coach W would be our go between? People change, I guess.

ANISSA GRANT

After Taylor and I watched *Britney & Kevin: Chaotic*, we watched *Britney: for the record*. And *Britney: for the record* was made after she and Kevin broke up and after she shaved her head and took the umbrella to the car and the ambulance came to her house and took her away and her daddy had to take guardianship of her.

The Britney you see in *Britney: for the record* is a much more subdued, much less wild, less in your face Britney. But she's still Britney, you know? She's still the most charismatic person you've ever seen. But she's been hurt. You can still see the hurt in her eyes. And at the very end of the movie, while you're watching her dance in various costumes, with fireworks going off behind her, beautiful as she's ever been, making her comeback, you hear her responding to the unseen interviewer, and she's talking about the cruelty and beauty of life. And she says something like, "You go from one extreme to the other and they're both worth it because you wouldn't see the other without the other one, but that cruel part is *damn cruel*, and you'll never forget it. But the heaven is heaven. So, it's like, I've been to both places."

And that's how I feel now. I'm waiting to see the light in my eyes again. One day you'll see it. Heaven.

TAMRA DAVIS, DIRECTOR, *SKIPPED PARTS* (speaking about Brad Renfro)

"And, you know, Brad is just the coolest.

He looks so unbelievably handsome and gorgeous and, you know, I don't know, I think Brad is one of our best actors—he's just crazy, so you have to take care of him. If there are any other directors working with him watching this, take care of the kid. Don't mess him up.

God…"

acknowledgments

Thank you Aaron Burch, Amanda McNeil, Garielle Lutz, Marston Hefner, Luke Goebel, Mathias Mietzelfeld, Andromeda, Destiny and Victoria.

Extra special thanks to CLASH Books for taking a risk on this novel and on me. I am forever indebted.

about the author

Elizabeth Ellen, photo by Miles Marie

ELIZABETH ELLEN is the author of several books including the cult classics *Fast Machine* and *Person/a*. She has been published in such places as *American Short Fiction*, *Catapult*, *BOMB*, *Muumuu House*, *Forever Magazine*, *Joyland*, *Salon*, and *Harper's Magazine*, and is the recipient of a Pushcart Prize for her story, "Teen Culture," published in the collection, *Saul Stories*. She is the founder of Short Flight/Long Drive Books and is the current publisher and editor of the literary journal, *Hobart*.

also by clash books

THE MISEDUCATION OF A 90s BABY

Khaholi Bailey

THE BULGARIAN TRAINING MANUAL

Ruth Bonapace

EARTH ANGEL

Madeline Cash

GIRL LIKE A BOMB

Autumn Christian

ALL OUR TOMORROWS

Amy DeBellis

DARRYL

Jackie Ess

PROXIMITY

Sam Heaps

HORSE GIRL FEVER

Kevin Maloney

SAD SEXY CATHOLIC

Lauren Milici

GAG REFLEX

Elle Nash

THE LONGEST SUMMER

Alexandrine Ogundimu

HEY YOU ASSHOLES

Kyle Seibel

WE PUT THE LIT IN LITERARY

CLASHBOOKS.COM

FOLLOW US

IG

X

@clashbooks

TikTok

@clashbook